THE TALE OF
CHO UNG

THE TALE OF
CHO UNG

A Classic of Vengeance, Loyalty, and Romance

TRANSLATED BY
SOOKJA CHO

COLUMBIA UNIVERSITY PRESS NEW YORK

COLUMBIA UNIVERSITY PRESS

Publishers Since 1893

NEW YORK   CHICHESTER, WEST SUSSEX

cup.columbia.edu

Library of Congress Cataloging-in-Publication Data
Names: Cho, Sookja translator.
Title: The tale of Cho Ung : a classic of vengeance, loyalty, and romance /
translated by Sookja Cho.
Other titles: Cho Ung chæon. English.
Description: New York : Columbia University Press, 2018. | Includes bibliographical
references and index.
Identifiers: LCCN 2018006944 | ISBN 9780231186100 (cloth : alk. paper) |
ISBN 9780231186117 (pbk. : alk. paper)
Classification: LCC PL989.A1 C45713 2018 | DDC 895.73/2—dc23
LC record available at https://lccn.loc.gov/2018006944

Columbia University Press books are printed on permanent and durable acid-free paper.

Printed in the United States of America

Cover image: Iljŏnhaewido, from the series Pukkwan Yujŏk Toch'ŏp, by anonymous
artist, ink and color on paper, 31.0 x 41.2 cm, approximately eighteenth century,
Korea University Museum

Book & Cover design: Chang Jae Lee

To my parents

CONTENTS

ACKNOWLEDGMENTS

This translation project is the acme of my teaching and research at Arizona State University. I completed a first draft in December 2012, which is when the real effort began. For the last five years, my spare time has been consumed by reading other old editions, consulting modern Korean collated editions, and revising my translation. Each time I began to flag, I was heartened by the help and support of my wonderful friends and colleagues. I deeply appreciate everyone who provided feedback during this long period.

In 2015, the Literature Translation Institute of Korea offered its support. It was a turning point for this project, driving me to wrap up long-standing questions and proceed to publication. My heartfelt thanks, therefore, to the institute.

I am grateful to the two anonymous readers who reviewed the manuscript and have embraced their suggestions as much as possible. I also extend my utmost gratitude to Jennifer Crewe at Columbia University Press, who immediately saw the value of the manuscript, and to Christine

Dunbar, Christian Pizzaro Winting, and Susan Pensak, with whom I have worked closely through the publication process. Their prompt and excellent work has made publishing with Columbia both an efficient and a valuable experience.

Although I have put my very best into this translation, I trust that it will be improved upon in future. As the project progressed, I realized again and again how much I owe to earlier scholars in the field, most of whom I know only from their books and articles. I have been able to mention only some of these trailblazing works in the present volume. My hope is that this translation will add to the understanding of this popular Korean tale among English-speaking readers and inspire scholars to build upon my work. I look forward to future research on and translations of the *Tale of Cho Ung* and other popular tales of premodern Korea, which will allow the Western understanding of Korean culture and literature to ripen.

INTRODUCTION

One day in the late Chosŏn (seventeenth-nineteenth centuries), a professional storyteller stood in a tobacco store on the main street of Seoul, recounting a heroic tale. One man listened enthralled until, losing track of the line between the real world and the imaginary one, he abruptly leaped to attack the storyteller himself. Recorded in anecdote, the bizarre behavior of this one man illustrates not only the prevalence of public storytelling in late Chosŏn Korea but the depth of Koreans' personal interest in such stories.[1] Those who listened in shops or on the street were the primary consumers of popular tales, although the stories circulated in manuscript form and were later published as commercial novels as well.[2] Though almost invisible to modern scholarship, aural audiences were instrumental in shaping these most beloved tales. Reading the stories now transports us into the minds and lives of those popular audiences whose daily experiences engaged them deeply with favorite stories that transmitted wisdom, reconfirmed their norms and values, and helped them make sense of their world.[3] The

Tale of Cho Ung encapsulates these late Chosŏn Koreans' passion for stories, allowing us to untangle and hear the multifaceted voices of those earlier Koreans in our modern imagination.

CHOSŎN BEST SELLER: THE *TALE OF CHO UNG*

The anonymously written *Tale of Cho Ung* (Cho Ung chŏn 됴웅젼 or 趙雄傳) unravels its young protagonist Cho Ung's journey, interlaced with romance, retribution, and military triumph, as he fearlessly confronts and overcomes obstacles and grows into a heroic man. The tale was the best-selling fictional narrative of the late Chosŏn period. There are approximately 450 surviving copies of different editions in manuscript or print (woodblock and movable-type) form—more than of any other popular narrative from the Chosŏn dynasty (1392–1910).[4] The surviving editions are written either entirely in Korean (woodblock print) or in Korean with occasional Sino-Korean characters (manuscript).[5] The woodblock-printed versions vary in length and format depending on which printing house produced them. Those from the printing houses in Wansan (present-day Chŏnju) and Seoul are considered the main editions. Those from Wansan comprise three volumes, and those from Seoul comprise only one.[6] Although there are minor differences in plot development and descriptions of events among the various versions, the overall narrative remains essentially the same.[7]

The Wansan editions are the longest and are considered representative commercial versions (*panggakpon* 坊刻本), in terms of popularity, quantity, and quality.[8] The earliest known edition consists of 104 leaves (70,700 characters) and its first volume dates from the *chŏngsa* year (1857). These Wansan editions provide an extended, more elaborate version of the tale, laced with descriptive and idiomatic expressions, enriched literary elements, and many popular sentiments common to *p'ansori* literature. Given that the Wansan area was the center of traditional literary works and publishing,[9] it is not surprising that the Wansan editions of the *Tale of Cho Ung* enjoyed the highest popularity. By contrast, the Seoul editions are generally very short. The longest one, comprising 30 leaves (22,170 characters), is only about one-third the length of a typical individual Wansan edition.[10] With an abbreviated treatment of events and many songs omitted, the Seoul editions were clearly aimed at an audience with different tastes. It is difficult to posit any direct relationship between these two editions. Just as the Wansan editions are not necessarily elongated versions of the Seoul editions, so the Seoul editions are not necessarily abbreviated versions of those from Wansan. Indeed, for all their brevity, the Seoul editions sometimes include elaborate scenes not found in the Wansan editions.[11]

The recent discovery of the tale's circulation through the book rental business opens up further dynamics of its multiplication in different editions within the context of the commercialization of reading and printing culture. For instance, a study of the relationship between different editions found that lending (or circulating) library editions (sech'aekpon 貰冊本) from Seoul preceded the Wansan editions and any other commercial versions, hinting that they were the fount from which different tellings of the tale sprang and competed with each other for commercial attention.[12] The apparently lengthy volumes of these lending library editions also serve to explain some traces of omissions in the surviving editions, suggesting that what we see today is not the whole, original best-selling tale of Cho Ung.

Despite its wide popularity, revealed by the numerous editions and copies published up to the early twentieth century, the *Tale of Cho Ung* did not initially attract a correspondingly strong interest among later scholars and audiences. In the new literary and cultural environment, which applied its own standards to canonical literature, the tale's unique literary value and importance as a best-selling story were gradually forgotten.[13] The *Tale of Cho Ung* was not introduced or researched as much as some tales that enjoyed great popularity in modern times, such as the *Tale of Ch'unhyang*, the *Tale of Hong Kiltong*, and the *Tale of Sim Ch'ŏng.*[14] Such gaps between the tale and modern audiences have also resulted in the lack of a complete, readable modern Korean or English translation. Though modern Korean renditions of the tale continued to emerge in the late twentieth century, they were often presented in abbreviated form, as a part of a larger anthology and with a focus on the tale's didactic message, their dry tone belying the wild popularity of the story over the ages. In recent decades, however, academic and official efforts to promote traditional literary works among Korean and global readers have brought new attention to the *Tale of Cho Ung*, as has a reprint of the early twentieth-century movable-type edition (Adan mun'go, 2007). The growth of academic and popular interest both in the tale and in classical Korean literature is anticipated at a greater level.

ORIGINS AND AUTHORSHIP: THE *TALE OF CHO UNG* IN HISTORICAL CONTEXT

There is little information about the identity of the author of the *Tale of Cho Ung*. None of the surviving editions or texts offers any evidence. This is not entirely surprising: most vernacular tales from the Chosŏn period were circulated anonymously or under aliases due to the low cultural esteem in which vernacular fiction was held.[15] Without a clearly identified author, however, it is difficult to precisely date the original text. It is generally believed that vernacular stories emerged after the ripening of the native Korean alphabet *han'gŭl* (promulgated in 1446) into a literary language—probably during the seventeenth century— and before the mid-nineteenth century, when surviving commercial editions began to appear on a large scale.[16]

The *Tale of Cho Ung* could have been composed at any time during the two hundred years or so between the inception and the blossoming of vernacular Korean stories. Based on the scale, themes, and the structure of the tale, however, most scholars hold that it probably emerged in the late eighteenth or early nineteenth century, when heroic martial and *p'ansori*-based Korean novels were in full bloom.[17] The fact that there is no record of the tale's popularity before the nineteenth century also seems to support this view. The first surviving record of Korean military tales (*kundam sosŏl* 軍談小說) did not appear until the late eighteenth century and does not mention the *Tale of Cho Ung*, although it does refer to stories such as the *Tale of So Taesŏng* (So Taesŏng chŏn 蘇大成傳) and *Tale of Chang P'ungun* (Chang P'ungun chŏn 張豐雲傳).[18] This omission suggests that the *Tale of Cho Ung* was not particularly visible before the late eighteenth century. In examining the surviving editions dating back to the mid-nineteenth century, it therefore seems most likely that the *Tale of Cho Ung* was written sometime during the late eighteenth or early nineteenth century.

The tale's popularity presupposes the presence of the strong historical readership of vernacular literature that began to form during
the seventeenth century, when the desire to write and appreciate stories
surfaced rapidly among Koreans, triggered by a variety of changing
social factors, such as the Japanese (1592–98) and Manchu invasions
(1627 and 1636), the development of commercialism, and the emergence of enriched reading materials and writing culture.[19] The native
Korean script, which was by this time widely used as the literary language, provided the means for common people, especially women, to
engage in the practice of reading and writing through the translating,
transcribing, and retelling of popular stories in Korean.

It is often said that Chinese historical novels such as the *Romance of
the Three Kingdoms* (Sanguo zhi yanyi 三國志演義), the *Romance of Chu and
Han* (Chu Han yanyi 楚漢演義), and the *Tale of Xue Rengui* (Xue Rengui
zhuan 薛仁貴傳), which were imported and circulated during and
after the sixteenth and seventeenth centuries, were instrumental in
widening the readership for the *Tale of Cho Ung* and other Korean heroic
martial tales of the eighteenth and nineteenth centuries.[20] These Chinese stories were initially available only to the literati but were soon
translated into Korean for a broader audience, by women such as Lady
Yun (1647–98), who hand copied a Korean translation of the *Romance
of Western Zhou* (Xi Zhou yanyi 西周演義) to share with her friends.[21]
This broadening of literary practice, driven by the increased demand
for writing in Korean and by the popularity of imported Chinese stories and their Korean translations, as well as the growth of the book
market (e.g., rental shops) and print culture of the eighteenth and nineteenth centuries,[22] all provided a favorable milieu for the composition
of new tales in Korean.[23] Against this backdrop, the *Tale of Cho Ung*
emerged.

Experts disagree as to the author's literary skill and knowledge.
Because the tale employs allusions and Sino-Korean poems more often
than other military tales with a similar structure, Cho Hŭiung argues
that the author must have possessed a considerable literary education
and knowledge of Chinese history.[24] Based purely on the quality of the
writing, however, Sim Kyŏngho argues that the author was a low-
ranking official, perhaps a clerk or military officer whose job did not

require a high level of literary education.[25] Although these two views may seem contradictory, each is valid in its own context. Together they highlight the heterogeneous authorship of the text; while the tale contains sophisticated references that would indicate literati involvement, it also contains unsophisticated sections with fundamental language errors indicative of a more common hand. This juxtaposition demonstrates that the original author was among those who were conversant with the prosody and patterns of military tales, with an average or higher-than-average level of knowledge and understanding of ancient classics and literary works.

Given that surviving editions may not accurately reflect the work of the original author, it is certainly possible that, for whatever reason, each volume of the original work was rewritten and edited by a different author and then evolved separately or randomly before being combined into a lending library or commercial edition as one complete set. This possibility is also suggested by flaws, simple mistakes, and certain gaps in literary sensibility in the surviving editions.[26] Perhaps the rapid success of the tale and concurrent increase in reading and transcribing practices caused a missing part of the original to be replaced in general circulation and then reproduced many times in cheap commercial prints. The first author's work may have been altered, deleted, or diluted as different versions of the story evolved to meet the demands of popular readers and the book market at large, or to better suit the intellectual and literary expectations of subsequent authors and readers. The extant editions, therefore, may be works of collaboration between authors and readers over time, rather than illustrative of the original author's qualifications.

A more detailed examination of surviving editions offers considerable information about the multiple author-readers and their education, literary tastes, and concerns. First, the sources cited in the tale indicate that most allusions in the text are culled from famous events in ancient Chinese history, Confucian classics, and popular historical narratives, such as the *Records of the Grand Historian* (Shiji 史記), the *Book of Songs* (Shijing 詩經), the *Book of Documents* (Shujing 書經), and the *Romance of the Three Kingdoms*. It is certainly possible that the original author intentionally used such early references because they were chronologically appropriate to the historical setting of the *Tale of Cho Ung*, which is the Song (Liu) dynasty (420–479 CE). It seems more likely, however, that using famous events from well-known texts was a reflection of the knowledge and interests of author-readers of the time; the tale was probably written by and aimed at an audience with an average level of classical Chinese education.

Second, the tale demonstrates a clear concern with a nonliterati or semiliterati audience. In books 1 and 2 of the Wansan editions, for example, Sino-Korean texts are presented in Korean, with a direct translation following.[27] The tale follows the conventions of vernacular literature, in which speaking and singing parts alternate to help narrate the story and express emotions; but further explanations of the quoted Sino-Korean texts also follow their Korean readings. This in-text translation aid illuminates how literature could have been appreciated by nonelite Korean readers such as peasants, artisans, and merchants—people who wouldn't have received enough literary education to understand or decipher the meaning of the Sino-Korean references.[28] This juxtaposition of Sino-Korean text and its translation serves as evidence of the enormous popularity of the *Tale of Cho Ung* among the illiterate and semiliterate common people of the late Chosŏn period.

Another fascinating element of the text is the way that changes in the descriptions of battle scenes in successive editions reveal the changing tastes or demographics of successive readerships. Descriptions of military events tend to be omitted or reduced in shorter editions of the tale. Yi Ch'anghŏn proposes that this reduction indicates a decline in Koreans' interest in the military as time went by.[29] Though it would be an oversimplification to suggest that reader tastes correspond directly to gender, if tradition indicates that a military tale engages masculine attention, then the gradual reduction of military scenes may indicate an increased female readership.[30]

In fact, the influence of female readers on book circulation and printing may have been greater than we tend to imagine. In his preface to *Four Books for Women* (Yŏ Sasŏ sŏ 女四書序), Ch'ae Chegong (蔡濟恭, 1720–99) disparaged women's reading practices, opining that many women in his time neglected their womanly duties because of their infatuation with vernacular stories.[31] He even went so far as to suggest that some avid female readers sold or pawned their jewelry to enable them to purchase and read more books.[32] The existence of this female readership suggests the possibility that women were actively involved in the evolution of the tale. Military scenes may have been omitted in favor of themes such as filial piety, love, and marriage (themes that dominate book 1)—that is to say, in favor of Cho Ung's character as a son, a lover, and a husband, rather than as a military general.[33]

The *Tale of Cho Ung* also shows a certain textual affinity to the world of performance literature, that is, to *p'ansori*-based novels. Its well-knit narrative structure, level of use of historical and literary allusions, and frequent insertion of dialogues and verse forms, including the 88-line song-poem that appears at the end of book 2, seem intended to achieve the syncretic blend of popular, dramatic, and emotional narration commonly seen in *p'ansori* novels, rather than being simple clichés of the written genre. These traits also point to the tale's long evolution among local Korean readerships, particularly of the Wansan editions, who loved *p'ansori* performance and the telling of tales based on it. The fervent literary creativity and skill that abound in the *p'ansori* literature can also inform our investigation into the authorship of the *Tale of Cho Ung*.

In short, the authorship of the tale's extant editions should be understood in a pluralistic way that embraces the work of the authors, readers, and transcribers who participated in the ongoing retelling and reprinting of the story. Like many other vernacular stories of Chosŏn Korea, the manuscript may have initially been written in classical Chinese before it was multiplied by translation,[34] transcription, and storytelling in Korean. Yet certain traits of the surviving editions reveal that the tale was widely read in vernacular Korean with the collaboration of various audiences, ranging from the illiterate to those with an average or above average literary education, including educated women. It is also important to consider the authorship of the *Tale of Cho Ung* within the context of a growing print culture. As a commercial book market develops, it caters increasingly to the demands of regular customers, rendering the relationship between the author and the reader even more malleable and, to some extent, interchangeable.

LITERARY BACKDROP: IMAGINARY CHINESE SPACE FOR JOURNEY, LOVE, AND CONQUEST

The *Tale of Cho Ung* is set in the Song (Liu) dynasty of premodern China. The use of a Chinese historical time and space was not unusual in late Chosŏn literature. While some tales were translated or adapted from Chinese literature, many popular Korean tales also deliberately used Chinese space, which offered a boundless landscape—familiar but still imaginative—in which to explore themes that could not be conveniently or appropriately pursued in a Korean context. It remains unclear why the Song (Liu) dynasty was selected for this tale, for the Tang, Song (Zhao), and Ming dynasties were more common choices.[35] However, the comparatively unknown Song (Liu) dynasty functions flawlessly as a flexible backdrop for the major events of the tale. The tale's deployment of the events in chronological order within the dynastic frame also maintains a certain objectivity and historicity within the diegetic world, despite several inconsistencies. The use of Chinese places and names in a past distant to the tale's readership also helped the author(s) design an environment in which to explore sensitive themes such as treason and the restoration of a dynasty.[36]

The tale's settings consist of a mixture of known and unknown places, seemingly in both China and Korea. The major locales are the capital city (Changan), the State of Wi, Kangho, and Kyeryangdo (Mount T'ae), which are interconnected through a variety of undefined areas of escape and travel, various military encampments and battles, and places of religious seclusion. Each backdrop becomes the site of a different narrative theme, and for this reason the locations follow the narrative, which downplays travel routes and geographical specificity.[37] For example, the capital city is where the conflict between Ung and Yi Tubyŏng begins and ends. The State of Wi is a transitional space in which Ung's military power and skills are tested against the army of the wicked Sŏbŏn king. Described as a thriving town, Kangho is home to Ung's romance with Maiden Chang. And whereas Kangho resembles the complex social realities of the real world, the religious spaces portrayed in the tale function solely as nurturing places for Ung and his family. When Maiden Chang and later her mother arrive at Kangsŏnam, where Ung's mother stays, they are understood to have arrived at a cozy, sacred, familial space built within the religious quarters. Kyeryangsŏm and Kyerangdo, with their similar names, are both places of imminent threat. Ung's mother and the crown prince are forced to escape from these places. Finally, nature—particularly mountains and rivers—becomes a neutral place fostering movement and evolution, a place of unforeseen ordeals and unexpected rewards. These places are all described in vibrant detail to inspire the imagination,[38] and the accompanying songs and poetry enliven the dry, lonely, and dangerous moments of Ung's journey, igniting readers' emotions and evoking a kaleidoscope of imagery: "The chattering of indifferent monkeys evoked the grief of lonesome travelers. Mournful cuckoos, shedding tears that spotted a cluster of flowers, sang 'Why Don't You Return?' How sad it was! The cuckoos' cries reminded the mother and son of their piteous plight, and they felt at one with the birds. Amid the empty mountains, even an iron-hearted man wouldn't have been able to resist the urge to sob" (book 1).

Travel between the major settings in the tale remains purely imaginary or fantastic; each distance is culturally symbolic rather than physically plausible. Ung and his mother, for example, travel 3,300 *li* on the night they escape from the capital. Since 3,000 li represents the greatest distance in physical space conceived by Chosŏn Koreans—Korea is typically referred to as 3,000-li land—a Korean audience would immediately realize that this first journey took Ung and his mother far beyond Korea, or a land the size of Korea, to start a new life. Most Chosŏn Koreans would have been fascinated by the idea of traveling with Ung to a barbarian land, a remote religious place, or a borderland between the worlds of immortals and the dead and the imaginative Chinese space. The recurring image of Ung traveling as though flying on his swift horse is vital to making his travels conceivable.

The space in the tale, though it is superficially Chinese, thus builds on the imaginations of Chosŏn Koreans, incorporating their literary and cultural tropes in a way that lends verisimilitude to the narrative. For example, the following scene, in which the king of Wi holds a banquet and enacts a ritual to console the eight dead generals, is drawn directly from the record of a ritual held by Wang Kŏn (877–943), the founder of Koryŏ (918–1392) Korea:[39]

The king [of Wi]'s men constructed eight human figures to sit at the banquet. They beat the drum of victory and poured wine into the glasses placed in front of the figures to offer solace. Mysteriously, the wine glasses went dry and the seats trembled. Everyone feasted on wine and meat. Some danced and some sang. The Wi soldiers overflowed with praise for Ung's achievement. The figures of the eight dead generals also appeared to make gestures of appreciation and to enjoy the banquet. (book 2)

The *Tale of Cho Ung* also employs many literary tropes commonly seen in other Korean literary genres, and this interpenetration and intertextuality operate to bring in echoes of the dialogic voices of different texts. For instance, Cho Ung's encounter with souls of the dead, particularly the soul of a dead general who wishes Ung to release his *han* (unresolved grudge), evokes the scenes and mood of the souls of the dead in the *Record of the Dream Journey to Talch'ŏn* (Talch'ŏn mongyurok 達川夢遊錄) by Yun Kyesŏn (尹繼善, 1577–1604). This particular narrative of a dream journey is a supernatural metanarrative developed to extend sociopolitical criticism and trauma healing from historical realities. Similarly, the scene of Cho Ung's entering a dream journey through the guidance of a butterfly, and meeting with the dead emperor and loyal subjects who warn him about upcoming threats, is part of the tale's adoption of compelling motifs from a different dream journey narrative and a novel, each carrying a specific literary sense and cultural meaning.[40] Also, the scene of the romantic affair between Ung and Maiden Chang is reminiscent of that of Ch'unhyang and Mongnyong, perhaps the most famous and beloved couple known to Chosŏn Korean audiences.

The story also uses the full-fledged appropriation of imaginative Chinese spaces as a vantage point from which to explore the size and topography of the entire literary landscape. The events during Ung and his mother's long life in exile, and the people they encounter, such as the old lady, the nuns, the monks, and the bandits, all present intriguing snapshots of lives envisioned in this literary space. Chosŏn readers would have been enthralled by how, when the nobly born Cho Ung and his mother are penniless wanderers, their interactions with people of lower status blur conventional social boundaries due to the characters' mutual understanding and compassion.

The *Tale of Cho Ung* demonstrates the ease with which Koreans utilized Chinese spaces to create stories that served them. The imagination, creativity, and political criticism that are embedded within this narrative along with literary and cultural elements familiar to Koreans causes the imaginary Chinese landscape to be simultaneously more realistic and more Korean.

CHO UNG'S SAGA: A MILITARY OR HEROIC TALE?

The *Tale of Cho Ung* recounts the arduous but spellbinding adventures of Cho Ung, a boy driven by his passion, righteousness, and sense of duty. Ung's stalwart character and martial achievements have often caused the tale to be labeled merely heroic or military, and then to be dismissed as typical of those genres. Like many heroic novels, the tale follows a young boy from early hardship to adulthood and final victory. However, the absence or reduced role of some elements essential to other heroic novels from Korea, such as an account of the hero's unusual birth, makes Ung's tale distinct.[41]

Similarly, a closer examination of military elements of the tale makes it difficult to define the tale as simply a military novel. Certainly, the story earned the title of most beloved military tale among the popular audience; it was said that "the best is the *Tale of Cho Ung*, and the second best is the *Tale of Yi Taebŏng* (Yi Taebŏng chŏn 李大鳳傳)."[42] Yet based on the extant versions, neither the quantity nor the quality of the tale's battle scenes dominates the entire story.[43] The tale also contains fewer scenes of Daoist magic than other military tales of the period, such as the *Tale of Chŏn Uch'i* and *Tale of Yu Ch'ungnyŏl*, which may have diminished the weight of the battle scenes for some readers of the story.

The fact remains, however, that each battle scene in this tale is carefully designed to yield its own delight and thrill to Chosŏn readers, who would have found the characteristics of each individual scene fascinating. The absence of the use of magical skills and some tactics seen in other military tales actually helps craft Ung as a more human hero, making his victory in each battle more meaningful. The difficulty in categorizing the tale as a military tale is thus rooted in the complexity of the themes the narrative represents, not in the descriptions per se of the battle scenes.

Indeed, the *Tale of Cho Ung* incorporates far richer themes than those found in typical military or heroic tales. Ung's journey unfolds in a complex tapestry of loyalty, honor, retribution, and love, interspersed with elements of romance and fantasy. Moreover, Ung's fearlessness in confronting and overcoming obstacles, from his innocent beginnings to his final vengeance, demonstrates a rare degree of free will, one that is revealed to be in harmony with the will of heaven—a remarkable feature of this tale. Furthermore, by paralleling personal tragedy with a dynastic collapse, the tale creates a heroic narrative that is deployed through the panoramic life events of the hero Ung.

With its emphasis on individual affection and ethics in the relationships between child and parent, husband and wife, subject and ruler, and pupil and teacher, the *Tale of Cho Ung* also presents human life in all its complexity, including irregularity and hierarchy, at times subtly dissenting from the social norms of the late Chosŏn period.[44] The tale navigates the labyrinth of emotions between people—hatred, anger, sadness, fear, disgust, surprise, love, happiness, gratitude, and humility. The deep emotions that Ung and his mother feel at each moment of their excruciating journey elicit a strong sense of humanity transcending time. The *Tale of Cho Ung* provides a glimpse into the vernacular fiction favored by late Chosŏn audiences, and hence reveals the vital aspects of life according to Chŏson Koreans.

CHO UNG: A REALISTIC AND MIGHTY HERO WITH POWER AND A STRONG WILL

The tale portrays Cho Ung as a heroic ideal, but also as a figure who is far more human than the heroes of other military tales from the late Chosŏn. Religious fatalism and divine intervention, which are dominant elements in many military or heroic tales, are also seen here, but they remain secondary because the tale instead renders Ung a mighty but realistic hero.

Ung starts off as a little boy who has nothing but who acquires the support, instruction, and tools he needs, one by one, through his own actions. While Ung and his mother are fleeing, he meets Monk Wŏlgyŏng, who gives them shelter in repayment for a donation made years before and offers to instruct Ung. Nevertheless, Ung's will to explore the world and fulfill his own plans prompts him to set off to become a warrior. During his journey, he meets a master who gives him a three-*ch'ŏk*-long sword and advises him to study under Master Ch'ŏlgwan. Ung's training with Ch'ŏlgwan earns him a magically swift horse. When he finishes his initial training with Ch'ŏlgwan, his meeting with Maiden Chang is unexpected, but he persuades her to be his wife. When Ung then decides to pursue his long-delayed aim of restoring the Song dynasty and avenging his father, he meets and impresses a spirit general who rewards him with armor and weapons. His subsequent success in the State of Wi as a military strategist and leader earns him command of the troops he needs to rescue the crown prince. An inevitable destiny appears to draw him onward, as his success at each step on his path earns him the means to triumph in his next endeavor.

Although Ung rarely uses supernatural power or paranormal skills to win his fights, he never falters in his personal war and receives unexpected support in times of exhaustion and trouble.[45] Yet readers soon discover that the fount of his power and success is none other than Ung himself. The tale makes a point of Ung's becoming a military hero through years of intensive training with masters and through field experience in actual battles. Ung doesn't outwardly request help from heaven or religious figures, nor does he ask what heaven's will is at each step. Instead, he maintains an optimistic and audacious mind. Though his mother often worries or despairs, Ung always cheers her up, emphasizing his determination to prevail and his confidence in the workings of heaven: "Mother, please do not worry. A person's life is determined by heaven, and his fame and shame are contingent upon his luck, so what is there to worry about? Also, as a man, I cannot stay idle when there is a sworn enemy before my eyes. However, I assure you that I will not do anything to avenge my father's death until I devise a good plan. Please don't worry" (book 1). Ung's pure and loyal heart, righteous determination, incessant efforts to improve himself, and dauntless pursuit of his goals earn him his luck and success and thus highlight the narrative's focus on a more realistic development of Ung's heroic character.

Ung's determination to learn and his respect for his teachers amplify his charm as a moral and heroic character. Throughout the story, he sincerely devotes himself to gaining skills and knowledge under his masters and wholeheartedly applies what he has learned. He listens to the words of the strange old men who approach him with the good intention of helping him. Heaven's help comes of its own accord, and the figures speaking on its behalf, be they ghosts of the dead or Daoist masters, do not guide Ung into taking heaven's side but instead simply strengthen him—for he is already on the right side. This volition reveals the increased value placed on self-reliance or self-fulfillment in late Chosŏn society, conveying the sense that "Heaven helps those who help themselves."

Interestingly, Cho Ung's idealistic popularity does not wane—but perhaps even increases—in the face of a surprisingly frank love affair with a maiden he meets during his journey. Accompanied by an exchange of songs, their first encounter evokes a romantic atmosphere more typical of love tales, but Ung then persuades the hesitant Maiden Chang to make love with him. He leaves her the next day, implying that he will return, but with no indication of when. The couple does not elope, nor is Ung pressed to succeed in the civil service exam to legitimize their encounter. This short but powerful depiction of a love affair adds a human flaw to Ung's heroic character and reveals an androcentric culture. Later in the story, Ung does not voice his love or concern for Maiden Chang. However, in light of Chosŏn culture's prioritization of a man's relationship to his parents over his relationship with his wife, Ung's negligence toward Maiden Chang does not necessarily mean a decline in his love for her. Indeed, Ung proves his love by visiting Maiden Chang later and by punishing the prefect of Kangho for what he has done to her and her family. Maiden Chang does not appear to doubt his love. Through mutual trust and understanding, the couple's love grows into a happy and ideal marriage.

It is important to mention that Maiden Chang and the other central female characters contribute to the construction of Cho Ung as a more appealing and respectful hero, revealing the tale's fulfillment of the male ideals of the time. Ung's ethical faculty is mirrored in the qualities of the women surrounding him. After their marriage, Maiden Chang recommends Ung's second marriage to a daughter of the king of the State of Wi, which Ung initially declines out of concern for his wife. Maiden Chang's advice reveals her virtuous character; she is not jealous of another woman[46] but supports her husband Cho Ung in a second alliance that has both personal and political benefits. Maiden Chang's behavior follows the model of "a wise mother and good wife" (賢母良妻), a term used in premodern Korean society to describe the ideal woman whom any man would want and an image that is still praised in some modern Korean families.

Both Lady Wang (Ung's mother) and Maiden Chang comply with social norms by epitomizing the virtue of chastity: Lady Wang decides that she and Ung must leave the village of Paekcha because their elderly hostess is encouraging her to remarry, and Maiden Chang determinedly rejects the marriage proposal of the prefect of Kangho. The one-mate-per-lifetime ideal of female chastity that these characters thus protect was considered a woman's most important virtue in late Chosŏn Korea, where Confucianism permeated all of society.[47] The institutional encouragement of both female virtue and polygamy is an undeniable historical reality in Korea, China, and other parts of Asia.[48] Female chastity and polygamy were also prominently represented in literature, particularly in the genre of the scholar-beauty romance (才子佳人小說).[49] The female characters in these stories, with their acceptance of polygamy, can be seen as a projection of male desire and a fantasy of the ideal woman. Yet in literary representation these archetypes can also serve as a space in which to experiment with the patriarchal reality.[50] The tales thus build upon the established social and cultural matrix of their time.

PUNISHING EVIL AND RESTORING POLITICAL ORDER

Another prominent motif in the *Tale of Cho Ung* is the merciless punishment of enemies or evildoers. Early in his military career, Ung allows the king of Sŏbŏn and several of his officials to return to their country after humiliating them; but aside from that one exception, Ung does not hesitate to kill enemy generals and those who are evil or treacherous, no matter how much they beg for forgiveness.

> Ung shouted an order to arrest the prefect of Kangho and pressed his soldiers to hurry. The soldiers cried out in acknowledgment of his order and swiftly went to arrest the prefect. They tied him up and brought him before Ung so fast it was as if their feet never touched the ground. Filled with anger, Ung exposed the prefect's wrongdoings one by one, and reprimanded him, "You are a civil servant to the country and receive a government stipend. However, you committed serious crimes that truly deserve serious punishment. Even if I were to consider sparing your life, you have already exhausted every means of saving yourself." In the end, the prefect was dragged around the town for the public to see and then executed.   (book 2)

There are many scenes in books 2 and 3 in which Ung and his soldiers are carried away by triumph; they dance and sing with decapitated heads skewered on their spears. These are scenes of unmitigated cruelty and of the violent vicissitudes of military life as imagined by audiences of the time. Ung's killing of the usurper Yi Tubyŏng and his officials is depicted as the perfect revenge, exactly what those evil characters deserve. These scenes reflect audiences' desire for justice in a time when the people were not deeply attached to softer virtues such as benevolence and compassion. When Ung and his mother suffer from Yi's persecution at the beginning of the story, readers of the time would have seen the foreshadowing of an ultimate, bloodthirsty revenge by Ung, pursued coldly until the moment justice is achieved. Even more than a device for Ung's revenge, the killing in the tale was a way for the audience to vicariously triumph over an undefeatable enemy.

By portraying Yi Tubyŏng as the perfect evil official, the tale harshly criticizes the corruption of those in power at the time and conveys a radical agenda of building a new political order or restoring the current dynasty to its ideal state. The death of Ung's father due to power struggles and factionalism and the exile of the crown prince by Yi Tubyŏng's coup d'état represent what governance by evil people does to society at large. Though it may seem like a trite plot device, the prefect of Kangho's evil plan to use his power to force marriage on Maiden Chang efficiently reveals the evils of a corrupt ruling class on a local level.

The *Tale of Cho Ung* may have been written to attack the royal class or certain groups of officials who wielded malicious power, and particular historical events may have inspired the popularization of the story.[51] Some even speculate that it may even have been an attempt to undercut the Chosŏn dynasty by attacking its founder, Yi Sŏnggye (1335–1408, who shares his surname with the evil character Yi Tubyŏng), who usurped the throne of the previous dynasty to start his own.[52] Given that the Chosŏn dynasty lasted more than five hundred years, some remarks made by court officials in the tale may support this interpretation. When one of Yi's cronies says, "Indeed, the land is not owned by one person, and there has been no imperial household that has lasted more than ten generations. As for the future of the country, how can we let the eight-year-old crown prince become the next emperor?" (book 1), readers are invited to think about the history and problems of their current dynasty, which had lasted well over ten generations when the tale became popular.

Likewise, the tale repeatedly reveals a concern with the weakness of the state in the wake of political conflict and disorder. Scholars of Chosŏn military tales have demonstrated that the employment of such political themes attracted a large readership and commercial success.[53] If episodes from the *Tale of Cho Ung* were based on real political incidents in which innocent people were hurt, it must have been a comfort to those who had fallen victim to false accusations and traps or had lost loved ones during political upheaval. It is an intriguing challenge for the reader to connect the world represented in the story with a historical reality, but, in any case, the tale undeniably gave voice to popular sentiments toward the Korean elite and the ruling class of the time. The character of Cho Ung served as an outlet for people's dissatisfaction with political realities and as a symbol of hope for change.[54] As the son of a noble family, Ung also represented the need for noblesse oblige among the ruling class of Korea.

The *Tale of Cho Ung* shows how premodern themes and characters can still speak to the sensibilities of modern audiences, offering pleasure, catharsis, and life lessons. As a coming-of-age story in which a heroic youth struggles to triumph over adversity, the tale can even galvanize readers while it simultaneously entertains them. The clichés that "Justice is served" and "Good efforts will be rewarded" were a source of reassurance to most late Chosŏn fiction readers, just as they are to readers today. The long-standing success of the tale is rooted in its role as an act of *tikkun olam* (repair of the world) that fulfills people's needs both for a champion and for an escape from everyday life.[55] The *Tale of Cho Ung* allows premodern and modern audiences alike to travel through a world of wonders and symbolically defeat that which has caused their disillusionment.

NOTE ON THE TRANSLATION

This translation is intended for both the scholar and the general reader with an interest in classical Korean fiction. It provides an approachable translation, detailed explanations of culturally specific terms, and in-depth commentary on obscure sections to further scholarly discussion.

The translation is based on the oldest extant woodblock edition from Wansan (*wanp'an*), which has 104 leaves in three volumes (33–33–38), the first of which dates from the *chŏngsa* 丁巳 year (1857).[1] It also draws upon invaluable modern collated editions, such as those by Yi Hŏnhong (Seoul: Koryŏ taehakkyo minjok munhwa yŏn'guso, 1996) and Cho Hŭiung (Seoul: Chimanji, 2009), whose annotations and interpretations are based on 104-leaf Wansan editions.[2] In addition, I consulted as many other commercial editions as possible to fill in gaps, correct errors, and ensure a more accurate and comprehensive translation. Examples of other editions I consulted include the following:

1. 97 leaves in three volumes (33–33–31), Wansan sin'gan 完山新刊, the *imjin* year (1892); at Sogang University

2. 89 leaves (30–30–29), n.p., n.d.; at Ewha Womans University, and also University of Tokyo (Ogura Collection)

3. 80 leaves (30–26–24), Wannam sin'gan 完南新刊, the *musul* year (1898); at C. V. Starr East Asian Library, University of California at Berkeley

4. 80 leaves, manuscript, Posŏng, Chŏlla-namdo, the *imja* year (1912?); at University of Tokyo (Ogura Collection)

This translation includes new research on available editions of the *Tale of Cho Ung*, and also on the references to classical texts found in the tale. As a result, it corrects some errors of earlier interpretations. The present volume also supplies a more elaborate context for the *Tale of Cho Ung* and a variety of alternate interpretations, inviting a detailed appreciation of the story.

Searching for a good translation model in modern Korean, I also consulted recent versions of the *Tale of Cho Ung*. Most of these are educational rewritings based on the short Seoul editions; the literary and cultural value and deep emotional world of the Wansan editions are largely absent. However, Yi Myŏngnang's rewriting of the *Tale of Cho Ung* in modern Korean (Ch'angbi, 2005), though abbreviated, reveals the core value and literary emotion of the original story, which is one of my aims in producing a translation that will appeal to modern readers.

In translating the *Tale of Cho Ung* into English, my first challenges were how to treat the traces of oral storytelling—for example, repetitions and the use of formulaic and idiomatic expressions—and how to interpret unidentified or abstruse terms and phrases. The complicated nature of the text makes a literal translation almost impossible. Crafting a reader-friendly translation that conveys the mood and savor of the original text requires delicate and careful judgment. To make this popular tale available to modern readers, I therefore set rules for translation.

First, this translation seeks to convey all the meanings expressed in the original text through a combination of direct and paraphrastic interpretations, applied to varying degrees on a case-by-case basis. Fixed terms and clear sentences are translated word for word, while other passages are paraphrased in order to communicate the full meaning of the text to modern readers. Likewise, the translated songs and poems do not always have the same numbers of lines as the originals.

Second, whereas the original text tends to use the same term or expression throughout to describe a similar or recurring situation, I have varied the corresponding English translation slightly depending on the specific context, particularly when translating honorific titles such as *kongja* and idioms or allusions such as *paekkollanmang* and *namga ilmong*. Exact repetition is not always helpful.

Third, the translation does not retain habitual repetitions from the original text when they are unnecessary or hinder the readability of the tale. This is especially true of juxtapositions of the Korean reading of Sino-Korean words and the explanation of those words within a sentence. However, when the original text narrates a Sino-Korean poem and then provides an explanation in Korean to instruct the audience, I include both cases so as to preserve the storytelling environment in which the tale is rooted.

Fourth, the translation uses brackets [ ] for any addition that is not part of the original text (e.g., for restored phrases from other editions or to supply a word the reader needs to know). Brackets also enclose paraphrased expressions that elucidate unidentified names, places, and times or that summarize earlier events (such as *mowŏl moil, irŏ kurŏ, iri iri,* and *yŏch'a yŏch'a*). When necessary, I elaborate on such expressions to help readers understand the context.

Finally, this translation uses the McCune-Reischauer romanization system and the Chinese pinyin system. Though the tale is set in China, the Korean reading is applied to names and places in the original text, so there are many places whose Chinese characters are not confirmed. In the notes, however, I use Korean, Chinese, or both, and include original Chinese characters for names and places whenever they could be readily identified or were already available in other manuscript editions. For modern Chinese place names, I use the Chinese reading, along with simplified Chinese characters. In translating official titles, I used both Chinese and Korean sources, including Charles Hucker's *A Dictionary of Official Titles in Imperial China* (Stanford: Stanford University Press, 1985) and the *Glossary of Korean Studies* by the Academy of Korean Studies.

These conventions will allow students and scholars of East Asian studies to engage more deeply with the textual characteristics of the original tale, discovering differences and commonalities between the Chinese and Korean languages and cultures. I hope that my efforts to create a readable translation that addresses the complicated nature of this story will enhance our understanding of premodern Korean and East Asian literature and allow a new generation of readers to enjoy the exciting *Tale of Cho Ung*.

THE TALE OF
CHO UNG

BOOK 1

The twenty-third year of Emperor Mun's reign in the Song dynasty was a time of peace.[1] In the absence of conflict, the people lived tranquilly and contentedly, free to sing the "Earth-Drumming Song."[2] In autumn of the twenty-fifth year,[3] on the day of *pyŏngin*[4] in the ninth month, Emperor Mun visited the Shrine of the Loyal Martyr—the tomb of Left Prime Minister Cho Chŏngin, the most loyal subject of the emperor.[5]

Minister Cho had been the chief steward of the Ministry of Personnel in the tenth year of Emperor Mun's reign.[6] At that time, a war broke out unexpectedly in the south.[7] The royal court suffered terribly during the war and was on the verge of collapse. With no stratagem to save the court, Minister Cho escorted the emperor with his royal seal through the Gate of Kyŏnghwa, over the Hill of Mubong, and finally to the Bridge of Kwangim.[8] The screams of people could be heard both inside and outside the city walls. Thrown into chaos, men and women, old and young, hurriedly fled. As Minister Cho hastily escaped with

Emperor Mun, the mountains were nearly covered by those seeking refuge—their robes veiled the mountains to the north and south like peach blossoms in the full bloom of spring, though spring had not yet come. The minister and the emperor traveled 150 li to the Pass of Noesŏng and spent the night there, resuming their journey the next day.[9]

The minister escorted the emperor from place to place, gathering reinforcements. In three months, they subdued the rebellion in the south and saved the royal court from collapse. Emperor Mun's grace and virtue were like the sky and the earth, while the minister's loyalty was like the sun and the moon. Emperor Mun bestowed the title of king of pacification on Minister Cho,[10] but Minister Cho respectfully declined it. Still wanting to express his gratitude, Emperor Mun granted Minister Cho the joint position of "grand master of the palace with golden seal and purple ribbon and left prime minister."[11] The minister's wife, Lady Wang, was given the title "lady of achievement."

For a while, time passed without hardship. But soon a time of misfortune came, as when the bow and arrow are stacked away because there are no more birds to shoot, and the hounds get cooked once all the hares are bagged.[12] Seized by jealousy, the villainous right prime minister, Yi Tubyŏng, made a false accusation against Minister Cho.[13] Upon learning of his slander, Minister Cho committed suicide with poison [to avoid being drawn into Yi Tubyŏng's evil scheme]. In his grief, Emperor Mun composed an elegy to the minister, built the Shrine of the Loyal Martyr, and commissioned his portrait. He housed the portrait inside the shrine and frequently visited it.

On one visit to the shrine, the chief steward of the Ministry of War,[14] Yi Kwan, son of Yi Tubyŏng, was attending the emperor. Reminding him of old times, the portrait of Minister Cho repeatedly overwhelmed the emperor with sadness. Kowtowing, Yi Kwan said to the emperor, "I am sure Your Majesty can find someone as loyal as Cho Chŏngin among your liege men. Ironically, while this place is named the Shrine of the Loyal Martyr [to honor his contributions], it only brings sorrow to your jadelike face. Even in death, a truly loyal liege man should never cause the emperor grief. Please, I beg you not to come to the shrine from now on and to destroy it." But the emperor denied his request

and ordered that Yi Kwan be interrogated for his offense. After staying at the shrine all day, the emperor returned to the palace as the sun
was setting. He decreed that Lady Wang be promoted to the title of
"lady of reverence and eminence"[15] and bestowed upon her a large
amount of gold and silver. He then sent an order to Lady Wang: "I have
heard that Cho Chŏngin had a son. Bring him to my presence. He will
relieve my feelings of despondence and grief."

Lady Wang had been seven months pregnant when she lost her husband. In the tenth month of her pregnancy, she gave birth to a boy. The
boy was extraordinary and full of spirit, and so he was named Ung, literally meaning "hero."[16] Lady Wang wore her widow's weeds for eight
years and relied solely on her son.[17] When she heard of the emperor's
visit to the Shrine of the Loyal Martyr, she felt her sorrow anew. But
soon after the emperor's return, the appointed official brought her new
title from the palace, along with gold and silver. Overwhelmed by the
honor, she descended the stone steps and bowed. After receiving the
emperor's decree, she faced toward the palace and made a deep bow four
times to pay respect to the emperor. She led the official into the reception room, offered him a seat, and expressed her gratitude to the
emperor. She felt very honored to see the wooden tablet with Emperor
Mun's order to bring Ung to the court and immediately asked him to
follow the official to the palace.

Ung was only seven-years-old, but his face was as handsome as jade,[18]
and his posture and gestures were more courteous and humble than
those of most adults. At the court, in front of the jade-decorated stairs,
he kowtowed to the emperor. After examining the boy for a long time,
the emperor praised him highly, saying, "The son of a loyal subject is
also a loyal subject, and the son of an inferior man is also an inferior
man.[19] How beautiful that your appearance tells me immediately that
you are nothing but loyal and filial. It is also splendid to know that you
are seven-years-old, the same age as the crown prince." The emperor
summoned the crown prince and said to him, "This boy is the son of
our loyal subject. He is the same age as you, a loyal subject and a filial
son. When the time comes, discuss state affairs with him. I am so
happy to have a trustworthy person beside me, now that I'm nearly
eighty, with whom I can discuss politics." The emperor's words made

the crown prince happy. Ung prostrated himself before the emperor and said, "I am most honored and grateful for your kind words, Your Majesty. However, your subject is still a little boy, and it could damage the prestige of the country if the son of a commoner's family were to reside in the palace. I am afraid I would be a burden to you if you were to discuss state affairs with me now, because they must be taken seriously. I beg you on my knees that I may request a leave of absence and be allowed to seek an audience with you when I am a more experienced and capable man." After listening to this earnest entreaty, the emperor realized that, although Ung was only a little boy, his words were wise. He also found Ung's attitude to be very serious and sincere. He told Ung, "Your remarks are most right. Do as you wish." He also said to the boy, "When you turn thirteen, you will be granted a government position. When that time comes, you will assist me with state affairs." Hearing this, Ung bowed deeply to the emperor four times and left the court. Before leaving the palace, he said goodbye to the crown prince, who was disappointed to see him go.

After the boy left, the emperor summoned all his officials to the court and praised Ung. He asked, "Is Yi Kwan among you? Where is he?" Right Prime Minister Ch'oe Sik, afraid of Yi's brothers' power like the rest, stepped forward and replied, "Your Majesty gave an order to interrogate him for his dishonorable conduct at the Shrine of the Loyal Martyr. He has been dismissed from his position." Thinking back on the incident, the emperor relented, saying, "His words were careless, but I will forgive him."

Yi Tubyŏng had five sons. They all held first-rank official positions in the government. All court officials feared the power of these sons so much that they obeyed any request from Yi Kwan and his brothers. After seeing the emperor openly displaying his fondness for Ung, Yi Kwan became anxious. He discussed the matter with the others, saying, "I am quite concerned that when Ung gets a position in the government, he will think about avenging his father's death. It would be wise to kill him before then. But how can we accuse this little boy of wrongdoing when he does not yet hold a position in the government?" They continued to plot against Ung.

Ung returned home and greeted his mother. She happily asked, "Did you have an audience with the emperor?" Ung replied, "Yes, I did, as soon as I entered the palace." "Were you not afraid to see the emperor in person? He must have had some questions for you—how did you answer?" his mother asked. Ung told her of how he had answered the emperor, the emperor's plan to grant him a position when he turned thirteen, and the emperor's love for the crown prince. Torn between joy and sorrow, Lady Wang said, "The emperor's grace is as broad as the sky and the sea. It is an impossible task to repay him. [However, the court is full of jealous people.] Once you have a position, I fear you will be falsely accused and arrested. What do you plan to do then?" Ung replied, "Mother, please do not worry. A person's life is determined by heaven, and his fame and shame are contingent upon his luck, so what is there to worry about? Also, as a man, I cannot stay idle when there is a sworn enemy before my eyes. However, I assure you that I will not do anything to avenge my father's death until I devise a good plan. Please don't worry." When their conversation ended, both mother and son wept bitterly. Their sorrow was beyond description.

It was the eighth day of the twelfth lunar month in the year of *pyŏngin*.[20] The emperor was greeted by officials as he sat on the throne in the palace courtyard. While discussing matters of the state, the emperor said to his officials, "Alas, my age is near eighty, and time only hurries one's death. I am concerned, for the crown prince is still young and unable to take care of state affairs. What, in your opinion, can be done to ease my worry?" All the officials said, "The rise and fall of a country is not determined by one's will. Our country will continue to be strong for a long time. So, do not be concerned about the crown prince's youth." Chŏng Ch'ung, chief steward of the Ministry of Rites,[21] stepped forward and said to the emperor, "Why are you so concerned about your old age and the crown prince's youth? You can rest assured that Minister Yi Tubyŏng will take good care of state affairs in the future." All the officials, fearing Yi Tubyŏng's power, agreed, "Minister Yi is like So Mu of the Han dynasty, so please do not worry about state affairs."[22] Initially, the emperor took them at their word, but he was not entirely convinced. Gradually he began to doubt.

On the same morning, during the hour of *chín*,[23] a white tiger appeared and passed through the Gate of Kyŏnghwa. It began to prowl around the palace. Every official and all three thousand soldiers at the palace were frightened and did not know what to do. As they panicked, the white tiger seized a court lady in its mouth and jumped into the rear garden, only to disappear without a trace, taking her with it. After hearing about the incident, the shocked emperor asked his officials to tell him about it in detail. They, however, did not know exactly what had happened either. Both the palace and the whole capital city were troubled and saddened by the incident,[24] not knowing whether it was a good sign or an ill omen. The emperor was so troubled by the incident, he was unable to eat or sleep. The officials reassured him, saying, "We have had a northern wind for days, and the fields and mountains are covered with more than a foot of snow.[25] The tiger must have been starving with nowhere to go and came here, thinking it was a grove. This is not unusual and should cause you no worry." The emperor was somewhat relieved, but he still had doubts, anticipating the worst.

Hallim Academician Wang Yŏl, a cousin of Lady Wang,[26] witnessed the incident and wrote her a letter.[27] Lady Wang was encouraging Ung to read books and teaching him about the country's history, when a servant entered with the letter. It read: "One day, sitting on the throne in the palace courtyard, the emperor was discussing the affairs of the country with his officials. Unexpectedly, a white tiger appeared. Prowling around, it seized a court lady in its mouth and disappeared. Because this was such a bizarre incident, the emperor is deeply concerned, and the court is unable to predict what will happen next. My sister, I hope you can tell me what this will lead to."

Lady Wang became pale with fright at what she read. She contemplated the event and wrote a reply to her cousin. She then told Ung, "A strange incident occurred in the country. When you get a position in the government in the near future, I fear that you will not be able to avoid persecution by treacherous officials." Ung replied, "Mother, please don't worry. One's fame and shame cannot be determined by someone else's will. The branch of a cinnamon tree sometimes flowers among pear or peach blossoms. It blooms as a cinnamon tree because pear flowers are pear flowers and cinnamon flowers are cinnamon flowers. They

don't simply mix and become one. Therefore, even if the court is full
of vile characters, as long as I am clear of any wrongdoing, like a white
jade, they could not possibly conspire to accuse me of any crime." His
mother replied, "You know only one thing, but not the other.[28] There
is a sorrowful aphorism that both jade and stone will burn together if
there is a fire on Mount Hyŏng.[29] Considering this wisdom, I doubt
that your enemies would deem you innocent and leave you alone when
misfortune is brought upon the entire state. Who would believe such
noble thoughts as my little boy has?" Ung replied, "When a person
confronts an obstacle in life, too much worry will cause him to be
overly anxious, which will not help to make things work out in his
favor. There is a saying: 'Place troops in mortal danger, and they will
fight to live; throw them into hopeless situations, and they will be preserved.'[30] I do not believe heaven will simply abandon us." Lady Wang
felt relieved by Ung's optimism.

Meanwhile, Hallim Academician Wang Yŏl received Lady Wang's
letter, which read: "How strange and bizarre! There will be trouble in
the country, and it will lead to rebellion in the near future.[31] Do not be
so foolish as to persist in your official post. Submit a request to resign."
Understanding, Wang Yŏl left the court by faking an illness and
departed for his hometown.

On the fifteenth day of the first lunar month in the year of *chŏngmyo*,[32]
all officials assembled to greet the emperor. The emperor announced,
"Some years ago I met Cho Ung. He appeared to be a loyal, filial, and
talented boy who could set a good example for the government.[33] For
the sake of the crown prince, I intend to bring the boy here and make
him an attendant in my study,[34] so that he can learn to understand
state affairs. What are your opinions?" None of the officials spoke a
word until Minister Yi Tubyŏng said, "The state must maintain its
prestige. Therefore, it would be unfortunate and unsafe to allow the
child of a commoner to reside in the palace without some special
reason."[35] To this, the emperor replied, "This is a question of recruit-
ing a loyal and talented person. He will be here for all the right reasons." Minster Yi Tubyŏng argued again, "If Your Majesty is looking
for a talented person, we will find hundreds of people in the capital
city alone who are ten times as loyal as Cho Ung. People with Cho

Ung's talent are too numerous to count."[36] The emperor did not agree and no longer wanted to hear the minister's opinion. There was no further discussion.

The minister walked out to the Chamberlain's Terrace and talked with the other officials. He threatened, "From now on, anyone who recommends that Cho Ung be allowed in the court will be punished." Everyone was cowed. Lady Wang and Cho Ung heard of the minister's warning as well. While the lady feared what the minister might do, Ung was infuriated.

Alas, the emperor's luck turned against him; he fell unexpectedly ill.[37] A month passed, but his illness only worsened. People throughout the country prayed to heaven for the emperor's swift recovery, but with the royal court full of vile, disloyal officials, it was difficult to maintain hope.

On the third day of the third lunar month in the year of *chŏngmyo*, the emperor passed away.[38] The crown prince was grief-stricken, and the people's mourning and lamentation filled the country. Lady Wang and her son were particularly saddened by the news. Shortly after the emperor's death Minister Yi took power, and his word was stronger than laws. Crowds began to sing the "Tune of Lament for Doomed Countries,"[39] and frightened people fled and hid in the mountains. In the summer, on the fourth day of the fourth lunar month, the officials buried the emperor in the West Hill according to the proper funeral rites.

One day, officials of all ages gathered at the Chamberlain's Terrace to discuss the affairs of the country. Yi Tubyŏng, harboring treasonous thoughts, conspired to seize the royal seal. The officials had no choice but to acquiesce.

It was the thirteenth day of the tenth lunar month, the birthday of the late Emperor Mun. The officials discussed the affairs of the country all day. Yi Tubyŏng said, "The crown prince is barely eight-years-old. Every state matter is of vital importance—the future of the country will be very dark if the eight-year-old prince ascends to the throne and becomes emperor. If he fails to enforce laws and our court falls into a dangerous state, what do you all plan to do?"

The officials replied at once, "Indeed, the land is not owned by one person, and there has been no royal court that has lasted more than ten generations. As for the future of the country, we cannot imagine letting the eight-year-old crown prince become the next emperor. While the emperor said on his deathbed that the crown prince should consult Minister Yi in making decisions, no country has two kings and no man has two heavens. It is unthinkable to have an emperor who relies on others to decide state matters."

As if the words came from the mouth of one person, all the officials spoke in unison, "Many days have passed now since we stopped discussing official business. We beg you to receive the royal seal of the former emperor and ascend to the throne, so that no one in this country will be dismayed." They then prostrated themselves four times before Minister Yi. His authority was as cold as frost and snow, and no one could challenge it. A great commotion ensued in the palace, and people cried and fled as if from a war zone—chaos and riots broke out across the capital.

Shortly, Yi Tubyŏng proclaimed himself emperor. After rewriting state laws, he sent official letters to all the administrative units of the empire and granted nationwide promotions. The officials gathered, deprived the crown prince of his title, and drove him out of the palace to live in a guesthouse built for hosting foreign envoys. Common people, attendants, consorts, concubines, eunuchs, and slaves inside and outside the palace shouted out to the heaven and the earth, deeply lamenting what had happened. The clear blue sky seemed to roar in rage, and the bright sun appeared to have lost its light.

Lady Wang turned pale with fright when she learned about the incident. She exclaimed fearfully, "Ung will be killed!" She prayed to heaven day and night, "Ung is only eight. Please spare his innocent life." No one could bear to witness such desperation. Ung held her by the arm and consoled her, "Don't think about the life of your unworthy son. Instead, take good care of your precious self. This short life is like a dream. I do not want to see you agonize over worries. I am afraid you will do yourself harm. Everyone dies eventually, even a conquering king. Although Yi Tubyŏng is our sworn enemy, I believe his sword cannot kill me, Cho Ung, since we did not wrong him. Please do not worry about me."[40] But Ung's heart was filled with anger.

Yi Tubyŏng named his eldest son, Yi Kwan, crown prince and renamed the dynasty. He fashioned himself the Emperor of P'yŏngsun[41] and announced the beginning of the first year of his reign called Kŏnmu.[42]

After being kept for some time in the guesthouse for envoys, the deposed crown prince of the Song dynasty, at the request of the officials, was transferred to the Kyeryangdo of Mount T'ae on which he was confined to a residence and guarded constantly so that none would hear news of him.[43] Hearing of the crown prince's exile, both Lady Wang and Ung cried, "We wish to follow and stand behind the crown prince in life or death. However, if the officials discover any trace of our loyalty, they will pursue and kill us both before we reach him. What should we do?" They wept day and night.

One evening, Ung was contemplating a scheme for revenge while gazing at the bright moon at twilight. Frustrated and laden with grief, his anger mounted; he strode toward the main gate unnoticed by Lady Wang. Walking along the main street of the capital, he came upon a crowd of adults and children singing a popular song:

> The kingdom is shattered and the lord is gone,
> There is a child born without a father.
> Emperor Mun has become Emperor Sun (Pyŏngsun);
> The time of peace is replaced by a time of trouble.
> If heaven and earth still remain the same,
> How can the mountains and rivers be changed?
> The *Samgang* (Three Bonds) have not disappeared;
> How can the *Oryun* (Five Relations) be altered?[44]
> The rain that falls on a bright, sunny day
> Is none other than the tears from a loyal subject's grieving heart;
> If not, it is the jealous mind of a vile person.
> Alas, common people!
> You'd better wait for the time to come,
> Either riding in a small boat on the Five Lakes or wandering on the
> Four Seas.[45]

The song intensified Ung's anger. In a mounting fury, he walked impetuously toward the Gate of Kyŏnghwa and looked at the palace. Not a human sound was heard, and the courtyard was serene, bathed in bright moonlight. Floating on the pond were pairs of ducks and geese, and the scenery within ten li had not changed since the last dynasty.

Recalling the affairs of the previous dynasty, Ung felt his loyal heart bursting with sudden waves of sorrow. He wished to immediately climb over the short wall of the palace to confront and kill Yi Tubyŏng. However, he knew he was no match for Yi, and there were too many soldiers behind the tightly closed gate. Feeling helpless, he was about to turn back, but, overcome by a burst of anger, he took out a brush from his bag and wrote several lines on the gate cursing at Yi Tubyŏng. He then returned home leaving no other trace.

That night, under the lamp, Lady Wang had a dream in which her husband, Minister Cho, appeared and shook her awake. He said, "You are sleeping too deeply. When the dawn comes, a terrible disaster will come with it. Hurry and run away with Ung!" In surprise, Lady Wang asked him, "Where can we go in the middle of the night?" The minister replied, "A few tens of li away from here, you will find someone who can help you. Hurry, leave now!" Waking up, she realized it was only a dream of the Southern Branch.[46] Yet Ung was nowhere to be found. Shocked and worried, she hurried outside the gate to look for him, but saw nobody. On the verge of fainting, she peered in the direction of the main gate. Then she saw Ung in the distance, hastily returning home. She called, "Where did you go in the middle of the night?" Ung replied, "I was overcome by anger, so I wandered around, following the moonlight, and have just returned." Choking with emotion, Lady Wang said, "I just dreamed of your father. He told us to run away. Even if we may die fleeing, how can we just sit here and await our death? We must leave now! Hurry and pack!" Ung said in surprise, "On my walk, I heard some people singing their grievances. In anger, I went to the Gate of Kyŏnghwa and wrote my own grievances."

Frightened, Lady Wang scolded, "My little child, what have you done? Like a little kid near deep water, you always worry me. How could you be so thoughtless! When people see what you have written at dawn, we are sure to be killed immediately—let us quickly pack our belongings and leave."

They packed a few clothes and supplies that they could carry and hurried to the Shrine of the Loyal Martyr. Inside, the portrait of Minister Cho was blushed red and covered with sweat. The mother and son approached the portrait, kneeling in front of it. They could not cry loudly but they sobbed. Their hearts were so deeply saddened that they could not help but beat their breasts with their hands to ease their sorrow. What a pitiful and miserable scene it was! Finally calming, they collected their thoughts, removed the portrait, and packed it with their belongings. With Ung leading the way, they hurried to leave the shrine, walked hastily for tens of li, and arrived at the shore of a large river. The water was rough and mounting high along the banks. The moon had already sunk, and dark clouds covered the sky. As they struggled to find the road in the pitch dark they noticed a lonely boat tied at the river bank. The skipper was nowhere to be seen. Lady Wang got on the boat and pushed it with a pole, but the boat was tied firmly to something and would not move. Daylight was already beginning to break in the east, and there were still many li to go. In desperation, she looked up at the sky, cried, and tried to jump into the water to drown. Ung restrained her and implored her not to despair. Lady Wang could not bring herself to commit suicide.

Suddenly, from the southeast, they saw a small boat. Lit with a lamp and skippered by an immortal lad,[47] it was moving quickly toward them like an arrow flying over a vast sea. Lady Wang and Ung happily waited for the boat to reach them, but it passed them by in the blink of an eye. Lady Wang called out, "Skipper, please help desperate people!" The immortal lad stopped the boat and asked, "Who on earth are you to stop a boat on an urgent mission?" Nonetheless, he urged them to get aboard quickly. Lady Wang boarded gratefully with her son. The boat was comfortably appointed. When it was not rowed, it still moved like the wind. Lady Wang asked the immortal lad, "What important business makes you travel the vast water so hastily, as though it were a road?" He replied, "I have an order from the Master of South Mountain[48] to rescue people in the world who are in need. I travel from place to place, to the four seas and the eight directions."[49]

In a flash, the boat reached a shore, and the lad instructed them to disembark. Lady Wang and Ung gathered their belongings and got off. Expressing her deep gratitude, Lady Wang said, "Thanks to you, we have traveled the vast water safely, but we don't know how to repay you. If you don't mind, could you tell us how far we are from the capital city?" The lad replied, "1,300 li by water and 3,300 li by land." Lady Wang asked, "Where should we go to survive?" The lad reassured them, "You will undergo a short period of difficult times, but you will not be killed. There are some villages over that mountain; you should set out in that direction." Then he rowed away.

That night, the emperor awoke from a nightmare. At daybreak, he summoned all the officials. As they were interpreting his dream, the keeper of the Gate of Kyŏnghwa rushed inside and cried, "I have come to report a writing that appeared on the gate overnight. Here is a copy." The emperor read:

The Song dynasty has become weak, and the court is full of corrupt officials. The people are so unfortunate that the emperor has passed away. The crown prince is still young, and villains in power are enjoying their golden time. Yi Tubyŏng is the worst of all. His rank was already first tier. What has made him become a traitor? Since the will of heaven is perfect, you will not live long. How could you take the royal seal when it rightfully belongs to the crown prince? When the fast deer,[50] once owned by the First Emperor of Chin,[51] was freed and allowed to roam about freely, the Hegemon King of Ch'o[52] tried hard to catch it with his strong courage and spirit. His efforts were supported by Pŏm Chŭng's marvelous plans.[53] Yet still he failed, and the deer fell to someone else's hand. You, vile traitor, you are also doomed to fail! Wealth and nobility are precious, but, if you value your life and your fate, you will not dare bring to an end the rule of the Song dynasty. You are unforgivable in any place in this endlessly broad world. Contemplating your crimes in detail, one by one, they are countless, so one single writing will not be enough to record them all. The writing on the right side is written by a loyal subject of the previous dynasty.[54] Cho Ung.

The emperor and officials were all shocked and enraged by the writing. They apprehended the gatekeeper and threw him out after beating him with a cudgel as punishment for not catching Ung in the act. They then shouted a command to capture Ung and his mother. The whole capital was in an uproar. The soldiers surrounded the house of Ung and searched inside but found it silent and empty. The constable returned to the palace and reported that they had already fled. Furious, the emperor pounded his fist on the table. He berated the officials, saying, "If you do not catch Ung and his mother, I shall have all of you punished. Go and capture them at once to alleviate my anger!"

The terrified officials surrounded the entire capital city. They encircled the thirty-li walls of the imperial castle with rings of troops, determined to capture Ung and his mother. But Ung and Lady Wang were already three thousand li from the city, where no one could capture them. The emperor, infuriated at his officials' failure to arrest the fugitives, yelled, "Bring to me the portrait of Minister Cho from the Shrine of the Loyal Martyr, now!" A constable rode to the shrine of Minister Cho, but he found that the portrait was no longer there. He rushed back to the palace and reported to the emperor that it was gone. The emperor pounded on the table even more furiously. Enraged and agitated, he ordered the gatekeeper to be brought to him again. The officials in attendance trembled with fear and anxiety. They brought the gatekeeper immediately into the emperor's presence. Livid, the emperor did not ask him anything, but ordered him beheaded and his head placed on public display.[55] In no time, his order was carried out. The emperor then cried, "Burn down the shrine and the house of Minister Cho."

In his anxiety, the emperor could no longer sleep or eat well. Noticing this, the officials spoke to him, "Ung is but an eight-year-old boy, and his mother is a mere woman. They could not have gone too far. If we post a capture order in every town of every province, it will be like catching a fish in a well, so Your Majesty does not need to worry." The emperor agreed and sent an order to each town announcing: "Whoever, regardless of rank, captures Cho Ung and his mother will be granted the reward of one thousand pieces of gold and the title of Marquis."[56] Officials throughout the country received the order and did their utmost to be the first to capture the pair.

Meanwhile, Ung and his mother left the boat and went over the mountain just as the lad had instructed. They saw a neat, clean village with rows of houses surrounded by bamboo and pine trees. Sitting near the entrance to the village, they watched people behaving tenderly with one another; the villagers seemed relaxed and unhurried. Ung and his mother begged a drink from someone fetching water at the well and

asked everyone who came there for a room for the night. Finally, someone led them to a house where they could stay. Entering the house,
they found it silent. No man dwelled there, only an aged lady and a
sixteen-year-old girl. Ung and his mother approached them, bowed to
show their respect, and looked inside the room. The room was as clean
as a jade; you could almost see your reflection in it.

The old lady asked Lady Wang, "Where are you from, and where are
you going?" Lady Wang replied, "Unfortunately, I lost my husband at a
young age, and later another tragedy befell our household. We narrowly
escaped, and I have been wandering with my little son. Thanks to
heaven, we found you. If I may, where is this place and what is its name?"
The old lady said, "It is called the Paekcha village of Kyeryangsŏm."[57]
She bade the girl cook dinner. The food was simple and plain, but
smelled good. Ung and his mother ate to their hearts' content and
thanked the old lady again and again. The old lady appreciatively said,
"I have treated you to a very simple meal; it makes me uneasy to be
thanked too much." Lady Wang thanked her again and asked after her
husband's whereabouts. The old lady replied with a deep sigh, "My husband was governor of Kyeryang. After he retired, we built this house to
settle down in this village which seemed quiet and remote. However,
due to ill fate, my husband died when he was just over fifty-years-old.
He left with me this little girl. Without a head of household, we couldn't
go back to our hometown, although we wanted to. So we became villagers and now lead a simple life here."

Hearing this, Lady Wang also sighed, and offered to join their household. She had a comfortable life there, but the thought of her hometown always brought terrible sorrow and uneasiness. Time is indifferent to a person's grief; seasons passed, and she grew older living in a
strange land. Nothing can compare to the resentments and anxieties
she endured as a result.

Time passed quickly. Lady Wang turned forty, and Ung nine. For
generations, the Paekcha village had produced one hundred kinds of
medicinal herbs. The villagers made their living by selling these herbs, and
so the village came to be called Paekcha, meaning "all kinds of resources."

One day, the old lady tactfully asked Lady Wang, "In this dreamlike
world our lives are like duckweed floating on the water. Even if you

were to live a comfortable life with us for a hundred years, you would still have many regrets. You are still young, and you are left destitute. How do you intend to endure all the hardships of the world by yourself?"

Smiling, Lady Wang replied, "I know that our lives are empty and meaningless in this world. However, because of my age and my lot in life, I do not expect to live much longer. I only hope to see my son carry on the family line. This hope alone drives me to live on." The old lady said, "How pitiful your words are! When heaven and earth came into existence, mankind and all other things were created by the opposition of clarity and obscurity. Opposite sexes were made so that they could enjoy the pleasure of union. Why do you still think of your long-deceased husband, spending the rest of your life without joy? Time does not wait for you, and your hair only turns gray. No matter how much you later regret the years wasted in faithfulness to your husband, it will be too late, and you will never regain your youth. All I ask of you is to meet my cousin, who also lives in this village. He lost his wife at a young age and was unable to find another suitable wife although he searched far and wide, day and night. Heaven dictated that we should meet each other. Now that I have known you for a while, I feel you are a good match for my cousin. Please don't think what I am saying is a curse. If you forsake a little of your noble faith, you will enjoy wealth and pleasure for the rest of your life. Please carefully think it over."

When the old lady had finished, Lady Wang felt a chill in her forehead and became very upset. She realized, however, that these were just the words of an elderly lady, and she tried to calm down. She said firmly, "Although it is said that being away from home makes a person humble, how could you be so inconsiderate as to insult me with such words, as if I were a slattern? Perhaps the nature of all mankind is the same, but individually we have different beliefs. Now that you have humiliated me so, how can I have the will to live?"

Seeing that Lady Wang was very upset, the old lady backed off. She realized that Lady Wang would not listen to her immediately. She changed her tone to one of appeasement, saying, "I only want what is best for you because I pity your situation. I am sorry and feel embarrassed that I have offended you." The old lady tried hard to soothe Lady

Wang and alleviate her anger. But day and night, Lady Wang worried that trouble awaited her.

The old lady told her cousin what had happened, stating, "There is no way to change her mind; her heart is as clean and cold as ice and snow." Her cousin was a rude and violent person. In a rage, he said, "Leave her be for now. She is like a netted fish. I have a plan for her."

One day Ung said to his mother, "It has been a while since we came to this village.[58] News from the capital city does not reach here, and when someone stays in a small village like this, he becomes foolish and fainthearted. I would like to leave, so I can hear the news and study with a good teacher." Since the day she had received the insulting proposal, Lady Wang had no longer wished to stay in the village, so she told Ung, "I cannot imagine staying here alone without you, and doubt I will be comfortable. You are right. Let us leave together." The following day, they packed their belongings and were ready to leave. They bade the old lady farewell, saying, "Your generosity is as broad as the rivers and seas. Sadly we must leave you without repaying your kindness. We do not want to trouble you any more." The old lady was surprised and sad to see them leave. She held their hands and asked them to come back to visit. Filled with sorrow, Lady Wang and Ung departed.

Little by little, they walked some tens of li. Their feet were swollen, and they were already tired. Ung noticed his mother limping, so he carried both of their packs. Walking little, they had to rest often, traveling barely another ten li. Soon they were exhausted and found an inn where they could rest. The next day, they divided their belongings between them and carried on. They walked for half a day but could not find an inn. Exhausted and starving, they sat down by the road. To their surprise, a man on horseback appeared from the distance. Ung asked the man for some food. He dismounted and said to them, "If my home were nearby, I would take you there. It is unfortunate, but I cannot." He gave Ung a small bag of food and tea. Ung thanked the man and returned to his mother. They ate all the food and drank the tea, but it was barely enough to ease their hunger and thirst.

Three days later, they managed to reach the Okkuyŏk village of the Haesan county.[59] Although it was still daylight, they decided to rest in the village for they were very tired, and their feet were swollen. Approaching the village, where there was a government way station, they heard a crowd of villagers chatting. Someone said, "The new emperor posted an order in every town of every province. It says that whoever apprehends Cho Ung and his mother will be rewarded with one thousand gold ingots and made a marquis governing ten thousand households. If, by divine intervention, we get lucky and capture them, we can become government officials." Fixated on the possibility of rewards, the villagers were clearly alert for suspicious travelers.

Ung and his mother overheard all this. Chilled to the bone, they felt their souls and bodies were crumbling.[60] They quickly fled from the village unnoticed, no longer feeling exhaustion or the pain in their feet. They went deep into the mountains and hid behind a boulder where they held each other and wept, "Wherever we go, we will surely be killed." As night fell and it grew dark, they cried bitterly, their sadness immeasurable. It was an early spring in the third lunar month. Hundreds of flowers were blooming, and the trees were growing dense and tall. In the darkness of the night and in the heart of the mountains, they had no place to go, so they spent the night resting against the boulder. Wild cats and wolves howled. Tigers and mountain lions came and went. However, the mother and son felt no fear of them.

Soon it was midnight during the third watch.[61] The moon softly cast the shadow of a tree, which looked like a drawing of mountain peaks and valleys. The chattering of indifferent monkeys evoked the grief of lonesome travelers. Mournful cuckoos, shedding tears that spotted a cluster of flowers, sang "Why Don't You Return?"[62] How sad it was! The cuckoos' cries reminded the mother and son of their piteous plight, and they felt at one with the birds. Amid the empty mountains,[63] even an iron-hearted man wouldn't have been able to resist the urge to sob.

Lady Wang held Ung and bewailed their lot in life. Her sorrow could have torn the green mountain apart, and even the trees and stones were sympathetic. They spent the night in despair, their eyes swollen and their faces wan. They looked as if they had become different people. Dawn broke, but where could they go? They were starving, with no strength to walk even a few steps.

Completely exhausted, Lady Wang lay down in the thick grass. Ung, still a little boy, brought his mother some flowers. "I cannot eat these even though I'm starving," she said, and she wept. Suddenly, they heard chattering. At first they were glad to encounter anyone, but then they became suspicious and frightened—they peered carefully along the track. Five or six nuns approached. Lady Wang asked them, "Which temple are you from, and where are you going?" [Ignoring her questions,] one of the nuns asked, "Where do you live? Why are you alone deep in the mountains?" Lady Wang replied, "We became lost and ended up here. We are too exhausted to move on. So we sit here helplessly." The nuns pitied Ung and his mother and gave them a little food, tea, and two bowls of cooked rice. Grateful for their generosity, Ung and Lady Wang replied, "Since you have saved us from the brink of death, we cannot thank you enough. How far is the temple from here?" The nuns said, "There is no temple on this mountain, and our temple is about one hundred li away. We would take you there, for it is not good to travel rugged mountain roads alone, but we are not heading that way. We are going to greet the new governor of this province.[64] Follow this road for some tens of li, and you will find a village."

Lady Wang bade farewell to the nuns and returned to Ung. They shared the food, which was enough to stave off their hunger. As soon as they finished eating, Ung got up and packed their belongings. He urged Lady Wang to get to her feet and proposed that they should leave immediately. Lady Wang said, "Where do you suggest we go? We would surely be caught by government officials, and I do not want to be killed at their hands. Perhaps it would be best to starve to death on this mountain." Ung said, "Heaven sets the course of a man's life. If heaven brings death to him, then he will die. If heaven brings life to him, then he will live. Why should we fear being killed by other men and let ourselves starve to death, becoming food for wild animals? Let's not worry but go on to the village," and he pressed her to move on.

Lady Wang replied in tears, "Don't say that with such confidence. If we travel together, we will stand out and get caught. How can you be unafraid? Perhaps we should alter our appearance. I will tonsure my head to look like a nun. You can then pretend to be my pupil. We won't be noticed." Ung said, "Our survival is important, but how can you simply give up your precious hair?"[65] Lady Wang tried to persuade him, "Don't worry. Tonsuring my head will not change how I live, for I am not a real nun. I have made up my mind." In tears, Ung said, "If you are going to shave your head, I will do so too." Lady Wang said, "Think. A child with a shaved head is going to look odd and attract suspicion. Don't be foolish!" Ung, knowing her determination, said, "Do as you wish." Lady Wang handed him a pair of scissors from her bag and instructed him, "Start cutting my hair." As he began, a torrent of tears gathered in his eyes, blinding him so he could not go on. He wailed bitterly and loudly. Lady Wang reproved him, "So far I have lived only for your sake. I expect you to be calm and comfort me. However, you are rousing my sadness, which I tried to repress, and not listening to me. How can I keep on living when you constantly defy me?"

Chastened, Ung stopped crying, picked up the scissors, and started cutting. It was an unpleasant sight that no one could have borne to watch. As soon as he finished, Ung threw away the scissors, wrapped his arms around his mother's head, and wept bitterly. The trees and rocks looked wet with tears, and the moon lost its light. Lady Wang and Ung both touched her head and wept, their suffering immeasurable. Lady Wang wiped the tears from Ung's face and soothed him, "Ung, do not cry. If you keep crying, I can't put my own mind at ease." Yet she could not stop her own jadelike tears from streaming down her cheeks. Ung stopped crying and tried to lift her spirits, saying, "Don't be sad. Compose yourself." Lady Wang tried to be strong and focused. She took a dress from her bag and altered it to look like a nun's robe. She covered her head with a one-ch'ŏk-long piece of cloth. When Ung saw her, he could not help but fall to his knees and weep bitterly. Lady Wang was also overcome by sadness, but she embraced Ung and allayed his sorrow. Before long, she urged him to get on his feet and start moving. She instructed Ung to walk ahead of her to the nearby village, following him with a bamboo cane in her hand. At the village, they begged for food, and no one recognized their true identities.

One day, they came to a village market. Lady Wang gave her sheared hair to Ung to sell at the market. He received only five *nyang*,[66] yet they were thankful, spending some of the money on food and keeping the rest in their bag. They decided to rest for a while at an inn. As it grew dark, they fell asleep. Lady Wang was woken by a tumult of loud voices outside. Soon the whole village was clamorous. Alarmed, she ran outside. A bandit holding a club charged toward her. Frightened, she jumped over the wall and ran away. Immediately her heart dropped; she realized she had left Ung behind. She turned around and saw pillars of fire rising from the town. The bandits shouted and chased the villagers. She beat at her breast and called Ung, but the bandits were already coming. She lost her sense of direction in the dark. Looking to the sky in grief, she called, "Ung, Ung!" Hearing a sound in the distance, she ran until she came to a house. She went inside, and realized it was a monument pavilion.[67] By hiding behind the monument, she was able to stay safe from the bandits.

Meanwhile, Ung was sleeping. Suddenly, a bandit grabbed his foot and threw him outside. Startled and disoriented, he looked into the room for his mother but could not find her. He saw a bandit taking away their belongings. Ung quickly pursued him. He clutched the bandit and, in tears, pleaded, "Our belongings are only worth a few coins. But there is some money inside them. Take the money, but please return the rest." Ung begged desperately. The old bandit took pity on him. He looked through the belongings and found three *nyang* and a portrait. He took the money and the portrait and returned the rest to Ung. "Kill me before you take away the portrait," Ung wept. The old bandit asked, "Whose portrait is this?" Ung said, "I am a pupil of a great master. My teacher carries the portrait of Buddha with him whenever he travels. Today, I was lodging at this inn, accompanying him, but now I am without him. If I lost the portrait, I wouldn't dare face my teacher. If I can't return to the temple, I, a child who has nowhere else to go, will die of starvation. Please take whatever you want, but leave the portrait behind. It won't be valuable to you anyway."

Deeply moved, the old bandit persuaded the other bandits to return the portrait. Ung put it in his bag and asked, "Do you know where I can find my teacher?" The old bandit replied, "Your teacher must have taken that road. Go that way." Ung thanked him and said, "I am alive because of your mercy. I am forever indebted to you, even after my death.[68] I don't know if we will meet again. Even so, I would like to know your name and home." The old bandit said, "Why would you want to know the name of a bandit? Leave quickly." Ung bade farewell to the old bandit and headed in the direction he pointed. Calling woefully to his mother, he wandered alone deep in the night. There was no response to his cries but silence.

Meanwhile, at the pavilion, Lady Wang drifted into a light slumber. In her short dream, Minister Cho appeared and said to her, "My dear, Ung will soon pass by. How can you be sleeping so carelessly?" She woke in astonishment and realized she was dreaming. She ran outside and heard someone crying. She listened carefully. It was Ung's voice! Fumbling in the darkness, she followed the voice, yelling, "Ung, is that you?" Ung replied, "Yes, it is I, Ung!" and ran to Lady Wang. Holding him in her arms, she wept, asking, "How did you escape from the raid?" Ung described how he had lost the money but, with the old bandit's help, had managed to save his own life and the portrait of his father. He also told how the bandit had led him to her. She said, in tears, "You went through a great ordeal to save our belongings. I am just glad you are alive, and the portrait is in our hands. I was chased by the bandits and fled here. Believing that you were dead, I had decided to kill myself without moving further in the darkness. Fortunately, I stumbled upon this pavilion and soon, in what might have been a dream or reality, your father appeared and spoke. . . ." She told Ung all that had happened. They decided to wait in the pavilion and leave at sunrise.

Soon, the roosters' crows announced the break of dawn, and the sun began to rise. Strangely, the inscription on the monument caught their eyes. From a distance, it looked as if it was wet with rain, but upon closer inspection they saw that it was written in shimmering gold. It read: "Inscription Forever Memorializing Cho Chŏngin, the Loyal Subject of the Great Country,[69] Vice Minister of the Ministry of War and Censor of Military Affairs of All Provinces."[70] It also read:

After the bright and exemplary emperor punished the king of the State of Wi,[71] innocent commoners suffered a famine and scattered to survive. The emperor dispatched a great official, who cared for the people like his own children. The weight of the emperor's virtue is heavier than Mount T'ae. It is impossible to recompense his goodness, as infinite as the sky and the earth. Listen, foolish people, will you forget to chant "Long Live the Emperor"?

Reading the inscription, Ung and his mother felt like they had been reunited with Minister Cho. They embraced the monument and wept bitterly. It appeared as if the trees and grasslands were crying, and that the birds and wild animals were all shedding tears with them. Consoling his mother, Ung asked, "Why is there a monument dedicated to my father?" She said, "It looks like we are at the border of the State of Wi. When your father was the vice minister of the Ministry of War, the king of Wi was Tu Ch'im.[72] He was atrocious and cruel, just as Emperors Kŏl and Chu of the Ha and Sang dynasties were.[73] The people of Wi, extremely distressed, composed a children's song that went, 'When will our king be doomed? One day feels like three years. When will his reign collapse?' This children's song spread over all the states. Meanwhile, the king of Wi conspired to revolt and seize the Great Country. Following the advice of a mysterious and wicked Daoist master,[74] the king kidnapped two fifteen-year-olds, a boy and a girl. They sliced the flesh from their bodies and dried it, complying with the principles of *ŭm* and *yang*,[75] and offered it as a sacrifice to heaven. Soon they gathered an army and marched toward the Great Country. When the army reached the Pyŏnyang area,[76] divine soldiers descended from heaven and crushed the king to death. For three years after the incident, it did not rain, and a period of severe famine followed, driving the people to scatter in all directions. Deeply concerned, the emperor selected your father to resolve the unrest. Your father overcame his reluctance and came to Wi, where he sacrificed cattle and sheep in a ritual to heaven, which brought light rain. He then gathered every grain from storage to provide relief to the people. On his way back, the people erected a monument honoring his deeds and fought to be the first to bid him farewell. When your father was still alive, he often talked about this place. I never imagined I would see the monument in person."

She then took a brush and ink from her pack and copied down the inscription from the monument. After she wept for a while, they prepared to leave. Yet which direction should they go? East, west, south, or north? What a sad moment! Being wanderers without supplies or money, they would surely die from hunger. Once they were dead, no one could bring them back.

Ung said to his mother, "It could be dangerous if we continue moving from inn to inn. Let us take shelter in a temple." His mother agreed. They searched for a temple and asked passing travelers for the location of a nearby one. Some told them, "If a monk does not know, how would a commoner know?," while others gave detailed directions.

Alas, time passed as quickly as flowing water. It had been three years since they started their journey. As they traveled, they often had to ask strangers for lodgings. Ung turned eleven-years-old. He had a healthy physique, and his strength could easily surpass that of an adult. Whenever they had to cross a stream, he carried his mother on his back.

Once they walked all day without seeing a single house. Hungry and thirsty, they sat down by the road. A group of mountain monks with iron canes appeared in the distance, coming from the rough, mountainous southeastern pass. Ung was happy to see them and eagerly awaited their arrival. The monks were glad to see Ung and his mother as well. One of them removed a light repast from his bag and handed it to Lady Wang, saying, "You must be very hungry from traveling. Allay your hunger with these." The mother and son were thankful and ate, alleviating their hunger. Grateful, Lady Wang said, "We have not met any other travelers on our way here. We were starving and on the verge of death. Fortunately we came across a Buddha saving human lives and filled our stomachs.[77] Your kindness will not be forgotten even after our death." The monk said with a smile, "If you feel so indebted for a little food, how will I repay you for the one thousand gold ingots I received from you?" Lady Wang said in surprise, "I am a poor nun who has to beg for food. How could I ever have possessed one thousand gold ingots?" He smiled again and said, "You are the wife of Lord Cho, loyal official of the Great Country, are you not? Despite your disguise, I know who you are." Lady Wang and Ung were petrified. They exclaimed, "We have been tracked down and finally exposed. Now we will die by the sword of our sworn enemy." In tears, they pleaded, "You will be awarded one thousand gold ingots and the rank of marquis to govern ten thousand households if you bring us to the capital city. However, one's wealth and nobility are only temporary and ephemeral in this world, just like a small cloud blown by a strong wind, or a bubble on the surface of water. Do not seek this short-lived opulence, but have mercy on us. You are also a disciple of Buddha. If you follow the teachings of Buddha and save lives, you will become a Buddha in your next life. On our knees we beg you to please show mercy and spare our lives." They clutched the monk and beseeched, in tears.

Smiling, the monk said, "My lady, do not fear. I am not here to apprehend you. Please relax and listen." When Lady Wang finally composed herself, he continued, "Please look carefully at me. Don't you recognize me? I am [Grand Master] Wŏlgyŏng. I came to your house to paint a portrait of Minister Cho. When I saw you after painting it, you made an offering of one thousand gold ingots to the temple, and I took them. How can you not remember me?" Lady Wang studied his face. She did think he resembled the painter. However, this uncertain world had made her suspicious. "I believe I did make an offering of one thousand gold ingots, but I don't recall exactly what it was for as that is not the sort of thing I normally remember. So please don't hesitate to tell me what you know," she said to him desperately. Wŏlgyŏng felt embarrassed and consoled her, saying, "My lady, you must have been under terrible strain while being away from home for so many years. With your poor health, your mind is not clear and you must have forgotten. However, I can prove myself. Please show me the portrait you have been carrying." Lady Wang's face turned pale in disbelief, and she asked, "Why would a beggar like me carry a portrait? Your Holiness, stop mocking my pathetic life and just do the right thing. I am like meat on your butcher block—do as you wish. Kill me or spare me." She wailed in sorrow. Understanding the strain she was under, Wŏlgyŏng asked, "Why are you so suspicious of me? When I met you after drawing the portrait, you were seven months pregnant. At the time, my intuition told me something about your future, so I read your facial features carefully and wrote my predictions of the hardships ahead of you on a piece of paper, inserting it into the back of the portrait. If you take out the portrait and find the piece of paper, it will allay your doubts and you will know the truth."

Curiosity led Lady Wang to pull out the portrait and detach the mounted paper from the backing. She examined it closely, and there indeed was a piece of paper with writing. It read:

What has made Lady Wang, who is as beautiful as flowers in full blossom, tonsure her head? She will meet a turtle in the waves of the rivers and the boundlessly vast water.[78] What fate does she share?[79] It must be the loyal soul of Kul Wŏn.[80] The little baby inside your belly is an extraordinary boy full of energy. Even though you make your childe[81] a pupil and disguise yourself as someone else, nothing will change, just as the portrait will not change, nor will this writing. The writing on the right side is written and sealed by Wŏlgyŏng from the Kangsŏnam[82] in the area of Sanyang[83] in the State of Wi, on the fifteenth day of the seventh month, in the fall of the year of kyŏng'o.[84]

After confirming that it was Wŏlgyŏng's writing, Lady Wang was filled with happiness. She held him and, in tears, cried, "I can't believe I could not recognize you! We have fled to save our lives from danger. We also heard the new emperor issued an edict throughout the country to apprehend us. Terrified, we traveled in disguise to avoid being caught. Thanks to heaven's grace, we met you here today. It is pleasant, though sad, to see you this way." Lady Wang was impressed by Wŏlgyŏng's accurate predictions. With her suspicion gone, she was relieved and spoke openly of her troubles. He exclaimed, "I have only a rough idea of what you have been through. However, the ups and downs and twists and turns of one's fortune are all determined by heaven. No matter how deeply you grieve, you cannot alter them. I have long anticipated meeting you here today. I intended to come much earlier and wait for your arrival, but I had urgent business to take care of at the temple. I am ashamed to say that I was late."

Wŏlgyŏng then led Lady Wang and her son along a rough mountain path. To their left and right stood steep cliffs that unfurled like folding screens, and tall trees grew densely, blocking the view of the mountain. In the deep woods, a stream wound its way through the forest, becoming a waterfall. The sound of a stone bell echoed from a distance and grew louder and louder. The travelers walked hastily as the sun set and rejoiced when they drew near their destination. They walked over a broken bridge and came to a stone gate.[85] Numerous mountain peaks and valleys surrounded the area like walls, but the middle was a broad open plain with a large pond whose water poured endlessly over its brim. At the shore, about ten monks were waiting for them in a boat. As they arrived, the monks disembarked and welcomed them politely. They boarded and sailed through lotus flowers in full bloom. The fragrance permeated their clothing. Above, impassive gulls flew to and fro. The travelers reveled in the sights, and before they knew it, they arrived at a heavenly palace, like the Land of the Immortals that floats in serenity.[86] The boat was moored at the temple gate, and they walked inside.[87] It was indeed like another world, not of humans—a fairyland.[88] It appeared as though the temple had been rebuilt from an older one. It was very neat and well kept. Lady Wang said, "Today I get to see your enchanting temple. But I am afraid I might taint it with my ordinary being." The monks said, "You are our honored guest, and your visit brightens our humble and modest home. Before, we lived in poverty and our temple was old and worn. It was about to give out, on the verge of collapsing after enduring many years of rains and winds. Some years ago, Wŏlgyŏng returned from the capital city with one thousand gold ingots, the gift he received from you as an offering. With them, we were able to rebuild the temple. As lowly monks living on a mountain, we don't know how to repay your generosity." The monks thanked Lady Wang again and again and praised her charity. She said, "I made a small offering, but in return I have received a huge reward. I am embarrassed." The monks treated the mother and son as if they were old friends. They ate well and slept comfortably in the annex. Perhaps it was a stroke of good luck in the midst of misfortune. As the days passed, Wŏlgyŏng discussed various texts with Ung and also taught him magical spells. Ung's mind was nimble—if taught one thing, he understood ten similar things. Lady Wang, on the other hand, relaxed and spent her time peacefully. As Ung grew up, her mind was relieved of some of its worries.

Time passed quickly. Ung turned fifteen, and grew tall and handsome, with exceptional strength and vitality. One day Ung said to his mother, "I have turned fifteen. This is indeed an enchanted land that anyone can live in comfortably. However, as a man, I should not grow old in one place. Even hermits enjoy moving around to broaden their horizons. I would like to be away from your care for a while and see the world beyond this mountain. I also want to hear news from the capital city." Surprised by his intentions, Lady Wang scolded him, saying, "We hide in this foreign land far away from our home and survive by relying on each other. It is unthinkable that you would leave me even for a moment! I will be worried sick about you if you leave. If you wish to travel, I will accompany you. Do not think you can go without me! It is an improper thought."

Ung could not continue the conversation with her. He went to discuss the matter with Wŏlgyŏng. Ung said, "I am now able to defend myself, so no one will trouble or harm me when I travel in the world. Though I am not a monk, I have been here for so long that I am unaware of what happens in the capital. I have had my own plans for quite a long time, so I asked my mother about my intention to leave the mountain. Yet she reprimanded me, and I could not argue with her. Would you please talk to my mother for me and persuade her to change her mind? I long to leave here and spread my wings." "Your words sound like those of a grown man," replied Wŏlgyŏng.

Wŏlgyŏng went to see Lady Wang. First he casually talked with her about the affairs of the past and present, and then he turned to Ung's intention to leave the mountain. Lady Wang said, "His words are indeed right, but I am in an isolated place without any family. Sending him far away will make me constantly miss him. Also, he is still a child who is unable to make important decisions. In a world filled with uncertainty, things might go terribly wrong for him." Wŏlgyŏng said, "What you say makes some sense, but Ung is no longer a child as you think. I would not worry at all for his safety even if he were placed against thousands of cavalrymen with a hail of arrows and stones pouring down upon him. Why are you so doubtful about his life? The Lord of P'ae [Yu Pang] survived the attempt on his life during the Feast at the Hong Gate,[89] and you yourself endured the furious waves of the river and boundless sea. Why would you need to worry about a life that is mandated by heaven? I would not recommend that he leave if I foresaw any misfortunes in his path. Besides, you will not worry alone during his absence; I am with you, and we will pray for him together."

Wŏlgyŏng invoked several other persuasive stories. Lady Wang pondered and asked, "What if things don't go as well for Ung as you said?"

He replied, "I foresee ups and downs throughout his entire life. So do not worry." She reluctantly agreed to let her son go, and Ung and Wŏlgyŏng were delighted to have her permission. On the following day, Ung bade farewell to his mother and the monks. She was despondent to see him leave and urged him to return soon. Seeing him off at the temple gate, Wŏlgyŏng shook Ung's hand and pointed to the safe path he should take. As Ung set out on his journey through the world alone, he felt very confident; there was nothing in sight to cause him fear.

Time passed peacefully. One day, half a year after he had left the temple, Ung arrived in Kangho.⁹⁰ It was a thriving place with many households and plenty of splendid things to see. Ung walked along the main road downtown and looked at the hundreds of items the merchants had on display. He noticed a gray-haired old man wearing a rough hemp garment with a black belt.⁹¹ Ung could tell from the old man's simple and coarse manner that he was not from the secular world. The man hung up a three-ch'ŏk-long sword and sat up straight behind it.⁹² Ung saw immediately that the sword was magnificent and of great quality. He had a powerful urge to buy it, but he had no money. Unsure if the sword was for sale, he watched the old man from a distance. Some shoppers approached the old man and expressed interest in the sword, but he said, "I would say it is worth more than one thousand gold ingots." They laughed and left.

Ung overheard the old man's asking price for the sword. Although he longed for the sword, the high price held him back from even asking the old man about it; he would have paid ten thousand gold ingots, but he knew he did not have the money. The market closed at sunset. The old man placed the sword under his sleeve and walked away. Ung followed him, but the old man was already far ahead, and he could not catch up. Disappointed, he went to an inn and spent the night there. The following day, Ung returned to the marketplace where the old man had been the day before, but the man was not there. Ung inquired of a nearby shopkeeper, "Yesterday, there was an old man selling a sword. Do you happen to know where he is now? Why has he not come today?" The shopkeeper said, "I don't know where he is. However, I do know it has been more than a month since he first came to the market to sell the sword. It is very expensive. Although some people showed great interest, he was not willing to sell it." Ung decided to sit down and wait for the old man to return while keeping some distance from the shop.

Time passed, and finally the old man arrived. He took the sword from his sleeve, hung it up, and sat behind it. Ung did nothing except stare at the sword. He pondered for a long time, could not think of a way to acquire it. Discouraged, he returned to the shopkeeper. In his frustration, he asked, "Could you ask the old man where he lives for me?" Complying with Ung's request, the shopkeeper told the old man, "There was a child who asked me about where you lived and the price of the sword." The old man was curious. He asked, "What did he look like?" The shopkeeper described Ung. The old man asked, "Do you know where he is from?" The shopkeeper replied, "I do not know, but he will come to you. Wait for him." Completely unaware that Ung had sat down to watch him from a distance, the old man anxiously awaited Ung all day. At sunset, the old man sighed sadly as he left the market with his sword. Ung likewise returned to the inn but was unable to fall asleep. He tried to think of a good way to acquire the sword, but nothing came to mind. On the following day, he went to see the old man, who again sat and hung the sword in front of him. For several days Ung simply watched the old man, resting covetous eyes on the sword. Eventually, the old man told the shopkeeper, "That child is destined to have the sword. I have awaited him every day but have not seen him. If he comes to you tomorrow, please persuade him to see me."

Meanwhile, Ung thought, "Tomorrow, I will negotiate the price of the sword with the old man. I will then go to Kangsŏnam and borrow money from Wŏlgyŏng to pay for the sword." On the following day, Ung went to the market to address the old man. The old man again hung up the sword in front of him, but this time he also had a hanging board with something written on it. Ung approached the board to see what it said. It read:

Hwasan tosa ilsujung-*hani*
Wŏlp'ae *kaŭi* maegŏmsa-*ra*
Inŏn ilgŏm-*i* kagihŏ-*o*
Ongdo samsi-*e* oyusa-*ra*

Punbun sijang-*e* kinamja-*rŏn'go*
Chŏn'gwa ch'ŏnin-*e* purwŏnmae-*ra*
Ung'a sosik-*ŭl* munsuji-*halgo*
Chwajŭk chii-*hago* kiwŏnsi-*ra*[93]

Meaning:

The sleeves of the Daoist Master of Mount Hwa are heavy.[94]
He appears to be selling a sword.
Whenever people ask the price of the sword,
The old man says he awaits its rightful owner.
Imagine how many men there were in the bustling marketplace;
Thousands have already passed by it, yet
He doesn't want to sell it.
Who can possibly know Ung's whereabouts?
When he sits down, he rests his chin on his hand;
When he stands, he looks toward the distance.

Ung read this with astounded delight. He cordially saluted the old man and asked him about the value of the sword. The old man gazed at Ung for a while. Then he held his hands and asked pleasantly, though in a loud voice, "Is your name Ung?" Ung replied, "Indeed I am Ung. How do you know my name, sir?" The old man said, "Of course I know your name. After heaven entrusted me with this treasured sword, I traveled over land and sea in search of its rightful owner. A few months back, I saw a General Star that belonged to you shining over Kangho.[95] That's why I came here and, for several months, awaited you. It is strange that I have not met you until now. Every night I looked up to the sky to see where you were but the star did not move. I presumed you were left destitute, wandering about to beg for lodging. Since I did not know of a better way to find you, I put up a hanging board and awaited your arrival. Indeed, it took quite a long time to finally meet you."

The old man handed the sword to Ung. Ung bowed to the old man to show his deep appreciation and received the sword. The sword was a little more than three ch'ŏk in length, and in the middle, the letters "Sword of Cho Ung" were engraved in gold. Ung bowed to the old man again and said, "You have given me the most precious sword, asking nothing in return. I am forever indebted to you, even after my death.[96] How can I repay you?" The old man replied, "It is your treasure, and I am simply delivering it to you. There is nothing to thank me for." The old man stayed with Ung for several days. He became very fond of Ung and was grieved to leave him. He said, "I feel relieved to have accomplished my mission. You have a long journey ahead. I hope you are prepared to fulfill your great destiny [from heaven]." Ung asked, "Where can I find a good teacher?" The old man replied, "Travel seven hundred li to the south to reach a mountain called Mount Kwan.[97] A Daoist master named Ch'ŏlgwan lives in the mountain.[98] If you are sincere and diligent, you will be able to see him; otherwise, you will not. Put your heart and soul into this matter." Shaking hands, they bade farewell and parted.

Ung fastened his three-ch'ŏk-long sword around his waist and headed south. Several days later, he reached the beautiful scenery of Mount Kwan. A steep cliff as tall as ten thousand *chang* was cracked in the middle,[99] and inside was an open plain that resembled heaven and earth. Several huts were built on the field behind a stone gate. Ung brought his left hand down to his right to show respect and walked slowly through the open gate.[100] Lotus flowers were blooming in a small pond, and chrysanthemums were planted around the steps leading to the outer chamber. It was quiet inside, with a few boys sitting together and playing *paduk*.[101] Ung approached and asked them if their teacher was home. The boys stood up and greeted Ung. They replied, "He indulges in fishing these days. He is out fishing with his close friends so he will probably come home late." Dispirited, Ung asked, "How late will he return?" They said, "He will return when the moon appears at twilight." Ung waited until dusk, but the teacher did not appear. Because he could not spend the night at a house whose owner was not home, he walked back down the mountain and spent the night in a nearby village. On the following day, Ung returned to see the teacher, but his thatched cottage was as quiet as the day before. He again asked the boys about the teacher. They said, "He returned around the third watch last night and went out in the morning when the rooster crowed." Ung was disheartened. He waited for the teacher all day, but to no avail.

Returning to the village, Ung rested there and went to the teacher's home around the third watch. The teacher was still not there when Ung arrived. Despondent, Ung asked the boys about the teacher again. They answered, "He usually goes out in the early morning at the rooster's first crow." Ung sighed and said, "For ten years, I have sincerely longed to meet a great teacher. I implore you to tell me where he went." The boys smiled and said, "When a woodcutter fails to catch a wild goose with a bow and arrow, he, unaware of his lack of skill and training, blames the bow and arrow and breaks them apart. You are just like the woodcutter. You do not realize your lack of sincerity and devotion, but simply complain of his absence. How amusing the situation is! Our teacher is somewhere on the mountain, but there are many high hills and deep valleys, so we don't know exactly where he is." Ung felt ashamed and couldn't ask them again. He awaited the teacher's return all day, but the teacher still did not come. Feeling wretched, Ung took a brush and wrote a message on the wall saying that he had come to seek an audience with the teacher but had left disappointed. He then said goodbye to the boys and departed. No one could imagine how heartbroken he was.

At that time, Daoist master Ch'ŏlgwan sat comfortably somewhere on the mountain and watched Ung's behavior. He felt sorry when he saw Ung write his message before leaving. In haste, he came down to his house and read the message:

A man who has been a wanderer for ten years,
Arrives finally from a place ten thousand li away.
In the Dream Pond, there is a dragon wanting to fly away,[102]
Things yet unaccomplished, indeed, hinder it from flying.[103]

Ch'ŏlgwan was astonished at these words. He promptly sent the boys to the village to invite Ung back. Ung saw them coming and asked, "Is the teacher back?" The boys said, "He has just returned and is asking you to come." Delighted, Ung followed the boys to the house, where Ch'ŏlgwan was waiting at the thatched gate. He held Ung's hands and happily said, "You must have exhausted your energy going back and forth on the rough mountain trail." He then urged the boys to quickly bring out an evening meal for Ung. Ung ate and thanked him, saying, "My stomach has not known food for several days, but now it's filled with this fragrant food. I thank you for treating me to such a delicious meal." Ch'ŏlgwan said, "There is no need to thank me. We were not aware of your hunger and simply prepared our usual meal." Then, Ch'ŏlgwan handed two books to Ung, saying, "Read these books." Ung thanked him on his knees and read them; they were the sacred texts written by saints and worthies. As soon as he finished reading, he asked Ch'ŏlgwan for another book. Ch'ŏlgwan smiled and gave him two military classics, the *Six Secret Teachings* and the *Three Summaries*.[104] Ung read them aloud, which greatly pleased Ch'ŏlgwan. He then gave Ung the *Astronomy Chart*.[105] Ung read the book and found it full of extraordinary skills and tricks. Ung also learned many other skills, feats, and arts of divination from Ch'ŏlgwan, which broadened his horizons and expanded his knowledge. He could now predict events that would take place in the immediate future.

One day, as the sun was setting beyond the western horizon and birds were returning to the woods to find shelter for the night, a raging wind rose up and a loud, thunderous sound resonated on the mountain. Astounded, Ung asked Ch'ŏlgwan, "Why, is there a beast in this place?" The master replied, "I will tell you a story. I used to have a feeble mare at my house. She grew thin, so I let her roam and graze freely on the mountain at first light. One day, a loud, continuous sound filled the air and there was a great commotion on the mountain. Thinking it queer, I went to where the horse roamed, but dense clouds of five colors covered the area, making it difficult to see. After a while, the din stopped and the clouds receded. There stood the mare, all wet and disoriented. I had to soothe her before I could bring her home. After the incident, I kept her home and fed her hay and porridge. In time, she gave birth to a foal, but in less than a month she died. The foal survived but was wild and could not be tamed. As it grew, no one dared to go near it. At first light, it vanishes into the mountains, but at night, it sleeps in the stable. It likes to race at the break of dawn, and when it does, it runs swiftly and neighs loudly. I fear it might hurt people."

Ung gazed at the mountain and saw the horse, as if in flight, climbing up a steep cliff of stratified rocks as tall as ten thousand *chang* and just as quickly descending. Not even an agile tiger could match its prowess. Before long, the horse returned home. Ung ran to it and shouted. The horse stared at Ung for a moment, then lifted its head and tapped the ground with its hooves, seemingly a sign of obedience. Remaining cautious, Ung said, "They say horses are similar to humans. Don't you recognize your new master?" The horse raised its head, sniffed at Ung, and swished its tail. It appeared to acknowledge him as its master. Ung rejoiced and hugged the horse. He put a halter on it and tied the lead rope to the stable. He inquired of Ch'ŏlgwan, "As to the horse's value, how much must I pay you for it?" Ch'ŏlgwan replied, "When heaven brought this dragon-horse into existence,[106] its rightful owner was already decided. The horse belongs to you. How can I speak of its worth when it is already another's treasure? I have been worrying that, without an owner, the horse might hurt people. Now I am very relieved and glad to pass the horse on to you." Gratefully, Ung said, "I already owe you so much for relieving me of hardship by allowing me to study ethics, morality, and the dharma under you.[107] I am immeasurably indebted to you now that you have given me this swift horse, easily worth one thousand gold ingots." Ch'ŏlgwan said, "When you are in a difficult situation, it is because of your fortune. It is also because of your fortune when things go well. You do not owe me anything." Ung's respect for Ch'ŏlgwan grew even greater. He continued to learn all kinds of secret arts and practices from Ch'ŏlgwan.[108] Within a year, he had mastered marvelous wizardry. What Ung achieved in such a short time would surprise many people and make them rub their eyes in disbelief.[109]

One day, Ung said to Master Ch'ŏlgwan, "I left my mother in a foreign place before I came here. With your permission, I would like to pay her a short visit, so I won't worry about her so much." Ch'ŏlgwan said, "You have my permission, but promise you will return promptly." Ung bade farewell to Ch'ŏlgwan. He led his horse outside the thatched gate and mounted. He touched the horse with the whip and took off at full gallop. He felt as if he were flying on great wings. In what seemed like an instant, he traveled seven hundred li and arrived in Kangho. The sun was still up, but he was very tired and decided to look for an inn.

Ung asked around until a person who stood by the road showed him to a well-maintained house with beautiful grounds.

The house belonged to Scholar Chang, a *chinsa* of the State of Wi.[110] He had died early, but had left behind a wife and a very beautiful daughter, Maiden Chang.[111] She was well-educated in poetry and calligraphy,[112] and people often praised her. Her mother, Lady Wi, wanted to find a worthy son-in-law, so she built a clean guesthouse and welcomed traveling young men. She would always look closely to see if they were suitable bachelors. On that day, Ung came to her house. In the outer chamber, Ung asked for the owner, but a maidservant of the house came out instead. She prepared the guestroom for Ung and treated him politely as a welcome guest. Ung was impressed by the cordial reception. When Lady Wi was informed that a guest had arrived, she called the maidservant and asked about Ung's appearance and manner.

The maidservant replied, "He is just a boy who is passing through the town." Lady Wi said with a sigh, "Time has passed quickly. My daughter is already sixteen-years-old, and it is difficult to find a suitable spouse for her." She blamed herself for the predicament. Maiden Chang tried to make her mother feel better. She said, "Do not be concerned with your unworthy daughter. Worry about your own well-being instead."

Meanwhile, Ung sat alone in the guesthouse, thinking, "I was told the people of this house were looking for a worthy bachelor for their beautiful daughter. It is unfortunate that they do not recognize me as one. While a white jade from Mount Hyŏng exists hidden under a pile of rocks, it is impossible for an undiscerning eye to discover it." Facing the full moon at dusk, Ung found himself reciting poems and singing songs. He fell silent when he heard the clear and exhilarating sound of the kŏmun'go zither from the inner chambers of the house.[113] He listened intently to the song, which went:

Trees were harvested from Mount Ch'o [Mount Hyŏng], and
A guesthouse was built for a hero to stay.
Yet no hero is seen, and instead come tawdry noblemen who are
   actually beggars.[114]
A paulownia tree on the rocks was hewn, and from it[115]

A zither was made so I could see a lovebird.
Yet no lovebird is coming, only chirping magpies.
Son!
Please bring a cup and pour me some wine!
May my ten thousand labyrinthine worries and regrets be released.

Ung was captivated by the song. In a frolicsome mood, he said to himself, "I can tell from the song that the singer is an extraordinary person. I should play in response, pretending to be a beggar who is a nobleman only in name." As soon as the music stopped, Ung sat near the guesthouse, on high ground under the moon, and took from his bag a flute, which he started playing sadly. Lady Wi and Maiden Chang were astonished by the sound of the flute. They quickly walked out to the middle gate to listen, and there they discovered that the sound was coming from the guesthouse. The deep, rich sounds of the flute spread through the clouds, calling:

My ten years of studying the *Astronomy Chart* were for traveling to
    the moon palace to meet the Goddess of the Moon, Hang-A.[116]
A karmic affinity ought to have formed between her and me in the
    world,
Yet unless the Ojak Bridge is found in the Milky Way,[117] I can hardly
    reach her.
All I wish is to see Hang-A, for whom a flute was made of bam-
    boo from the Sosang Rivers,
Wistfully playing the flute in the moonlight.[118]
Yet would there be anyone who could understand my music?[119]
Never mind!
Since it is likely no one can understand me,
I, a guest from afar, shall simply console myself.

As the song ended, Lady Wi and Maiden Chang felt uplifted, as if their bodies were floating in the air. Leaning against the gate, they peeked at the boy. His face was as appealing as jade,[120] and there was something special about the way he moved. They had never seen a man quite like him before. Lady Wi rejoiced, "Just as a saint is born after a unicorn appears,[121] so a hero appears when my daughter, a jadelike child, is born."[122] Maiden Chang felt embarrassed by her mother's remark and retired to her inner chamber. She lit a candle and leaned against her soft bedding. She soon dozed off, and her late father appeared in her dream. He said, "I have brought an eligible bachelor to you. Do not miss this blissful opportunity to be united with him as husband and wife. He is a wanderer without a home, so once he leaves it will be very difficult for you to meet him again." Her father took her hand and led her to the guesthouse. There she saw a yellow dragon playing with seven stars amidst clouds in five colors. Sensing her entrance, the dragon raised its head and stared at her. Startled and frightened, Maiden Chang tried to flee back to her room. But the dragon chased her and seized her skirt in its teeth. It took her to her room and started to coil around her body. She was horrified until she realized that it was only a dream, perhaps the most important dream of her life. She was shaken and soaked with sweat, but gradually she became calm. She wrote her dream on the wall as a poem and recited it.

Meanwhile, Ung finished playing his flute and walked under the light of the moon, hoping to receive a response, but there was nothing. Disappointed, Ung said to himself with a sigh, "Alas, she appears to know the tunes of the zither but not those of the flute. She must have thought it was an ordinary traveler playing." Suddenly the sound of verses drifted through the air. Ung listened closely. The sound was like striking a jade plate with a coral mallet.[123] His curiosity aroused, he opened the middle gate and walked into the inner garden. Nobody was there. Judging by the brightness of the moon, it was about the third watch of the night. He noticed that a separate chamber in the rear garden was brightly lit with candles, and someone within was reciting verses. He opened the door quietly, then boldly walked in and sat down. He looked around the room. The walls were beautifully painted in white, the windows were decorated with silks, and folding screens enclosed a private space. The jade girl who had been reciting verses started, huddling in her bed.[124] As she caught sight of Ung, she covered her body with a blanket. Sitting under the candle light, Ung said to her in a proper and polite manner, "Maiden Chang, don't be alarmed. I am the traveler who is staying at the guesthouse. I have been away from home for a while, and the moon made me feel lonesome. So I walked aimlessly until I heard someone reciting verses. I thought it was the young master of the house and ventured here, led by my desire for poetic inspiration. Now, I find myself in a rather awkward situation . . . I am a male stranger in a woman's private bedroom. Please tell me what I should do."

Under the cover of the blanket, Maiden Chang was not sure what to do, but she knew she had to say something. [Driven by the desperate need to protect herself,] she said, "The sky and land have not changed, and people still observe etiquette. Without regard for your life, you are perpetrating a crime. I urge you to leave at once and save yourself." Ung replied, "When a butterfly sees a flower, it does not see the fire nearby. A goose is not afraid of an old fisherman when it sees water. If I had cared for my life, I would not have been so impudent. I beg you to thaw your ice-solid chastity a little and be a neighbor to a lonely soul?" He moved to sit closer to her. Her situation was becoming dire. She thought quickly and said to Ung, "In the ancient *Book of Songs,* there is a poem in which a virtuous couple sings, 'Gentle maiden, pure and fair / Fit match for a prince.'[125] I do not intend to go to bed alone forever. When I think about the tombs of my ancestors, however, I remember that I am a descendant of nine generations of *chinsa.* I can't offend my ancestors by giving my body to a man without having my parents' consent and completing the Six Rites of a formal wedding.[126] If I taint my house's name, I cannot dare to live. I beg you to change your mind, leave now, and look forward to another time."

Ung knew her words were indeed right, but he was blinded by his love for her and could not discern what was proper. He said, "Even virtuous men from the past saw women in secrecy. A formal wedding, mediated by a matchmaker and consisting of the Six Rites, is a luxury that only a great king and a lady from a wealthy and noble family can afford. I cannot expect such indulgences since I am all alone in a foreign land. However, if you consider me a matchmaker and our union as the Six Rites, I will promise to be with you for a hundred years." Then he went into her bed. Like a small force that could not overcome a greater one, Maiden Chang's will could not defeat Ung's desire.[127] Like a fish in a well, she was powerless to avoid being caught. They then were like a pair of lovebirds; no one could stop their union. Once together, they could not tear themselves apart!

Maiden Chang lamented, "I am a gentry girl from the inner chambers and a descendant of nobility. Now I do not deserve to live, for I have committed a sin and tainted my house's name." She broke down and sobbed. Ung tried to console her, "I am also a sinner. I took you to be my wife without asking consent from your parents, which is unfilial conduct. However, the songs of our flute and zither did call to each other. Does that not show that we are a perfect match for one another? Indeed, our fate was already decided by heaven and not by my will."

They grew affectionate in the course of the night. It was already past the third watch, and a rooster from a distant village crowed. As Ung was getting up, Maiden Chang spoke to him, "My mother would like to see you. Please stay here for today and meet her. You can always leave later." Ung said to her, "It has been three years since I left my mother a thousand li away, and a moment feels like three years. It makes me uneasy to stay in one place even for an hour." Maiden Chang grabbed Ung's clothes and sobbed. She said, "If you go now, when will I hear from you? I barely know who you are. How can I recognize you if I see you again in the future? Please give me something that will serve as proof of our union." Ung agreed with her. He looked inside his bag and found nothing, but he had a folding fan in his hand. He opened it and wrote a couple of verses on it, then handed it to Maiden Chang. He said, "Take this fan. It will serve as proof of our union in the future." She received the fan and read the writing:

T'ungso-*ro* changhwa ongnyŏgŭm-*hago*,
Chŏngmak simgyu-*e* kwangbuji-*ra*.
Kŭman yarang-*i* sugaa-*o*?
Changssi pangyŏn-*ŭi* choungsi-*ra*.
Munjang ch'wibyŏk-*i* kwaeilp'o-*hani*,
Pundo hwayŏn-*e* nonggahŭi-*ra*.
Sinp'ung suŏ ŏmnusa-*hani*,
Sosik-*i* mangmang pudosi-*ra*.[128]

The passage meant:

> After playing the flute in response to a jade woman's zither,
> A reckless man finally arrives at the deep and lonely inner chamber.
> A young, handsome dandy—whose child is he?
> It's none other than Cho Ung, who has a beautiful karmic affinity
>   with a daughter of the Chang family.
> On the jade-colored wall, covered with decorated curtains, hangs the
>   gown of the man
> Who rushes to the gorgeous mat on which he plays with the beauty.
> With a few words in the wind of early morning, they part from each
>   other, fighting their overflowing tears, and
> Giving no promise of any news or date of a future union.

Ung bade a final farewell to Maiden Chang and urged his horse on its way. She followed him as far as the gate. She clung to it and watched Ung for a long time, but he sat on his horse upright, as if nothing had happened, and rode like a cloud in a high wind.

That same night, Lady Wi had a dream. In it, a blue dragon entered the hall and rose above the clouds with Maiden Chang on its back.[129] Lady Wi was horrified by this sight. She stomped her feet on the ground and called her daughter loudly. Startled by her own yelling, Lady Wi woke up in a daze but soon realized it had been a dream. She opened the window to look outside and saw that day had already broken. She got up and went to see her daughter in her chamber. Maiden Chang was still in a deep sleep. Lady Wi woke her and said, "The day has broken and you are still asleep?" Maiden Chang woke up with a start and asked, "Why are you up so early?" Her mother said, "You seem bewildered. Are you tired?" Maiden Chang replied, "Last night I appreciated the moonlight and went to bed late. So naturally I am still tired." Her mother said, "You know well that being dazed by the light of the moon will make you sick. You should behave better." Lady Wi then asked the maidservant to bring some food [to the guesthouse]. The maidservant said, "The guest who stayed at the guest house has already left." Lady Wi was upset and asked, "When did he leave?" The maidservant replied that she did not know when the guest had departed. Lady Wi said, "He must have left without notice because you servants did not treat him well." She then called another servant and commanded, "Bring him back if he has not gone too far." The servant ran as fast as he could to the top of a nearby mountain but, unsurprisingly, he could not locate Ung who was riding at the speed of a thousand li a day on his swift horse. Seeing that Ung was already far away, the servant came back and told Lady Wi that he was unable to find Ung. In her disappointment, Lady Wi said, "How futile my life is! I have awaited someone special like him for years, but have quickly lost him. I have no will to continue living." She wept in grief. Maiden Chang, consoling her mother, said, "Please don't be sad. If he is meant to have a close connection to our family, he will contact us even though he is gone now. We cannot gain everything we wish in this world. Please do not be sad about him." Maiden Chang made every effort to relieve her mother's suffering.

Far away, Lady Wang was anxious for Ung and had been unable to sleep well since his departure. The monks at the temple consoled her day after day, helping her pass the time. One day, Wŏlgyŏng said to her, "Do not worry about Ung. He has met a great teacher and studied under his roof. He has also acquired many treasures to decorate himself with. We should be excited for him." Lady Wang asked him, "How do you know all this?" Wŏlgyŏng replied, "I met Ung in a dream last night. He wrote on the wall and I read it aloud. I woke up, startled by my own sleep-talking, and realized it was just a dream. It was indeed a mysterious dream, so I prayed to Buddha and tried to interpret Ung's writing, which read: 'Samdal Wisu-*hago*, yangdŭk Ch'ŏnji-*ra*.' As I have some knowledge of discovering the meaning in dreams, I have unraveled its message. 'Samdal Wisu' means Ung is with a great teacher like Kang T'aegong at the Wisu and doing well.[130] Concerning the phrase 'yangdŭk Ch'ŏnji,' I'm sure that Ung acquired a great horse, since 'Ch'ŏnji' implies a lake that contains a dragon-horse.[131] Then, 'yangdŭk' means 'attaining two things.' So, what kind of treasure would 'yangdŭk' suggest? Ung must have acquired gold because it is said that 'Gold is abundant in Yŏsu [where Ch'ŏnji is located].'[132] However, gold can also be a sword.[133] It seems, therefore, that Ung is with a great teacher and has acquired a great horse and sword. Lady Wang, please don't think this insignificant monk is talking gibberish and do not scorn me. When your son returns, what I have said will be proven, but for now you should rest easy." With delight, Lady Wang replied, "If what you have said is indeed true, then I have nothing to worry about."

Time passed uneventfully. One day in her dream, Lady Wang took a tiger in her arms, but she did not feel fear. She was startled out of her slumber and quickly realized it was a dream. She called Wŏlgyŏng to discuss her dream. Pleased, he said, "Your son will return very soon." Lady Wang wanted to know exactly what her dream implied. Wŏlgyŏng said, "What appears to be an ill omen in a dream can be a good sign. The Chinese character for the tiger is *ho*, and the character for 'good' is also *ho*.[134] What would be the greatest good that could happen to you right now? Your dream is a sign that your son will return soon; it is indeed a joyous day for us." Happy now, she asked him, "When will I see my son?" He considered and then said joyfully, "I sense Ung is already within one hundred li of here. Perhaps, we will see him by the *chin* hour today."[135] She replied, "Since you said this with such confidence, how about making a bet with me?"[136] He accepted her wager. Together they went past the stone gate and awaited Ung's arrival.

Suddenly, the sound of small stones scattering could be heard from the narrow road just beyond the approach to the temple, and soon there appeared an immortal lad on horseback, moving through a cloud. With a whip raised in his hand, the lad made his way to the temple. Lady Wang and Wŏlgyŏng peered closely at him. It was Ung.

Ung dismounted from his horse and politely greeted his mother. Lady Wang embraced Ung and shed tears of joy. Overcome with emotion, she was unable to respond to his greeting. Wŏlgyŏng had to intervene to calm her down, and Ung was finally able to properly make his bow to her. He asked, "Have you been well, both physically and mentally while I was away?" Still emotional, she said to him, "I have been well, but where have you been and how did you get that sword and horse?" Ung explained to her how he had acquired them, how he had managed to feed and lodge himself, and how he had met and spent time with Master Ch'ŏlgwan. Lady Wang and Wŏlgyŏng rejoiced at Ung's story. She said to her son, "What you experienced could only be accomplished by the guidance of heaven! While you were away, I was healthy, but I missed you each day of the year and every hour of the day. At the full moon, Wŏlgyŏng dreamed of you and predicted that you had met with your teacher and obtained two things: a horse and a sword." She also said, "I had a mysterious dream last night and made a bet with Wŏlgyŏng that you would return today. We eagerly anticipated your arrival today and waited at the stone gate, but I still had some doubt. Who would believe you have actually returned as we hoped?" Lady Wang was over-joyed. Thanking Wŏlgyŏng and the other monks, Ung said, "You have eased the worry of an undutiful son for many years. I don't know how to repay you," and repeatedly expressed his gratitude. Wŏlgyŏng insisted Ung's constant praises were not necessary and said to him, "I can only imagine what you have gone through. Despite your years of hardship, we are all happy that you have returned home safe, after traveling ten thousand li alone." Everybody welcomed Ung with open arms.

One day, the monks arranged a large banquet and seated Ung and Lady Wang as the guests of honor. They said, "Our poverty made us unable to repay even one-ten-thousandth of what we owe you for your generosity, which has pained us for a long time. Now that you are reunited with your beloved son, whom you have missed for years, we can congratulate you. We have humbly prepared some local delicacies to eat together in celebration." The monks struck a metal bell, stood up, and bowed to Lady Wang and Ung. The atmosphere was delightful. Lady Wang and Ung stood up and thanked them saying, "It is we who are greatly indebted to your generosity. You kindly took in people who had no place to go and provided for us for many years. Moreover, you have always showed deep concern for the well-being of our family. We are not sure that we truly deserve all your great kindness. For that, we feel ashamed to stay here." The monks were much moved by their humility and expressed their appreciation.

Time passed, and Ung turned sixteen. One day, Lady Wang said to Ung worriedly, "You are an adult now. Sadly, you have no relatives and are a stranger in a distant foreign land. Who will volunteer to be a match-maker for me and find a wife for you? How sad it is! Time only hastens this old lady's death. I am afraid I will not see a daughter-in-law in my life time." Tears coursed down her face. Her crying made Ung sad. He hid his sorrow and tried to console her, saying, "Mother, please do not be sad. No thing in this world lives its life alone. I doubt I will be alone forever."

Then he suddenly knelt with his face down and asked her to forgive him for being an unfilial son. Astonished, Lady Wang said, "We are fugitives now, and I feel like a bird hiding in the woods. Have you done anything wrong while you were away?" Terrified, he told her, "How could I ever do harm to others? Though I was unfilial when I left my teacher . . ." Ung explained his infidelity and went on to tell his mother about his affair with Maiden Chang in Kangho. To his surprise, Lady Wang was delighted. She said, "I am so relieved. The old saying that 'those who commit crimes will find it difficult to survive' is indeed right. I knew you would be too cautious to commit a crime, but, as we are fugitives, I jumped at the thought that you might have committed a serious crime and was shocked and afraid for a moment." She then said, "Although I have not seen Maiden Chang, from your description, she seems a perfect match for you. This must be heaven's wish, not an act of man. Considering our current circumstances, how could you have anticipated needing proper manners? Do not take it too seriously. You have done nothing wrong." She then asked Ung for more details, including the Chang family's background. Ung told her everything in detail. Lady Wang and the monks were amazed by Ung's story and congratulated him, "Heaven guided him, and it is praiseworthy!" Wŏlgyŏng said to Lady Wang, "Do you remember what I told you some time ago? Given what you have just heard, you must now decide the credibility of my prediction." Lady Wang praised the monk, saying, "My foolish mind cannot fully grasp your marvelous ability!" She willingly admitted that she had lost the bet. Over the next three years, Wŏlgyŏng again tutored Ung in various skills.

One day, Ung said to his mother, "I promised my teacher Ch'ŏlgwan I would return to him. I would like to leave you for a while, so that he will not be disappointed." Ung's words brought a new sadness to Lady Wang. She answered, "I missed you dearly when you were gone before. I have just started to recover from the emotional turmoil, but you wish to leave again. Yes, indeed, you should keep your promise to your master, but I'm concerned. No one can foresee what will happen in human affairs, and things easily grow tense. Should your return be blocked by unexpected circumstances and delayed indefinitely, how would I reach you?" Wŏlgyŏng interrupted her and said, "Lady Wang, please rest easy. I foresee his whereabouts." Fully trusting in his ability, she said,

"Without you, how could we, a mother and son, decide things in a strange land? I could not dare to send Ung far away again without your words of prophecy." She then urged Ung, "Pay a visit to your teacher, but please return promptly." Ung bade farewell to all and spurred his horse to run as fast as it could.

Several days later, Ung reached Mount Kwan. The familiar scenery of the mountain range and streams welcomed him. As he arrived at the stone gate, the boys came out and greeted him. They held hands and bowed to each other. Ung went inside to see Ch'ŏlgwan, who greeted him delightedly, "You are a man of your word. You kept the promise you made. I praise you!" He continued, "How is your mother? Is she well?" Ung stood, made a bow, and thanked him for his concern. Ch'ŏlgwan said with a smile, "You seem different. I presume that you now have a wife. I am very happy for you." Ung blushed at his teacher's remark and felt ashamed. He knelt with his face down and asked for his forgiveness, saying, "Out of my ignorance, I broke the sacred trust between a pupil and his teacher. I have terribly mistreated you." Ch'ŏlgwan held Ung's hands and said, "You did not mistreat me, nor did you break our trust. It was all guided by heaven's wish. Don't be ashamed of yourself. I understand all."

Back under Ch'ŏlgwan's guidance, Ung continued to acquire new skills. Ch'ŏlgwan said to Ung, "You are proficient in reading and writing. I have a book that will be useful for you. Study it." Ch'ŏlgwan went on instructing Ung with military books like the *Six Secret Teachings* and the *Three Summaries* and all kinds of strategy and tactics required to become a general.[137] Because he could remember everything he read, Ung quickly became very knowledgeable in many things. In light of this capacity, Ch'ŏlgwan grew even more fond of Ung and enjoyed having discussions with him day and night.

One day, Ch'ŏlgwan said to Ung, "Do you realize your destiny? Based on my observation of heaven's will and the movement of stars, including the General Star, I predict that the Great Country will be restored by your own hands." Ung did not know what to say to his teacher, though he felt great joy and confidence. But in the early morning of the following day, Ch'ŏlgwan was stunned by the look on Ung's face. He said, "Bad signs are on your face. I am afraid that your near future looks very ominous." Horrified, Ung urged, "Please tell me what you mean in detail." Ch'ŏlgwan took a moment to gaze at Ung's face and finally said, "At your in-laws' house, someone is about to pass away." Handing Ung three pills, he ordered, "Leave immediately and take these with you so that you can save a life." Ung immediately left for Kangho, whipping his horse to run ever faster.

After Maiden Chang bade farewell to Ung, she did not hear from him nor did she know his whereabouts. She became so ill with worry that she was unable to get out of her bed. Lady Wi was very worried and tried hundreds of medicines, but to no effect. She prayed desperately to heaven to save her daughter's life, but it seemed that only a special elixir could save her. Any moment, poor Maiden Chang might die. That day, Ung arrived at the Chang house. He could faintly hear a wailing cry from inside the house and see the servants moving urgently about. Ung was shocked by the sight. He stopped a maidservant and asked what was going on. The maidservant recognized Ung and, although the situation in the house was dire, told him in quite a welcoming tone, "In the women's quarters, Maiden Chang's serious illness has reached its peak; she may pass away any minute now. It may sound harsh, but you must find another house for your lodging." Ung told the servant, "Go tell the lady of the house that there is a traveler passing by who happens to know medicine. If she gives the traveler a list of her daughter's symptoms, he might be able to discern the cause of her illness. Please tell the lady what I just said."

The maidservant went inside and told Lady Wi about the visitor, "The young gentleman who lodged at our house some time ago is outside." The maidservant then gave Lady Wi Ung's message. The news gave her hope, and she stopped sobbing. She asked the maidservant to tidy the guest room and treat the visitor well. She then quickly prepared a list of her daughter's symptoms and sent it to Ung. Ung looked at the list and handed the pills that he had brought to the maidservant. He said, "These pills will ease her symptoms soon. Immediately provide her with some food and encourage her to eat often." The servant took the pills to Lady Wi and passed on the visitor's instructions. Lady Wi ground the pills and gently shook her daughter awake so she could administer the medicine. With the medicine in her mouth,

Maiden Chang groaned, but soon she was able to sit up in her bed and asked Lady Wi for some food. Lady Wi was very happy to see her daughter so improved. She gave Maiden Chang some food and then immediately went to see Ung. She held his hands and thanked him again and again. She said, "I have long regretted that I did not get to see you the last time you were here. However, you came back during this desperate time and saved a precious life from certain death. Our family owes you a great deal. I have a favor to ask, if I may. I have a daughter who has come of age and is ready to find a husband, but we have not found a suitor yet. She is not special and is unworthy of boasting, but you are the one to whom I would like to entrust the rest of my daughter's life. Please do not break my heart by hesitating, but grant my wish."

Ung replied pleasantly, "I thank you for not viewing me as a dirty vagabond and for sincerely asking me to be your son-in-law. I dare not decline your gracious offer, but I must ask my mother for her opinion. I will ask her immediately and return with news." Lady Wi was very happy at his decision, but she wished they could have a wedding much sooner. On the following day, Ung bade farewell and was about to leave. Lady Wi was already missing him. She said, "Please tell us what your mother says as soon as possible," and gave him a pair of unthreaded pearls as big as chicken eggs. She said, "It is difficult to get in touch with someone once he leaves. I do not have a son but I would like to think of you as my own. These are my precious belongings, and I would like you to keep them as a symbol of my trust." Ung gratefully accepted the pearls and returned to Mount Kwan directly to see Ch'ŏlgwan.

Ch'ŏlgwan welcomed him and said, "If it were not for you, it could have been very serious." Ung said, "Yes, indeed. Without you, I could never have saved her," and thanked him profusely.

Later, Ch'ŏlgwan took Ung up to a large boulder in the mountains to sense the aura in heaven. He said to Ung in surprise, "Did you sense it? My observation of the stars and directions in the sky, and of the situation of the Central State,[138] tells me that the Kak Star is not in its right place.[139] This surely means that the land is now in an uproar. These days Sŏbŏn has grown very powerful and is trying to take over the Great Country.[140] It is time for you to achieve great things. Wait to reconnoiter, then assist the State of Wi and consequently recover the

Great Song!" Ung replied uncertainly, "I do not think I can accomplish great things with my limited ability. I doubt I could survive the showering arrows and stones of battles." Ch'ŏlgwan said, "Fear not. You will achieve great things. Go out to the Central Plain, recover the Great Song, and have your revenge." Ung obediently packed his belongings, obtaining a map of Wi from Ch'ŏlgwan. As Ung was leaving, Ch'ŏlgwan was sorry to see him go. He held Ung's hands and said, "I am afraid that this time we will part for a long while. Take care of yourself and accomplish great things." Ung finally said goodbye to Ch'ŏlgwan and rode to Kangsŏnam to see his mother for several days. Lady Wang embraced her son, happy to see him. Ung told her about the way he had cured Maiden Chang's illness. Lady Wang was amazed at Ch'ŏlgwan's mysterious ability and praised him.

BOOK 2

A short while later, Ung spoke to Lady Wang, "Sŏbŏn has become very powerful and intends to seize control of the Great Country. Although my intervention could change nothing, I want to see how the situation unfolds." Lady Wang replied, "How could any mother expect the son she bore to return home alive after sending him off to a battle-field? Do not speak such nonsense." Ung spoke again. "Going to battle and leaving you alone and lonely is the last thing I want to do, but it is my teacher's command. What do you think I should do?" Lady Wang paused a moment, then said, "If that is what the master commanded you to do, I cannot stop you. The king of the State of Wi is the same rank as your father. His name is Sin'gwang. Help him and accomplish a great meritorious deed. After that, return immediately so I can see your face again." So Ung bade her farewell.

Following the directions given to him by the Daoist master Ch'ŏlgwan, and equipped with his three-ch'ŏk-long sword, Ung headed to the State of Wi. On his great horse capable of traveling one thousand li a day, he passed over high mountains as if flying above the clouds. No one could come close to his prowess. He traveled all day but could not find a place to stay. He rode his horse aimlessly along a narrow rocky road for some time. Suddenly, he heard a dog barking. He gladly followed the sound and came upon a small village consisting of only a few houses. Under the light of burning pine knots, the villagers were discussing agricultural matters. Ung knocked on the thatched gate of a house, looking for its owner. An old man came, greeted him, and showed him to a guest room. They treated each other with the respect customary between guest and host. Ung looked around and realized the house was unoccupied. He asked the old man, "Why does no one live in this house?" The old man replied, "We did not have a place for weary or sick travelers who passed through the village, so we have built a house just for this purpose." He then briskly prepared dinner and brought it to Ung.

After the meal, Ung lit a lantern and started to read a book on military tactics. Just before the third watch, a beautiful woman walked in, wearing a green blouse and red skirt [like those worn by brides] and a crescent-moon-shaped amulet. She was incredibly lovely. Ung asked, "What sort of a woman are you to walk around in the middle of the night seeking a man?" She replied, "I live in this village. You seem lonesome, so I've come to comfort you." Ung was immediately certain she was a ghost. He chanted a spell for warding off ghosts, and the beauty fled the room sobbing.

Ung was so disturbed that he could not fall asleep, so he recited a passage from the book on tactics. Some time after the third watch, a strong roaring wind blew around the house, lifting sand and stones into the air and knocking down tree branches. It was as though the world were turning upside down. The door repeatedly swung open and closed by itself. Startled and shaken, Ung was unable to calm himself.

A moment later, Ung heard the sound of a servant clearing the road for his master,[1] and a general walked into the room. Standing eight ch'ŏk tall, the general was wearing chest armor and holding a three-ch'ŏk-long sword high in the air. Clearly visible, he strode in and sat down, leaning against the writing table. His stern look made Ung uneasy. Yet, wanting to make a strong impression, Ung glared at him fiercely, pulling out his sword and hitting the writing table hard. Ung yelled like a

thunderclap, "They say the wicked cannot be victorious over the righteous. How dare a malignant ghost like you carelessly venture into the
room and sit in front of a great man!" Startled, the general got up and
took a seat farther away from Ung. Ung yelled at him again and this
time struck him with his sword. Shocked, the general hastily left the
room. Shaken by this second ghostly encounter, Ung was again unable
to fall asleep, so he sat up by candlelight.

Soon, a man wearing a coronet, a martial garment, and a black belt
came into the room and greeted Ung. Ung greeted him in return and
said, "In the dead of night, it is difficult to tell a man from a ghost. What
brings you here so late into the night?" The man replied, "I was once a
man of magnanimity. Having risen through the ranks as a military officer in the Kwansŏ area, I fought in many battles.[2] However, I died
without achieving my highest aspirations, and my spirit has become a
restless ghost fuming over a grudge. A short time ago, I appeared before
you in my armor to test your prowess as a general. I am delighted to find
that your unanticipated visit here is an opportunity to complete my
unrealized purpose. The pretty woman you saw earlier is my beloved
concubine." He opened the door to call her inside. She strode in with
the general's armor, helmet, and sword in her arms and sat down. The
general said, "With the armor, helmet, and sword that my most loved
concubine has brought, I hope you will win the battle in my name. Your
success and victory will end my years of resentment and bring serenity
to my restless soul, for which I will be forever grateful to you. I also ask
you to bury the armor, helmet, and sword in my grave on your return
journey." He and his concubine bade Ung farewell and departed. Still
unsettled, Ung awaited daybreak. At dawn, he found the golden armor
and helmet, and the three-ch'ŏk-long sword placed before him. He
called the old man and asked, "Is there a grave nearby?" The old man
replied, "There is a grave behind the village that belongs to a general of
yore." Ung went to the site, and there indeed was the grave. On the
tombstone was written: "The Grave of Hwang Tal, General of Kwansŏ."
Below it was a smaller grave with the epitaph: "The Grave of Wŏllang,
Lady Wi." Ung felt sorry for them after seeing their graves. He departed
for the State of Wi with the armor, helmet, and sword in his possession,
feeling as if he had been given wings.

Several days later, Ung arrived in the State of Wi and saw the opposing armies of Wi and Sŏbŏn positioned along a sandbank that stretched for one hundred li. The army of Sŏbŏn camped with a mountain at its rear. The army of Wi camped with a river at its rear. The Sŏbŏn encampment looked well fortified and garrisoned by many capable generals. Over the course of a month, the two armies had battled every day, but Sŏbŏn was always victorious. Defeat after devastating defeat, Wi was on the verge of total collapse.

A dense fog lay over the battlefield. Like two dragons fighting over the Wish-fulfilling Pearl,[3] the two armies fought again. In the heat of the battle, the Sŏbŏn general encountered his enemy general and engaged him in a duel. After fighting ten bouts, the Sŏbŏn general slashed off the head of the Wi general in an instant. With his fighting spirit mounting, the Sŏbŏn general dashed wildly toward the enemy's encampment and shouted, "Generals of the State of Wi, come out and receive my sword!" His loud voice caused both encampments to tremble. Wi was in peril; there was no general to fight the enemy, and the surviving soldiers were greatly weakened. Seemingly faced with total defeat, the king of the State of Wi, wailing, wrote a capitulatory letter. He handed the letter to the commander of his rear troop to deliver to the enemy. The Sŏbŏn general rushed fiercely at the Wi commander as he came out of the gate. Startled, the Wi commander quickly showed him the letter.

After reading it, the Sŏbŏn general bellowed angrily, "How arrogant it is that your king sent a capitulatory letter from his comfortable seat when he should have come in person and presented his neck. I am outraged! I will cut off your head to ease my anger." With a flash of his sword the head of the Wi commander toppled to the ground under his horse. The general skewered the head on the tip of his sword and danced wildly toward the Wi encampment. Petrified by the spectacle, the king of the State of Wi was convinced that he had no choice but to commit suicide to avoid humiliation.

Looking on, Ung felt his anger mounting. He put on the armor and helmet, and held up the three-ch'ŏk-long sword. As if flying, he mounted his horse and galloped onto the battlefield. Like a thunderclap, he shouted, "Sŏbŏn generals, come out quickly and receive my sword!" His thunderous voice caused the sky and the land to tremble, and his sudden appearance stunned the soldiers on both sides and caused their hands and feet to go numb. Ung rode directly to the Sŏbŏn encampment and engaged the enemy general. Ung's sword flashed in the air and, after several bouts, the enemy general's head was slashed off and fell below his horse. Ung skewered the head on the tip of his sword and rode to the Wi encampment as if flying, dancing on horseback.

Meanwhile, the king of the State of Wi was at his command post gazing hopelessly over the battlefield. To his astonishment, an unknown general had come to Wi's aid, decapitating the enemy general. Now he was racing toward the Wi encampment with the enemy general's head. Ung's appearance was undoubtedly like a dream. Marveling at Ung's extraordinary feat, the king quickly emerged from his encampment to welcome him, and, heaping praise upon praise, seated Ung beside him at the command post. But Ung quickly came down from his seat, knelt down before the king, and begged his forgiveness, "As an outsider to your army, I took part in the battle without your permission. I beg you to punish me for my offense."

The grateful king replied, "Please pardon me for not reaching out and welcoming you into my army much sooner—I was simply unaware of you. My life was about to come to an end but, in an astonishing turn of fate, you came and saved me. I would like to know your great name and history."

Ung kowtowed before the king and told him in detail about his life. The king was amazed to find out who Ung was. He sighed deeply as he held Ung's hands and said, "General, your father was a dear childhood friend of mine. Looking at you now is like seeing the face of an old friend; it makes me feel very happy, yet sad at the same time." He continued, "It has been a long time since I heard news about your family and the Great Country of Song. Tell me what has happened there and how you have ended up in Wi." In tears, Ung told the king how Yi Tubyŏng had usurped the throne of the Kingdom of Song, proclaimed himself the new emperor, and exiled the crown prince of the Kingdom of Song to Kyeryangdo. Ung also explained that he and his mother had been on the run ever since Yi Tubyŏng took the throne. Upon hearing

Ung's story, the king collapsed. The court officials who were standing nearby leaped to revive him. Finally coming to his senses, the king bowed four times facing toward the Great Country and wept remorsefully, for his loyalty was strong. Ung comforted him, saying, "Please do not grieve over the Great Country but be reminded that you have a great problem at hand. Your enemy has not yet been defeated. Once your country returns to peace, you will be able to take care of many things." The king eventually regained his composure and discussed strategies to win the war.

Meanwhile, on the other side of the battlefield, the king of Sŏbŏn exclaimed, "Who was that enemy general? His skill in wielding a spear tells me he is not an ordinary man. I cannot help but worry." Maeng Sang stepped forward from the crowd of generals and said loudly, "That general's head is as good as skewered on the tip of my sword. Your Majesty should not worry about him." As soon as he finished speaking, Maeng Sang seized his weapon and swiftly rode out of the encampment. He shouted at the enemy, "Enemy general, come out quickly and receive my swift sword!" Ung immediately jumped on his horse, pulled out his sword, and dashed to engage Maeng Sang in a duel. Ung moved like a fierce tiger leaping out of the woods.

Before they could exchange more than a few cuts and thrusts, Ung's sword flashed through the air and slashed Maeng Sang's head to the ground. Whirling his sword, Ung proceeded to the enemy encampment without fear and shouted like a clap of thunder, "King of Sŏbŏn, come out promptly and accept your defeat. If you delay, I will bring peace to the land by chopping off your head." Sŏbŏn's soldiers were scared and did not know what to do. When Ung returned to his encampment, the king of Wi, feeling even more fond of him, expressed concern that he might get wounded if he kept fighting so fiercely.

Meanwhile, the shocked king of Sŏbŏn said, "What can we do to capture the enemy general?" Before he could finish speaking, General of the Left Yi Hwang stepped forward from the crowd of generals and said, "I will go out tomorrow and capture the enemy general alive."[4]

The king of Wi quickly made Ung the grand field marshal of his army.[5] The grand field marshal's banner was rewritten in gold: "Loyal Servant to the Kingdom of Song, Grand Field Marshal of Wi." On the following day, Ung raised his banner outside the encampment. Spear in hand, Ung rode to the enemy encampment and shouted, "General of Sŏbŏn, come forth and stretch out your neck!" His voice rumbled through the sky and the land. Responding to Ung's taunts, Yi Hwang came out of the encampment on horseback. Just as they were about to engage in a duel, a gust of sand blew and clouded the air, obscuring both encampments. With a battle cry, another enemy general attacked Ung from behind. This enemy seemed tough and ruthless, and perhaps not so easily defeated. The three men spurred their horses on in their private battle—two against one. They clashed like two dragons violently striving for the Wish-fulfilling Pearl. In the chaos of their fight, neither side's soldiers could discern the three generals.

Dozens of blows were exchanged among them, but it was not enough to decide the victory. Suddenly, a sword flashed in the air, and the head of one of the generals fell to the ground. The soldiers from both sides strove to see first whose head it was. It was Yi Hwang's. The death of the enemy general instantly raised the morale of the Wi soldiers. In high fighting spirit, they charged the enemy encampment while the air rumbled with the sound of drums and bugles and shouting. Then, another sword-flash and another head fell to the ground. This one belonged to the second Sŏbŏn general.

With their morale higher than ever before, already beating the drum of victory, all the Wi soldiers attacked the enemy encampment. The Sŏbŏn soldiers were unable to stop the overwhelming charge. Grand Field Marshal Ung had beheaded two Sŏbŏn generals, turning the tide of battle definitively in Wi's favor. Seizing the opportunity to end the battle, Ung rallied his horse and charged toward the enemy encampment, wielding his mighty sword. As if there were nobody opposing him, Ung decapitated the enemy gatekeeper and strung his head on a flag pole at the gate. Like a god of war,[6] Ung continued his whirlwind assault on the enemy encampment, inflicting heavy casualties. The bodies of Sŏbŏn soldiers were piling up like a massive graveyard. In the chaos, some of the Sŏbŏn soldiers started to flee and caused a stampede. Many were crushed to death when they stumbled and were trampled by the feet of their fellow soldiers. The remaining Sŏbŏn soldiers were no longer able to withstand the attack of Wi and scattered. In the heat of the battle, the king of Sŏbŏn disguised himself in the clothes of another, and escaped to safety. Ung captured most of the enemy generals who had fallen behind. He returned to his encampment with them in shackles.

The king of Wi welcomed Ung at the gate and clasped his hand as they walked up to the command post together. Once there, the king of Wi praised Ung's glorious achievement. However, Ung again prostrated himself before the king and said, "What happened today is all due to Your Majesty's virtue."

Not wasting any time, Ung quickly took leave of the king and ordered the chief military officer of Wi to collect the weapons and provisions that had been left behind in the enemy encampment.[7] He also ordered the troops to bring in the fourteen captured enemy generals. He pointed out their wrongdoings one by one before declaring, "I should have you all executed, but I am letting you go. Return and tell your king never again to have such wrong ideas." Finally, he said, "Leave." After having the characters *Defeated General* permanently inked on their foreheads, they were released.[8] The enemy generals thanked Ung for sparing their lives and left in tears.

The king of Wi ordered the chief military officer to organize a large banquet. The Wi soldiers were seated at the banquet in order of rank and ate until their stomachs were full. The king of Wi lamented, "Had I met our grand field marshal sooner, none of my generals would be dead now, but eight were killed. I am sorry for their poor souls." Ung consoled the king, "They had run out of luck and there was nothing Your Majesty could have done. Let's just focus on comforting their souls."

The king's men constructed eight human figures to seat at the banquet.[9] They beat the drum of victory and poured wine into the glasses placed in front of the figures to offer solace. Mysteriously, the wine glasses went dry and the seats trembled. Everyone feasted on wine and meat. Some danced and some sang. The Wi soldiers overflowed with praise for Ung's achievement. The figures of the eight dead generals also appeared to make gestures of appreciation and to enjoy the banquet.

When the banquet came to an end, Ung escorted the king of Wi back to his state. The army marched with great discipline and high spirits because of the triumphant victory over Sŏbŏn. They marched as far as

Pyŏnyang and camped with the base of a high mountain to their rear. Ung instructed the chief military officer to allow the soldiers to rest. Wanting to enjoy the spectacular scenery of the area, Ung climbed the mountain to admire the views, bringing with him the supreme commander[10] and the chief commander.[11] The sun was already setting when they came across a horde of people talking loudly around a big fire that burned brightly, illuminating the sky.

Grand Field Marshal Ung and his two lieutenants were surprised to discover the gathering, but quietly hid themselves in the tall grass and surveyed the crowd. They recognized the routed Sŏbŏn generals and their soldiers, who had slowly regrouped on the mountain. The king of Sŏbŏn said, "Don't make a big commotion. The enemy encampment is just below. If they find out we are here, we will be in great trouble. However, because they are weary, they will let their guard down and sleep deeply tonight. When they fall asleep, we will storm their command post and capture the king of Wi and Grand Field Marshal Cho. Capturing them will be like catching fish in a well." He quietly issued orders to his army before declaring, "Whoever disobeys my orders will be court-martialed."

Ung overheard everything and laughed softly at the enemy king's plan. At the same time, however, he grew angry. He assigned missions to his two lieutenants. They departed swiftly to relay the plans for an upcoming battle to the camp at the base of the mountain. A short time later, the lieutenants reported back to Ung on the mountain. Ung put on his armor, mounted his horse and rode out with his sword drawn. At the sound of cannon fire, the Wi troops, waiting in ambush, rushed to surround the Sŏbŏn encampment. Ung called to his soldiers to quickly tie up the enemy king. The king of Sobon's face turned a dark blue. Petrified with terror at the sudden attack, he was easily captured along with a number of his generals. The rest of the enemy soldiers panicked and stampeded. Again, many of them were crushed to death as they stumbled and were trampled by their fellows.

Ung made the captured enemy king and generals walk before his horse and descended to the base of the mountain. One hundred thousand Wi soldiers at the encampment stood stunned at the sight. The king of Wi was startled out of a deep sleep by the loud chatter of the soldiers and immediately called Ung to explain the commotion. Ung came into the king's quarters and bowed. The king asked, "What is all the fuss about in the encampment?" Ung replied, "The moon is bright and the air is cool. Our soldiers are steaming their rice and eating their late evening meal. That's what you hear. But there is one more thing that may have caused some fuss as well. A while ago we had an incident that resulted in the capture of the enemy king along with his fourteen generals. I have them bound outside." The king of Wi was dumbfounded, but he quickly exclaimed in joy, "This is the most incredible and admirable achievement!" He praised Ung affectionately and majestically.

First, the king of Wi had the enemy king and his generals dragged around his encampment to humiliate them. He then issued his soldiers an order to behead his enemy and put his head on display for everyone to see. In tears, the enemy king pleaded with the king of Wi. In a last desperate attempt to save his life, he said, "Yi Tubyŏng rebelled against the Great Country and declared himself the new emperor. People all over the land loathe him. I only started the uprising in hopes of destroying Yi Tubyŏng and recovering the Great Country. Now, I've learned that Your Majesty also wishes to recover the Great Country. I hope only for your mercy, so that I can rebuild my army and help you fulfill your wish."

The king of Wi and Ung thought the king of Sŏbŏn seemed sincere and appealing; they decided to make an exception and pardon him. After receiving a written surrender, they said to the king, "You should be executed. Yet, after generously considering what you have said, we will release you. Return to your country and do not disappoint Wi." The king of Sŏbŏn thanked them with a hundred bows and left.

As the king of Wi approached his palace, people of the capital city traveled from as far as one hundred li outside of the city to welcome him. They shouted, "Hurrah!" and looked happily for their relatives in the marching army. Their joyous chatter could be heard both far and near. Three days after his return, the king of Wi hosted a lavish banquet at the Chŏngsŏ Gate and asked Ung to punish and reward soldiers at his discretion. Sitting at the Chŏngsŏ Gate, Ung oversaw and drilled the army and implemented a fair distribution of rewards and punishments. No one contested his judgment, and everyone praised him warmly. The banquet finally came to an end, and, at the sound of cannon fire, soldiers beat drums and gongs to announce the disbanding of the army. Before letting the soldiers go, Ung gave them his final order, "Soldiers, go back to where you came from and lead a peaceful life." Transported with joy, the thirty thousand soldiers rose up and bowed to Ung, praising his accomplishments, before they slowly regained their senses and left, dancing and singing as they went.

After the army had scattered, Ung went to see the king of Wi, who was in conference with his court officials about Ung's accomplishments and the proper reward due to him. The king said to the officials, "A country is not led by just one person. Since I am getting old and cannot think clearly, it is my intention to pass down the royal seal to Grand Field Marshal Ung." Awestruck by the king's announcement, Ung groveled before the king and said, "This land is not for your loyal servant to stay in. How can I be greedy for money and power and betray the people of my old country? I beg Your Majesty not to discuss my accomplishments." Ung continued, "I am ordinary. I lack both talent and skill. However, due to help from heaven and the gods and Your Majesty's virtue, I was victorious in battle. Furthermore, meeting an old friend of my deceased father made me happy, like meeting my own father or an elder brother. However, I left my widowed mother in a desolate place and I do not know whether she is well. As a son, I cannot help but think about her all the time. Now I plan to bring the crown prince of Song back from his exile, and with him I will visit my mother. I cannot say when I will see Your Majesty again." Surprised, the king said, "I also longed to serve the crown prince. Let us go together and bring him here." But the court officials and Ung said, "The State of Wi should not be without Your Majesty even for one moment." The king nodded and spoke to Ung, "I am sorry that circumstances prevent me from accompanying you. I hope I will see the crown prince in my lifetime, so that in my death I can face Emperor Mun in the underworld as his loyal servant. I consider myself a loyal servant to the emperor; I would look absurd if I did not at least do that. Woe is me! My title was conferred by the emperor, but I am unable to uphold the sacred oath between the emperor and his servant."

Facing the direction of the crown prince's place of exile, the king wept bitterly. Ung and the court officials consoled him, saying, "Don't be so hard on yourself. Besides, we have no new information on the Great Country." The king responded by exhorting Ung, saying, "The crown prince no longer has a suitable place to dwell. Bring him here, and we will discuss the restoration of the Great Country. Please remember, so I do not become a disloyal servant in this world." The king then placed one thousand elite enlisted soldiers and dozens of great generals under Ung's command, and said, "Please bring these assigned soldiers with you. You may encounter some obstacles on your long journey." Ung thanked the king, bade him farewell, and marched toward the crown prince's place of exile.

All that time, the household of Chang *chinsa* had not heard from Ung. Since his departure they had worried day and night, until their worries resembled chronic illnesses. When they heard about the war in the State of Wi, their worries multiplied. For a time, they even speculated that Ung had not contacted them because he had been killed in the war. Finally, an official announcement arrived, which read, "Sŏbŏn was defeated in the war and people in the border area should not worry." When they heard this, Lady Wi and Maiden Chang happily exclaimed, "Sŏbŏn is defeated. It is still possible that Ung has survived the war, and if he is alive, he will contact us soon." They waited for Ung day and night.

Unbeknownst to them, the prefect of Kangho,[12] an eastern frontier land of the State of Wi, had recently become a widower and had not yet chosen his new wife. When the prefect was informed that Sŏbŏn had been defeated in the war, he opened the main gate of the city and ordered his soldiers, who had been guarding the walls since the war started, to search for a suitable wife for him. Shortly after, he heard of Maiden Chang's great beauty and character. He asked his child's wet nurse to find out whether Maiden Chang would make a good wife. The wet nurse went to the house of Chang and asked for an audience with Lady Wi. She said, "I am here to see your daughter, whose great beauty and character are much spoken of throughout the region." Lady Wi said, "You must have heard wrong. My daughter is just a child and cannot think on her own yet. Moreover, she has been ill all of her life and cannot even walk around the house. There is nothing special about her to see." The wet nurse said, "What I heard was quite the opposite. Please allow me to see her." Lady Wi could no longer deny her request, so she reluctantly sent a maid to notify Maiden Chang of the visitor.

Maiden Chang was upset by the news. She said, "Why would someone want to see a sickly stranger? That is highly unusual and I am not comfortable hosting a visitor now." The maid returned and conveyed Maiden Chang's words to the wet nurse. However, the wet nurse kept insisting on seeing Maiden Chang. Unable to stop her, Lady Wi asked the maid to show the wet nurse to the separate chamber. Maiden Chang was lying on her bed reading a book when they entered. Startled by their unannounced entrance, Maiden Chang asked, "Who is this person with you?" The maid replied, "This is the visitor who wanted to see you." Maiden Chang became angry and said to the maid, "When a visitor comes inside, you must notify me beforehand. How could you bring a visitor in without giving me any notice?" Maiden Chang called another servant to pull the maid aside and whip her legs as a punishment. After sending away both servants, Maiden Chang lay back down on her bed and said to the wet nurse, "Because I suffer from a disease, I am unable to sit for a long time and receive a visitor, so please understand." She then pulled a blanket over her entire body. The wet nurse was unable to speak a single word to Maiden Chang and soon left her alone; nonetheless, she did get a good glimpse of her. She was indeed a great beauty, and her voice was like shattering jade. Baffled, the wet nurse left the hall and told Lady Wi about the awkward interlude with Maiden Chang. Lady Wi apologized to her, saying, "My child is a spoiled brat and her behavior was unacceptable. I should not have let you see her in the first place. Please forgive her." She asked a maid to treat the wet nurse to some wine and food before she left.

The wet nurse returned to the prefect and told him, "Maiden Chang is truly an exceptional beauty with refined manners, and her great conduct and dignity show in many different ways." The prefect was delighted to hear what the wet nurse had discovered. Without delay, he sent a marriage proposal to the Chang family. Stunned, Lady Wi said to Maiden Chang, "What are we supposed to do?" Maiden Chang comforted her, "Do not worry. Just tell him that I am already engaged to someone else." Lady Wi duly informed the prefect of Maiden Chang's previous engagement, and the prefect was disappointed. The wet nurse suggested, "Why don't you find out if Maiden Chang has already received the betrothal gifts from her groom-to-be?" The prefect thought this was a good idea, and asked the Chang family about the betrothal gifts. Although his inquiry took Lady Wi and Maiden Chang by surprise, but they remained calm and gave the prefect false dates for the betrothal gifts and the wedding. Nonetheless, the prefect saw an opportunity and said with delight, "She has not received the betrothal gifts yet! Whoever submits them to her first will become her groom." He immediately notified the Chang family of his dates for sending the betrothal gifts and holding the wedding, saying, "I've heard that Maiden Chang has not yet received the betrothal gifts from her groom-to-be. Since a woman who has not received the betrothal gifts is no one's bride yet. I will send the gifts before anyone else." Lady Wi was shocked by his behavior, and Maiden Chang outraged. In utter disbelief, Maiden Chang wrote a letter scolding the prefect: "Every man or woman has his or her own soul mate. Only an animal could suggest that a woman who has not yet received betrothal gifts is no one's bride. If someone could steal a marriage by force, people without authority and power would not be able to marry. Your suggestion is unheard of in this world! You should never speak of it again."

Her reprimand infuriated the prefect so much that he wanted to arrest and execute her. However, the wet nurse intervened and persuaded him to proceed with the original plan. Still yearning for Maiden Chang, the prefect hastily prepared the betrothal gifts and sent them to the Chang family along with the message: "If my marriage proposal is not accepted, I will arrest both mother and daughter and beat them to death."

Lady Wi and Maiden Chang paled with horror at this missive. The mood of the household was as if someone had already died. Lady Wi said, "What should we do? We don't know what happened to the young nobleman Cho, and how can we evade the prefect's power and influence? If we decline his betrothal gifts, he will certainly kill us. I am not afraid to die, but I cannot stand to see you die so innocently, which I would not forget even in my death." They put their arms around each other and wept. At their grief, the sun and the moon seemed to lose their light, and even animals appeared to cry for them. Having no other option, they decided to accept the gifts. They unwillingly asked their maid Maehyang to receive the betrothal gifts and store them in her room. After that, the mother and daughter cried day and night.

Time passed implacably, and soon it was the day before the wedding. The prefect sent his servants to set up a large banquet in front of the Chang house and prepare for the wedding ceremony. That night, Maiden Chang decided to take her own life. She looked up at the sky and wept bitterly. Suddenly, she recalled that her father had handed her a sealed letter on his deathbed, saying, "In the future, you will find yourself in a desperate situation. When that happens, open this letter and proceed as it directs." Maiden Chang immediately opened the letter, which read: "You will not be able to evade the demand imposed on you by the prefect of Kangho. Go to Sŏgang,[13] and you will find a boat. Board the boat and head to Kangsŏnam in Sanyang. There you will find someone who can help you."

Maiden Chang's father had made an accurate prediction. It echoed an old saying: "Happy events are often accompanied by a great deal of hardship."[14] When she finished reading the letter, Maiden Chang was overwhelmed, wavering between happiness and grief. She called her maid Kaae to help her pack, and they quickly went to Sŏgang together. Maiden Chang paid a sizable sum of money and boarded a fast boat. During the night, she traveled three hundred li along the waterway. At dawn, she left the boat and set out on foot to find Kangsŏnam, her maid following faithfully. Unfamiliar green mountain peaks and quietly flowing shallow streams lay in her path. What an extraordinary mountain and waterway! It was indeed a very special place under the sky. Just then, Maiden Chang heard the sound of a stone bell ringing. She was happy that a temple was nearby and looked around to find it. Finally approaching the temple's stone gate, she noticed that the main prayer hall stood very high. Large servants' quarters were built on both sides of the gate and decorated with exquisite colors and designs that would fill any heart with rapture. At the ringing of the stone bell, monks started to gather for supper. The monks looked neat, spoke politely, and bore themselves with dignity. Their appearance was rustic, very different from the monks found in a city. She felt rejuvenated as she sat on a bench and admired the scenery around her. Monks approached her and were taken by surprise at her look and manner. They asked her, "Where are you from? Because our temple is within a deep mountain range, it is difficult for a passerby to simply come and go. With your frail body, how and why did you come up here?" Maiden Chang replied, "Disaster struck my family. I used to live in Kangho in the State of Wi, but I lost my parents during the war. Having no place to go, I wandered, and by a stroke of good luck, I ended up here. I hope that you great monks can save my wretched life," she begged.

Pitying her, the monks went to see Wŏlgyŏng and Lady Wang for their opinions. One of the monks said, "Two women from Kangho of Wi are here. One has a face and figure of a rare beauty. We have traveled to many countries and seen perhaps ten million people, but we have seen no one as beautiful as her." Lady Wang said, "Bring them to us." The monk brought the women to Lady Wang, who saw that one of them was indeed extraordinarily beautiful. Lady Wang immediately felt a connection to the beauty, affection pouring from her heart. She approached her and held her hands. She consoled the girl, saying, "Look at you, how young you are! How did you end up here? I heard that you were from Wi. Do you happen to know the current state of the war there?" Maiden Chang stood up, bowed to her, and replied with composure, "On the way here, I heard that Wi emerged victorious and Sŏbŏn was defeated." Lady Wang and Wŏlgyŏng were happy at the news. They said, "We have been worried about our young nobleman's safe return, but this news eases our minds." Maiden Chang said to Lady Wang, "I can see that this place is not easy to find. How did you end up here all alone?" Lady Wang sighed deeply and said, "Something bad happened to my household. I am here to treat the sickness that I acquired as a result." Wŏlgyŏng looked closely at Maiden Chang. He said to her, "You appear to be married. If I may ask, to which family are you married, and did you lose your husband in the war?" Maiden Chang said, with an innocent face, "I have yet to know the principle of ŭm and yang,[15] so how can I have a husband?" Wŏlgyŏng was suspicious of Maiden Chang but, swayed by her words, he did not inquire further.

Later, Wŏlgyŏng said to Lady Wang, "I had a close look at her, and, indeed, she is not of this world. I have never seen the famed Maiden

Chang of Kangho, but in my opinion she must be at least equal to Maiden Chang. However, she looks to be married and hiding her true identity. I thought she might be a prostitute, but after scrutinizing her carefully, I concluded that she was not. She is like a toad that is alarmed by a heavy storm and finds shelter under the cinnamon tree in the moon.[16] Is she possibly Maiden Chang? In fact, no one but Maiden Chang herself could have such beauty. I feel confident that she is Maiden Chang." Lady Wang said, "I also have not seen Maiden Chang, but I doubt she is the kind who just wanders alone." Wŏlgyŏng said with a smile, "How can we predict a person's fate? Lady Wang, how did you end up here yourself?" Lady Wang just smiled without saying a word.

From that day on, Maiden Chang stayed with Lady Wang in the temple. Maiden Chang often gazed into the distance and wept quietly to herself. Lady Wang consoled her, "This is also part of your fate. Do not be so sad." Yet, in sadness Maiden Chang passed her time. One day, in casual conversation with Maiden Chang and Wŏlgyŏng, Lady Wang said, "I have heard Maiden Chang of Kangho is a rare beauty, but in my opinion, she could not be as beautiful as you are." Maiden Chang was filled with dread and astonishment, but she remained calm and asked, "How do you know about Maiden Chang?" Lady Wang replied, "I happened to hear of her a long time ago, but do you know her?" Maiden Chang replied, "How could I know a girl from another household? I was always confined in the women's quarters of my own home." Maiden Chang thought it was strange that Lady Wang brought up the question. Knowing nothing about Maiden Chang's past, Lady Wang remained deeply suspicious.

One night, Maiden Chang was overcome with emotion at the sight of a full moon. She took some objects from her bag, placed them on the altar in front of a statue of Buddha, and said a prayer. By chance, Lady Wang saw her burning incense and bowing twice at the altar. She overheard Maiden Chang's prayer, "I pray to the spirits of the mountains that I will see my mother and husband soon." After Maiden Chang prayed for a while in her grief, she removed every trace from the altar and left. Lady Wang thought Maiden Chang had acted strangely and told Wŏlgyŏng what she had seen. He said, "She must have a husband, but she consistently hides this truth from us. If we could only search her belongings, we could find some clues." They formed a plan to examine her things.

One day, while Maiden Chang was out for a bath with her maid, Wŏlgyŏng and Lady Wang took the opportunity to search her belongings for clues as to who she really was. They did not find anything particularly unusual except for a young nobleman's fan. Looking closely, they saw that something was written on its face. It read, "This is my token of affection given to Maiden Chang," and further read, "Cho Ung hereby signed." Lady Wang and Wŏlgyŏng were delighted to finally know who Maiden Chang was. Lady Wang praised Wŏlgyŏng, saying, "Not even a ghost can come close to your intuition. I wonder what happened to her. It is mysterious indeed." As they continued to chat about her, Maiden Chang returned from bathing. Seeing that Lady Wang was in an unusually good mood, Maiden Chang said, "Happiness is in your face. Did something good happen to you?" Lady Wang replied, "Since I sent my son to the war, I did not know if he was alive or dead. Moments ago, Wŏlgyŏng and I were devoutly praying in front of the Buddha statue and received good news. I am indeed happy." When Maiden Chang heard that Lady Wang's son had gone to the war, she was surprised but, strangely, her words came as a great joy in her heart. Maiden Chang asked, "How did you receive this news?" Lady Wang replied, "The Buddha statue in this temple is of miraculous efficacy. If your prayer is sincere, it listens and makes your prayer come true. If you have a wish, accompany Wŏlgyŏng and sincerely read your prayer at the Buddha statue."

[Maiden Chang prepared eagerly to make a prayer at the Buddha statue.] Delighted, she immediately brought out her belongings and began to search for something for the prayer. Not finding it, she grew increasingly alarmed. Lady Wang noticed her distress, and, feigning surprise, asked her, "Is something missing from your belongings?" With a grave countenance, Maiden Chang replied, "I kept a token of affection with my other belongings, but it is now missing." "Did it belong to your parents?" Lady Wang asked innocently. Maiden Chang remained silent, but tears coursed down her jadelike face. Maiden Chang's maid, standing beside her, broke her silence and said, "It belonged to her husband. He gave it to her when he left soon after meeting her for the first time." Lady Wang could no longer pretend or contain her emotion. Grasping Maiden Chang's hands, Lady Wang said, "Without any doubt, you are Maiden Chang, my daughter-in-law!" and returned to Maiden Chang the fan that she had been hiding. With immeasurable happiness, Lady Wang explained, "This fan belonged to my son, Cho Ung. He told me that he had become a son-in-law of the Chang family when he traveled in Kangho. He told me all about you. I was afraid I would not meet you in my lifetime and lamented day and night. No one could have dreamed that we would finally meet today."

Maiden Chang was a little suspicious at first, but she quickly banished her distrust. She politely stood up, bowed to Lady Wang, and said, "I was told that my mother-in-law was in a remote place, but I never guessed that I would find you here." Maiden Chang was overcome with joy and relief. Lady Wang asked, "My fortune turned for the worse and I ended up here, but under what circumstance did you come here?" Maiden Chang collected herself and told Lady Wang all the details of how she had met Ung, how she had been cured of her sickness, and how she had fled from the prefect of Kangho. Lady Wang and the monks lauded her wise actions. From that day on, Maiden Chang honored her special bond as daughter-in-law to Lady Wang and treated her with great respect. Her filial conduct was so zealous that no comparison to it existed.

Meanwhile, Grand Field Marshal Cho was about to set out for the crown prince's place of exile. He sent an official letter to Kwansŏ bearing advance notice of his arrival. The towns along his route were shaken by his approach. All the prefects and chief magistrates competed to give Ung the warmest welcome and farewell, standing in rows beside the road.[17] When he eventually reached the Kwansŏ area, where General Hwang's tomb lay, Ung instructed his troops to lodge inside the city walls and ordered the local officials to promptly refurbish the tomb and prepare for the interment ritual. Then he personally wrote a prayer of invocation and began the rite. In keeping with tradition, swords and spears were arrayed facing in the proper directions, and incense was carefully arranged. It was the third watch when Ung prepared to bury the armor and the sword General Hwang had given him according to the great man's instructions. He found a suitable stone box, placed the items within, and buried them. Then he ordered cannon fire, along with shouting and beating the drum of victory; arrows were shot into the sky. Suddenly, a cold wind blew around the banners of the five directions, and the ghostly figure of the deceased general appeared.[18] Wearing chest armor and holding a mighty sword, the ghost general stood arrogantly. His commanding presence and invincible spirit seemed powerful enough to bend swords and spears.[19] Several cups of sacrificial wine that were offered mysteriously disappeared.

When the ritual finally came to an end, Ung instructed his chief military officer to provide the troops with plenty of food and bid them rest. Ung went to his room, lit a lamp, and devoted his attention to a military book. Sometime after the third watch, General Hwang appeared at the doorstep and announced himself. Ung stood up and greeted him, saying, "Although we live in the separate worlds of the living and the dead, we share a deep friendship. With your divine intervention, Wi emerged victorious from war. Your spiritual power is indeed worthy of praise." The spirit general thanked Ung and said, "I feel rejuvenated and am in your debt forever, because you, with your dignity and virtue, alleviated the suffering I endured before and after my death. I am also deeply moved and grateful that you comforted my soul by holding a military ceremony at my tomb and providing me with the wine and meat which eased my thirst and hunger. You have also cleaned my tomb, which is my lodging in this world.[20] How can I dismiss your kindness even for a moment? Yet unfortunately, it is time to leave. It saddens me to part from you so quickly, but I must now bid you farewell. The distinction between the worlds of the living and the dead prevents me, a ghost, from remaining much longer in this complex world of the living. I wish you may restore the ancient glory of the Great Song, and leave your illustrious name in history for many generations to come." After this, he left the room. Ung felt much obliged for the general's kind words. The next day, he gathered the villagers and ordered them, "Guard the tomb with diligent care, and hold rituals in the general's honor each spring and fall."

Later that day, Ung and his troops left the village. They traveled for several days and eventually arrived at Mount Kwan. Ung ordered his troops to stay at the base of the mountain and ascended alone, on horseback. The landscape appeared to be the same as before, but he noticed that the stone gate was wide open. He walked past the gate to approach the thatched cottage, expecting to see someone, but found no sign of people. He looked around the premises, which were strangely lonely and desolate. The familiar things were all gone, and the house looked like it had been abandoned for a long time. Gazing upon the bleak and dilapidated remains, Ung was overwhelmed with billowing solitude and immeasurable desolation. The shade from the indifferent white clouds above fell softly on the stone statue, and sympathetic monkeys cried sadly, deepening his loneliness. Unable to contain his sadness, Ung sighed deeply to the sky and walked around aimlessly. He climbed a large boulder nearby and, from that vantage, noticed some writing on the wall. He did not recall its having been there before. Curious, he climbed down to take a closer look at the writing. It read:

Has the Daoist Master of Mount Hwa returned on time?
The passes and mountains in the frontier regions are full of spears, swords, and barbarians.
Having not completely swept the dirt from between heaven and earth,
At which pass can I meet a delightful hero?[21]

After reading this, Ung's face paled with surprise. He wiped his tears and sighed as he descended from the mountain. Before marching on with his troops, Ung sent an official letter to Kangho to announce his arrival and his intention to stay at the Chang family's residence. The prefect of Kangho was racked with anxiety. In a panic, he could not think what to do. Finding no way to hide his wrongdoing against the Chang family, he instructed his servant on how to deal with the situation. The servant went out to greet Ung and said, "The Chang family has committed a murder. With the lady of the house in prison and the daughter on the run, we are afraid you will not be able to stay in the Chang's house, but we are prepared to have you stay in a guesthouse."

The news shocked Ung. He quickly went to the guesthouse and prepared orders for the town. He ordered the officials of Kangho to bring before him every prisoner, regardless of the severity of their crimes.

Perplexed and urgently carrying out Ung's order, the officials moved about like boiling water. About a hundred prisoners were brought before Ung. One by one, he asked the prisoners about the allegations against them. He determined that every one of them had been wrongfully accused. Among the prisoners, Ung saw Lady Wi wearing a large cangue on her frail, delicate body.[22] It was an unpleasant sight. He bade her sit close to him and asked her what crime she was accused of. She could not speak a word, but instead she took a detailed note from her breast and presented it. Overcome by emotion, Ung issued an order to remove the cangue from Lady Wi and called her old servant to take her to her house. He then decreed that all the prisoners were innocent of the charges against them and that they should be released immediately. In a body, the prisoners stood up and thanked Ung. They expressed their unexpected happiness by dancing, and their delighted chattering could be heard all over the town.

Ung shouted an order to arrest the prefect of Kangho and pressed his soldiers to hurry. The soldiers cried out in acknowledgment of his order, and swiftly went to arrest the prefect. They tied him up and brought him before Ung so fast it was as if their feet never touched the ground. Filled with anger, Ung exposed the prefect's wrongdoings one by one, and reprimanded him, "You are a civil servant to the country and receive a government stipend. However, you committed serious crimes that truly deserve serious punishment. Even if I were to consider sparing your life, you have already exhausted every means of saving yourself." In the end, the prefect was dragged around the town for the public to see and then executed. Ung appointed So Yŏnt'ae, a former general of Song, as prefect of Kangho, and reported the matter to the king of Wi.

Later, Ung went to the house of Chang. With the walls crumbling there was nothing pleasant to see; loneliness pervaded the house. Ung stepped inside to see Lady Wi. She felt honored by a visit from such a high-ranking official. She said, "Oh, grand field marshal, you saw through the right and wrong and saved my pitiful life. I am so grateful to you." Ung replied, "It appears that you don't recognize me. Perhaps you are out of your senses due to the hardship of being in a jail cell for so long. I am Cho Ung, who benefited from your kindness." Lady Wi slowly gazed at his face and was astonished. Holding his hands, she burst out crying loudly and could not speak a word to him. After consoling Lady Wi, Ung asked what had happened to her. Lady Wi took a deep breath, and said, "My daughter disappeared with her maid Kaae one day, and to this day I don't know where she is, or if she is alive or dead. It fills me with anxiety and sorrow." She gave a despairing wail. No one could bear to watch the scene. Ung, likewise, was speechless with grief at learning that Maiden Chang had disappeared. Only after some time was he able to regain control of his emotions. Ung consoled Lady Wi, saying, "Only heaven determines a person's longevity in life, and fate decides his life and death. Although we do not know her whereabouts, I doubt she is dead." He continued, "I am sure someday we will see her, so please don't let anxious thoughts assail you. I will do my best to find her, but in the meantime, please come with me to Kangsŏnam, where my mother lives." Ung sent a letter ahead to his mother to notify her of his imminent arrival and left for Kangsŏnam with the Chang household. The letter included the following signatures:

Loyal Subject of Song,
Grand Field Marshal and Surveillance Commissioner of All
    Provinces of Wi[23]
Cho Ung.

Lady Wang, Maiden Chang, and Wŏlgyŏng were all delighted to receive the letter from Ung. They climbed up to the mountain peak to watch for his arrival. After a short while, thousands of troops and horses began to appear through the pass. Standing out in the middle of the troops, the young commander, wearing golden armor and holding his great sword, rode the golden saddle of his swift stallion. He looked like a golden dragon, surrounded by clouds of five colors, outshining the light of the sun and the moon.

Ung ordered his troops to wait outside the stone gate and entered the temple. The monks accompanied Lady Wang to welcome him. As soon as Lady Wang saw her son, she held him tight. Wavering between joy and sorrow, she said, "Is this a dream or reality? Are you really Ung or someone else?" Overwhelmed by emotion, she looked as if she had lost her mind. Ung told her, "Mother, please calm down." He had to hold her down to get her to sit, and when she did, he comforted her. Finally calm, Lady Wang said to Ung, "After you left for the war, we lost contact with you for such a long time. We could not do anything but hope for your safe return. Briefly tell us about your journey." Ung lowered himself to the ground and started to tell them his story.

First, he explained how he had dealt Sŏbŏn a huge blow in battle, forced its surrender, helped the State of Wi bring peace to the land, and become the grand field marshal of Wi. Then he spoke of how he had stopped in Kangho on his way to Kangsŏnam and found the Chang household in turmoil and of the action he had taken to resolve the situation and punish the prefect's crimes. He explained how he had freed all the innocent prisoners of Kangho and, in the end, executed the prefect of Kangho because his crimes were too grave. Finally, he told them how Maiden Chang had disappeared with her maid, apparently to avoid the prefect's forced marriage, and how, since Lady Wi was alone and without a family, he had decided to bring her to Kangsŏnam.

As Ung finished his tale, Lady Wang, Wŏlgyŏng, and the other monks praised Ung's deeds. Lady Wang said to Ung, "By your own efforts, you have returned in glory. Look at your success! Your honor is immeasurable, and you cannot imagine how proud of you I am. I have already heard about the Chang family. One day, Maiden Chang fled here to save her own life. We have shared what is in each other's hearts. I am so happy that you brought your mother-in-law with you today." And she called Maiden Chang.

Hearing that her mother was there, Maiden Chang hurried out. At the sight of her daughter, Lady Wi ran toward Maiden Chang and hugged her tightly. They sank to the floor together, weeping uncontrollably. Bittersweet emotions washed through the cottage in the temple, the joy of reunion tempered by all the sorrows that passed during their separation. Lady Wang consoled Lady Wi, "Don't be sad. Now that you are reunited, there will be nothing to worry about." Lady Wi collected herself and said to Maiden Chang, "Are you dead and standing before me as a spirit? Or are you living and standing before me as a survivor?" Still overcome with emotion, Lady Wi looked at her daughter again and again as if to decide whether or not she was dreaming. Those who watched their reunion could not help but also shed tears. Maiden Chang stopped sobbing first and, with her arms around her mother, consoled her, saying, "Mother, please calm down for the sake of your health. You are weeping bitterly for your child, who is the most disrespectful and disobedient under the sky. If I have caused you sorrow and pain, I do not deserve to be your child. However, thanks to heaven's grace we are reunited today. I bow before you and beg you, mother, please calm down for a moment." Under Maiden Chang's assiduous consolation, her mother finally managed to calm down. Ung brought the two ladies and Maiden Chang to a separate house, where they spent a pleasant night sharing their stories of hardship and salvation.

The next day, Ung instructed his chief military officer to have his troops bring in the rolls of silk and jewels he had received as gifts from the towns he had passed through. The soldiers brought the items in twelve carts. Ung had the gifts piled up in a mound inside the temple and called Wŏlgyŏng and the other monks. He spoke to them, "Grand Master and each monk of this temple, your grace is as great as the rivers and seas. There is no way I will be able to fully repay your favor but in the meantime, I would like to present a small gift to you as a token of my gratitude. Please keep it in your temple and use it as you wish." The monks were deeply moved by the kind gesture and thanked Ung again and again.

After ensuring that his family would be comfortable and safe at Kangsŏnam, Ung prepared to set out for the crown prince's place of exile. He decided to take the route that passed Sŏbŏn to reach Kyeryangdo in Mount T'ae Prefecture. His generals spoke up, warning, "We are concerned that Sŏbŏn is still an enemy of Wi." Ung reprimanded them loudly, "The likes of you ought not to be generals. If you are afraid, don't follow me." Ashamed, they could not speak another word. Ung saw that he had been too harsh and tried to cheer them up, saying, "You are anxious about trivial things; that is not the way a general should behave. When we reach Sŏbŏn, the king will most likely try to lure me into a trap. How could I not be worried? [But that does not stop me from passing through Sŏbŏn]." Ung bade farewell to everyone in the temple and they were all miserable to part from him. He sent out an official letter to notify each town that lay on the route to Sŏbŏn of his passing. As Ung's troops passed through each town, the magistrates, one by one, came to the outskirts of their towns to await his arrival, fearing they might provoke Ung's anger.

The king of Sŏbŏn was also informed of Ung's passing. He discussed the matter with his generals, asking, "What can we do to please Grand Field Marshal Cho?" Several of them said, "We have heard Grand Field Marshal Cho covets wealth and likes beautiful women. First, treat him well and then have beautiful women available to attend and entertain him. Finally, offer him the title of marquis with one thousand gold ingots and entice him into accepting it." The king of Sŏbŏn agreed to the plan and awaited the grand field marshal's arrival.

Time passed and Ung reached Sŏbŏn. The king of Sŏbŏn sent out a special envoy to greet him and escort him into the capital city. The envoy presented Ung with a list of valuable gifts he had brought along. Ung showed it to his troops and had the gifts distributed among the soldiers as rewards. The envoy was amazed by his conduct. Ung ordered his troops to camp inside the city walls and instructed his chief military officer, "Feed the soldiers heartily and let them rest well."

The king of Sŏbŏn promptly had some lambs and cattle butchered and sent the meat, along with one hundred large bags of white rice, to Ung's troops. Ung thanked the king of Sŏbŏn, saying, "What happened in the past was only intended for the good of each country. I have no hard feelings and have already forgotten all about it." Ung also said with a smile, "We have to go our separate ways, but it is so good to see you again." Very pleased by his friendly response, the king of Sŏbŏn said, "Grand field marshal, you are not originally from Wi . . . I have something to ask of you, and I hope you will not refuse. Although Sŏbŏn is a relatively small country, its domain stretches one thousand li across. It has one million soldiers in armor, two towns that are known for scenic beauty and relics, and rivers that flow for more than ten thousand li. I would like to confer upon you the title of marquis of Yangnam.[24] Please do not refuse, and please stay in Sŏbŏn for a while to help us rebuild our country, which suffered a great defeat in the war and is now in turmoil." Ung was displeased by the king's request, but was compelled to veil his feelings, saying, "Because I am simple and dull-minded, I am afraid I cannot do as my heart desires. Also, I am on the way to my country, so I cannot accept your offer."

After returning to his quarters disappointed, the king of Sŏbŏn discussed things with his retainers, "The grand field marshal seemed determined not to accept the title. What are we going to do now?" Several of his retainers said, "Of course, he would not accept the title at the first offer. Tonight, we will have a beautiful woman attend and entertain him. He will be lured into changing his mind." The king of Sŏbŏn immediately put the plan into action. He called the most beautiful court maid, Wŏltae, who was a talented singer and dancer, to the palace. She was, perhaps, one of the most talented court ladies under the sky. He said to her, "If you can please Grand Field Marshal Cho and convince him to change his mind tonight, I will bestow on you a great reward and allow you to stay with him. To the best of your ability, carry out this task."

After receiving the king's order, Wŏltae dressed in beautiful clothes and jewelry. She then asked for an audience with Ung. Ung noticed her exceptional beauty and asked her, "What brings you here?" Wŏltae replied, "I came here on the king's order to make your lonesome stay more comfortable." Ung conversed with her and pretended her company helped ease his travel fatigue. He asked her, "Can you dance and sing?" She replied, "I am not very good at either, but I have learned the rudiments." He thought her humble words polite and laudable. He asked her to sing. She opened her red lips halfway, and, in her beautiful and tranquil voice, started to sing a song. Her tone was as clear and elegant as the crane's sunset song at the Sosang Rivers. She sang:

> Why bother missing a temple on a mountain?
> Yangnam is the prefecture of the emperor.
> The magnificent palace [in Yangnam],
> For whom is it kept empty?
> Perhaps, to the person desiring to become its owner,
> It must be the land allotted by heaven.

The lyrics of her song disturbed Ung. He knew she was deceiving him and involved in some treachery. Yet, hiding his feelings, he praised her performance and asked her for another song. She took heart and sang again:

I wish for you to hate the title of marquis, the ministerial post worthy of one thousand gold ingots, and not to accept it.
Recalling the death of the Hegemon King of Ch'o under the misty
moonlight of the O River,[25]
I am afraid your lifetime's resentment will never be forgotten.[26]

When her song was over, Ung was furious. In outrage, he scolded her
loudly, "You are a cunning woman. With foul intentions, you try to
bring down a man's loyal heart. How outrageous this is!" Ung pulled
out his sword, slashed her head off, and threw it outside the door. He
was still hot with anger even after the killing.

The incident was reported to the king of Sŏbŏn. "That wicked
woman must have botched the job," he said. He summoned all the court
ladies and asked them, "Can any of you change the grand field marshal's
mind?" The ladies had heard what had happened and were very frightened. Some cried, some ran away, and the rest were silent, all except one.
Holding the kŏmun'go zither in her arms, Kŭmnyŏn said, "I will comfort the grand field marshal and change his mind." The king of Sŏbŏn
was happy to have a volunteer and entreated her, "You must devote
yourself to the task and succeed."

Receiving the king's order, Kŭmnyŏn presented herself before
Ung. He gazed at her and found her to be exceptionally beautiful. He
asked, "How old are you?" Kŭmnyŏn replied, "I am nineteen-years-
old." Enchanted, he let her sit beside him. She held the zither in her
arms and started to play with her delicate hands. She sang along to the
tune of the zither. Her singing tone was loud and elegant, like a coral
mallet striking a jade plate. She sang:

The moon terrace, moon terrace, the moon-viewing terrace!
His loyal heart that shines like the sun and the moon,
How could you change it just by singing an elegant song?[27]
How beautiful he is, the treasure of the Song dynasty, the treasure
of the Song dynasty.

After she finished playing, Kŭmnyŏn set down her zither and pleaded
tearfully, "I am not a native of Sŏbŏn, but a daughter of Tu Yusŏng from

Sŏgang of the State of Wi. My father died young and my dependent, aging mother and I made a meager living before Sŏbŏn's war drove us to flee. In the turmoil, I was separated from my mother and captured by Sŏbŏn soldiers. I could not end my life at that time because it would have been unjust. I grieved day and night because I did not know whether my mother was dead or alive. I am so happy to meet you, Grand Field Marshal of Wi, thanks to heaven's grace. I kowtow before you— please take me with you, so that I can find out what happened to my mother." He felt deep sympathy and noticed an extraordinary quality about her, so he agreed to let her accompany him. He asked her about her lineage and her deeds when she had lived in Wi and then he slept with her.

The next day, before leaving the city, Ung wrote to the king of Sŏbŏn: "I thank you for your generosity. The court lady that you sent to me was from Wi. Learning that she wants to see her mother, I have decided to take her with me. Please understand." The king of Sŏbŏn was angry, "I have lost many treasures and extraordinary court ladies and received nothing in return. I am outraged." Unable to calm himself, the king of Sŏbŏn summoned his retainers and proposed an evil plot, "The grand field marshal will have to pass through Sŏbŏn again. We will capture him then."

Several days passed. Ung reached the outskirts of the prefecture of Mount T'ae as the sun was setting. He ordered his troops to find a suitable site for camping and [scout the region] for news from Kyeryangdo. [The scouts soon returned with the news that] the prefect of Mount T'ae Prefecture had just arrived in Kyeryangdo, where he planned to administer a lethal dose of poison to the crown prince of Song. Ung was shocked and asked the local people for details. They said, "The emperor sent the poison to put the crown prince to death and ordered the capture of any officials who are still loyal to the former dynasty." Stricken, Ung asked how far it was to Kyeryangdo. They told him it was seventy li away. He ordered the chief military officer to hold the troops in their current position and await his return. Alone, Ung rode urgently toward Kyeryangdo.

It was already deep into the night when Ung arrived. He scouted the area and found the house where the crown prince was being held. Spears and swords were arrayed around the house like jagged frost. Outside, many soldiers stood guard as if to prevent even a swallow from flying over the walls. Ung decided to hide and observe the area first. Inside the walls glowed bright lamps, and there was a crowd of officials, young and old, loyal to the crown prince. At the center of the crowd, a lovely woman was playing the zither in her arms. She was singing a farewell song:

A jade ax, a gold ax!
Sharpening both sides of their blades,
I cut down the cinnamon tree on the moon.
In Kyeryangdo we gather,
To serve, to serve,
To serve our crown prince.
With icy wind blowing over it,
One branch of the plum tree, braving the snow, is in full bloom.[28]
Coming together, coming together,
Coming together are the loyal officials of the Song court, in which
The towns were built in the second year, and
The capital was built in the third year.
The music from the last Emperors Kŏl and Chu of ancient dynas-
    ties was no longer heard.[29]
Oh heaven, I pray and pray;
May the fifth watch[30] tonight stay in the pond in which the sun
    bathes.[31]
Alas, I ask, "What time will it be tonight?";
While the cold wind blows, rustling in the air,
He bids farewell in tears,
Ardently embracing the loyal officials.
[If he dies,] won't he become a soul that does not return?[32]
All I wish is that beside his tomb,
The plum tree of the green mountain be planted.

As the beauty finished playing the zither, tears trickled down her face like raindrops. Moved by her sadness, the officials all stood, bowed to the crown prince, and departed. Once the area was clear, Ung rose up from his hiding place and leaped into the house as if he were flying. He strode to the crown prince, kowtowed, and said, "I am the son of Cho Chŏngin, loyal servant of the former dynasty. Your Majesty, are you well?" Ung's sudden entrance astonished the crown prince. In disbelief, he grasped Ung and asked, "Is this a dream or reality? Are you a ghost or alive?" He wept, saying, "Only a ghost could have come here." Ung reassured him, saying, "Please take heart for a moment."

The crown prince wiped the tears from his face and asked, "Why did you enter the jaws of death?" He continued, "My luck has abandoned me and I am on the verge of death. Not in my wildest dreams did I think I would see you again. Thinking about our past feels like a dream. We met at the age of eight, and only now are we able to see one another again. I am delighted to meet you, but also sorrowful that we meet under such unfavorable circumstances." Ung asked, "Who was that woman singing?" The crown prince replied, "She is a maidservant in the employ of this province's government. In fact, the garrison commander of this province sent her here to tend to me, so I can pass the time more cheerfully."[33] Ung also asked, "What is the name of the commander?" The crown prince replied, "His name is Paek Sŏngch'wi, and he is with our cause. He looks after me, and I live here quite comfortably, which I did not anticipate. Indeed, what he did for me will not be forgotten."

The crown prince went on to explain that the maidservant sent by Paek greatly helped him to assuage his agony and loneliness and that the loyal officials had followed him to Kyeryangdo. He also told Ung that he was to receive the poison tomorrow at the hour of chin, after which the loyal officials would be arrested. These events had been set in motion by a report from the prefect of Mount T'ae Prefecture to the imperial court. He wept bitterly when he finished speaking. The news brought great sadness to Ung's heart. After consoling the crown prince, Ung said, "This is an urgent matter. My soldiers are camped one hundred li from here. I came alone, not aware of your fate. I must leave you for now but will return with my troops to escort you to safety. Until then, please take care of yourself." He bade the crown prince farewell and left.

It was the fifth watch and the rooster crowed. In their quarters, the loyal officials had been unable to fall asleep. After a time, they came back to the crown prince to wish him a goodnight. Candles were brightly lit in his room, and, to their surprise, his face was radiant. They knelt before him and said, "We sense happiness in Your Majesty's face, but we do not know the reason. Has something auspicious happened?" The crown prince replied, "Maehwa knows why I am so delighted." The curious loyal officials asked Maehwa about it. She smiled, opened her red lips, and sang in her clear voice:

> After the rain last night amid the mountains,
> Did you hear the news of spring?[34]
> Whether or not the news of spring has come indeed,
> You, the plum blossom in the snow, should know.
> I, the plum blossom, know,
> Yet, perhaps not the willow.[35]

The song made the loyal officials very happy, and they looked forward eagerly to Ung's return.

Ung made it back to his encampment while it was still dark. He quickly summoned his lieutenants and gave them instructions. After they made a plan, Ung hastily led his troops to Kyeryangdo, but the day had already broken, and the hour of *chin* was approaching. Sword in hand, Ung anxiously rushed into the house. The emperor's envoy was already bringing out a bowl of poison, and the loyal officials were all bound. Infuriated by the sight, Ung struck the bowl away and smote the envoy with his sword. The man's head fell to the ground. Ung pressed his soldiers to immediately release the loyal officials and bowed deeply to the crown prince four times. After his close brush with death, the crown prince was barely himself. He grabbed Ung's hand and said, "Am I in a dream? If so, I fear to wake up." Ung consoled him, saying, "Your Majesty is safe now." The loyal officials looked as if they had lost their souls, so Ung led them to the main hall.

A moment later, with the sound of drums, bugles, and cries shaking the sky and the land, General of the Main Troop O Wŏnch'ung arrived with his soldiers.[36] To the sound of the drum, Wŏnch'ung's troops encircled Kyeryangdo and arrested the prefect and the magistrates of every village, bringing them before Ung in restraints. Ung then exposed their wrongdoing and had them dragged around to be humiliated by his troops before their executions. He then reported their crimes to the crown prince.

The crown prince and the loyal officials were all pleased with this felicitous outcome and praised Ung, "Your virtuous accomplishment is as broad as the sky and the sea. We doubt there has been a loyal servant quite like you in all antiquity. Your swift action saved the life of the crown prince and the lives of one hundred people. We are forever indebted to you." They were filled with delight.

Ung ordered Wŏnch'ung to arrange a banquet celebrating peace, and everyone enjoyed the event. About one hundred loyal officials got up from their seats and danced joyously. The sight was too grand to describe in words. Sixty of the loyal officials, including Yi T'ae and Sŏ Hwang, were at least eighty-years-old, but they danced happily nevertheless, with their white hair waving in the air. The younger officials enjoyed the banquet just as much. The peasants of Kyeryangdo also feasted, danced, and sang. The sound of their happiness was heard all over the area. Overcome by delight and wine, the crown prince called Maehwa, had her sit at his table, and asked, "How can you not be part of this joyous banquet of peace? Compose a song of peace for the grand field marshal about his accomplishment today, to comfort and cheer the troops."

She lowered her head to acknowledge his order. She held the zither in her arms and sat neatly in her seat. After tuning the zither, she started to pluck the strings and opened her red lips halfway, singing beautifully to the melody of the zither. Her voice was clear and elegant like the ringing sound of a shattering jade and lonesome like a crane's cry to its mate. Hearing her plaintive melody, the crowd grew calm and quiet, feeling refreshed by the music and enjoying the atmosphere of the banquet. The song went:[37]

What a pleasure, what a pleasure it is
To feel the spring wind in the snowy weather!
How slow, how slow it is
Your coming on a swift stallion!
What made you come so late?
Was it because you were coming from ancient times, traversing
    these events?
Did you [impersonate the Yellow Emperor and] classify sounds to
    develop music?[38]
Did you [like Yŏwa] fill in the holes
With five-colored stones that you had ground?[39]

During the phase of Emperor Yŏm's decline,
Were the defiant princes punished?[40]
Indeed, did you taste all kinds of herbs and make all kinds of medicine [like Sinnong]
To save human lives?[41]
Did you become Kon, who worked hard to control floods for nine years, and
Reported the completion of the work [to the emperor]?[42]
After seven years of drought,
Did Emperor T'ang of the Sang dynasty pray for rain?[43]
Did Yi Yun behead Kŏl of the Ha dynasty,
Who built magnificent palaces and terraces decorated with jade?[44]
Were Sun the Great and Chŭng Sam indeed
Devoted filial sons?[45]
Did you become Yŏ Sang [Kang T'aegong] and
Feed thin fish at the Wi River?[46]
Did you [as Paegi and Sukche] live deep in the Suyang Mountain,
Only collecting fiddlehead ferns?[47]
On your way back,
Did you meet Kul Wŏn and sing of loyalty and filiality?[48]
Did you console a woman
Who wailed bitterly before the graves of her men?[49]
Did you become Chach'u from the Kae Mountain,
Whose death caused people to serve cold food?[50]
Did you become Ye Yang, who painted his body with lacquer to impersonate a leper,
And sharpened his sword in the Changha River?[51]
At the banquet in Minji,
Did the king of Chin play the pu [at the request of In Sang'yŏ]?[52]
Did you become a problem solver
By finally ending the half-day discussion about the State of Cho's receiving relief from Ch'o to fight against Chin?[53]
Did you ridicule the assassin Hyŏng Ka,
Singing at the cold Yŏksu River, over which a lonely wind blows?[54]
Did you become the deer of Chin[55] and
Find your new lord?

Did you as the Lord of P'ae safely return

From the Feast at the Hong Gate?[56]

By playing the bamboo flute [of Chang Ryang] in the Kyemyŏng
   Mountain,

Did you have eight thousand soldiers [of Hang U] scattered?[57]

Did you meet an old lady washing clothes

Under the castle wall of Hoeŭm and alleviate your hunger?[58]

Did you meet the soul of Ki Sin and

Hold a ritual for him with a written prayer?[59]

Did you make your name known to the world and display it in the
   first floor of the Unicorn Hall,[60]

Responding to the energy of the twenty-eight constellations of stars
   in the sky?

Did you become the spring rain in the snowy mountains, and

Help the myriad things grow?

Did you save people

Like streaks of rain during a drought?

Did you see jade and save it

When fire ignited in the Kunlun Mountains and burned jade
   together with stone?[61]

Did you travel to the Great Wall and

Explore the lay of the land?

What made you come so late?

Your coming on a swift stallion,

Why was it so belated?

May you be like the sun when one approaches you, and

Like a cloud when one beholds you.[62]

Alas!

The life of our emperor was at stake.

The bowl of poison was brought forth;

The loyal servants with gray hair were all tied up.

The sun lost its light;

The vast blue sea trembled.

At the end of the *myo* hour[63] and the beginning of the *chin* hour,

When his souls were about to fly

And scatter away,[64]

Suddenly there blew a gust of strong wind, and
There came a man on a swift stallion,
With a treasured sword acquired in the O area,[65]
In which the energy of the Big Dipper and Altair came down.
His coming seemed like that of King Yama,[66] who
Broke into the room unceremoniously like an arrow and
Exchanged life and death.
The bowl of poison has disappeared.
The loyal servants who were tied are now dancing happily.
Oh, behold, all the people!
Let us brew the wine of peace and
Drink with our lord,
Sharing happiness for all ages.
The virtuous deeds will be enumerated and
Immortalized for posterity.

The loyal officials, both young and old, recited the song and joyously danced. The banquet continued for three days, and grain from storage was distributed to peasants to provide relief. The peasants were very pleased and praised Ung's deed day and night. Later, Ung said to the crown prince, "The prefect of Mount T'ae Prefecture and all the magistrates were removed, and their vacant positions should be filled immediately. I recommend that Your Majesty grant the positions to some of your loyal officials and set them to protect the regions."

After everything was settled in Mount T'ae Prefecture, Ung selected an auspicious day to depart, escorting the crown prince and the remaining loyal officials. It was on the fifteenth day of the third lunar month of spring. They passed the Barracks Gate and arrived at Yangmu, where the soldiers were fed until their bellies were full and allowed to rest before marching on to Sŏbŏn.

Meanwhile, the king of Sŏbŏn had spent a long time planning to capture Ung upon his return. One day, a spy reported to him that Grand Field Marshal Cho was on the way to Sŏbŏn with the crown prince of Song under his protection. The king of Sŏbŏn was excited at the news. He gathered his retainers and discussed the situation with them, "Last time, I lost many treasures and two great beauties, but in the end, I did not achieve what I intended. Words cannot describe how infuriated I am. What can we do to avenge this affront and ease my suffering?" All the retainers said, "We heard the grand field marshal was coming here with the crown prince of Song. First, let us lure the crown prince into the palace and hold him inside. Then, if we suggest that we combine our forces with theirs to recover the Great Country, they will agree to our offer and follow our lead. If this scheme does not work out, we will destroy the villages and barracks along the way to Wi and strategically place fortified buildings in pairs, a remount station and a lodge for our soldiers, at regular intervals along the road. This will allow us to build a separate fort where our soldiers may lie in ambush and carry out our plot. We are sure that we can capture Grand Field Marshal Cho within three days. There is nothing to worry about." The king of Sŏbŏn thought the idea commendable and bade them proceed with their plan.

Several days later, as Ung was approaching Sŏbŏn, the king of Sŏbŏn traveled ten li from the outskirts of the capital city to greet him. Ung spoke to the king, "You are welcoming me with open arms although you and I quarreled the last time we met. I feel guilty, for I do not deserve such a welcome." The king of Sŏbŏn responded, "It is said that the wrath of a warrior does not outlive the battle. How can I mistreat a guest of my house? There is no need to thank me, and please request whatever you need. Although Sŏbŏn is considered poor, she does well enough to provide for you. Her soldiers are the best among the many neighboring countries, so her people can rest easy. On my knees, I request: If there is any military affair or task you are considering, please allow us to join you, so that we may help you complete it. With a generous heart, please reflect on our offer."

Ung laughed aloud and said, "You are being greedy. Do you not know even the moon and the sun have moments of waxing and waning? You would do well to keep your expectations low. Otherwise, you will be at risk. I witnessed Sŏbŏn's great prosperity as I passed back and forth. Indeed, although Sŏbŏn is relatively small in size, she is rich and produces the finest soldiers. Furthermore, neighboring countries pose no major threat to Sŏbŏn. Your reign as king is perfectly secure for your lifetime. Given that, why do you rashly desire more? It concerns me to see you this way."

Smiling rather smugly, the king said, "What you said may seem sensible; however, since time immemorial, people have fought in wars merely for the glory of their countries. If everything were just as you suggested, what need would there be for soldiers and weapons?"

"From what you say," replied Ung with a smile, "I can see that you are full of greed and unable to maintain peace. In an unfortunate country, war breaks out when a traitor tries to usurp the throne in a rebellion and soldiers are only needed then to suppress the rebels. A king like you believes only in his strong army and vast wealth and tries to conquer other countries by force. It is heartbreaking."

The king of Sŏbŏn said, "Poverty has always been nearby in a barbarian country like this. For this reason, whether king, officials, generals, or soldiers, we have all long wished for our country's prosperity."

Ung replied, "Each country tends to have its own rightful king in accordance with the status and size of its economic power and territorial resources. Now you fail to understand your situation and attempt to conquer other countries in order to gain wealth and resources that do not rightfully belong to you. Without some kind of a divine intervention, what you desire so desperately cannot be achieved simply because you want it. Even the collaboration between the powerful Hang U and his talented tactician Pŏm Chŭng to kill the Lord of P'ae at the Feast at the Hong Gate failed, and, as a result, they lost their supremacy over the whole land. Why do you intend to do such a wrongful thing? Why do you try to make me an accomplice to your scheme by praising me in an untruthful manner for hours on end? You should realize that I am the kind of person who wants to be rid of the likes of you. Do not bring your unjust scheme to my attention."

Feeling embarrassed, the king said, "My wish is not outside the realm of possibility, as you think. Sŏbŏn is small and overpopulated. She needs to expand just a little for a bit of breathing room."

Ung said, "You are starting to annoy me, and I am tired of repeating myself. One cannot simply chop off the legs of a crane because they look a little too long. Likewise, one cannot simply elongate the legs of a duck just because they seem too short. Does adding some length make much difference? I have no interest in knowing what you consider an ideal country, whether it is large or small, good or bad."

The king of Sŏbŏn was unable to offer further contention, and their argument came to an uneasy end. Ung went to instruct his chief military officer, telling him, "We will stay here today. Allow the soldiers to rest," and then paid a visit to the crown prince. Ung greeted the crown prince and recounted his conversation with the king of Sŏbŏn. After he finished listening, the crown prince said with a smile, "We should not listen to a rebel like him." Ung spent some time with the crown prince and then went to his own quarters to rest.

The king of Sŏbŏn discussed the situation with his retainers, "I had a long talk with the grand field marshal, but his determination was as straight as the pine and bamboo. He will not easily give in to my request. How can we lure him now?" Minister of the Right Chang Kan said,[67] "Currently, beneath all of the heavens, there is no great general like Grand Field Marshal Cho. He is a major threat to our purpose. With him out of the way, the conquest of the land would be in the palm of your hand. You must take this opportunity to eliminate him." He continued, "I recently heard of a Daoist master who was as capable as Chegal Ryang.[68] Let us prepare some fine silks and send a trusted messenger to request his guidance." The king of Sŏbŏn liked the idea, so he dispatched Minister of the Left Chu Ch'undal.[69]

That night, the king of Sŏbŏn prepared a banquet and instructed Chang Kan to lure the crown prince out of his quarters by pretending he had been sent by the grand field marshal to pass his words on to the crown prince. "The king of Sŏbŏn invited me, your servant, to a farewell banquet. Unable to decline his cordial invitation, I am already at the banquet. We all would be honored by your presence at the banquet as well," Chang Kan lied to the crown prince. Another Sŏbŏn official knelt before the crown prince and implored him, "My king presented precious gifts to the grand field marshal; however, he thinks only about Your Majesty and has not touched his chopsticks to any food at the banquet. With all due respect, I dare to request your presence at the banquet." Seeing the king of Sŏbŏn already standing by the door, ready to escort him to the banquet, the crown prince was unable to decline their request and followed them into the palace.

Many candles were brightly lit inside the annex at the rear of the palace of Sŏbŏn. Music was playing, and beautiful women were ready to attend to the crown prince, who was seated at the main table. There were many delicious dishes. Everything was arranged in a magnificent manner. The crown prince asked, "Did the grand field marshal just step out?" The king of Sŏbŏn answered, "He is outside." Sensing that something was wrong, the crown prince kept asking for the grand field marshal. Yet how could Ung, who was sleeping in his room, know what was happening? The king of Sŏbŏn spoke, "I, an insignificant king, brought you, a great king, here to make a request." He continued, "I have a daughter who is of peerless beauty and is talented in poetry and calligraphy. I would like to offer to you my daughter's hand in marriage. Please do not think it is an improper gesture from an insignificant king. Please accept my request." The crown prince now realized he had been deceived. He could not suppress his anger and became infuriated. He poured scorn upon the king, "King of Sŏbŏn, your title as a king is pitiful and undeserved. You call yourself a king, yet treat your own daughter like a prostitute. Your conduct is filthy and foul." Yelling the grand field marshal's name, the crown prince demanded that the king be seized and removed immediately. Alas, how could the grand field marshal know what was happening and come to his aid?

Feeling ashamed and uncomfortable, the king of Sŏbŏn withdrew, leaving the crown prince behind. He returned to his chamber where he could discuss the matter with his retainers behind locked doors. Some leaned toward killing the crown prince outright, but others were inclined to free him. With their opinions divided, they could not agree upon a single plan.

Meanwhile, Grand Field Marshal Cho woke up from his sleep and went to see the crown prince. However, he could not find him in his quarters. Alarmed, Ung asked Maehwa, who explained how the crown prince had left with the king of Sŏbŏn.

In a mounting fury, the grand field marshal pulled out his sword and rushed to the palace as if he were flying. When he arrived, the king of Sŏbŏn was still consulting with his retainers. With a single blow Ung broke the door apart, then he swung his sword high and struck the king's desk. The king, directly in the path of the flying desk, was thrown out of the room. Wrathfully, the grand field marshal yelled, "I should have killed you a long time ago, yet foolishly I let you live." His sword was now at the king's throat, ready to strike. At the sight of Ung's lethal intent, the king fainted, collapsing to the ground, and his retainers, fearing for their lives, scattered. In a trembling voice, the reviving king implored, "Please, I would like to know why you are so upset." In a fury, Ung brandished his sword and yelled, "Where did you take the crown prince? Tell me at once!" His voice shook the palace and sent a shock, like thunder, throughout Sŏbŏn. The king groveled on the ground, begging for mercy. Ung raised his sword, poised to strike down the king. The terrified king quickly responded, "Grand field marshal, please calm down. The crown prince is in the annex at the rear of the palace." Ung strode towards the annex. The king, trailing along, begged, "Please, could you stop for a moment and listen to me? I have a small wish."

It was nearly midnight. The moonlight was dim, and it was very dark outside. Unaware of the king's wicked scheme, Ung rebuked him, "Don't say another word, but take me to the crown prince." In an effort to deter Ung from finding the crown prince, the king recanted his earlier statements, pretending he did not know the crown prince's whereabouts. He groveled before Ung, saying, "When you furiously rushed into the room and demanded to know where the crown prince was, I panicked and uttered some words out of confusion and fear; but the truth is, I don't know where the crown prince is." Ung swung his sword toward the king's neck, but in a split-second reflex, the king ducked, and the sword slashed off his topknot instead. Seeing his topknot roll to the ground, the king fainted again. As he slowly regained consciousness, he thought for a moment that he had just been beheaded. Dazedly, he touched his neck and could feel it was intact. He soon realized that only his topknot was missing. Pale and trembling, he pointed toward the hall in which the crown prince was being held. Ung quickly ran to the hall and found the crown prince sitting with several beautiful women. He knelt before the crown prince and asked him what had happened. The crown prince explained. Although Ung had found the crown prince safe and well, his anger did not subside, even after they left the palace.

Their terrible fright over, the king's retainers gathered around him. They were trying to make the king feel better when they noticed, to their dismay, that blood was dripping from his body. Upon closer inspection, some of the king's fingers were cut off and bleeding, soaking the dragon robe that he was wearing.[70] The retainers were infuriated and vowed to seek revenge.

On the following day, Ung instructed his chief military officer, "We will leave as soon as possible. Prepare the soldiers for an immediate departure and report back on their progress." General of the Main Troop O Wŏnch'ung came and said, "About forty soldiers, suffering from extreme fatigue, did not recover and their symptoms have become severe overnight. We acquired some medicine from a generous donor, but it will be some time before there is any significant improvement. What shall we do?" Concerned, Ung reported to the crown prince, "Many of our soldiers are sick from their long march. They need treatment before we can march again." The crown prince was worried, "I fear what ill plans the king of Sŏbŏn may have in mind." Ung comforted him, "Please don't worry about the king of Sŏbŏn. Your servant will take care of him." Ung then instructed the chief military officer to postpone their departure and treat the sick soldiers.

Meanwhile, Minister of the Left Chu Ch'undal met with the Daoist master. The master said, "Four days ago, I looked up at the sky and saw an auspicious star shining above Sŏbŏn. I said to myself, 'There must be a great general approaching.' Later, I recognized it as Cho Ung's star. This general cannot be captured easily. There is no way to capture him except the way I am about to tell you. Hamgok of Yŏnju is deep in the mountains.[71] The front of these mountains is called Sword Pavilion and Mount Iron,[72] as it is very difficult for even a bird to pass through freely. On a certain night, Ung's troops will camp in Hamgok. We will use that chance. First, erect walls along both sides of the valley and pile up many stalks of dry grass to start a fire. Then, have your soldiers lie in ambush nearby and act on my instructions. Even if he could fly, Ung would not be able to escape the trap. However, you must proceed with caution and secrecy. Once Ung is killed, I will come to serve your king." Chu Ch'undal returned to the palace and told the king of Sŏbŏn all that the Daoist master had said. The king promptly put the scheme into action. Chu Ch'undal, thinking of the king's wounds, kowtowed four times to the king and said, "Seeing Your Majesty harmed like this, how can I, as your servant, sit and do nothing?" He expressed how his heart boiled with anger.

Ung's sick soldiers were treated for several days, but they showed no improvement. Not wishing to delay further, Ung decided to place the sick soldiers on horses and depart. He ordered, "Bring thirty horses from Sŏbŏn." However, the king of Sŏbŏn repeatedly refused to give up the horses, which angered Ung. He sent out heavily armed soldiers to seize and bring the king of Sŏbŏn before him. Ung's voice shook the air. All the officials of Sŏbŏn were terrified and they promptly dispatched forty horses to Ung [of which he selected thirty]. The sick soldiers were placed on the horses, and the troops marched forward.

As they marched, Ung's soldiers noticed that all the houses beside the road had recently been deliberately destroyed. At the end of the road, a fortification that had not existed before was blocking their path. They approached it, but the gate was shut tight, and they saw no sign of anyone inside coming to open it. The commander of the vanguard, Wi Hongch'ang, yelled, "Gatekeeper, open the gate at once. Grand Field Marshal Cho is escorting the crown prince." The gatekeeper peered outside and yelled, "It is said that soldiers should obey their commanding officer before anyone else, even before an imperial order, so why should I listen to a lowly thug like you and open the gate?"

Infuriated, Ung commanded his sappers to break down the gate and charge inside. However, the Sŏbŏn soldiers quickly assumed a battle formation and resisted their enemy's advance. After settling the crown prince safely in the gatehouse, Ung charged single-handedly, beheading the gatekeeper in a single blow. He tied the gatekeeper's head onto his banner pole and rode into the enemy's formation, rushing this way and dashing that. Horrified by Ung's might, the Sŏbŏn soldiers opened the east gate and fled. The crown prince watched the battle from the top of the gatehouse, and, deep in his heart, he was impressed by Ung's valor. After the battle, Ung fed his horse, gathered the abandoned enemy provisions, and distributed the food among his soldiers before issuing an order to march.

While marching, Ung came to realize that what had happened had been Sŏbŏn's plot to capture him. Anticipating more enemies ahead, Ung carefully scouted the roads before him. Upon reaching a resting place, Ung encountered another recently built fortification guarded by Sŏbŏn soldiers. A Sŏbŏn general emerged on horseback with a spear in his hand, shouting, "Traitor Cho Ung, stretch out your neck and receive my sword! Today, I will have revenge for yesterday's defeat."

Ung responded, "You are the traitor. You are a fool to be so confident. You should flee and save your life!" Before Ung could finish, the Sŏbŏn general charged at him. Ung spurred his horse forward. The general did not have a chance to fight several bouts before Ung slashed off his head and threw it to the ground. He challenged, "Is there anyone in the Sŏbŏn encampment who can defeat me? Any of you, come out all at once!"

Soon, a Sŏbŏn general wearing a golden helmet and a breastplate emerged from the encampment with a polearm. He mounted swiftly and fiercely charged toward Ung. However, with a single blow of Ung's shining sword, the Sŏbŏn general's head tumbled down by his horse's feet. Ung shouted, "How many generals are there in your encampment? All of you, come out at once, so that I can hasten your impending death."

Shaken and horrified, the enemy soldiers did not dare come out, instead barring the gate tightly. With his soldiers, Ung attacked the fortification and slaughtered the guards inside. The dead bodies of the Sŏbŏn soldiers piled up and blood flooded the area, forming small streams. Nobody could match Ung's prowess. The might of his one sword was equivalent to that of a million soldiers.

On the following day, Ung's troops reached an outpost, and yet another fortification built by the Sŏbŏn soldiers blocked the road. Ung first cut down the commander of the enemy vanguard and then charged the enemy encampment. Suddenly, he found himself surrounded by about ten enemy generals. They circled, exhibiting their most lethal fighting moves, about to strike Ung all at once. Unafraid, Ung raised his sword and slashed off their heads one by one until not one lived. He threw the heads over the fortification, and the horrified Sŏbŏn soldiers scattered and fled.

As his army moved forward, Ung continued to destroy the fortifications in his path. When he arrived at the sixth one, the gate was wide open, and it was very quiet inside. It was an eerie sight, but Ung thought, "They must have feared my valor and lost the courage to fight." He instructed his troops to camp inside the fortification and allowed them to rest for the day.

After the third watch, there was a sudden commotion. Shouts, drumbeats, and loud bugle calls shook the air. Startled, Ung ran toward the sounds and saw a large number of Sŏbŏn soldiers rushing in. Ung quickly took the crown prince and all his troops to the north gate and quietly hid them. He then climbed up to the top of the gate and surveyed the area. He could see that the Sŏbŏn soldiers had torches in their hands and were entering the command post. In spite of their torches, the darkness of night impaired their vision greatly so that they collided with each other and swung their weapons around blindly. This chaos soon caused a stampede, and many were crushed to death under the feet of their fellows. Not realizing what had happened, the remaining Sŏbŏn soldiers declared victory and brought enough torches to light the whole area. They began counting casualties, but the wounded and killed were all soldiers of Sŏbŏn—not a single soldier was one of Ung's troops. The Sŏbŏn soldiers were petrified and turned pale.

From the top of the north gate, Ung raised a flag, and at his command, his troops encircled the Sŏbŏn soldiers with shouts and drumbeats. Their morale quickly declining, the Sŏbŏn soldiers were overwhelmed. Wielding a long spear, Ung rampaged through the enemy formation. Dead bodies were piling up like a hill, and their blood formed a stream. Those who escaped Ung's spear fled. After the battle ended, Ung took the crown prince back to his quarters and the loyal officials praised Ung's great victory, "Only Grand Field Marshal Cho could defeat the elite troops of Sŏbŏn!"

The surviving Sŏbŏn soldiers returned to their king and delivered news of the battle, "We at the sixth fortification were utterly defeated and unable to capture Cho Ung. We are all ashamed. How can we face Your Majesty, and how can we consider ourselves generals of our soldiers?" They asked the king to execute them as punishment for their failed assault. The king consoled them, saying, "Victory and defeat in battles are normal in military affairs. There is no one to blame."

Very angry, nonetheless, the king of Sŏbŏn wrote official letters to the prefect of Yŏnju regarding Ung's movement and their plan at Hamgok. He also wrote: "Grand Field Marshal Cho took thirty horses that belonged to Sŏbŏn, but he did not return them to us. When he comes to Yŏnju, demand the return of these horses on behalf of

Sŏbŏn. If he does not comply with our demand, retrieve the horses by force and return them to us."

Ung and his troops marched for several days and eventually arrived in Yŏnju. He allowed his soldiers and horses to rest. Ung was also resting in his quarters when a pair of butterflies flew above his bed, and, mysteriously, wings grew on his body. Ung flew up, following the butterflies, and arrived in an open field deep in the dense forest of a high mountain. It was unlike the human world. There was an immense palace, tall enough to reach the sky. He approached it and noticed a door with a plate on top. The plate was clearly inscribed, "Door of the Most Loyal." Ung looked through the open door and saw an old man sitting on a high platform. His face was handsome like a jade, and he was wearing a golden crown and dragon robe. Many people were sitting beside him in a row, enjoying what appeared to be a banquet. Beautiful women were sitting at the table, which was laden with wine and food. What a splendid sight!

The people seated spoke distinctly about the rise and fall of emperors and the generations of all ages. The unknown emperor sat on a high platform and commanded everyone, "Write about your accomplishments and submit them." One of their writings read:[73]

"Pokchibon-ŭn hansin-ira," which means:
I am originally a subject of the Han dynasty.
"Simjŏng-i pulli-roda," which means:
There are not many deep thoughts, but,[74]
"Chŭgyŏnggongja-hani pokch'an-iroda," which means:
If I recall past events, my achievements outshine the Big Dipper and
the Sun.[75]

Another said:

"Chinjeangŏm-hani chehusŏhi-roda," which means:[76]
By wielding a sword and executing ferocious bandits, the Emperor
of Chin showed signs of becoming a feudal lord.
"Saeksŏngch'ŏnha-hani tongmungongju-roda," which means:
By protecting the world under heaven as if he defended a castle,
His name shook the whole world.

Their achievements were too many to list. The people at the palace all expressed their feelings about the past. Some, angry beyond measure, were taking out their swords and shouting in outrage.[77] Yet others were singing and dancing. While Ung was carefully observing them, a person among them came forward and took a seat, saying, "What we discuss are ancient affairs, which are difficult for us to believe or to fully understand, despite our regret over them. Let me ask you about the current matter: If the Great Song were indeed destroyed by a traitor, could she be restored? If so, when could that happen?"

Another person remarked, "The luck of the Great Song is still great and will last forever. Do you doubt her fate? I am sure there will be a restoration."

A third person interjected, "Don't you know? Heaven has sent Cho Ung to restore the Great Song. Yet, alas, Cho Ung! What a pity for him! A time of great trouble and difficulty is upon him. At dawn tomorrow, Cho Ung's life will be at stake due to the evil plot of Sŏbŏn, and it looks like he will not survive. Alas! He is going to follow in our footsteps, not consummating the full life determined for him by heaven! What a pitiful man he is!"

Suddenly a guard at the gate reported an urgent message, "Emperor Mun deigns to come here." All the people descended from the hall and greeted the emperor. After the emperor was seated on his throne, the officials asked what had made him come late to this meeting. The emperor replied, "The person who will save the Great Song is Cho Ung. On my way here, however, it came to my attention that Sŏbŏn is plotting to capture him. Ung faces unfavorable times ahead, and it looks like he may be unable to overcome his own misfortune. I am so worried about his fate that I visited the master to ask him to intervene and save Ung." All the people exclaimed, "We all thought Ung was going to die and we discussed his pitiful end publicly. However, it has turned out that his great luck has not yet been defeated. Their evil plot against Ung won't affect his lifespan now." Ung woke abruptly, and realized it was just a dream of the Southern Branch.

Please find and read the next volume if you are curious to know what happened next.

BOOK 3

Ung awoke from his dream and sat up. Before long, he heard the clamor of military horns and shouts and the noise of thousands upon thousands of soldiers and horses outside. Alarmed, he summoned Wŏnch'ung, general of the main troop, and asked, "What is the commotion about?" Wŏnch'ung replied, "The prefect of Yŏnju claimed we stole thirty warhorses from Sŏbŏn and demanded the horses back. When we refused to yield to his demand, he came back with troops to retrieve the horses by force. We captured them inside our encampment. I have them just outside, bound with ropes," and he quickly brought in the captives.

Infuriated, Ung ordered the captives bludgeoned before sending them away. However, the prefect of Yŏnju was beheaded, and his head was hung on the gate of the encampment. After reporting the incident to the crown prince, Ung continued, "I think Your Majesty should know, I had a dream," and described the details. The crown prince was astounded at the account of Ung's dream [it was apparent that the people who appeared in Ung's dream were the deceased emperor and his loyal retainers]. Grief-stricken, the crown prince wept bitterly to the sky. Ung did not want to trouble the crown prince with any other problems, so he instructed his troops to be vigilant on their march. Later, while he marched, Ung thought pensively about the deceased emperor who had appeared in his dream and felt a lingering sadness; it was a day filled with woe.

The sun was sinking behind the western mountain range and the moon was rising above the eastern ridge when Ung arrived at Hamgok. Under the moon, indifferent monkeys cried and cuckoos quietly sang the song "Why Don't You Return?"[1] Between the sheer, lofty slopes of Mount Ak to the east[2] and the pavilions of the pass at jagged Mount Kŏm to the west,[3] the path that lay before Ung was treacherous. Steep and rugged mountain peaks, one after another, threatened to pierce the heart of any traveler who dared to venture into the gorge in darkness. Undeterred, Ung pressed his vanguard into Hamgok. As he rode, Ung glanced up casually and was surprised to see an old man wearing simple clothes made of coarse hemp on a small eastern ridge. The old man urged his blue donkey[4] hastily downward, waving his white feather fan[5] for Ung to stop.

Awed by the portentous sight, Ung reined in his horse and waited for the old man to join him. When the old man arrived, he immediately asked, "Are you coming from Yŏnju?" "Yes, I am," replied Ung. The old man then asked, "Did you chance to meet Grand Field Marshal Cho who was traveling to Wi? Please answer me quickly!" His sudden appearance puzzled Ung and raised his suspicions, but he politely replied, "Yes, I am indeed Cho Ung. What urgent business do you have with me?" The old man happily said, "I am a hermit who likes to visit famous mountains and places of scenic beauty. While traveling throughout the land, I met Daoist Master Ch'ŏnmyŏng at the Oro Peak[6] and stayed with him for several days. When I was about to leave, he asked me to deliver a letter to you at the hour of o [11 A.M.–1 P.M.] today.[7] I hurried my donkey to arrive earlier, around the hour of chin [7–9 A.M.], but it tired along the way, and the time was already past the hour of o. I was so worried that I would not find you here after the delay. You don't know how glad I am to see you here!" He pulled a letter from his sleeve and handed it to Ung. He then raised his arm in a gesture of farewell and departed.

Ung gazed at the sealed letter in wonder. When he looked up from it, the old man was already long gone. Although the mysterious encounter left Ung speechless, he promptly opened the letter, which contained only a warning: "Do not blindly enter Hamgok. Sneak inside the fortification first and fire one shot with the cannon." Ung's face turned pale in horror. He quickly summoned General of the Left Wi Hongch'ang and ordered, "Stop the soldiers from entering Hamgok." However, Hongch'ang reported, "The vanguard troops have already entered Hamgok." Ung urgently ordered him, "Immediately pull them back without causing a commotion. Make it appear that we are camping in Hamgok. Bring out one or two soldiers at a time while keeping out of sight. Do not delay. Hasten their return."

After carefully attending to Ung's instructions, Hongch'ang relayed the order to the vanguard troops. Soon, the commander of the vanguard returned with his soldiers. Ung was relieved to see them return safely from harm's way. Having directed his soldiers to camp in an open field, Ung issued another order, "Lay the banners, swords, and spears on the ground. Do not stir and keep quiet." Ung then ordered O Wŏnch'ung, general of the main troop, "Take command of the vanguard troops. There is an enemy fortification in Hamgok. Lay an ambush at the left and right flanks of the gate and wait for the signal."

At the third watch, Ung ordered General of the Rear Yu Yŏnt'ae, "Infiltrate the fortification in Hamgok, fire a round from the cannon, and immediately retreat." Before long, Yu Yŏnt'ae had carried out his order. At the cannon's fire, a tremendous commotion surrounded the fortification and a large number of Sŏbŏn soldiers burst out. At the gate, Wŏnch'ung's troops fell upon them and took about three hundred captives.

After the battle, Wŏnch'ung brought the captives to Ung, who, excited by the successful mission, had the drum of victory beaten. He released all low-ranking captives but kept about twenty high-ranking officers for interrogation. Ung spoke to the enemy officers, "I should have you all executed, but I, out of mercy, have decided to release you. Tell your king that the head of the prefect of Yŏnju was hung on the gate of my encampment for his petulance, a quality he shared with your king," and released them.

That night, a fire erupted, spread, and reduced the entire mountain range to ashes. Unable to endure the blaze, Ung decided to relocate the encampment far away from the fire for the night. The intense heat drenched the backs of the soldiers with sweat as they retreated to the new encampment. Later that night, when they attempted to pass through Hamgok, the mountain ridges were collapsing from the fire and the enemy fortification was still burning. With the ground scorching hot, it was impossible to continue. Ung's troops had no choice but to pull farther back to Yŏnju and camp in a peasant village nearby. Scared by their unexpected arrival, the villagers ran away. After spending three days in the village, the troops returned to Hamgok, which still emitted enough warmth from the fire to film the soldiers with sweat as they walked.

Days later, they reached Kyeyang in the State of Wi. The welcoming governor of Kyeyang presented a letter to Ung from the king of Wi. Ung was as happy to receive the letter as if it were from his own parents. He promptly opened it and read:

> On this day, the king of Wi writes a letter to Grand Field Marshal Cho. It has been some time since you left. Because I have not heard any news, I am eager to know whether you were able to travel tens of thousands of li safely and if the crown prince is well. Day and night, I, an aged king, am filled with worry and anxiety about you and the crown prince, and my feelings of longing for your safe return have become an incurable illness. I have invited your mother to come here to relieve your worries for her. She is doing well. Please do not fall into worries and loneliness while travel-ing in a distant place but come back as soon as possible so that your mother's worried countenance and my restless mind will be relieved.[8]

Ung shared the king's letter with the crown prince. They both happily said, "There is nothing to worry about now." The crown prince and the loyal officials cried cheerfully, "We are officially in Wi territory. There will be no trouble awaiting us now. All this way, we have constantly worried about Sŏbŏn's raids," and chattered together with relief. The soldiers also praised Ung and the crown prince for keeping them safe from undue danger.

Ung sent out an official notice to the capital of Wi, which read: "Loyal servant of the Great Country and the Grand Field Marshal of Wi, escorting [the crown prince, who will be restored as] the great king of Song, will depart from Kyeyang shortly." The king of Wi received the notice and happily anticipated Ung's arrival. He instructed his retainers to be ready to receive orders at any moment and sent out an official letter to every village in his kingdom ordering them to accommodate Ung's troops with proper manners and the utmost respect. As Ung's troops passed by each village and county on the road, all the prefects and governors came out and greeted them. Several days later, Ung's troops finally arrived at the capital city of the State of Wi. The king and officials of Wi were waiting at the outskirts of the city to welcome them. The king of Wi knelt before the crown prince and lamented, "This humble king of Wi has committed a sin of disloyalty. I dare not face Emperor Mun in the underworld after my death." He went on apologizing. The crown prince consoled him, offering words of gratitude instead, "It was because of your efforts that I was able to come here alive. How grateful I am to you!"

The king of Wi turned delightedly to the loyal officials and said in tears, "Even in a dream, I did not expect to see all of you alive." The king of Wi walked down to the troops who accompanied Ung and said, "I am glad to see all of you returned home safely from a campaign that ranged across tens of thousands of li." The troops bowed in unison and thanked their king, "Because of your prayer, we were able to preserve our lives and return home unharmed. We do not know how to repay your favors and kindness." They praised the king highly. When the king of Wi returned to his palace with Ung and the crown prince, all the people of the capital city praised the king's virtuous deeds.

Ung's mother and wife were excited beyond description when they heard of Ung's arrival. They both clasped his hands as soon as Ung entered the room to greet them. Lady Wang happily said, "I would regret nothing even if I were to die right now because I am so happy to see you. I am also delighted that you have brought the crown prince." After Ung had spoken briefly with his mother, he turned to see his wife, saying, "I owe you a great deal."

After spending some time with her son, Lady Wang entered the crown prince's quarters. She knelt down, bowed to the crown prince, and said in tears, "Great King, how is your health? I can die now with-out regret because I am so happy to see you alive." The crown prince said in tears, "I am like a man reborn. I almost died, but by Ung's efforts the rest of my life has been preserved. I am so happy to be here and to see you in person," and he consoled her.

Ung arranged a large banquet, for the king of Wi wished to honor the crown prince. Ung also invited the loyal officials to the banquet so that they could all enjoy it together. Ung suggested to the king of Wi, "The soldiers loyally fulfilled all their duties on the campaign. Your Majesty should reward them." The king of Wi said, "Do as you wish. There is no need for you to report and discuss the matter with me. Do not be a stranger here, nor think that I would countermand you. Do not be afraid to speak up—this is the court of Wi, but the peasants, officials, and king of Wi are all here because of you. It makes me feel uncom-fortable when you act like a total stranger." Ung bowed to the king and said, "I did not mean to estrange you, but I am not in a position to deter-mine the promotion and demotion of Wi officials. How dare I order it? There is a saying, 'Consult the chamberlain for law enforcement in matters of crime and punishment,[9] and consult the chamberlain for the national treasury in matters of grain and money.'"[10] The king of Wi agreed with Ung, "Your words are indeed right. Please forget what this humble king said before," and called up the generals and common sol-diers that served in the campaign. He said to them, "You carried out my orders and returned home safely from the campaign that traveled ten thousand li. Your meritorious service should not go unnoticed." He then promoted each general one by one and presented the common sol-diers with rewards worth one thousand gold ingots in total. All the sol-diers thanked and praised the king. Soon after, the general of the West Pass[11] arrived to report that the king of Sŏbŏn had died from a severe abscess on his back and his eldest son, Tal, had ascended to the throne. After listening to the report, the king of Wi and Ung said without sym-pathy, "His death is well deserved."

Time flowed by. One day, the king of Wi, Ung, and the officials were having a conversation. The king of Wi said to the others, "I have some-thing to discuss, but I am afraid I might sound foolish." The others said, "Let us hear what it is first." The king of Wi said, "I am very happy that the crown prince is with us. Although he is still young, I am afraid that he will not find a suitable bride when he eventually returns to his country. As you know, this old king has two daughters: fourteen and sixteen. For several years, I looked at eligible bachelors, but I was never able to decide. The crown prince is unmarried and Ung, although he already has a wife, did not have the Six Rites for marriage.[12] What I have in mind is to ask the crown prince to marry my older daughter and entrust the younger to Ung. I would like to hear your opinions."

The officials all said, "Your Majesty's words are righteous and touching. We are sure that the crown prince will accept your proposal and Ung will not decline either." However, Ung responded, "Since I already have a wife, please leave me out of the discussion and focus on the crown prince's marriage." Respecting Ung's decision, the officials did not push him further. Praising the king's devotion to the crown prince, they immediately went to the crown prince's quarters and proposed the marriage. He happily accepted.

Later, Ung told his mother, Lady Wi, and Maiden Chang about the king's marriage proposal and asked their opinions. Ung's mother was not enthusiastic, and Lady Wi expressed outrage, "The king of Wi is very rude," she said, overcome by anger. Maiden Chang tried to calm her down, saying, "As the father of two unwed daughters, what the king of Wi said is understandable—do not take it too seriously. Please calm down and forget about it." She then said to Ung, "I understand that you are reluctant to have a second wife because you do not want to hurt my feelings. However, that is not the way a hero should behave," and continued, "The king of Wi asked you out of a father's worry and desperation. It is impolite to outright decline him. Let us not discard the opportunity right away. It could lead to a good relationship. Allow me to see the king's daughters and decide." She then secretly went to the palace with her maidservant to see the princesses, who were elegant and well mannered. Maiden Chang could see from their countenances that they respected their parents and were loyal to their country. She praised them inwardly.

Maiden Chang returned and told her mother-in-law and mother about the princesses' great beauty and conduct. She also said to Ung, "A virtuous man deserves to be with well-mannered and elegant women.[13] The princess is worthy to be your spouse. The idea is lovely and meant to be," and she insisted that he accept the king's marriage proposal. The two ladies remained silent, but Ung finally determined, "I never thought about having a second wife or concubine, but since you sincerely insist, I shall obey your wish." Shortly after, Ung told the king of Wi about his change of heart. Delighted, the king promptly selected an auspicious date and planned to have the two weddings on the same day.

On the wedding day, a grand banquet was laid inside the palace. The wedding candles gave off brilliant light, which shone on gold, silver, and myriad jewels. Court ladies, wearing jades resembling the moon, were standing beside the two brides, whose splendor outshone the sun and the moon. The grooms and brides came forward to take a wedding bow[14] and perform the rite of Plighting Troth.[15] When the ceremonies were over, each couple went to their nuptial room and spent their first night together. Their affection that night was not the same as that of ordinary couples.

Three days later, Ung and his newlywed wife came to show their respect to Lady Wang. Lady Wang and Maiden Chang held the princess's hands and welcomed her into the family. However, the crown prince, also a newlywed, was without a parent to visit and was overcome by sadness. The crown prince had one wife and two concubines. Ung had two wives and one concubine [Kŭmnyŏn].

One day, Kŭmnyŏn approached Ung in tears, "Because of your gracious deed, I was able to return to my home country and to live a comfortable life. I could ask for nothing more except that I do not know what happened to my mother. Please, help me find her." For the first time Ung realized how much Kŭmnyŏn had been grieving over her mother. After describing her situation to the king of Wi, Ung had drawings of her mother posted on government buildings throughout the country in an effort to find her.

The mother of Kŭmnyŏn, Lady Yang, had been separated from her daughter during the chaos of war. She pined for Kŭmnyŏn every day and night until she heard of Ung's coming to Wi from Sŏbŏn. She hurried to Wi and submitted a petition to Ung explaining her situation. The letter read:

My daughter and I were separated in Sŏbŏn during the war. As I had no one to rely on, I had to look for my daughter alone and was unsuccessful. I lamented day and night before hearing of your coming from Sŏbŏn. I thought you might have knowledge of the events that took place in Sŏbŏn and perhaps, know the fate of my daughter.

Astonished by the letter, Ung immediately arranged a meeting between Lady Yang and Kŭmnyŏn. Finally reunited with her mother, Kŭmnyŏn wept, "Mother, is that you? Am I seeing a ghost or a living being? I am your unworthy daughter, Kŭmnyŏn." They embraced each other and cried aloud. Overcome by emotion, Lady Yang fainted and maidservants rushed to revive her. Soon both mother and daughter regained their composure and talked happily about how much they had missed each other.

One day, Ung said to his mother [and his wives], "I am going to be away for a while. I will return after I see my teacher and gather news of the Great Country." His words caught them by surprise, but after a speechless moment, they said to him, "We wish you a quick and safe return." After bidding farewell to his mother and his wives, Ung said to the king of Wi and loyal officials, "I am going to be away for a while to gather news of our country and will return." He then bade farewell and left.

Ung traveled alone for several days to arrive at Kangsŏnam. It was very quiet and there was no living creature in sight. Disappointed, Ung gazed around and saw a young girl on a steep ridge singing a song while picking herbs. Her singing sounded as if it were breaking apart the mountains. Surprised and curious, he listened carefully to the song:

The person running on the stone path,
He must be an unexpected visitor from the outside world.
Where did your eight thousand soldiers go now?
Why do you travel alone over one thousand li?
Even though you have come to look for your master, thinking of the
    old favor,
He is now assisting the immortals at the Silver Terrace.[16]
Riding white clouds,
No one knows his movements.

The general on the rocks must now be pressed for time.
Something is going on at the Hak Mountain,[17]
Please go there without delay!

When the song ended, Ung quickly climbed up the cliff to question the girl but she had disappeared without a trace. Unhappily, he descended the mountain and came to a nearby village. He asked a villager about the location of the Hak Mountain and was told it was in Pyŏnyang of the Great Country.[18]

While on his way to the Hak Mountain, Ung met a man on horseback with a short sword at his side hastening the other way. Ung approached the man and, from his saddle, bowed to the stranger, asking, "How far is Pyŏnyang from here?" The man replied, "Follow this road for several hundred li and you will reach Pyŏnyang." Ung asked him again, "Where are you going to?" The man replied, "I am from the Great Country. By the emperor's order, I am urgently going to Kyeryangdo of Mount T'ae Prefecture." Surprised, Ung asked, "On what business are you going there?" He replied, "An official was sent there to carry out the emperor's order to put the former crown prince to death by poison. However, we have not heard back from the official for several months. In his wrath, the emperor ordered me to perform the task in that official's place and arrest him as a criminal." In a mounting fury, Ung yelled, "I, Cho Ung, am a loyal servant to the former dynasty. I will not allow the followers of Traitor Yi Tubyŏng to live."

As he cried out, Ung raised his sword and beheaded the emperor's messenger. His body fell upside down, and his head toppled to the ground. Ung picked up the head and put it in his saddlebag. In the blink of an eye, he reached Pyŏnyang and met an old man. Ung asked, "Can you direct to me to the Hak Mountain?" The old man said, "The Hak Mountain? The mountain range over there is called Ch'ŏnsudong. There is an old saying in this area that the Hak Mountain is somewhere over that mountain range, but no one has ever seen it. I never have seen it with my own eyes either."

Cuckoos cried sorrowfully as Ung ventured into Ch'ŏnsudong along a narrow gravel path leading to a high mountain lush with green trees.

The mountain was very steep and rugged, but Ung pressed on. Further along, Ung saw an old monk who was composedly reading a book on a large flat boulder under a short pine tree by the path. His cone-shaped hat was hung on the top of the pine tree and his nine-headed cane was pushed into a crack in the boulder a little so that it would stay upright. Although Ung's coming startled the old monk, he nonetheless ignored Ung, pretending not to notice him. Upset by this strange behavior, Ung shouted at the old monk who, this time, played deaf. Outraged, Ung pulled out his sword to strike the old monk. Like a bird flying away in horror, the old monk evaded the attack by fleeing to a nearby cliff, leaving behind a piece of paper with some writing on it. Ung chased the old monk, but he quickly disappeared. Astonished, he returned to the tree and read the paper:

On the endlessly vast teal mountain, a visitor is staying.
White clouds are deep in the Immortals' Land.
The crystal clear water flows over one hundred li along the mountain valley.[19]
What a splendid place for a home!

Ung looked curiously around for the house mentioned in the writing. Spotting it, he approached and called for the master of the house. A boy opened the thatched gate and led Ung inside. Ung requested, "I would like see the master of the house." The boy replied, "Our master, Ch'ŏnmyŏng, went out a while ago. He said that a guest would come today and told me to hand this to the guest," and handed a sealed letter to Ung. It read: "Go quickly to the Hak Mountain and behead Yi Tubyŏng." The letter was a pleasant surprise to Ung since it offered him an opportunity take his revenge, but the name Yi Tubyŏng also provoked his anger. Ung asked the boy, "Show me the direction to the Hak Mountain. Also, where did Ch'ŏnmyŏng go?" The boy said, "This path will lead to Ch'ŏnmyŏng and that path will lead to the Hak Mountain." Ung wanted to meet Ch'ŏnmyŏng first, so he climbed up the cliff.

Suddenly, a flood of roaring white tigers appeared and stalked Ung. Ung desperately ran away but could not escape the fiercely pursuing tigers, which quickly overtook him. In desperation, Ung threw the head of the emperor's messenger to the tigers. They bit and batted it and, after playing with it for a while, ate it and left.

After that horrid encounter, Ung decided to immediately fulfill his duty at the Hak Mountain. He soon came across thousands of disciplined soldiers and warhorses encamped on a vast open land surrounded by mountain peaks that stretched to reach the sky. Alarmed by the sight, Ung hid to observe them. From the south terrace, they brought out a bound man and forced him to kneel in front of the command post. Someone yelled at the man, "You were none other than a pillar of the Song dynasty and a subject from a renowned family receiving government salaries for generations. Your grain was piled up like a mountain and your status was of the first rank. You have always enjoyed what your eyes and ears wanted and what your heart desired. Indeed, there has been nothing lacking in your life. It is hard to understand why you became a traitor. Why did you exile the crown prince in a place ten thousand li away? Even though you are a person who knows but little of the world,[20] why did you send poison to the crown prince? After standing in the endlessly broad world and reflecting upon your wrongdoings one by one, you more than deserve to die. The common people are eager to see your corpse." They tied the man to a pole raised in a wagon with a board written: "Traitor Yi Tubyŏng," and began to move north.

Seeing his archenemy, Ung leaped onto the wagon with his sword drawn shouting, "Traitor Yi Tubyŏng, stretch your neck and receive my sword!" Ung swung his sword at Yi Tubyŏng's neck, and saw his head fall down near the cart horse. Blind with rage, Ung repeatedly stabbed Yi Tubyŏng's stomach and eventually ripped it apart. When Ung finally came to his senses, he found that the Yi Tubyŏng whom he had killed was merely an effigy. Nonetheless, Ung felt satisfied. He walked up to the command post and said, "I am the son of the former dynasty's loyal subject, Cho Chŏngin. I, an outsider, insolently intervened and offended you. Please pardon my interference." Ung's precipitous appearance had surprised everybody at the encampment. They seated Ung at the command post and asked, "How did you survive all these years? Do you happen to know the fate of the crown prince?" Ung said, "The crown prince dodged Yi Tubyŏng's evil plot and is very well." The people at the encampment prostrated themselves in a deep bow to the sky. They happily cried, "Heaven saved us! Our great king is well! We would not have any regrets even if we were to die now."

Ung asked them, "Who are you people and what is this gathering about?" A silver-haired old man grabbed Ung's hand and said in tears, "Don't you recognize me? I am your mother's cousin, Governor Wang. Perhaps, you do not know me since I ran away when you were very young. When Yi Tubyŏng raised a rebellion, we all fled our separate ways but, just a few months ago, we started to gather here. Commoners who also fled the rebellion heard of our gathering and began to join us. They voluntarily enlisted in our army, which now has five thousand soldiers. This situation resembles the moment when Emperor Mu of the ancient times was to punish Emperor Kŏl.[21] What an exciting event! However, we lack a great commander to lead our army. We could do nothing but wait for heaven to grant us an opportunity to strike Yi Tubyŏng. In our frustration and anger, we made an effigy of Yi Tubyŏng and acted so as to ease our pain and suffering. I have many questions for you. Please tell me where you grew up, where your mother and the crown prince are now, how you dodged Yi Tubyŏng's plot, and how you managed to rescue the crown prince." Ung lay prostrate and said in tears, "Your nephew is so happy to see you alive. I can now die a happy man."

Ung told his tale to his uncle from the beginning: how he had fled with his mother in the chaos of war; how they had drifted from place to place, praying to heaven; how he had met his masters[22] by chance and learned many skills from them; how he had gone to Wi, conquered Sŏbŏn, and became the grand field marshal. He also told him that he had gone to Kyeryangdo when all the loyal officials were bound and the crown prince was about to drink the poison brought by the emperor's messenger, and that he had killed the emperor's envoy and saved the crown prince just in time. He went on to explain how he had saved the crown prince from grave danger again while they stayed in Sŏbŏn on their way back to Wi, how he had become a son-in-law of the king of Wi, and finally how he had received a message at Kangsŏnam to come to the Hak Mountain, killing another messenger of the emperor along the way. As Ung recounted the events of his journey, the people were astounded. They held him and cried, "We have never heard a story as incredible as yours!" They became ever more fond of Ung, and their happiness was beyond description. They said, "Illustrious heaven was moved and gave us a hero to restore the royal line of Song and to punish the traitor. How could we not be overjoyed?"

Meanwhile, a surviving soldier of the emperor's messenger killed by Ung in Nŭngju returned to the palace and told the emperor how his messenger had died. The news infuriated the emperor. Pounding on the desk, the emperor reprimanded his officials, "Cho Ung was within our reach, only a few hundred li away, but you could not capture him. Now he has killed a messenger of mine—I am enraged. If you do not capture him soon, I will execute all of you." The officials were frightened, but Left Prime Minister Ch'oe Sik said, "Your Majesty should not be so concerned over catching petty Cho Ung. Simply select valiant warriors and order them to capture Cho Ung." Following Ch'oe Sik's advice, the emperor assigned one thousand soldiers to General of the Gentlemen-of-the-Household Yi Hwang and ordered him to capture Cho Ung.[23]

Meanwhile on the Hak Mountain, the officials loyal to the former emperor unanimously elected Cho Ung as their commander in chief and the grand field marshal of their main army and launched a great campaign against Yi Tubyŏng.[24] Ung put on a consecrated helmet,[25] wore armor stitched with iron scales, and carried at his side a bow decorated with many jewels. He mounted his dragon-horse that could travel a thousand li a day and held a dagger in his left hand and a spear in his right. He pressed his vanguard troops to move forward and, to the rousing sound of drumbeats, the soldiers quickly broke down the encampment. Their spears blocked the sun and their morale reached the blue sky. Ung's words of command were like autumn frost. The loyal officials approved, "Ung marches his army like Han Sin[26] and P'aeng Wŏl."[27]

Soon, Ung reached the East Pass[28] and ordered his lieutenants to commence an assault on the emperor's forces. The enemy soldiers could not withstand the ferocity of Ung's vanguard troops and surrendered. When Ung arrived at Pyŏnyang, the terrified Governor T'aewŏn called up soldiers to block Ung's path. Outraged, Ung yelled, "Governor T'aewŏn, come out quickly and receive my swift sword. I am a loyal servant of Song, Cho Ung. I am on a march to destroy the traitor Yi Tubyŏng." To Ung's astonishment, the governor eagerly threw away his sword and dismounted his horse. On his knees, he pleaded to Ung, "I did not know who you were and mistakenly tried to fight off your great army. With your generous heart, please forgive me. I implore you, allow me to be part of your army—I will follow you to the end with all my strength." In a mounting fury, Ung yelled, "You are a wicked thug no different from Yi Tubyŏng. I am not going to allow any of his followers to live," and impaled the governor with his sword. After seizing the enemy's arms and provisions, Ung marched on to the capital city.

People in rural villages nearby heard of Ung's righteous army, and many came to join him. On its swift march toward the capital city, Ung's army encountered an unidentified troop of about one thousand men in battle order blocking the road. Suspicious, Ung sent out a scout and found that it was the emperor's envoy going to all provinces. Ung shouted, "Stretch out your neck and receive my sword. I am a loyal servant of Song, Cho Ung." The enemy soldiers retreated at once, but the emperor's messenger came forth with a sword in his hand, shouting, "Traitor Cho Ung, we should have met sooner. With heaven's blessings, I am going to capture you. I am already very happy for the honor and glory I will receive. Today, I will cut off your head and grant His Majesty's lifelong wish." Infuriated, Ung cursed him, "There is no use in letting a wicked thug like you live. I will finish you off first to ease my anger," and rushed at the enemy. Before the messenger could lift his sword, a single blow from Ung slashed off his head, dropping it to the ground beneath the horse. Ung skewered the head on the tip of his spear and returned to his encampment. Soldiers, heedless of rank, congratulated him, and officials, both young and old, praised him.

The remnants of the defeated enemy troops escaped back to the palace. They reported to the emperor that Cho Ung had struck Pyŏngyang, killing both the governor and the emperor's messenger, and that Ung's army was quickly approaching the capital city. Shocked, the emperor was at a loss. A spy of the general of the West Pass came in and reported,[29] "Commanding an army of eight hundred thousand men, Cho Ung has already conquered Kwang'ŭm and will strike Sŏju next.[30] I urgently request that Your Majesty muster soldiers and stop those bandits." The emperor was horrified at the news. He looked around at his retainers and cried, "What should we do?" Before the emperor finished talking, General of the Left Chang Tŏk stepped forth and said,[31] "I am not very talented, but in a single beat of the war drum, I will capture Cho Ung and bring him to your presence." The emperor was pleased, saying, "Go quickly and ease my indignation." Chang Tŏk kowtowed to the emperor to bid farewell. He quickly conscripted soldiers and marched.

By now, Ung's army reached the base of the Kyeyang Mountain in Sŏju. In the valley, a general wearing plate armor with a long spear in his hand waited with three hundred soldiers. He came to Ung and made a bow. He said, "I am Kang Paek, the son of the former dynasty's loyal servant, Kang Kul.[32] During Yi Tubyŏng's rebellion, I lost my father and mourned bitterly. Because I had a little bit of valor and knowledge in military tactics, I put together a troop of several hundred soldiers and waited for heaven's sign. Thanks to heaven, I heard of your marching to the capital city and awaited your arrival here. I am so glad finally to see you today. Please allow us to join your army—together, we can slay Yi Tubyŏng and recover the Great Song. In doing so, I will also avenge my father." Delightedly clasping his hand, Ung said, "Your father accompanied the crown prince to Kyeryangdo, and then moved to the State of Wi with him. He is alive and well in Wi. You should not worry." In a confusion of joy and sorrow, Kang Paek expressed his deep gratitude to Ung. In this way, many people voluntarily joined Ung's army, and their numbers rose to nearly one hundred thousand.

Soon, Ung's assault on Sŏju commenced. The prefect of Sŏju, Wi Kiltae,[33] commanding an iron-armored cavalry of three thousand men, took up a defensive position on the road, blocking Ung's way. Infuriated, Ung called Kang Paek, now new commander of the vanguard troops, and ordered, "Go and fight him. Today, I want to test your skills." Kang Paek immediately rode out with his long spear raised high and approached the enemy's encampment. He shouted, "I am the commander of the vanguard troops, Kang Paek. Enemy general, come out quickly, stretch out your neck, and receive my swift sword." Wi Kiltae angrily rode out of his encampment shouting, "Today, I will capture Cho Ung and ease the emperor's indignation," and rushed at the enemy. Kang Paek spun his spear and engaged Wi Kiltae. They fought like two tigers. After ten bouts, neither had yet emerged victorious. Compared to Wi Kiltae, Kang Paek's attack showed greater agility, but lacked power. Impatient and increasingly incensed, Ung rode out of his encampment, sword in hand. He shouted, "Wi Kiltae! You are a traitor. Are you not scared knowing you are going to die?," and rushed at him. Without a word, the infuriated Kiltae engaged Ung. Before a single bout, Ung's sword flashed in the air and slashed off the head of Kiltae. Ung picked up the head with his spear and hung it on the top of a flagpole at the gate of his encampment. Then, like a leaping tiger, he charged at the enemy army from the west to the east.

Kiltae's son, Wi Yŏng, was also a great warrior capable of single-handedly fighting off ten thousand men. Grief-stricken by the death of his father, Wi Yŏng shouted, "I will avenge my father!" He rode out in anger, sword in hand, to confront Ung. Wi Yŏng said, "Traitor Cho Ung, come out quickly and face me. Today, I will cut off your head and have my revenge." Wi Yŏng was about eight ch'ŏk tall, and his face was swarthy, with eyes that shone like bells.[34] Ung angrily said, "You are just a child. You are no match for me. It is unfortunate to kill both father and son at the same time, but, alas, that looks to be your fate." He called Kang Paek and ordered, "Fight him."

Kang Paek jumped on his horse and rushed at Wi Yŏng whirling his spear. Wi Yŏng rode to meet him. They exchanged twenty bouts, but were evenly matched. Suddenly, Wi Yŏng's sword flashed and struck down Paek's horse. Startled, Paek leaped clear and evaded Wi Yŏng's attack on foot. He quickly seized an opportunity to counterattack—incredibly, he leaped up and landed behind Wi Yŏng on his horse. Before Wi Yŏng could react, Paek slashed off his head and seized his horse. Impressed to see Paek riding Wi Yŏng's horse back to his encampment, Ung praised Paek, "You are a great warrior of valor." The deaths of the prefect and his son so shocked the enemy soldiers that they scattered, and Ung blew the horn of victory.

Ung continued his march toward the capital city and soon arrived at the Kwan Mountain.[35] Ung saw a large army from the capital taking up a battle position at the base of the mountain, apparently expecting Ung's arrival. Ung's army took up a position with a mountain to its rear and the enemy at its front. Ung instructed his chief military officer,

"Stay still and do not engage the enemy yet." Ung was studying the enemy formation when a general yelled, "Traitor Cho Ung, stretch out your neck and receive my sword." The enemy general moved in a circle in front of Ung's encampment yelling insults. Incensed, Ung came forth and taunted him, "You are an insignificant traitor. How can I let you live? I will send one of my lieutenants to deal with you. In return, send me your soul on the tip of his sword." He then sent Kang Paek to fight.

Obedient to Ung's order, Kang Paek rode out on horseback with a spear in his hand. He shouted at the enemy, "Listen, ignorant traitor, you do not know heaven's wish and you try to fight us. How absurd it is!" Like two dragons fighting for a Wish-fulfilling Pearl,[36] Paek and the enemy general dueled. After about ten bouts, Kang Paek's spear flashed in the air and the head of the enemy general tumbled down from his horse. Paek fixed the head on the tip of his spear and returned to the encampment dancing. Ung was delighted with his victory.

After watching Kang Paek's intrepidity, the enemy soldiers from the capital city grew anxious and worried, saying, "Cho Ung has acquired another great general." Nonetheless, on the following day, another enemy general came and shouted, "Traitor Cho Ung come out quickly and receive my sword. Yesterday, you boasted of killing one of our weakest generals and bragged of victory. Today, I swear that I will cut your head off to bring serenity to the land and ease our emperor's indignation." He continued to rampage in front of his enemy's encampment.

In response, Kang Paek came forth on horseback, saying, "How many generals do you have in your army? Have them all come out, and let's end this," and engaged the enemy general. With a sudden flash of his spear, Kang Paek knocked the helmet of the enemy general to the ground. Terrified, the enemy general fled. From the enemy encampment, another general rushed out, shouting, "Traitor Cho Ung, you are a fugitive from the law. You are still alive only because we have allowed you to live. However, you did not repent of your crimes and continue to act like this. For that, you do not deserve to live. Come quickly and stretch out your neck. By the way, where is your mother? If she is with you, give up the rest of her life as well," and hurled himself at Kang Paek. The enemy general was Grand Field Marshal Chang Tŏk. Furious, Kang Paek yelled, "Traitor Chang Tŏk, how dare you to raise your head and say such words? Do you not fear heaven? You do not deserve to live another hour!"

As Ung watched, they fought. At the outset, neither had the advantage; however, Kang Paek started to struggle and was soon fighting for his life. Seeing that Kang Paek was in grave danger, Ung rode forth and relieved him. In a mounting fury, Ung raised his long spear and attacked Chang Tŏk. Before long, Chang Tŏk realized that he could not defeat Ung—he spun his horse around and fled to his encampment. But Ung chased him right into the enemy encampment[, where he unleashed a confounding strategy]. When Ung appeared to attack the western flank, he actually assaulted the southern part. When Ung appeared to head to the north, he actually dashed south, wielding his devastating sword. Ung's bizarre maneuvers created chaos in the enemy encampment. Enemy soldiers of every rank could not believe their eyes and, in complete disorder, many of them stumbled and were crushed to death by the feet of their comrades. Horrified, Chang Tŏk spurred his horse to escape the chaos. Ung charged after Chang Tŏk, shouting like thunder, "Traitor and incompetent commander, do not run away from me!"

With all of his strength, Chang Tŏk attempted to escape from Ung. Suddenly, a white tiger jumped out of nearby woods blocking Chang Tŏk's way and trying to maul him. Shocked, Chang Tŏk faced the heaven and cried in frustration, "A white tiger is blocking the path before me, and Ung is chasing me from the rear. How can I survive between the two? In this moment of life or death, where can I go? What am I supposed to do?" Before he could finish, Chang Tŏk heard the sound of a horse approaching. He turned around and saw Ung on horseback, drawing nearer as if he was flying. In desperation, Chang Tŏk dismounted his horse and desperately begged Ung on his knees, "Before you do anything, please let me explain. I ended up fighting you briefly in the battle only because I was following the emperor's order; I hold no grudge against you. They say the wrath of a warrior does not outlive the battle. Please show mercy and forgive me. I will join your army and follow you to the end. Together, we will achieve a glorious victory and leave our names in history." But, his begging only angered Ung who scolded him, "I pity you but, considering the unspeakable sins that bandit Yi Tubyŏng has committed, I cannot let you live." In a flash of Ung's sword, Chang Tǒk's head fell to the ground. He skewered the head on the tip of his sword and returned to his encampment. Everybody praised his valor.

In the capital, Yi Tubyǒng had been impatiently waiting for news from Chang Tǒk ever since his departure. A scout finally reported in, "Cho Ung conquered seventy provinces of Sǒju. Our main force battled him at the Kwan Mountain. Field Marshal Chang Tǒk has fallen. The enemy force's invasion of the capital city is imminent. They are advancing like a flood."

The report horrified Yi Tubyǒng. He looked around at his retainers in shock and demanded, "How do we deal with this situation?" Before he could finish, Commander in Chief Chu Ch'ǒn stepped forth and said,[37] "Chang Tǒk was a slow-thinking man. There was no way he could defeat the enemy. Although I lack skills, if Your Majesty grants me the seal and sword of a field marshal, I will capture Cho Ung in battle and bring him to your presence."

Pleased, Yi Tubyǒng replied, "Proceed with caution when you confront the enemy. Achieve a great victory and return soon." Chu Ch'ǒn received the emperor's order and set out. Yi Tubyǒng looked at Left Prime Minister Ch'oe Sik and said, "Should you assist Chu Ch'ǒn in battle and return with Cho Ung in tethers, I will divide my kingdom and grant half to you." Ch'oe Sik replied, "How can I refuse Your Majesty's command? Victory and defeat in battle are usual in warfare, but even if I anticipated a sure defeat, I would not disobey your order. Should Your Majesty assign some troops to my command, I will accompany Chu Ch'ǒn to battle and capture Cho Ung, bringing peace to the land! Your Majesty should rest easy."

Very pleased, Yi Tubyǒng made Ch'oe Sik the grand field marshal and Chu Ch'ǒn the commander of the vanguard, and assigned one thousand officers and eight hundred thousand men to their command. The emperor also granted them a spear with a white tassel attached, an axe with a yellow tassel attached, a flag on a pole carved with a dragon and a phoenix, military uniforms, and royal swords representing their absolute power in the army.[38] The newly appointed Grand Field Marshal Ch'oe thanked the emperor and left. Ch'oe Sik immediately began drilling his well-disciplined army, strengthening their military prowess so that even a ghost could not predict his tactical maneuvers. Yi Tubyǒng personally came out to see off Ch'oe Sik and his army. With their spears raised high to reach the sun and the moon, the soldiers shouted war cries, beat drums, and blew bugles. The sound of the marching army caused the land and the sky to tremble, and its merciless passage was like an autumn frost.

For some time, Ung's army moved forward without encountering any resistance. When it arrived at the East Pass of the O Mountain, however, it was confronted by Ch'oe Sik's army of eight hundred thousand men, waiting in a battle position along the mountain ridges. After a brief examination, Ung called the commander of his vanguard troops, Kang Paek, and instructed, "Encamp in the grassy area," and continued to observe the enemy position. With a volley of cannon fire, a general emerged from the enemy encampment. Standing under the flag at the gate, he shouted like a thunderclap, "Traitor Cho Ung, quickly come out and receive my spear."

Angered, Ung ordered Kang Paek to fight him. Brandishing his own spear, Kang Paek rode out on his charger and approached the enemy encampment. He shouted, "Listen, generals and soldiers of Traitor Yi Tubyŏng. Don't you understand heaven's wish? How dare you confront us! I will cut you down first and ease my anger," and rushed at the enemy general. Martial flags, swords, and spears veiled the sun and the moon. A gust of sand arose and obscured visibility on the battlefield. The two combatants exchanged dozens of bouts, but neither emerged victorious. As it grew dark, Ung struck a gong to recall Kang Paek from the fight. Returning to his encampment, the infuriated Kang Paek restlessly awaited daybreak when he could continue.

At this moment, a shout came from the encampment of the emperor's army, which said, "What a pity! Cho Ung trusts such a reckless general and invaded our country. It is indeed laughable." Grand Field Marshal Ch'oe Sik devised a plot and commanded his army, "Apparently Cho Ung does not know the art of war; he encamps in a grassy area. Prepare some gunpowder. In the calm of night, we will attack the enemy encampment with fire. We will commence the attack at the third watch tonight and destroy the enemy. Let us capture Cho Ung and bring peace to the land." His soldiers received the plan enthusiastically.

At the first watch,[39] Ung called Kang Paek and instructed, "The enemy must have seen that we have camped in a grassy area—they will try to attack us with fire. We are not going to fall victim to their plot. We will relocate, but be sure to make no noise." Kang Paek quietly began to pull back the entire army. When they were clear, Ung sent out a dozen of his soldiers to the old camp site. He instructed them to rustle the grass and call out to each other as if on watch so as to deceive the enemy before returning very late to the new camp.

That night, a brigade of the emperor's army waited in ambush in a nearby mulberry grove. At the third watch, they fired one cannon shot to commence the attack and set fire to the grass on the left and right flanks of where they thought Ung's encampment lay. The blaze engulfed all of the vegetation in the area, including the mulberry grove, and reduced it to ashes. The enemy rejoiced, "There is not a single enemy soldier left! Not even their souls!" Suddenly, Ung alone charged out from hiding on horseback, shouted, "Cho Ung came back to life from death!" and killed a large number of enemy soldiers before returning to his new encampment.

After deploying the brigade, the remaining enemy troops on the ridges looked up to the sky at the third watch and saw the enormous fire that had started after the artillery fire. They rejoiced, "Now Cho Ung is dead," and awaited the return of the brigade. All too soon, a few surviving soldiers stumbled back, weeping, "We were terrified. Cho Ung rose from the dead, killed many of us, and disappeared. How could we not be scared?"

Astounded by their experience, Ch'oe Sik and Chu Ch'ŏn exclaimed, "Cho Ung must have been an uncanny general! He became a ghost and killed our soldiers. Unless we completely destroy his soul, we will face another disaster!" Then, they realized, "The emperor is waiting for a report; we should not delay news of our victory," and immediately sent out a letter. They also blew horns to celebrate their victory while they waited for the day to dawn. Soon, the rooster crowed and daybreak came. They distributed food to the soldiers and urged the vanguard to advance. Suddenly, there was a crack of cannon fire, then the sound of horns and shouts shook the sky and the land. Startled, the soldiers looked around for the source of the sound and saw a general moving quickly toward them from the east, shouting, "The emperor's army, stop! Receive my sword! Today, I will destroy all of you." The unknown general went berserk, his sword a blur. Shocked, the soldiers retreated and huddled behind the tightly closed gate of their encampment. Chu Ch'ŏn said to Ch'oe Sik, "We sent word to the emperor saying that we killed Cho Ung, but apparently Cho Ung is still alive. If we don't do something to correct that letter, we will be punished for deceiving the emperor. We must send him another dispatch." Ch'oe Sik quickly sent out another letter.

Cho Ung arrived before the enemy encampment, all the while shouting, "You ignorant traitor, come out quickly and surrender," and exhibiting his skill with the sword. The enemy soldiers were afraid and did not know what to do. Ch'oe Sik said to Chu Ch'ŏn, "We don't have any general in our army who comes close to Cho Ung's valor. It might be better to surrender to him and escape with our lives." Ch'oe Sik's words angered Chu Ch'ŏn. Chu Ch'ŏn drew his sword and pointed it at Ch'oe Sik, scolding him, "Grand Field Marshal Ch'oe, you are a high-ranking government official, but your idea is utterly disgraceful. How could you suggest such a thing when you are on the government payroll? You should feel ashamed to call yourself a general!" Ch'oe Sik responded, "I am not trying to save myself, I worry about our country. But if we are dead, what good is our country to us, regardless of its fall or rise? You should think it over." Grabbing a spear, Chu Ch'ŏn scolded Ch'oe Sik again, shouting, "You should not be the grand field marshal," and stormed out of the encampment.

He shouted to Ung, "Traitor Cho Ung, come quickly and receive my sword. Yesterday, luck saved your life, but your luck ends today," and rushed toward him. Enraged, Ung engaged him in a duel. They exchanged over twenty bouts, but neither emerged victorious. Chu Ch'ŏn soon realized that he was no match for Ung. Hoping to flee, he spun his horse around; however, in a swirl of his sword, Ung struck Chu Ch'ŏn, whose head fell to the ground by his horse as light gleamed from Ung's sword. Ung impaled the head on the tip of his spear and charged toward the enemy's encampment. He shouted, "How many generals do you have left? Come out all at once, stretch out your necks, and receive my sword!" His voice was like a thunderclap. Shocked and frightened, the enemy soldiers began to scatter.

Seeing his army's morale collapse and its will to fight gone, Ch'oe Sik wrote a letter of surrender and came out of the gate in tears. Kneeling before Ung, he begged, "I committed a serious error by fighting you.

But please have mercy and spare the rest of my life." Ung immediately saw through Ch'oe Sik's wickedness and scolded him aloud, "What good is your letter of surrender? You are the most villainous official of all, and Yi Tubyŏng is the most evil of traitors. How can I let you live?" Ung raised his sword, slashed off the head of Ch'oe Sik and threw it toward the enemy ranks. Horrified, the remaining enemy soldiers cried, "We are doomed!" and fled.

After dispatching his enormous army to battle, Yi Tubyŏng had waited anxiously for news. Finally, he received a letter from Ch'oe Sik. He quickly opened it and read:

> Minister and Grand Field Marshal Ch'oe Sik bows one hundred times and writes to Your Majesty. Your retainer confronted the enemy on a certain day at the East Pass of the O Mountain. In accordance with our plan, we were victorious in battle and killed Cho Ung. Your retainer hereby reports that peace has been restored to the land, and Your Majesty can rest easy.

Yi Tubyŏng rejoiced and, looking around at his retainers, said, "Grand Field Marshal Ch'oe Sik has killed Cho Ung in a single battle. He has eased all my worries. How could I not be overjoyed?"

Yi Tubyŏng immediately arranged for a banquet and enjoyed it with all his officials. Soon, however, another letter came. He opened it and read:

> Minister and Grand Field Marshal Ch'oe Sik bows one hundred times. I should be punished for deceiving Your Majesty. In the previous letter, I reported that Cho Ung was killed in battle. The next day, as our army was en route to return, one general stood in the way. Upon careful inspection, we discovered that it was Cho Ung, who had apparently relocated his encampment to escape our plot and now confronted us again. I am most ashamed.

The emperor was shocked and deeply disappointed at the letter. A short time later, a spy arrived and reported, "Cho Ung killed Grand Field Marshal Ch'oe Sik and his lieutenant commander Chu Ch'ŏn. His army of eight hundred thousand men approaches the capital city like a flood. We request that Your Majesty send out an able general to deal with this urgent situation."

Yi Tubyŏng was appalled at the report. He looked around at his retainers and felt only pity for himself. Suddenly, there was a clamor outside the palace gate. The worried emperor summoned the gatekeeper to ask what all the commotion was about. The gatekeeper said, "Three unknown warriors have arrived and caused a commotion." Wanting to examine the warriors in person, the emperor instructed the gatekeeper to bring them to him. He asked them, "Where are you from and what brings you here? Tell me!" The three warriors bowed to the emperor and said, "We live near the East Sea. We were shocked to learn of the death of our beloved uncle, the prefect of the Mount T'ae Prefecture, by Cho Ung's hand. We also heard that our country was in danger and felt uneasy. We are three brothers. Our names are Iltae, Idae, and Samdae.⁴⁰ We are not talented, but we are not afraid of Cho Ung. We humbly request that Your Majesty assign some troops to our command so that we can capture him. We will make him kneel before Your Majesty."

Pleased and relieved, Yi Tubyŏng immediately mustered five hundred thousand soldiers. He appointed Iltae as grand field marshal, naming Idae his lieutenant and Samdae the commander of the vanguard. He awarded each a spear with a white tassel, an axe with a yellow tassel, a flag on a pole carved with a dragon and a phoenix, military uniforms, and royal swords representing their absolute military power. He instructed them, "Do your best to bring peace to our country. When Cho Ung is captured and our country is finally at peace, I will divide the land and grant half to you." Yi Tubyŏng poured wine into a cup and handed it to the newly appointed grand field marshal, then personally saw the three brothers off. The three brothers felt very honored. They made a deep bow to thank him and departed. Pushing their valiant, well-disciplined soldiers ever forward, they marched for several days to reach Kokkang where they encamped on a sandy beach near the river and let their troops rest.

Suddenly, the gatekeeper dashed into their command post and said, "We caught a suspicious person, claiming to be a Daoist master, who attempted to enter the encampment. I await your orders regarding him." Suspecting that man might be an acquaintance of his, Iltae ran to the gate. Iltae held the Daoist master's hand and brought him to his command post. He apologized profusely to the master, "We have disgraced our teacher-student relationship. We mistreated you by leaving you without permission." The Daoist master said after a deep sigh, "You are making a terrible mistake now. Heaven has had a different plan for you since your birth. Aware of heaven's wish, I took you in as my students and guided you. Why didn't you listen? Why did you leave? Disband this army and follow me back to the mountain." Samdae replied, "Do not worry. Together, we three brothers have enough talent to capture Cho Ung, so why would you be afraid? Also, if we stayed idle in a time of disorder, we would waste our talents and miss a great opportunity to be successful as generals. Teacher, set aside your doubts and have faith in us. You should join us in the march and teach us some clever tactics." Determined to stop them from marching further, the Daoist master grabbed the three brothers and said, "I am on your side. Why won't you listen to me? This battle is not in your favor. Do not be foolish and let us go back together."

The Daoist master tried valiantly to sway them, but they ignored him and marched on. Following the army, the Daoist master argued with the brothers day and night. "Do not go against heaven's plan. Let us go back." But the three brothers would not listen to him. Several days later, they reached Sŏch'ang. Cho Ung had already arrived and encamped across from them in Tongch'ang. Iltae encamped in Sŏch'ang, Idae in Hwaŭm, and Samdae in Kangjin. The Daoist master examined Ung's battle formation from a distance and said in astonishment, "You three, look at Cho Ung's battle formation. A great Daoist master must have taught him. His position is also enshrouded in heavy fog, which indicates that he might possess a dragon-horse and a heavenly sword. I am very upset that you have not listened to me. Let us not fight a losing battle but go back. Your time will come later." Iltae did not listen to him, insisting, "Let's see what Cho Ung is capable of." He issued an order to his chief military officer, "Send out a general to fight." Supreme Commander Sŏl Int'ae responded to the call. He emerged from his encampment on horseback, shouting, "Traitor Cho Ung, come out quickly, stretch out your neck, and receive my spear," and rampaged in front of Ung's encampment. Ung responded, "You are like a rooster that cannot crow and a dog that cannot bark." Ung grabbed his spear and rode out, shouting, "You worthless traitor, you are already a dead man. Dismount from your horse and surrender!" They fought, but before they could exchange a dozen bouts, Ung's spear struck Sŏl Int'ae's horse. Frightened, the horse whirled around and fled. Ung did not chase him but returned to his encampment where his soldiers all praised him.

After watching Ung's fight, Iltae laughed aloud, "I have heard people speak highly of Cho Ung. Today, though, I watched him fight like a child. He is insignificant, no cause for worry." The Daoist master said, "You cannot determine someone's full ability with just one look. I watched him briefly and could tell he is no ordinary man; the spirit of a flying dragon circled in the air in front of him, and the auspicious light from the Purple Star shone at his back.[41] He wielded a heavenly sword and rode a dragon-horse. Do not fight this losing battle. Let us go back." Iltae was out of patience and did not respond to his teacher. Upset by Iltae's rude attitude, the Daoist master said, "You shall not see me ever again," and left.

The Daoist master went next to Idae's encampment, and Idae came out to greet him. The Daoist master said to Idae, "Your older brother is stubborn and won't listen to me, so there is nothing I can do for him anymore. However, why don't you end this fight and go back with me?" Angered by his words, Idae utterly ignored the Daoist master. The Daoist master was dismayed. He said, "You also shall not see me ever again." Arriving in Samdae's encampment, the Daoist master told him face to face, "Your brothers won't listen to me, so there is nothing I can do for them anymore. You three brothers do not understand heaven's intention. If you listen to me now, your time to shine will come later. Why don't you disband your troops and go back to the mountain with me?" Samdae became surly with him and said, "Teacher, why do you worry so much? If we do not strike Cho Ung now, he will become a bigger threat later. Don't be anxious, but stay with us to watch the outcome." Overcome by anger, the Daoist master told Samdae, "You three brothers shall not see me ever again. But perhaps this misfortune might also be heaven's plan." In sorrow, he bade a bitter farewell to Samdae and left.

With deep regret, the Daoist master crossed to Ung's encampment. He said to the gatekeeper, "I am a traveler who is just passing by. I would like to have an audience with Grand Field Marshal Cho." The gate-keeper went inside and informed Ung of the visitor. Ung thought it strange to have a visitor on a battlefield but invited him to come inside. Ung offered him a seat at his table and treated him politely, saying, "Seeing you in person tells me a great deal about who you are. I beg you to teach me." The Daoist master replied, "How extraordinary you are, Grand Field Marshal! How can you tell who a stranger really is at first sight? I have come to tell you the secret plans of heaven," and he pulled a sealed letter from his sleeve and handed it to Ung. He said, "Do as it is written in the letter," and made to leave, saying he did not belong to this world. Astonished, Ung tried to persuade him to stay, but the master insisted on leaving. Ung grasped his guest by the sleeve, but he shook it free, took two steps down the stone stairs, and disappeared—there was simply nothing Ung could do to stop him. Ung faced the sky and humbly expressed his appreciation to the Daoist master.

Ung opened the letter and read: "When you confront Iltae, do not enter his encampment; when you confront Idae, rub your sword with the blood of a white horse and recite the words that repel spirits; when you confront Samdae, do not go near the left side of his body." Although Ung was dubious about the veracity of the letter, he was nonetheless very pleased to have advance warning.

On the following day, Ung girded himself for battle and rode out. He sat his horse in front of the enemy encampment and shouted, "Traitor, come out quickly and receive my spear." Ung's voice was like a thunderclap, but the gate remained tightly closed and Iltae did not respond. Ung continued to provoke the enemy, but no one came out. Ung eventually got tired and returned to his encampment. Ung spoke to Kang Paek, "It is strange that the enemy general stays behind the closed gate and does not come out. He must have some scheme. Stay alert."

The next day, Ung again went to the enemy encampment. He was eager to fight, but to no avail—the enemy remained behind the closed gate and did not respond. Ung again returned to his encampment disappointed. Ung continued to taunt the enemy for several days, but Iltae kept the gate shut and would not come out. However, on the tenth day, Iltae raised the commander's flag and opened the gate wide. He shouted,

"Traitor Cho Ung, you are still a juvenile. You do not understand heaven's wish and are disrupting this reign of peace. Your sin is grave. Today, I will capture you and alleviate the chaos you have caused." As he rode out to face the enemy, Ung saw nine-ch'ŏk-tall Iltae standing in iron plate armor decorated with inlaid gold thread. His beard was over two ch'ŏk long and his eyes shone like stars. Ung called Kang Paek and ordered, "Go out and fight him." Ung added, "The enemy general will fake his defeat and flee. Do not chase him."

Acknowledging his orders, Kang Paek rode out on horseback to engage Iltae in a duel. They exchanged thirty bouts, but neither emerged victorious. Suddenly, Iltae feigned defeat and fled. Wielding his spear, Kang Paek yelled and chased him to the enemy encampment. As Iltae approached the gate, his troops on both flanks followed him inside the encampment. Kang Paek stopped his pursuit and, for a long time, rode around the enemy encampment taunting Iltae before returning to his own side. He told Ung, "I chased the enemy general to the front of the enemy encampment. As he entered the gate, the enemy troops on both flanks followed him inside. It was strange." Kang Paek's account made Ung suspicious of the enemy's actions.

The next day, Ung raised his spear high and shouted, "Traitor Iltae, do you have the courage to fight me? Come out quickly and receive my swift spear. I am destined by heaven to behead Yi Tubyŏng and restore the Song dynasty. What sort of a person are you, indifferent to your own life?" Iltae had heard enough of Ung's taunts and rushed out to engage him. They fought like a pair of tigers. A cloud of sand arose from their fight, and soldiers from both sides, armed with swords and spears, circled around them to watch the duel. Ung and Iltae exchanged dozens of bouts, but neither emerged victorious. Suddenly, Iltae feigned defeat and fled. Ung yelled, "Traitor, do not flee but receive my spear," and chased Iltae to the enemy encampment. Iltae appeared to enter his encampment, but spun back to reengage Ung.

Spears and swords obscured the sun, and the two horses whirled around one another in a violent dance. Soldiers from both armies dared not watch the fierce fight, but could only listen. After exchanging many bouts, Iltae again fled to his encampment, but Ung did not chase him. By the end of the day, Iltae had feigned defeat three times, but Ung never chased him into the enemy encampment. At his encampment, a suspicious Iltae said to his lieutenants, "It is strange that Ung did not chase me inside the encampment when I faked my defeat and fled several times." He warned them to be careful not to reveal their scheme to anyone.

Meanwhile, Ung conferred with his lieutenants in secrecy, "Iltae is not an ordinary general. It won't be easy to capture him. Tomorrow, Kang Paek shall go out to fight. Fight Iltae until the sunset and fake your defeat before he can do the same. When you run away from him, flee into his own encampment. The enemy soldiers will mistake you for Iltae and carry out their scheme. Tomorrow, we will find out what they are up to."

The next day, Iltae came to Ung's encampment and provoked him to come out. Ung kept the gate closed and did not respond. Just before sunset, Ung ordered Kang Paek to fight Iltae. Wielding his spear, Kang Paek charged out on horseback to confront Iltae face to face. He shouted, "Listen, you ignorant peasant. Today, I will cut off your head and ease the grudge between heaven and earth," and hurled himself at Iltae. They exchanged dozens of bouts, but neither emerged victorious. When the sun finally began to set, Kang Paek faked his defeat and ran into the enemy encampment. Enemy soldiers mistook him for Iltae and led Kang Paek's horse toward their command post. Surprised by Kang Paek's unexpected action, Iltae spurred his horse after Kang Paek into the encampment. Mistaking him for Kang Paek, Iltae's soldiers quickly encircled Iltae's horse and struck it with their swords. In terror, Iltae's horse fell into a hidden pit. The soldiers swarmed the pit, hacking with their swords. Iltae yelled at them with frustration, "Soldiers, don't you recognize your own general?" Startled, the soldiers lit torches and looked carefully into the pit. To their surprise, Iltae glared back. Horrified by what they had done, they scattered, leaving Iltae in the pit.

Ung and Kang Paek were very pleased with the outcome of the battle. They went to the pit and saw Iltae dying inside, riddled with spears. Showing no sympathy, Ung ridiculed Iltae, "Listen, traitorous Iltae. You went against heaven's wish and devised an evil plan. Now, you will die by your own scheme. If you still have some courage left in you, try climbing out of the pit alive." At Ung's insult, Iltae's anger exploded, and he died instantly. As it was very late and dark, Ung and Kang Paek decided to return to their encampment for the night. The next morning, they came back to the enemy encampment. By daylight, they saw that, around the gate, hundreds of pits had been dug and studded with innumerable spears and swords. Their hearts shook at the sight. Before leaving, they stripped the enemy encampment of provisions and flags.

As Ung prepared to march on to Idae's encampment, he slaughtered a white horse and rubbed its blood on his sword. Idae, meanwhile, was reeling from the news that Iltae had been killed in battle. He wept over his brother's death and vowed his revenge. When Ung arrived, Idae ground his teeth in anger and emerged from his encampment wielding a sword. He shouted, "Traitor, you are but a child. I will avenge my brother's death," and rushed at Ung. Ung wielded his sword rubbed with the blood of the white horse. When Idae swung his blade at Ung, it flew toward him but was repelled by Ung's sword. Furious, Idae raised his blade high in the air and wielded it with tremendous force such that even a vigorous tiger could not have evaded it. Idae's flying blade made several strikes at Ung, but each was repelled by Ung's sword. Idae returned to his encampment in vain and said to his lieutenants, "I am suspicious of Cho Ung's sword. I struck several times at Cho Ung, but each time my blade failed. That is strange." He was deeply concerned.

The following day, Idae opened the gate of his encampment and was ready to fight Ung again. He raised his blade in the air and rushed at Ung. Facing his enemy, Ung focused his mind and raised his sword high. Riding toward Idae, Ung scolded loudly, "Traitorous Idae, your older brother Iltae was killed by my sword. Do you think you can do better and defeat me? Don't waste time trying to save the remnant of your life. Dismount your horse and surrender to me!" They dueled. Idae was a fearless warrior whose valor was ten times that of Ung and his flying blade was fearsome. They exchanged more than eighty bouts, but neither emerged victorious. Ung was exhausted, and the fight was not going in his favor. He turned his horse and attempted to return to his encampment, but Idae's flying blade blocked his way. Idae yelled, "Cho Ung, you ignorant peasant, where are you trying to go? Today, I will cut off your head and avenge the soul of my dead brother." He raised his blade and struck down at Ung. With all of his remaining strength, Ung blocked Idae's blade with his blood-stained sword, while reciting an incantation to repel spirits. Stunned, Idae dropped his blade to the ground. Seizing the opportunity, Ung overcame his weariness, raised his sword, and slashed at Idae's neck. As Idae's head fell to the ground, the sky darkened with pouring rain and a roaring wind. In the pitch-darkness, Ung continued to recite the words that expel spirits. Suddenly, the rain stopped and the wind calmed. Before Ung's eyes, a ghostly eight-ch'ŏk-tall general rose up from the dead body of Idae and disappeared into the clear sky, weeping. Ung was speechless at the sight and thought, "Idae must have been possessed by a ghostly general!"

Upon witnessing their commander's death, Idae's soldiers scattered as if they shared a single mind. Ung skewered Idae's head on the tip of his spear and returned to his encampment. His soldiers heaped praises upon his triumph. Blowing the horn of victory, they marched to Samdae's encampment. Ung threw Idae's head into the enemy encampment and taunted them, "Listen, Traitor Samdae. I beheaded your eldest brother Iltae at Sŏch'ang and your second brother Idae at Hwaŭm. Like your two brothers, you are destined to die in vain. Come out quickly, stretch out your neck, and receive my sword," and he stalked back and forth along the front of the enemy encampment.

The enemy soldiers were afraid of Ung. However, the outraged Samdae, holding a long spear in his left hand, rode out of his encampment on horseback to confront Ung. He shouted, "Today, I will capture you and avenge the deaths of my two brothers," and rushed at Ung. Ung thrust his spear at Samdae's right side. Handling his spear only with his left hand, Samdae attacked Ung from his left. Ung dodged his one-sided attack while counterattacking Samdae's right side. By day's end, they had exchanged about eighty bouts but neither was victorious. As night fell, they broke off the fight and parted until the next day.

In his encampment, Samdae said suspiciously to himself, "Cho Ung might have discovered something. I wonder how." He feared that his secret was exposed. In the other encampment, Ung said to Kang Paek, "Samdae fought with incredible valor. He is not an ordinary warrior. It won't be easy to defeat him. General Kang, initiate a fight with Samdae tomorrow. I will come to your aid later." He added, "Do not attack Samdae's left side and don't underestimate him."

The next day, Samdae rode out of his encampment. With his spear pointing toward his enemy, he shouted, "I swear I will slash off your head and ease my anger today," and paced back and forth along the front of the enemy encampment. Kang Paek also rode out with his spear toward his enemy. He taunted, "Listen, lowly Samdae. The souls of your two brothers are confined in our encampment and weep day and night. They cry, 'We will bring the head of our youngest brother to you, so let our souls go free,' and make an eerie noise. They are certainly dead, and it is too late for you to save them," and he rushed at Samdae. Because Kang Paek attacked only on Samdae's right side, Samdae could not make the most of his extraordinary talent with his left-handed spear and could not fight Kang Paek at his full strength. Samdae grew leery of Kang Paek's tactics and increasingly frustrated. After they had exchanged about thirty bouts, neither emerged as a victor, however, General Kang was beginning to flag.

In front of his encampment, Ung had been watching. Seeing that the fight had turned against Kang Paek, Ung grabbed his sword and joined the fight, attacking Samdae's right side. Samdae, though very skilled with a spear, was now laboriously fighting two enemies at once. After the three men exchanged about twenty bouts, General Kang's spear abruptly impaled Samdae's horse, causing it to collapse, and throwing Samdae to the ground. Seizing the opportunity, Ung rushed at Samdae with his sword raised high to finish him off. However, Samdae miraculously sprang up, evaded Ung's attack, and instantly counterattacked. Ung and Kang Paek continued to hurl coordinated attacks at Samdae. Eventually, Samdae was overwhelmed and fled on foot. Ung urged his horse to chase Samdae. Before he could escape, Ung raised his sword and struck off Samdae's left hand. In shock, Samdae dropped his spear, and soared into the sky. Ung jumped up to reach Samdae and slashed off his head. With a strong gust of wind, the head fell to the ground. Suddenly, blue fog rose from the ground and a pair of rainbows appeared above the enemy encampment. Awed by the strange phenomena, Ung looked around and noticed a wing under Samdae's left arm.[42] Having witnessed their commander's death,

Samdae's soldiers scattered in dismay. Ung and Paek returned to their encampment and blew the horn of victory. Their soldiers praised them and were euphoric in the triumph. Having defeated Samdae and his two brothers, Ung was in high spirits. He treated his soldiers to wine and food and immediately marched on to the capital city. The dead bodies of the enemy piled up wherever they passed.

Meanwhile, in the emperor's palace, a spy for the general of the East Pass delivered an urgent message: "Cho Ung has killed Iltae, Idae, and Samdae. Ung is unstoppable and fast approaching the capital city. We humbly ask Your Majesty to deal with this urgent crisis." The emperor and his retainers were panicking. Looking to his retainers, the emperor demanded, "Find a solution and ease my troubled mind." All together, his retainers replied, "Iltae and his brothers were heaven-sent generals. Their valor was beyond extraordinary, but they were killed at Cho Ung's hand. We now barely have enough soldiers to defend ourselves. Furthermore, we are afraid we don't have a capable general to lead an army. We think it would be wise to surrender."

Just then, a message from the general of the West Pass arrived. The emperor and his retainers opened and read it:

Commander-in-Chief of China, Grand Field Marshal and Head of the Resistance Army Cho Ung sends a message to Yi Tubyŏng on behalf of the resistance army of eight hundred thousand men. Obliged by heaven's decree, I will put you to death, bring peace to the land, and restore the court of Song. If you are going to confront us, come out quickly and fight. If you are afraid, surrender and preserve your pitiful life.

The message stunned the emperor and his retainers. Staring at each other, they asked, "What are we supposed to do?" They could not decide.

Suddenly, Crown Prince Yi Kwan and his four brothers stepped forth and said, "Your Majesty should not worry. After selecting a capable man to be the commander of the vanguard troops, Your Majesty should personally lead the army. Your disloyal retainers would make things worse. They only think about themselves and do not sincerely care about the country. We loathe them! Once we overcome this crisis, Your Majesty should punish them for treason and to ease your anger." The retainers were struck speechless and kept their heads down. Faced with no alternative, the emperor made up his mind and prepared to personally lead the army, however no one seemed willing to follow him into battle.

That night, Minister Hwang Tŏk called up the officials of the court for a secret discussion. He asked them, "We will witness the fate of our country any moment now, and I have no doubt that our lives are already in grave danger. What do you all plan to do?" They replied, "We all think it would be best if we run away. Minister, do you have another idea?" Hwang Tŏk drew his sword in a decisive gesture and asked again, "Are you all willing to follow me?" They all replied, "We are faced with our worst enemy and are doomed. Knowing this to be a matter of life or death, we are willing to do anything." Hwang Tŏk paused a moment and then said, "If we run away, what about our many family members? Even if we succeed in fleeing, how are we going to live? I have an idea that will save our families and preserve our government positions. Do you want to hear it?" Delighted, they said, "Our minister's words sound right. How can we not follow you now?" Hwang Tŏk said quietly, "Among us, let us select sixty strong and courageous men with military backgrounds. In stealth, we will enter the palace, tie up the emperor and his five sons, and bring them to Cho Ung. He will deem our effort the most worthy achievement in his entire campaign against the emperor and will praise us. What do you think?" Everyone agreed, "That is an excellent idea."

Later that night, a band of sixty courageous men entered the palace and hid in ambush. They waited until it was very late and then took their chance and jumped upon the emperor and his five sons. They said, "It is useless for you to continue on; your luck has already run out," and tied up the emperor and his five sons. At dawn, the officials of the court put Yi Tubyŏng, Yi Kwan, and the other four sons in a caged wagon and went to Grand Field Marshal Cho's encampment.[43]

By now, the people of the capital city heard of Grand Field Marshal Cho's approach. They were delighted at the news, and a great number of them, too many to count, traveled far to see Ung's coming. They also heard that Yi Tubyŏng was in custody. People both young and old happily said, "Evil Yi Tubyŏng took advantage of his position and proclaimed himself emperor. He coveted everything, from the land to the sky, but was unable to prevail, and his reign has quickly come to an end.

Heaven knew about his sins all along, and even ignorant commoners, in their hearts, knew and wanted to cut the flesh off his body. Grand Field Marshal Cho, who is great and illustrious like the sun and the moon, freed us from the emperor's reign of terror. He is indeed a welcome rain to us! We wonder if the scattered officials who were loyal to the former dynasty have heard the news as well. Everyone, both young and old, in the capital, let's go watch Yi Tubyŏng's last breath!"

Ung led his army of eight hundred thousand men toward the capital city. Welcoming men and women, both young and old, crowded the main road, blocking Ung's path. They joyfully greeted Ung, "Glorious and majestic are Ung's deeds. Where have you been all these years? Why are you only coming here now? By heaven's grace, the Great Song will rise again!" and cheered. Ung said to them, "I am also very glad to see you again."

Ung pressed his army to march on and arrived at the Hwangja River several days later.[44] The scenery of the river was just as he remembered, and it brought back sad and painful memories of his past. Ung urged the skipper of a nearby boat to carry him across. Once he arrived at the opposite bank, Ung saw the officials of the court awaiting him at the gate of the capital city. With Yi Tubyŏng, Yi Kwan, and Tubyŏng's other four sons in the caged wagon, they welcomed Ung's arrival. They stepped forward, kowtowed to Ung, and said, "We deceived our former emperor and for that we deserve to die. However, at that time, we were not able to run away like the others and to go against Yi Tubyŏng's authority. We had no choice but to reluctantly participate in his schemes. However, we held the rightful crown prince of Song in our hearts and grieved every moment without him. By heaven's grace, we heard of your coming. We put our shameful bygone days aside and bring before you Yi Tubyŏng and his sons in shackles. We hope you will have mercy and forgive us, so that we can live out the rest of our lives," and they continued to beg desperately.

Ung was furious to see Yi Tubyŏng. He immediately halted his marching army and shouted out, "Bring Yi Tubyŏng to me at once!" Ung's soldiers ran forward, took Yi Tubyŏng into their custody, and forced him to kneel at the center of the army. Ung yelled at him, "Yi Tubyŏng, raise your head and look at me. You deserve to die for your grave crimes. You first expelled the crown prince and then sent a messenger to put him to death by poison. Is this not your crime? You also sent troops to capture me, which brought chaos to the land. Is this not your crime as well? Confess!"

The guards repeatedly jabbed at Yi Tubyŏng with swords and spears and yelled, "Confess quickly!" Yi Tubyŏng barely retained his self-command under his wounds and cried, "My retainers were vicious and disloyal servants. They accused and captured me and my sons like this. What can I say now? Just do as you wish." His words infuriated Ung, who ordered the guards to have Yi Tubyŏng bludgeoned to death. With a shout, the guards ran to Yi Tubyŏng and started to beat him. Yi Tubyŏng could not bear the beating and screamed, "Please stop! Since things seem to have already been disclosed, I am going to tell you everything. Those narrow-minded officials were responsible for stealing the royal seal of Song, banishing the crown prince, and trying to kill him with poison. In trying to hide their crimes and avoid punishment, they came up with a scheme to frame me. They are the ones who committed the crimes against Song. I never intended to harm the court of Song. However, in a twist of fate, I am facing your accusations and they are not."

In mounting fury, Ung yelled at Yi Tubyŏng, "You are wicked and cunning. I shall let you live for now only because I want the crown prince to see your final moment," and he set to torturing Yi Kwan and his brothers. Finally, Ung ordered the guards to put Yi Tubyŏng and his five sons back in the caged wagon and proceeded into the capital city dancing.

As Ung's army moved into the city, their prowess was like the frost of autumn. Having secured the city, they comforted the people there. Soon Ung chose a date for his departure to the State of Wi. When he left, Ung asked the loyal officials to stay behind and guard the capital. When Ung arrived in the State of Wi, he was lauded by the crown prince of Song and the king of Wi. He took a short leave from them to greet his mother, who was happy to see her son. Ung then turned to his wife, Maiden Chang, and greeted her with a happy countenance, "I hope you have been well with our mothers." Kŭmnyŏn also made a bow to Ung, asking him, "Did you stay safe and well during your ten-thousand-li campaign?" Ung happily replied, "I have returned safe and sound from the campaign. How is your mother?" and expressed his love.

Later that day, Ung bowed and made a suggestion to the crown prince of Song, "For a long time, the capital city has been without a true ruler. Please allow us to prepare for your prompt return." The crown prince agreed with a smile, "I was just about to do that. Prepare a palanquin for my crown princess!" The crown prince of Song bade his last farewell to the king of Wi. The king of Wi was sad to part from him, saying, "I, the king of a small country, would like to personally escort you, the king of the Great Country, to your palace. However, because Wi borders Kadal,[45] I am afraid I cannot be absent even for an hour. Please forgive me." The crown prince of Song was also heartbroken to leave the king of Wi.

On the same day that Ung arrived in Wi, he escorted the crown prince, the crown princess, his mother, his mother-in-law, his wife Maiden Chang, Kŭmnyŏn, and Kŭmnyŏn's mother to the Great Song. The king of Wi traveled one hundred li to see Ung's company off. He was despondent to bid them a final farewell. They were equally grieved to part from the king of Wi. As they headed toward the capital city, their melancholy was beyond description.

As Ung's company approached the capital city, loyal officials both young and old and common people of the capital city from all walks of life traveled one hundred li from the outskirts of the city to welcome the company and sang the "Earth-Drumming Song."[46]

That day, the crown prince returned to his country and finally ascended the throne, becoming the legitimate emperor. Yi Tubyŏng, along with Yi Kwan and his other sons, were brought into the court and the new emperor interrogated them about their crimes. Immediately after their confessions, they were taken outside the palace walls and executed. At the emperor's order, their bodies were grotesquely mutilated and displayed along the main road. Their crimes and consequent punishments were officially made known all over the empire. The members of Yi Tubyŏng's household were arrested and their property confiscated. They were then scattered through the empire to work as slave laborers.

Later that day, the emperor sat high on his throne and hosted a banquet to reward those who had served him in the conflict. Grand Field

Marshal Cho was made king of a state in the borderlands and his wife Maiden Chang the queen of chastity.[47] Ung's maternal uncle, Governor Wang, was made right prime minister. Kang Paek's father was made left prime minister. Kang Paek was given the titles of commander in chief, grand field marshal, and grand academician.[48] The rest of the soldiers were rewarded in accordance with their merit, and no one complained of the suitability of their reward.[49]

Finally, the emperor ordered the guards to bring in Yi Tubyŏng's retainers and forced them to kneel down in the court. The emperor condemned them, "You are wicked and vicious. You conspired against your own emperor and brought him down. You are worse traitors than Yi Tubyŏng. I shall not let you live," and he sentenced them to death by dismemberment.

Later, the emperor clasped Cho Ung's hands before sending him to his new realm. Shedding tears, the emperor said to Ung, "I can see your loyalty and devotion, but, instead of making you king of another realm, I intended to bequeath my throne to you, as the land under the sky does not belong to me alone. However, because you understand the importance of being loyal, I know you will not accept my offer and I fear that our close relationship will fall apart if I insist."

King Cho Ung walked down the stairs, made a deep bow to the emperor and said, "Exiled ten thousand li away, Your Majesty has suffered greatly. People all over the empire grieved over your exile. Today, Your Majesty returned to the royal court because of your grace and virtue. Still, Your Majesty took pity and rewarded me generously so that my indebtedness to Your Majesty cannot be paid back even in my death. As your servant, I only did what I had to do. Because of this, Your Majesty's words make me uncomfortable; I fear that future generations will see me as a traitor."

The emperor realized that his comment had upset Ung. He put his hands on Ung, asked him to sit, and said, "I will miss you dearly from ten thousand li away. You must visit me at least once a year." Ung made a bow, bade farewell to the emperor, and left for his new country with his family.

Year after year, once the crown prince of Song had ascended the throne, there were bountiful harvests in the land. With abundant food for everyone, people showed no interest in taking items that were dropped on the ground. They were not driven to become bandits in the mountains. People enjoyed singing the "Earth-Drumming Song" and led the illustrious life of those during the reigns of the great emperors of ancient times such as Emperors Yo and Sun.[50] Peace prevailed throughout the land, even on the frontiers; no one conspired to rebel. All the people praised the emperor of Song's virtue, singing:

> Long live the emperor!
> Let us study and learn so that we can be loyal to our country.
> Long live the emperor, who is like Emperors Yo and Sun!

Ung left for his new country after his name was recorded for illustrious loyalty on the first floor of the Unicorn Pavilion. His virtue as a king benefited his realm such that all the people there sang a song of peaceful times and shouted, "Long live our King!"

The great virtue of the emperor and the loyalty of Grand Field Marshal Cho are indeed unprecedented. As the writer of this story, I find it difficult to record their great deeds in a single brushstroke, so I urge you, readers, to use your sound judgment in understanding their great virtue and ardent loyalty.[51]

NOTES

INTRODUCTION

1. This anecdote is found in "The Tale of Ŭnae" (Ŭnae chŏn 銀愛傳)" in Yi Tŏngmu's 李德懋 (1741–93) *Ajŏng yugo* 雅亭遺稿 (Ajŏng's Posthumous Work), included in vol. 20 of the *Collection of Ch'ŏngjanggwan* (Ch'ŏngjanggwan chŏnsŏ 青莊館全書). For the original text and its Korean translation, see *DB of Korean Classics*. A slightly different version of this incident is seen in the 1790 record in vol. 31 of the *Veritable Records of King Chŏngjo* (Chŏngjo Sillok), http://sillok.history.go.kr/id /kva_11408010_003. Neither record gives a specific time of this incident, but it appears that it took place during the eighteenth century, since both records are from the late eighteenth century and tobacco was first imported into Korea in the late sixteenth or early seventeenth century.

2. Yi Minhŭi, *Chosŏn ŭi pesŭt'ŭsellŏ: Chosŏn hugi sech'aegŏp ŭi paltal kwa sosŏl ŭi yuhaeng* (Seoul: P'ŭronesisŭ, 2007), 54; see also Michael Kim, "Literary Production, Circulating Libraries, and Private Publishing: The Popular Reception of Vernacular Fiction Texts in the Late Chosŏn

Dynasty," *Journal of Korean Studies* 9, no.1 (2004): 11–13. Oral storytelling was the most common way of appreciating vernacular stories in the late Chosŏn. Professional storytellers such as *chŏn'gisu* 傳奇叟 were still found in the early twentieth century, and their main audience at that time was commoners, particularly working-class people. The *Tale of Cho Ung* was a favored part of their repertoire.

3. For these functions of storytelling, see David Herman, *Storytelling and the Sciences of Mind* (Cambridge: MIT Press, 2013), esp. 227–308.

4. This number 450 is borrowed from Kan Hoyun. According to Kan Hoyun, the tale's number of surviving copies is more than that of the *Tale of Ch'unhyang* (Ch'unhyang chŏn 春香傳) and of the *Nine-Cloud Dream* (Kuun mong 九雲夢), with the surviving copies numbering 241 in manuscript form, 178 in woodblock, and 31 in movable type; see Kan Hoyun, *Arŭmdaun uri kososŏl: Chŭlgŏun sangsang kwa haehak ŭro kadŭkhan Han'guk kososŏl ch'ŏnnyŏn ŭi segye* (P'aju: Kimyŏngsa, 2010), 461. The tale also has the largest number of woodblock prints from the Wansan printing house. Based on different reports by Cho Hŭiung, Ryu T'agil, Sŏ Taesŏk, and Yu Ch'undong, at least 29 different commercial editions (22 woodblock and 7 movable type) were printed multiple times; see, for example, Yu Ch'undong, "Wanp'an Cho Ung chŏn ŭi p'anbon," *Yŏlsang kojŏn yŏn'gu* 38 (2013): 37–62; and Cho Hŭiung's introduction to *Cho Ung chŏn* (Seoul: Chimanji, 2009), 11, and his "Cho Ung chŏn ibon'go mit kyojubo," *Ŏmunhak nonch'ong* (1993): 41–58. The number of surviving copies is subject to change, particularly when those in private or overseas collections are included. However, the tale's popularity has been surpassed by the *Tale of Ch'unhyang* from the late nineteenth and early twentieth century onward.

5. For example, the manuscript edition from Posŏng transcribed in the *imja* year (1912?) uses a number of Chinese characters for names and poems.

6. Editions from Ansŏng, in the Kyŏnggi area, are also reported, but there is only one known surviving copy, which differs little from one of the Seoul editions. The editions from Wansan, Seoul, and Ansŏng are called *wanp'an*, *kyŏngp'an*, and *ansŏngp'an*, respectively. *Talsŏngp'an*, editions from another famous print house in Taegu, were also well known, but no surviving edition from this print house has been reported.

7. Cho Hŭiung, "Cho Ung chŏn ibon'go mit kyojubo," 57.

8. For general information on the Wansan editions, see Ryu T'agil, *Wanp'an panggak sosŏl ŭi munhŏnhakchŏk yŏn'gu* (Taegu: Hangmunsa, 1981).

9. The Wansan area was the Mecca of traditional print culture. The local production of good wood and paper and the popularity there of *p'ansori* and vernacular literature boosted the publication of many best-selling stories, among which the *Tale of Cho Ung* was the most popular; for more information on this background, see Ryu T'agil, *Wanp'an panggak sosŏl ŭi munhŏnhakchŏk yŏn'gu*, 15–37. The area also frequently appears as a backdrop in famous fictional narratives such as the *Tale of Ch'unhyang*, the *Tale of Sŏl Kongch'an* (Sŏl Kongch'an chŏn 薛公瓚傳), the *Record of a Chŏp'o Game at Manbok Temple* (Manboksa chŏp'o ki 萬福寺樗蒲記), and the *Tale of Ch'oe Ch'ŏk* (Ch'oe Ch'ŏk chŏn 崔陟傳). Recently, more and more official and scholarly attention has been paid to the value of the Wansan editions and their meaning within the history of Korean literature, resulting, among other things, in the launch of a museum (Wanp'anbon Munhwagwan) in the area in 2011.

10. Cho Hŭiung, "Cho Ung chŏn ibon'go mit kyojubo," 47. The number of characters in the longest *wanp'an* and *kyŏngp'an* editions provided here are borrowed from Yi Yunsŏk's research on commercial editions; see his "Panggakpon Cho Ung chŏn ŭi wŏnch'ŏn," *Tongbanghakchi* 166 (2014): 130.

11. For a detailed discussion of the relationship between Seoul and Wansan editions, see Chŏn Sŏngun, "Cho Ung chŏn inmul hyŏngsang ŭi punjang," *Uriŏmun yŏn'gu* 44 (2012): 265–69; Yi Yunsŏk, "Panggakpon Cho Ung chŏn ŭi wŏnch'ŏn," 140–44.

12. See Yi Yunsŏk, "Panggakpon Cho Ung chŏn ŭi wŏnch'ŏn," 125–48. According to Yi Yunsŏk, a more than nine-volume lending library edition of the tale is reported to have existed, although only one volume (the sixth) is extant. Recent scholars seem to agree that the lending library editions preceded both the Wansan and the Seoul editions and that the Seoul editions were separate, abbreviated versions of the lending library versions and evolved in a different way. However, the edition on which the lending library editions were based remains unknown.

13. Cho Hŭiung. "Cho Ung chŏn," in *Kojŏn sosŏl yŏn'gu*, ed. Hwagyŏng Kojŏn Munhak Yŏn'guhoe (Seoul: Ilchisa, 1993), 712. In his book on

premodern Korean fiction, W. E. Skillend also says that "the story [the *Tale of Cho Ung*] does not seem to have received the attention it deserves." See his *Kodae sosŏl: A Survey of Korean Traditional Style Popular Novels* (London: School of Oriental and African Studies, 1968), 204.

14. Until the 1990s, only two studies appeared on the *Tale of Cho Ung*, whereas the other three tales were actively researched: there were 223 publications on the *Tale of Ch'unhyang*, 93 on the *Tale of Hong Kíltong*, and 95 on the *Tale of Sim Ch'ŏng*. For these statistics, see Han'guk Kososŏl Yŏn'guhoe, *Han'guk kososŏllon* (Seoul: Asea munhwasa, 1991), 399–406.

15. This tendency is related to Confucian thought that prioritized "transmitting and not creating" (述而不作) and seeing literature's value as one of "conveying the teaching or truth" (文以載道). The literati's composition of fictional stories was limited for this reason, and those they did write were often in classical Chinese, emphasizing the factuality of a story or its utility in the education of readers. This situation was exacerbated in the case of compositions in vernacular Korean, a native Korean language initially known as women's script (*amgŭl*) and seen as secondary to literary Chinese. The belated development of vernacular fiction and drama as entertainment in Korea is often attributed to this devaluation both of fiction writing and of the native Korean language among the elite Confucian literati. For general information on the view of vernacular fiction and the hierarchy of genre, see the introduction to *A History of Korean Literature*, ed. Peter H. Lee (Cambridge; New York: Cambridge University Press, 2003), 5–9.

16. Ōtani Morishige, *Chosŏn hugi sosŏl tokcha yŏn'gu* (Seoul: Koryŏ taehakkyo minjok munhwa yŏn'guso, 1985), 43; Chŏng Pyŏngsŏl, "Chosŏn hugi ŭi Han'gŭl sosŏl param," *Han'guksa simin kangjwa* 8 (2005): 142–45. According to Yi Ch'anghŏn's research, most surviving commercial editions (*kyŏngp'an*), including those of the *Tale of Cho Ung*, date back to the mid-nineteenth century; see Yi Ch'anghŏn, *Kyŏngp'an panggak sosŏl p'anbon yŏn'gu* (Seoul: T'aehaksa, 2000), 552–67.

17. Cho Hŭiung, "Introduction to *Cho Ung chŏn*," 24. Cho Hŭiung's view that the tale emerged during the late eighteenth and early nineteenth century is widely accepted. Im Ch'igyun also states that it was not until the mid-eighteenth century that we see the emergence of the military novels; see his "Han'guk kojŏn sosŏl ŭi hawi changnŭ wa yuhyŏng," in Yi Sangt'aek et al., *Han'guk kojŏn sosŏl ŭi segye* (Seoul: Tolbegae, 2005), 76.

18. The earliest account on military tales is found in the *Record of Observances from the Interpreting Officials* (Shoshokibun 象胥紀聞, 1794) by Oda Ikugoro (小田幾五郎, 1755–1831). The first record in Korea is found in the *Literary Collection of Ch'ujae* (Ch'ujaejip 秋齋集) by Cho Susam (趙秀三, 1762–1849). For more information, see Sŏ Taesŏk, *Kundam sosŏl ŭi kujo wa paegyŏng* (Seoul: Ihwa yŏja taehakkyo ch'ulp'anbu, 1985), 22–23.

19. During the seventeenth century, the desire for personal expression through stories was growing rapidly among Koreans as they endured violence, tragedy, and displacement during both the Japanese invasion, which began in the *imjin* year of 1592 and continued until 1598, and the Manchu invasions in 1627 and 1636. Scholars consider these war periods to be a watershed for Chosŏn history, demarcating either the early and late Chosŏn or the mid and late Chosŏn. Many accounts of war were written and read for the memory, healing, education, and entertainment of those who survived, and this literary environment brought more attention to the practice of reading and writing. See, for example, So Chaeyŏng, "Imjin waeran kwa sosŏl munhak," in *Imjin waeran kwa Han'guk munhak*, ed. Kim T'aejun et al. (Seoul: Minŭmsa, 1992), 231–32.

20. The *Romance of Three Kingdoms* and the *Romance of Chu and Han* were already circulating among Korean literati in the second year of King Sŏnjo's reign (June 1569), according to the recorded official history of the Chosŏn dynasty (Chosŏn wangjo sillok). The *Romance of Chu and Han* was believed to be a translated Korean version of the *Romance of Western Han* (Xi Han yanyi 西漢演義); see Han'guk Kososŏl Hakhoe, *Kojŏn sosŏl ŭi sot'ong kwa kyosŏp* (Seoul: Pogosa, 2013), 88. Yet Min Kwandong et al.'s recent study presents a different view—namely, that the *Romance of Chu and Han* was a separate Chinese novel popular among Koreans; see their *Chungguk t'ongsok sosŏl ŭi yuip kwa suyong* (Seoul: Hakkobang, 2014), 167–90. The *Tale of Xue Rengui* was very popular in the eighteenth and nineteenth centuries, appearing in broad outline in Korean vernacular tales and folk narratives. While there is little evidence for the direct influence of these novels on Korean military tales, it is generally believed that the characters, plots, and themes of these novels were influential and that some of this material was integrated into Korean military tales. For more information on the circulation of these Chinese novels, see Claudine Salmon, ed., *Literary Migrations: Traditional Chinese Fiction in Asia* (reprint, Singapore: ISEAS, 2013), 39–72; and Jinhee

Kim, "The Reception and the Place of *Three Kingdoms* in South Korea," in *Three Kingdoms and Chinese Culture*, ed. Kimberly Ann Besio and Constantine Tung (Albany: State University of New York Press, 2007), 143–52.

21. Im Ch'igyun, "Chosŏn hugi sosŏl ŭi chŏn'gae wa yŏsŏng ŭi yŏkhal," in vol. 5 of *Han'guk sŏsa munhaksa yŏn'gu*, ed. Sa Chaedong (Taejŏn: Chungang munhwasa, 1995), 1682; see also Kan Hoyun, *Arŭmdaun uri kososŏl*, 140–43. The *Romance of Western Zhou* is better known as the *Romance of Enfeoffment to Deities* (Fengshen yanyi 封神演義) because the former is a Korean translation of the latter. For more information on the popularity of the *Romance of Western Zhou*, see Ōtani Morishige, *Han'guk kososŏl yŏn'gu* (Seoul: Kyŏngin munhwasa, 2010), 218–30.

22. Scholars generally agree that the book-lending service (*sech'aegŏp* 貰冊業) appeared during the eighteenth century; see Yi Chuyŏng, "Han'guk kojŏn sosŏl ŭi tokcha," in Yi Sangt'aek et al., *Han'guk kojŏn sosŏul ŭi segye* (Seoul: Tolbegae, 2005), 123–24. Chŏng Pyŏngsŏl estimates that it was already available in Seoul around 1710–20; see Chŏng Pyŏngsŏl, "Chosŏn hugi ŭi Han'gŭl sosŏl param," 145. For a comprehensive discussion of the reading practice and print culture of late Chosŏn Korea, see Michael Kim, "Literary Production, Circulating Libraries, and Private Publishing," 1–31; and Chŏng Pyŏngsŏl, *Chosŏn sidae sosŏl ŭi saengsan kwa yut'ong* (Seoul: Sŏul taehakkyo ch'ulp'an munhwawŏn, 2016).

23. Yi Yunsŏk stresses that the practice of translating and transcribing Chinese stories played an important role in enriching and widening Koreans' fiction writings, particularly those composed in Korean; see Yi Yunsŏk, "Han'gŭl kososŏl ŭi t'ansaeng kwa yut'ong," *Inmun'gwahak* 105 (2015): 9.

24. Cho Hŭiung, "Introduction to *Cho Ung chŏn*," 17. This view coincides with the general view that heroic or military novels were composed by groups of professional writers. Most of these people were declassed literati from the gentry (*yangban*) class who wanted to pursue money and actualize their frustrated political dreams in their writings. See Yi Chuyŏng, "Han'guk kojŏn sosŏl ŭi tokcha," 94.

25. Sim Kyŏngho, "Cho Ung chŏn," in *Han'guk kojŏn sosŏl chakp'umnon*, ed. Wanam Kim Chinse Sŏnsaeng Hoegap Kinyŏm Nonmunjip Kanhaeng Wiwŏnhoe (Seoul: Chimmundang, 1990), 376–78.

26. Such flaws are common throughout *panggakpon* novels. However, the low quality of the woodblock prints and manuscripts in fact proves the great popularity of the tale, with the demand for copies exceeding the desire for a high-quality product; see Yu Ch'undong, "Ilbon komajawa tae-hak tak'usok'u mun'go sojang Chosŏnjŏnjŏk kwa kososŏl e taehan yŏn'gu," *Han'gukhak nonjip* 48 (2012): 315. In this translation, I also note a few important discrepancies and mistakes in the original text, mostly in the names and ages of the characters. For example, Ung's master (either Wŏlgyŏng or Ch'ŏlgwan in book 1) is named as Ch'ŏnmyŏng in book 3, while Ung's age often remains ambiguous, not necessarily matching the sequence of events narrated in the text. Differences in the use of literary language and expressions are also apparent. While book 1 shows a poetic sensibility and descriptive language, book 3 tends to use simple narration with fewer allusions and idiomatic expressions, evincing a more monotonous and repetitive use of language.

27. For examples, see notes 93 and 128 in book 1 of this translation, and note 75 in book 2.

28. These nonelite readers had enough money and leisure time to enjoy works of literature and art—an activity that had previously been monop-olized by the ruling class. At the core of their participation in the reading and entertainment culture was their aspiration to attain a higher social class. See Ryu T'agil, *Wanp'an panggak sosŏl ŭi munhŏnhakchŏk yŏn'gu*, 29–34. Ōtani Morishige argues that these traits of the commer-cial editions were in a way the necessary outcome of their targeting a different readership in the nineteenth century, whose members were mostly lower-class people with little if any literary education, unlike the seventeenth- and eighteenth-century readers of the manuscript and lending library editions of the novels. See his *Han'guk kososŏl yŏn'gu*, 68–70, 81–82.

29. Yi Ch'anghŏn's research on the Seoul editions (*kyŏngp'an*) also proves that in a shorter edition, with 17 leaves, military elements are often omitted; see his *Kyŏngp'an panggak sosŏl p'anbon yŏn'gu*, 333–34. The *wanp'an* editions with 97 (1892) and 88 leaves (1903) also omit a considerable portion of the descriptions of Ung's battles against Yi Tubyŏng's troops.

30. Ch'ae Chegong, "Yŏ Sasŏ sŏ," in *Han'guk kososŏl kwallyŏn charyojip II*, ed. Muak Kososŏl Charyo Yŏn'guhoe (Seoul: Ihoe munhwasa, 2005), 108.

31. Ch'ae Chegong, "Yŏ Sasŏ sŏ," 108.

32. It is well known that the women of the late Chosŏn played a dominant role in developing vernacular fiction. Those who were educated and who had leisure time and money, such as palace ladies and gentry women, were regular customers at book lending libraries (or rental shops). Ōtani Morishige even states that vernacular fiction was developed in Korea as part of women's culture; see his *Chosŏn hugi sosŏl tokcha yŏn'gu*, 35–42. Although we know that female readers enjoyed the transcribed manuscript and lending library editions, which maintained better quality than commercial editions, the extent to which they enjoyed the commercial editions needs further research.

33. The *Tale of Cho Ung* was also favored by gentry women from Yŏngnam (present-day Kyŏngsang Province) because of Ung's heroic character and familial concerns. See Kim Chaeung, "Yŏngnam chiyŏk p'ilsabon kosoŏl e nat'anan yŏsŏng hyangyuch'ŭng ŭi yongmang," *Han'guk kojŏn yŏsŏng munhak yŏn'gu* 16 (2008): 11–17. In fact, Professor Im Ch'igyun alerted me to the influence of the local dialect of this region in later editions of the *Tale of Cho Ung*.

34. Whether or not the original tale was written in classical Chinese has been a significant question in the history of vernacular Korean fiction. Written in 1689 by Kim Manjung (1637–92), the *Nine-Cloud Dream* has both Sino-Korean and vernacular Korean versions, and scholars think that the production of editions in both languages would have been common.

35. The Tang, Song, Yuan, and Ming dynasties are common backdrops for vernacular fiction, and among them the Ming is used most frequently. This preference for the Ming is attributed to the Chosŏn court's close relationship with and favoritism toward the Ming dynasty—an attitude that persisted even after its collapse in 1644; see Kim T'aejun, *Chosŏn sosŏlsa* (Kyŏngsŏng: Ch'ŏngjin sŏgwan, 1933), 159.

36. There are a number of reasons for the use of Chinese space in Korean literature: 1. the imaginary space of China had long been a dreamland among Koreans; 2. it provided more room for developing characters and plots without the risk of embarrassing mistakes; 3. it gave the Korean literati a feeling of symbolic participation in Chinese literary space; and

4. it offered a safe venue in which to express potentially risky criticism. In military tales that involve a hero's fight with non-Koreans, and that extend beyond the country's territory, the use of Chinese places and names from the distant past avoided any diplomatic offense and thus permitted long-term success in the book market. See Kan Hoyun, *Arŭmdaun uri kososŏl*, 62; T'ak Wŏnjŏng, *Choson hugi kojŏn sosŏl ŭi konggan mihak* (Seoul: Pogosa, 2013), 31–39.

37. The accuracy or impossibility of the travel routes in a tale is sometimes used to gauge the nationality of an anonymous author. See O Hwa (Wu Hua), "Yu Sorang chŏn ŭi kukchŏk munje e kwanhan koch'al," *Hanminjok ŏmunhak* 67 (2014): 221–50.

38. I have attempted to identify the actual locations of the places named as much as possible in my translation. However, my overall observation is that the names and locations are selected randomly, rather than being based on a certain map of an actual place. The traveling distances remain symbolic, and the order of places mentioned in the narrative of Ung's travels does not allow me to trace a route on any available map of China.

39. This ritual is called *kasanghŭi* 假像戲 (Effigy Play). Wang Kŏn (877–943), the founder of Koryŏ Korea (918–1392), ordered that a *kasanghŭi* take place as part of a Buddhist performance called Palgwanhoe 八關會 (The Eight Precepts Observance Ceremony) to console the souls of generals Sin Sunggyŏm and Kim Rak, who had died in his battle against the Latter Paekche (900–936) in 927. Kyŏng Illam has found that the description in the original *Tale of Cho Ung* is similar to what took place in the *kasanghŭi* performance; for more information, see his "Cho Ung chŏn ŭi kasanghŭi hwaso suyong kwa kŭ ŭimi," *Inmunhak yŏn'gu* 85 (2011): 77.

40. The former motif is seen in the *An Ping mongyurok* 安憑夢遊錄 (Record of An Ping's Dream Journey) by Sin Kwanghan (申光漢, 1484–1555), and the scene of meeting up with the dead emperor is best represented by that in the *Wŏn saeng mongyurok* 元生夢遊錄 (Record of Scholar Wŏn's Dream Journey, ca. 1598) by Im Che (林悌, 1549–87), and the *Wang Hoe chŏn* 王會傳 by Kim Chesŏng (金濟性, ca. 1840).

41. Cho Hŭiung, "Introduction to *Cho Ung chŏn*," 7–9. The definition of the heroic or military novel in Chosŏn Korea requires further discussion.

The *Tale of Cho Ung* resonates with other anonymously written heroic martial tales such as the *Tale of Yu Ch'ungnyŏl* (Yu Ch'ungnyŏl chŏn 劉忠烈傳), *Tale of So Taesŏng*, and *Tale of Chang Paek* (Chang Paek chŏn 張白[伯]傳) in its implementation of a similar backdrop and plots. However, the *Tale of Cho Ung* differs significantly in its literary treatment of events and also in its characterization. A detailed comparison of the plots of military tales is available in Sŏ Taesŏk, *Kundam sosŏl ŭi kujo wa paegyŏng*, 19–68.

42. Cho Hŭiung, "Introduction to *Cho Ung chŏn*," 10.

43. The evolution of the *Tale of Cho Ung* has rendered its battle scenes less dramatic and extreme compared to those in military and heroic tales such as the *Tale of Chang Paek*, the *Tale of Ch'oe Koun* (Ch'oe Koun chŏn 崔孤雲傳), and the *Tale of Chŏn Uch'i* (Chŏn Uch'i chŏn 田禹治傳), which focus more on fight scenes and the use of Daoist magic.

44. This intricate relationship between popular literature and social norms has been carefully explored by Haboush, who demonstrates that the popular vernacular literature of late Chosŏn Korea formed an alternative, or antihegemonic discourse through its embodiment of different views and sentiments, in which emotion outweighs or challenges social norms. For more on this subject, see JaHyun Kim Haboush, "Filial Emotions and Filial Values: Changing Patterns in the Discourse of Filiality in Late Chosŏn Korea," *Harvard Journal of Asiatic Studies* 55, no. 1 (1995): 129–77.

45. In many tales, religious figures such as the Buddha or Daoist masters play the role of a savior. In this story, however, the characters are frequently helped by the dead at critical moments. For example, Ung's father materializes to give timely advice to save his family, and the ghosts of Emperor Mun and the general of Wi offer vital assistance and guidance.

46. In Chosŏn society, men could abandon their wives legitimately when their wives committed any of the acts categorized as "the seven evils for expulsion" (七去之惡): 1. not obeying her in-laws; 2. inability to bear a son; 3. lewd behavior; 4. jealousy; 5. a serious disease; 6. being talkative; and 7. stealing. Maiden Chang's support for Ung's having a second wife demonstrates that she is not jealous.

47. For a brief outline of the Confucianization process in Korea, see the introduction to *Women and Confucian Cultures in Premodern China, Korea, and*

Japan, ed. Dorothy Ko, JaHyun Kim Haboush, and Joan R. Piggott (Berkeley: University of California Press, 2003), 9–12; for a rigorous analysis of the changes brought by Confucianization, see Martina Deuchler, *The Confucian Transformation of Korea: A Study of Society and Ideology* (Cambridge: Harvard University Asia Center, 1995).

48. Having multiple wives was prohibited by law in the fifteenth century, allowing only one legal wife. But this law was primarily to ensure a patrilineal line by reducing conflicts in the distribution of inheritance and power among children of the first and other wives. Polygamy was thus legitimately practiced in the form of one wife and many concubines. See Eugene Y. Park, *A Family of No Prominence: The Descendants of Pak Tŏkhwa and the Birth of Modern Korea* (Stanford: Stanford University Press, 2014), 11.

49. In the scholar-beauty romances of China, both male and female characters go against social norms in the pursuit of their love. In many cases, the male character becomes successful and is blessed with multiple wives. The *Tale of Cho Ung* and most other Korean romance and military tales of the period follow the genre grammar of the scholar-beauty romance of China. For a discussion of polygamy in literature and culture, see Keith McMahon's books: *Polygamy and Sublime Passion: Sexuality in China on the Verge of Modernity* (Honolulu: University of Hawai'i Press, 2010) and *Misers, Shrews, and Polygamists: Sexuality and Male-Female Relations in Eighteenth-Century Chinese Fiction* (Durham: Duke University Press, 1995). According to Pak Chaeyŏn, the scholar-beauty romance was introduced to Korea after the seventeenth century; to date, copies of thirty-eight different novels of this genre have been found, though the total number of scholar-beauty tales that circulated in Korea would have been higher. For more information, see his "Chosŏn sidae chaeja kain sosŏl ŭi chŏllae wa suyong: saero palgultoen Paek(Poek)kyuji rŭl chungsimŭro," *Chungguk ŏmunhak nonjip* 51 (2008): 466–74.

50. I argue against the androcentric view that the female readers of this popular tale were supporters of polygamy and the other patriarchal traditions depicted in the story; an enhanced representation of the patriarchal themes can evoke many different readings, depending on a given reader's perspective and intention. JaHyun Kim Haboush presents an enriched discussion of how we posit the relationship between the

Confucian moral values manifest in the texts and their female readers and writers. She argues that female readers and writers, though influenced by the dominant Confucian (i.e., neo-Confucian) ideology, were able to find subversive ideas and create an alternate space for themselves through their reading and writing of those texts. See her "Versions and Subversions: Patriarchy and Polygamy in Korean Narratives," in *Women and Confucian Cultures in Premodern China, Korea, and Japan,* 279–304.

51. For example, the author of the *Tale of Cho Ung* may have been inspired by two failed coups known as the Rebellion of the Musin Year (Musillan 戊申亂; 1728), led by Yi Injwa (李麟佐, 1695–1728), and the Naju Graffiti Incident (Naju kwaesŏ sagŏn 羅州掛書事件; 1755), led by Yun Chi (尹志, 1688–1755). Accounts of these incidents show some similarities with the *Tale of Cho Ung* (book 1), such as "the usurpation of the throne" (Musillan), "writing complaints on the wall," and "the appearance of a tiger in the palace" (Naju kwaesŏ sagŏn). This likeness could indicate merely the intertextuality of historical records and literary works, but it could also help us more accurately date and identify the author of the *Tale of Cho Ung*. For information on the relationship between the tale and the Naju Incident, see Sim Kyŏngho, "Cho Ung chŏn," 378–79.

52. Cho Hŭiung, "Introduction to *Cho Ung chŏn*," 19.

53. Sŏ Taesŏk, *Kundam sosŏl ŭi kujo wa paegyŏng,* 96–107.

54. In his interesting article on a hero's era, Kim Yongch'ŏl argues that Cho Ung is characteristically representative of a Chosŏn hero, fully embodying the common people's long-standing desire for a messiah during the nineteenth century. The increasingly common perception of Cho Ung as a messiah, combined with his charm as a romantic hero and a conqueror loyal to the throne, surely contributes to the story's great popularity among the people and is the element that makes the story a classic. See Kim Yongch'ŏl, "Yŏngung ŭi sigan/yŏngt'o kŭraep'ŭro pon Cho Ung chŏn: Han'guk ŭi kojŏn'gujo siron 1," *Inmun'gwahak* 51 (2013): 1–26.

55. Joseph Campbell, introduction to *The Hero with a Thousand Faces,* 3d rev. ed. (Novato, CA: New World Library, 2008), xlv.

NOTE ON THE TRANSLATION

1. The *chŏngsa* date (1857) is written at the end of the first volume. Each of the three volumes of this earliest Wansan edition shows traces of its own respective evolution, based on somewhat different renderings of the tale; see Ryu T'agil, *Wanp'an panggak sosŏl ŭi munhŏnhakchŏk yŏn'gu*, 93–99. The full three-volume text is available in vol. 3 of *Kyŏngin kososŏl p'an'gakpon chŏnjip*, ed. Kim Tonguk, W. E. Skillend, and D. Bouchez (Seoul: Nason sŏsil, 1975), 147–99.

2. Cho Hŭiung's book is based on the 104-leaf edition from the *chŏngsa* year included in vol. 3 of *Kyŏngin kososŏl p'an'gakpon chŏnjip*. Yi Hŏnhong also says he uses the 104-leaf edition, but the original text included in his book is slightly different from the one included in the *Kyŏngin kososŏl p'an'gakpon chŏnjip*, and he provides no further information about the original edition he uses.

BOOK 1

1. "Emperor Mun of the Song" (宋文帝) refers to Yu Ŭigyŏng 劉義慶 (Liu Yiqing, 407–453 CE) of the Song dynasty (420–479 CE), which was part of the Southern Dynasties period (420–589 CE). This Song dynasty was generally called the Yu Song (C. Liu Song), following the surname of its founder Yu Yu 劉裕 (Liu Yu, 363–422 CE), to differentiate it from the Great Song (960–1279 CE), whose founder's surname was Cho 趙 (C. Zhao). Emperor Mun governed for twenty-nine years during the reign of Wŏn'ga 元嘉 (424–453 CE), which is known as the most peaceful time of the Yu Song dynasty. The dynasty, particularly the reign of Emperor Mun, was the period in which poets such as To Yŏnmyŏng 陶淵明 (Tao Yuanming, 365–427), Sa Ryŏngun 謝靈運 (Xie Lingyun, 385–433), and An Yŏnji 顏延之 (Yan Yanzhi, 384–456)—beloved and admired by Korean literati—were active. Yet Emperor Mun was involved in a major war with the Northern Wi 魏 dynasty (Wei, 386–534 CE) in 430 and 450 over the area of Hoebuk 淮北 (Huaibei; present-day northern Anhui Province). Soon after his defeat in this war, Emperor Mun gave up his throne. Though Chinese dynasties are frequently employed as a backdrop in Chosŏn fiction, Yu Song rarely appears in Korean literature. The detailed years

presented in this tale, such as the twenty-third year of Emperor Mun's reign—that is, 447—do not match the time setting that follows, as indicated by *pyŏngin* 丙寅 (426, or 486), *chŏngmyo* 丁卯 (427, or 487), or *kyŏngo* 庚午 (430, or 490), nor the chronology of Yu Song. This time displacement or inaccuracy might be culturally symbolic or simply anachronistic, which is often the case with popular literature.

2. The "Earth-Drumming Song" (*kyŏgyang* 擊壤; C. *jirang*) originated during the peaceful reign of Emperor Yo 堯 (Yao, 2356–2256 BCE) of ancient China. It refers to a pastime in which common people (peasants), free from any worries in their daily lives, enjoyed singing while they drummed on the earth. Both "singing the Earth-Drumming Song" and "playing the Earth-Drumming Game" are commonly used tropes for peaceful times.

3. The original text has *wŏlmyŏngnyŏn* 越明年, literally meaning "the year after the next year," that is, the twenty-fifth year of Emperor Mun's reign.

4. *Pyŏngin* is the third term of the Chinese sexagenary cycle (*yuksip kapcha* 六十甲子; C. *liushi jiazi*). The cycle, also known as the Stems-and-Branches (*kanji* 干支; C. *ganzhi*), is used for recording days or years throughout the text. The exact meaning of *pyŏngin* day (day 3) mentioned in the text remains unclear.

5. Left prime minister (*chwasŭngsang* 左丞相; C. *zuochengxiang*): one of the highest positions in the central government. It has been ranked higher than the right prime minister (*usŭngsang* 右丞相; C. *youchengxiang*) since the Han dynasty (206 BCE–220 CE); see Charles O. Hucker, *A Dictionary of Official Titles in Imperial China* (Stanford: Stanford University Press, 1985), #483, 126–27.

6. The chief steward of the Ministry of Personnel (*ibu sangsŏ* 吏部尚書; C. *libu shangshu*): head of one of the six ministries (*yukpu* 六部; C. *liubu*), top-level administrative agencies (*sangsŏ*; ranked 3a in Tang China) in the central government. The chief steward of the Ministry of Personnel (also translated as minister of personnel) was always considered preeminent among the six ministers; see Hucker, *A Dictionary of Official Titles*, #5042, 410–41.

7. In the *kyŏngp'an* edition, the Southern Barbarians (Namman 南蠻; C. Nanman) brought about a war.

8. These place names, including the Pass of Noesŏng (雷城關) which appears later in this paragraph, could have originated from actual places in the capital city of Song. A Gate of Kyŏnghwa (景化門) corresponds to both Chinese and Korean places. In the case of the Hill of Mubong, "Mubong" could simply mean a hill that has no peak instead of being the name of a particular hill. It's difficult to find any references to the Bridge of Kwangim (Kwangnim 光臨 in the 80-leaf University of Tokyo edition).

9. The definition of the li, a unit of distance, has varied across time and region; in Korea, 1 li often indicates approximately 400 meters, following the standard of the Han dynasty (206 BCE–220 CE), while in modern China it has a standardized length of half a kilometer or 500 meters. The li is often translated as a "mile" in the West, but if we count the length of 150 li based on the Korean value, the total distance of 150 li would be approximately 37 miles.

10. King (prince) of pacification (*chŏngp'yŏng wang* 靖平王 or 征平王): an honorary title, given posthumously to emperors, princes, individuals of high standing, and members of the literati.

11. Grand master of the palace with golden seal and purple ribbon (*kŭmja kwangnok taebu* 金紫光祿大夫): an honorific title conferred on officials of high distinction; see Hucker, *Official Titles*, # 1159, 168.

12. These expressions originate from *pijo chin yanggung chang* 蜚鳥盡良弓藏 and *kyot'o sa chugu p'aeng* 狡兔死走狗烹 from "Wŏlwang Kuch'ŏn sega" 越王勾践世家 (C. Yuewang Goujian shijia) and "Hoeŭmhu yŏlchŏn" 淮陰侯列傳 (C. Huai yin hou lie zhuan) in vols. 41 and 92 of the *Records of the Grand Historian* (*Sagi* 史記; C. *Shiji*) by Sama Ch'ŏn 司馬遷 (Sima Qian, ca. 145–86 BCE). They both describe the idea that good tools or methods will be abandoned after they are no longer needed.

13. Right prime minister (*usŭngsang* 右丞相): one of the highest positions in the central government; see note 5, book 1. In the manuscript versions such as the 80-leaf University of Tokyo edition, Yi Tubyŏng appears as 李斗炳.

14. Chief steward of the Ministry of War (*pyŏngbu sangsŏ* 兵部尚書): the head of a top-level administrative agency in the standard six ministries.

15. Lady of reverence and eminence (*kongnyŏl puin* 恭烈夫人): an honorific title granted to the wife of a loyal official. The title also appears in other stories, such as the *Tale of Yang Chubong* (梁朱鳳傳) and the *Tale of Chang P'ungun* (張豐雲傳).

16. The Chinese character for Ung is 雄 (C. *xiong*), which has various connotations such as powerful, grand, masculine, or heroic.

17. It was typical in both China and Korea to observe a three-year mourning period. Lady Wang's eight-year mourning period in the text demonstrates not mere obedience to the rite but unusual faithfulness to her husband.

18. The original text says "a jade or jewel on a cap" (*kwanok* 冠玉), which is a common expression referring to a handsome man.

19. "An inferior man" is a translation of *soin* 小人 (C. *xiaoren*), literally "small man." *Soin* is often interpreted as an inferior, selfish, lowly, vile, or unworthy man as opposed to *kunja* 君子 (C. *junzi*), which means a superior, noble, and great man. *Soin* appears several times through the text, and I have used different words in translating the term, depending on the context of each instance.

20. The original text says "the day of *nabil* of the month of *nabwŏl.*" *Nabwŏl* 臘月 is the twelfth lunar month, and *nabil* 臘日 refers to the eighth day, when the year-end worship of *napche* 臘祭 is being held.

21. Chief steward of the Ministry of Rites (*yebu sangsŏ* 禮部尙書; C. *libu shangshu*): head of one of the standard six ministries; see note 6, book 1.

22. So Mu 蘇武 (Su Wu, 140–60 BCE) was a high minister of the mid-Former Han period (206 BCE–8 CE). When he was sent by the emperor to the Xiongnu people as an ambassador, the Xiongnu detained him and asked him to surrender and work for them. But So Mu steadfastly refused to surrender, despite extreme hardships and suffering, which made him known for his courage and loyalty.

23. *Chin* 辰: 7 to 9 A.M., the hour of the Dragon, the fifth Chinese hour in the double-hours based on the Chinese zodiac.

24. In the original text, "Changan" 長安 frequently appears to mean the capital city. Changan was an ancient capital of many Chinese dynasties, such as Han, Sui (581–618), and Tang (618–907). Its name was changed to its present-day name, Xi'an 西安, during the Ming dynasty

(1368–1644). This anachronistic use of Changan as the capital city is common in Korean literature.

25. The original text uses *cha*, a traditional Korean unit for measuring length, which is equal to one *ch'ŏk* 尺 (C. *chi*). Until the Three Kingdoms period of China (220–280 CE), the value of one ch'ŏk remained at approximately 23 cm to 24 cm, and in Chosŏn Korea the value was almost the same (23 cm). From the nineteenth century on, it changed to equal 30–33 cm.

26. Hallim academicians or royal secretaries (*hallim haksa* 翰林學士): a title for scholars at the Hallim Academy of Arts and Letters (*hallim wŏn* 翰林院). These scholars were well versed in literature and the arts. They drafted imperial edicts and provided counsel to the throne. Wang Yŏl appears as 王烈 in the manuscript editions.

27. In the *kyŏngp'an* edition, Lady Wang is described as being well versed in the Purple Star Astrology (*chami tosul* 紫微道術), which centers on the Purple Star (*chamisŏng* 紫微星), commonly known as the Emperor Star. Purple Star Astrology was used for both fortunetelling and other everyday consulting among East Asian people; for more information on this astrology, see Peng Yoke Ho, *Chinese Mathematical Astrology* (New York: RoutledgeCurzon, 2003). For this reason, Wang Yŏl, who is described as a cousin of Cho Ung in the *kyŏngp'an* edition, consults Lady Wang for her interpretation of the strange event.

28. "Know only one thing, but not the other" (*chiji kŭl puji kŭ* 只知其一, 不知其二) is an idiom meaning having a one-sided perspective. Its earliest appearance is found in "Ch'ŏnji" 天地 of *Changja* 莊子 (the *Zhuangzi*).

29. Mount Hyŏng 荊山 (C. Jingshan) is located in the Nanzhang county of Hubei Province in China. It was known for its production of jade, as seen in the story of Pyŏn Hwa 卞和 (C. Bian He), in which a person from the state of Ch'o 楚 (Chu, ca. 1030–223 BCE) during the Period of the Warring States (475–221 BCE) found a famous jade disc called Hwassi pyŏk 和氏璧 (C. Heshi bi) in Mount Hyŏng. The sentence describes a situation in which both good (jade) and bad (stone) people face the same misfortune. In the 80-leaf University of Tokyo edition, Mount Hyŏng appears as 衡山 (C. Hengshan), one of the Five Sacred Mountains; see note 48, book 1.

30. The entire passage is originally from the "Kuji" 九地, chapter 11 of *Sonja Pyŏngpŏp* 孫子兵法 (the Art of War by Sunzi). It means that experience of dangerous situations or areas makes people (soldiers) capable of crafting victory out of despair or defeat.

31. The original text has the expression *sojang chi hwan* 蕭牆之患, meaning "the trouble within the walls of the palace." The expression, which came from the chapter "Yongin" 用人 of *Han Pija* 韓非子 (the Han Feizi), became a cliché descriptor for rebellions inside the country.

32. *Chŏngmyo*: the fourth year of the Chinese sixty-year cycle, one year after the *pyŏngin* year.

33. The original text contains the expression *ijŏng chi p'yo* 釐正之表, literally meaning "an exemplary that helps to put things in the right order."

34. The original text has *sŏdong* 書童, literally meaning "book boy," which generally refers to "a boy serving a scholar in his study."

35. "A child from a commoner's family": in the absence of Cho's father, who was a high official, Cho's family would revert to the humble status of commoners. Cho Ung also refers to himself as a child from a commoner's family when he meets the emperor for the first time.

36. The original text reads *kŏjae turyang* 車載斗量, meaning "measured in cartloads and gallons."

37. The literal translation of the beginning part is "[the emperor's] fate ordained by heaven became unfortunate." The original text has the expression *winyŏnhi*, whose meaning remains unclear; I translate it as *uyŏnhi* ("unexpectedly" or "suddenly"), following Cho Hŭiung's edition.

38. According to the *kyŏngp'an* edition, Emperor Mun was seventy-seven years old when he passed away.

39. "Tune of Lament for Doomed Countries" (Manggukcho 亡國調) refers to the music of a dying country. It has also been considered the cause for the fall of a dynasty. Manggukcho appears in "Hwayongdo" 華容道 (Kim Chongch'ŏl edition), one of the *p'ansori* songs based on the episode of the legendary Battle at the Red Cliffs (赤壁) in the *Romance of the Three Kingdoms* (三國志演義).

40. During this scene in the *kyŏngp'an* edition, Ung calls his mother *t'aet'ae* 太太 (C. *taitai*), a Chinese term used to refer to a wife or mother during the Ming-Qing period, adding to the sense of Chinese culture.

41. P'yŏngsun 平順 (Peace and Harmony).

42. Kŏnmu 建武 (Building Military): this title was used by Emperor Guangwu (5 BCE–57 CE) for the first years of his reign (25–57 CE) after he founded the Eastern Han (25–220 CE) dynasty.

43. Kyeryangdo of Mount T'ae [Prefecture]: Mount T'ae (T'aesan 泰山; C. Taishan), located in Shandong Province, is one of the most famous among the five sacred mountains in China. Kyeryangdo may be translated either as Kyeryang Island or Kyeryang Province, depending on the meaning of *do (to)*. Like many other place names in the tale, it is very difficult to link the name in the story to an actual place; it is not clear where Kyeryangdo actually is and whether it is located near Mount T'ae.

44. *Samgang Oryun* 三綱五倫 (C. *Sangang Wulun*), originally initiated by Tong Chungsŏ 董仲舒 (Dong Zhongshu, ca.179–104 BCE) of the Han dynasty, indicates the principles and rules in human relations, that is, between ruler and minister, father and son, husband and wife (the three bonds), plus those between the old and the young, and among friends (the five relations). These relationships indicate the hierarchical nature of Confucian society, in which all people have distinct roles and positions in their relationships with others.

45. The expression "Five Lakes and Four Seas" (*oho sahae* 五湖四海; C. *wuhu sihai*) is commonly used to indicate "everywhere under the sun." The phrase "riding in a small boat on the Five Lakes" probably refers to the Chinese story of Pŏm Ryŏ 范蠡 (Fan Li, b. 517 BCE) and Sŏ Si 西施 (Xi Shi, b. 506 BCE) of the Wŏl 越 state. Pŏm Ryŏ, a minister of Wŏl, helped King Kuch'ŏn 勾踐 (Goujian, d. 464 BCE) of Wŏl destroy the O 吳 (C. Wu) state by using the beauty of Sŏ Si. After completing their mission, the couple became hermits, roaming the Five Lakes in a fishing boat.

46. The expression "a dream of the Southern Branch" (*namga ilmong* 南柯一夢; C. *nanke yimeng*) originates in a mid-Tang tale titled "Namga T'aesu chŏn" 南柯太守傳 (C. Nanke Taishou zhuan; the Tale of the Governor of the Southern Branch), written by Yi Kongjwa 李公佐 (Li Gongzuo, ca. 778–848). In this story, Sunu Pun 淳于棼 (C. Chunyu Fen) drinks with his friends, and, in his intoxication, he experiences another life consisting of both blessings (e.g., marriage to a princess and service as the governor of the State of the Southern Branch for twenty years)

and misfortunes (e.g., defeat in a battle and the death of his wife). When he suddenly wakes up, he comes to realize that everything that has happened is merely a dream and that the kingdom he lived in and the county he was governor of are actually an ants' nest inside a hole in the southern branch of a large scholar tree (*koesu* 槐樹; C. *huaishu*). After this, he understands the brevity of life and devotes himself to Daoism. For more information and a translation of this tale, see William H. Nienhauser Jr., *Tang Dynasty Tales: A Guided Reader* (Hackensack, NJ: World Scientific, 2010), 131–87.

47. An immortal lad is *sŏndong* 仙童 (C. *xiantong*) in Korean. It generally means an immortal servant boy in Daoist terms.

48. South Mountain (Namak 南岳; C. Nanyue) refers to Mount Hyŏng (Hyŏngsan 衡山; C. Hengshan), one of the five sacred mountains, which is located in China's Hunan Province. The mountain is famous for a number of temples, one of which is the Grand Temple of South Mountain (Nanyue damiao 南岳大廟).

49. The Four Seas (四海) and Eight Directions (八方) represents the whole world and all directions accordingly. The "Four Seas" constitute the boundaries of the earth, which is flat and square in ancient Chinese thought, and the "Eight Directions" consist of the four cardinal directions (East, West, South, North) and four intercardinal directions (NE, NW, SE, SW). See also note. 45, book 1.

50. A deer is often used metaphorically to indicate the Chinese kingdom or the political power of China, more frequently referred to as "the central plain" (*chungwŏn* 中原; C. *zhongyuan*). The deer and the central plain are thus used in combination to mean "to attempt to seize the throne," as in the expression "hunting deer in the central plain" (逐鹿中原). In "Hoeŭmhu yŏlchŏn" in the *Records of the Grand Historian*, it is also written that the deer lost by the State of Chin 秦 (C. Qin) was chased by all under heaven (秦失其鹿, 天下共逐之). The text here mentions the failure of former attempts to seize power and emphasizes the role of heaven in obtaining power. This prediction will eventually turn out to be right.

51. The First Emperor of Chin: Chin Si Hwang 秦始皇 (Qin Shi Huang, 259–210 BCE), the founding emperor of the Chin dynasty (221–206 BCE). In this passage, the deer probably represents the Chinese kingdom, unified by Chin Si Hwang.

52. The Hegemon King of Ch'o refers to Hang U 項羽 (Xiang Yu, 232–202 BCE) from the Ch'o 楚 (C. Chu) state, a prominent military leader and political figure during the late Chin dynasty. He fought Yu Pang 劉邦 (Liu Bang, 256–195 BCE) over China, specifically the central plain, but was defeated. Yu Pang became the first emperor of the Han dynasty.

53. Pŏm Chŭng 范增 (Fan Zeng, 277–204 BCE) was the adviser to Hang U. He was known for his expertise in military strategy and politics. He assisted Hang in rebelling against the Chin dynasty. Pŏm realized that Yu Pang would become a future threat to Hang U and urged Hang to kill Yu, but Hang did not heed Pŏm's advice.

54. "The writing on the right side": in traditional writing, one writes vertically from top to bottom, and the lines advance from the right to the left side of the page. In this style of writing, when the page is finished, the signature lies on the far left side while the main writing is located on the right side.

55. The original text has the expression *sosi* 燒弒, possibly meaning "burning to death." But it could also mean "displaying the decapitated head in public" (*hyosi* 梟示), as seen in the *kyŏngp'an* edition. Following the *kyŏngp'an* edition and the interpretation of scholars such as Cho Hŭiung and Yi Hŏnhong, I translate the sentence based on the meaning of *hyosi*, which makes more sense than "burning to death" both in general and in the situation described, since the execution was completed quickly.

56. Marquis (*hujak* 侯爵; C. *houjue*): a feudal vassal who owned the land of ten thousand households (*ho* 戶; C. *hu*).

57. The original text says that Paekcha village (百資村) is in Kyeryangsŏm. Kyeryangsŏm can possibly mean "Kyeryang Island," but, based on the description of the Kyeryang area in the text, the place does not appear to be an island. It is also a different place from the Kyeryangdo, where the crown prince is exiled; see note 43, book 1.

58. The original text says, "It has been almost eight years since we came to this village." But "eight years" looks like an error here. The question of how long Ung stays in the village is unclear, but based on the information in the latter part of the story, it should be less than three years: Ung leaves the capital at the age of eight, and he is eleven when he meets Daoist master Wŏlgyŏng some time after leaving the village. This means Ung's residence in the village could not have exceeded three

years. It is possible that the intention of the original text is, "It has been a while since I came to the village at the age of eight." The 80-leaf University of Tokyo edition states one year instead, and the 97-leaf *imjin* edition from Sogang University preserves a reader's crossing out of the character "eight," suggesting that "eight" is an error.

59. There are no Chinese characters provided for these place names in the original text. The name of the village Okkuyŏk indicates that the village is a post town (*yŏkch'on* 驛村) that has a relay station for mail horses.

60. The original text has *samhon ch'ilbaek* 三魂七魄 (three immortal souls and seven mortal souls), a term for two distinct human souls: *hon* 魂 (C. *hun*; immortal souls) and *paek* 魄 (C. *po*; mortal souls). According to *Un'gŭp ch'ilch'ŏm* 雲笈七籤 (C. *Yunji qiqian*; the Seven Lots from the Bookbag of the Clouds), the three immortal souls are T'aegwang 台光, Sangnyŏng 爽靈, and Yujŏng 幽精, and these souls, along with the *ch'ilbaek* 七魄 (seven mortal souls), are crucial to one's illness and death; for example, one must secure the three souls (拘三魂) due to their tendency to fly away. For more information, see Fabrizio Pregadio, *The Routledge Encylcopedia of Taoism: vol. I, A–L* (London: Routledge, 2005), 521–22. The 88-leaf and 97-leaf editions from 1903 have *chanhon ch'ilbaek* 殘魂七魄 (remaining immortal souls and seven mortal souls) instead of *samhon ch'ilbaek*.

61. Third watch (*samgyŏng* 三更): 11 PM–1 AM, the third of the five night watch periods, from 7 PM to 5 AM (7–9 PM; 9–11 PM; 11 PM–1 AM; 1–3 AM; and 3–5 AM).

62. "Why Don't You Return" or "Better Go Home" (Puryŏgwi 不如歸; C. Burugui): a name for the cuckoo, Tugyŏn 杜鵑 (C. Dujuan), as well as the name of the song sung by the cuckoo. According to a legendary tale, Tu U 杜宇 (C. Du Yu.), king of the State of Ch'ok 蜀 (C. Shu), during the Three Kingdom Period of China, was betrayed by a person called Pyŏllyŏng 鼈靈 (C. Bieling)—whose life he had saved and whom he had treated well—and was then forced into exile, and died of grief. After Tu U died, he was transformed into a cuckoo, singing sadly every morning, "Puryŏgwi, puryŏgwi." Since then, *puryŏgwi* has become another name for the cuckoo. A record of this story is found in "Ch'okchi" 蜀志 (C. Shuzhi) of *Hwayanggukchi* 華陽國志 (C. Huayang guo zhi; the

Records of the States South of Mount Hua) by Sang Kŏ 常璩 (C. Chang Qu, fl. third century CE).

63. Empty mountain (*kongsan* 空山): this expression evokes the famous passage in the poem "The Deer Enclosure" (Nokch'ae 鹿柴; C. Luchai) by Tang poet Wang Yu 王維 (Wang Wei, 699–761) that reads: "In the empty mountain, no one is seen / Only the echo of the human voice is heard" (空山不見人, 但聞人語響).

64. Governor of a province (*t'aesu* 太守).

65. In Confucianism, one should keep his/her body, skin, and hair intact, as they are given to one by one's parents (*sinch'e palbu su chi pumo* 身體髮膚, 受之父母). Thus, shaving one's hair is a disgraceful and unfilial act. For the symbolic meaning of hair and its cultural significance, see Alf Hiltebeitel and Barbara D. Miller, eds., *Hair: Its Power and Meaning in Asian Cultures* (Albany: State University of New York Press, 1998).

66. *Nyang* 兩: traditional currency widely used in East Asia. Like other units, its value has changed over time and in different regions. Based on records from seventeenth-century Korea, one could buy one *sŏm* or *sŏk* 石 of rice (about 80 kg in the modern standard) with one *nyang*.

67. A monument pavilion 碑閣 (K. *pigak*; C. *beige*) is a small building that protects a monument (called a stele or stela) commemorating patriotic and honorable deeds.

68. The original text has the expression *paekkollanmang* 白骨難忘, literally meaning "I will not forget your kindness even when my body turns into white bones."

69. The Great Country (*taeguk* 大國) refers to the country governed by the emperor of the Liu Song dynasty. The setting of the story reflects China's feudal system, best represented by that of the Zhou dynasty (1050–256 BCE) in which the feudal overlord (*ch'ŏnja* 天子; the Son of Heaven or the emperor) governs the entire Chinese land while giving vassals (*chehu* 諸侯; royal relatives, loyal generals, and other personnel) control over fiefdoms (*chehuguk* 諸侯國; vassal states). Based on this system, the State of Wi is a vassal state, and the Song dynasty represents the authority and ownership of the entire land of China.

70. The Loyal Subject of the Great Country, Vice Minister of the Ministry of War and Censor of Military Affairs of All Provinces (*Taeguk*

ch'ungsin pyŏngbu sirang kyŏm kakto chinmuŏsa 大國忠臣 兵部侍郎 兼 各道
鎮撫御史).

71. The king of the State of Wi (Wiguk 魏國; C. Weiguo): "Wi" is the
Chinese state that appears frequently in vernacular fiction of the late
Chosŏn, which is often set against a backdrop modeled on the Warring
States period (475–221 BCE). It is difficult to know which of the two
Chinese Wi (魏 and 衛) states is indicated here because there is no Chi-
nese character provided in the original text.

72. Tu Ch'im 杜侵.

73. Emperors Kŏl and Chu of the Ha and Sang dynasties: tyrants and the
last emperors of their dynasties of China. Emperor Kŏl 桀 (C. Jie) of
the Ha (C. Xia) dynasty (twenty-first–sixteenth century BCE) was corrupt, neglected his duties, and persecuted even loyal subjects. His
infatuation with drinking and women, particularly his beautiful concubine Marhŭi 妹喜 (C. Moxi), who lacked virtue, has often been
identified as a direct cause of the fall of the Ha dynasty. Similarly,
Emperor Chu 紂 (C. Zhou) of the Sang (C. Shang) dynasty (sixteenth–
eleventh century BCE) ruled tyrannically and practiced all kinds of
cruelty, including severe punishments of innocent officials to please
Talgi 妲己 (C. Daji.), his beautiful but evil concubine.

74. A Daoist master (*tosa* 道士; C. *daoshi*) frequently appears throughout the
story, characterized by his special martial arts ability, power, and talent rather than his pursuit of religious enlightenment.

75. *Ŭm* and *yang*: *yin* 陰 and *yang* 陽 in Chinese, which describe two com-
plementary principles in Chinese philosophy that maintain the harmony of the universe.

76. With no Chinese characters provided for this place, Pyŏnyang may
refer to Bianyang 邊陽, in Guizhou Province, or to Bianliang 汴梁, in
the Kaifeng area of Henan Province. The latter seems more likely
because Bianliang is close to the historical location of the State of Wi
in northern China.

77. A Buddha saving a human's life (*hwarin chi Pul* 活人之佛): this expression is often used to describe unexpected help from a person, particularly a monk.

78. "Meet a turtle in the waves of the rivers": this phrase refers to Lady
Wang's encounter with helpers, such as the immortal lad. It reminds

the reader of the belief that a person who donates money to a Buddhist temple or frees captured turtles during the Buddhist ceremony called *pangsaeng* 放生 (Releasing Life) will later receive help from a turtle during a desperate situation. In fact, there are many reports among Buddhist laypeople of a turtle that appeared and ferried them to shore when they were adrift at sea. In Buddhism this turtle is also considered a transformed body of the Bodhisattva.

79. The original text has *sŏngsu*, whose meaning remains unclear. It seems to make the most sense to translate it as a "constellation" (星宿) that is related to one's birth and fate. In the text, the term suggests a particular star god or related spirit that governs Ung's mother and her family.

80. Kul Wŏn 屈原 (Qu Yuan, 343–278 BCE): a poet and minister of the Chu (K. Ch'o) state during the Warring States period. After being wrongfully accused by vile and jealous officials, Qu Yuan fell into great despair and committed suicide by jumping into the Miluo River. Here, Kul Wŏn represents Minister Cho.

81. Childe is a translation of *kongja* 公子, referring to a son of an aristocrat or a high official. In this tale, Wŏlgyŏng calls Ung *kongja*.

82. The original name of this place is unclear. The name of this temple in the surviving editions is either Kangsŏram or Kangsŏnam 降仙庵 (Hut of Descending Immortals). I use "Kangsŏnam" throughout this translation because its meaning is relevant to the religious context of the story.

83. Places with the name of Sanyang 山陽 (C. Shanyang) are found in many parts of China, but the one from Henan Province, southeast of modern Jiaozuo 焦作 county, is probably most pertinent to the story.

84. *Kyŏng'o*: seventh year of the sixty-year cycle. Historically, 430 is the *kyŏng'o* year during the Song dynasty.

85. The original text says *tan'gyo*, which could mean either a broken bridge (斷橋) or a bridge painted in red (丹橋). The former is common in poetry and fiction, and the latter evokes the religious (Buddhist or Daoist) mood of this scene; see Cho Hŭiung, *Cho Ung chŏn* (Seoul: Chimanji, 2009), 96.

86. Immortal's Land (*sŏn'gyŏng* 仙境): an enchanted place deep inside the mountain. The description of this immortal place is similar to the ideal

land of "Peach Blossom Spring" in Tao Yuanming's famous essay "Tohwawŏn'gi" 桃花源記 (Taohuayuan ji; the Tale of Peach Blossom Spring).

87. The original text says "They entered Hyŏngdang [possibly, 荊堂]." Hyŏngdang seems to refer to the name of a hall within the temple, but there is no further clue.

88. This passages evokes the last line of a poem titled "Question and Answer in the Mountains" (Sanjung mundap 山中問答) by the Tang poet Yi Paek 李白 (Li Bo, 701–762 CE), which reads: "You ask me why I reside in the turquoise-colored mountains / With no answer, I smile, feeling at ease / Peach blossoms on the flowing water fade away gradually; / There is another world that is not of humans" (問余何意棲碧山, / 笑而不答心自閑. / 桃花流水杳然去, / 別有天地非人間).

89. Feast at the Hong Gate (Hongmunyŏn 鴻門宴; C. Hongmenyan) refers to a meeting between Yu Pang, Lord of P'ae (Peigong 沛公; K. P'aegong), and Hang U (C. Xiang Yu) at the Hong Gate outside Hamyang 咸陽 (C. Xianyang), the capital city of the Chin (C. Qin) dynasty. Yu and Hang were fighting for rule of the entire empire after the collapse of Chin, and Yu occupied the capital city first. Infuriated, Hang held a banquet for Yu, planning to kill him, but failed. His adviser, Pŏm Chŭng (C. Fan Zeng), regretted the failure and predicted the defeat of Hang U. See notes 52 and 53, book 1, for more information on Yu Pang, Hang U, and Pŏm Chŭng.

90. Kangho 江湖, originally meaning "Rivers and Lakes": as a literary trope, the term often indicates the world of warriors or simply the mundane world. In this text, it indicates an actual place that is thriving and, according to book 2 of the story, is located in the eastern frontier land of the State of Wi.

91. Rough hemp (ch'up'o 麤布): a low-quality hemp fabric. In this text, it is used to reveal the unusual, particularly hermit or Daoist-like, character of the person who wears it.

92. Three-ch'ŏk-long sword (Samch'ŏkkŏm 三尺劍): If "three-ch'ŏk" describes the actual length of the sword, then it is roughly 70 to 100 cm long, though standards of measurement differ; see note 25, book 1, for more information on ch'ŏk. Later in the text, Ung's sword is described as more than three ch'ŏk long. In either case, the sword's title indicates

a long and powerful weapon, regardless of its length. In this tale, moreover, the sword's symbolic meaning is of great interest: it signifies the conquest of the world and foundation of a dynasty. This reference may be traced back to the story of Yu Pang (C. Liu Bang), the founder of the Han dynasty, whose sword also represents conquering the world and founding a dynasty. The *Romance of Three Kingdoms* by Luo Guanzhong (ch. 80) says that Yu Pang's killing of a white snake with his three-ch'ŏk-long sword led to the rise of a righteous army, the conquest of the Chin dynasty, the defeat of Hang U (C. Xiang Yu), and the founding of the Han dynasty (朕想高祖提三尺劍, 斬蛇起義, 平秦滅楚, 創造基業). This symbolic meaning is also recorded in vol. 8 of "Kojo pon'gi" 高祖本紀 (C. Gaozu benji) of the *Record of Grand Historian*: "Whilst I was only a humble commoner, I carried a three-ch'ŏk-long sword to take the world. Is this not the will of heaven?" (吾以布衣提三尺劍取天下, 此非天命乎). These references in famous historical and fictional narratives must have been well known to Korean audiences; indeed, the tale has many references to those two sources. As a result, in the *Tale of Cho Ung*, this particular sword represents Ung's military prowess and destined restoration of the dynasty as fulfillment of heaven's mandate. This subtle placement of Ung in a position comparable to that of Yu Pang strengthens the political theme of the story as well as the image of Ung as a hero. The sword also appears in several other, anonymously written fictional narratives from the late Chosŏn period, such as *Kim Ch'wigyŏng chŏn* 金就景傳 and *Hyŏn Sumun chŏn* 玄壽文傳.

93. The original text shows a typical Korean way of reading classical Chinese text, namely, a combination of Korean reading of Chinese characters and *kugyŏl* (a mnemonic rhyme). The poem in Chinese characters is as follows: "華山道士一袖重 / 月牌可擬賣劍士 / 人言一劍價幾許 / 翁道三時吾有俟 / 紛紛市場幾男子 / 前過千人不願賣 / 雄兒消息問誰知 / 坐則支頤起遠視"; Yi Hŏnhong, *Cho Ung chŏn, Chŏk Sŏngŭi chŏn* (Seoul: Koryŏ taehakkyo minjok munhwa yŏn'guso, 1996), 75.

94. In China, a sword symbolized the authority of a place and a person, and there were stories of a sword associated with Mount Hua 華山 (K. Mount Hwa). For example, Emperor Wu of the Early Han dynasty made eight swords and buried them at Mount Hua and at the

other sacred mountains of Heng 恒 (K. Hang), Song 嵩 (K. Sung), Huo 霍 (K. Kwak) and Tai 泰 (K. T'ae). Another story states that Emperor Xiao Wu 孝武 (362–396 CE) of the Jin 晉 (K. Chin) dynasty had a divine sword 神劍 buried on the peak of Mount Hua in the first year of the Taiyuan 太元 era (376). For more information, see Jin Yiming, *Long xing jian* (Taibei: Yiwen wushu wenhua chuban, 2005), particularly "Jianshu yuanliu."

95. General Star (*changsŏng* 將星): the second star of the Big Dipper (Ursa Major). This auspicious star represents authority and military prowess.

96. A translation of the Korean expression *paekkollanmang*; see note 68, book 1.

97. Mount Kwan (冠山).

98. Ch'ŏlgwan 鐵觀.

99. *Chang* 丈 (C. *zhang*): a traditional unit of length. One *chang* is ten ch'ŏk, and one *ch'ŏk* is ten *ch'ŏn* 寸 (C. *cun*); see note 25, book 1.

100. "Bring his left hand down to his right" (左上右下) is a translation of the word *kongsu* 拱手 in the original text. Men used this gesture of *kongsu* to show respect to a person higher in status or age than themselves. This greeting ritual is still practiced in China.

101. *Paduk* is the Korean *go* game (in China, *weiqi* 圍棋). The game, also known as "the encircling game," involves two parties' competition over surrounding territory. It originates from ancient China and is still popular in East Asia.

102. The Dream Pond (Mongt'aek 夢澤; C. Mengze) is said to have been located in the Chu (Ch'o) state, the present-day Yunmeng 云梦 Lake area in Hubei Province. The use of the name in Tang poems is helpful for understanding the meaning of the passage. In the High Tang poet Meng Haoran's 孟浩然 (K. Maeng Hoyŏn, 689–740) poem "Climbing Mount Xian with Friends" (與諸子登峴山), the "dream pond" represents a person's dark side or unfulfilled dreams as opposed to heaven['s will]. The Late Tang poet Li Shangyin 李商隱 (K. Yi Sang'ŭn, 813–858 CE) wrote a poem with the same title, which tells how a king of Chu led numerous talented women to starve themselves to death because he favored women with tiny waists. In the poem, the pond is depicted as the women's burial place. In both cases, the dream pond represents frustrated dreams or thwarted wills.

103. In the original text, only a Korean reading of the Sino-Korean poem is presented without any interpretation of its meaning, suggesting that the audience would already know what it meant. However, the rendering of this poem, particularly its hidden Sino-Korean characters, varies slightly among scholars. This translation is based my own interpretation: 遽作十年客, 迎見萬里外, 夢澤龍有飛, 是誠未達也.

104. The *Six Secret Teachings* and the *Three Summaries* (Yukto samnyak 六韜三略; C. Liutao sanlüe) refer to two of the Seven Military Classics of ancient China. The authorship of the *Six Teachings* is unclear, but is generally attributed to Kang Chaa 姜子牙 (Jiang Ziya, fl. eleventh century BCE), who helped King Wen 文 found the Zhou dynasty in 1046. His original name was Yŏ Sang 呂尚 (C. Lü Shang), but he was more commonly known as Kang T'aegong 姜太公 (Jiang Taigong; Grand Duke Jiang) or T'aegong Mang 太公望 (Taigong Wang; Grand Duke Wang), and was particularly known for his bizarre way of fishing—with a straight hook and no bait—to pass the time while waiting for better days. The authorship of the *Three Summaries* is more problematic. It was probably written by either Kang Chaa or the Daoist immortal Hwang Sŏkkong 黃石公 (C. Huang Shigong), who is thought to have conveyed it to the Han-dynasty strategist Chang Ryang 張良 (Zhang Liang, ca. 186 BCE). It later became known as Hwang Sŏkkong's *Three Summaries*. For an English translation and more information on the two classics, see *The Seven Military Classics of Ancient China*, trans. Ralph D. Sawyer (Boulder: Westview, 1993).

105. The *Astronomy Chart* (Ch'ŏnmundo 天文圖).

106. Dragon-horse (*yongch'ong* 龍驄) refers to an excellent horse resembling a dragon. According to the *Book of Changes*, it was a mythical horse that emerged from the Luo River, marked with eight trigrams (八卦) on its back.

107. The original text says "Todŏk mun" 道德門, which means the gate of ethics and morality. In religious teaching, this term is often considered a synonym for the gate of precepts and rules (戒律門) that one must learn to observe the practice of Dharma.

108. The original text says "Work of the Way [or Dharma]" (*toŏp* 道業; C. *daoye*). The "Work of the Way" has many connotations in both practical and religious senses, ranging from virtuous acts and religious

practices and arts (Buddhism and Daoism) to beneficial occupations. In the text, *toŏp* seems to make more sense when translated as "magic arts and practices of Daoist [immortals]" called *sŏnsul* 仙術, since this rendering emphasizes the possession of supernatural power and the mastery of magical skills.

109. This sentence is a translation of *kwalmok sangdae* 刮目相待, originating from the story of the Chinese general Lü Meng 呂蒙 (178–220 CE) during the Eastern Han dynasty (25–220 CE). Lü originally did not receive any literary education, but when Sun Quan 孫權 (182–252 CE), the king of the Eastern Wu (220–280 CE), asked him to read books, he quickly mastered them. The expression is Lü Meng's response to Lu Su 魯肅 (172–217 CE), who was surprised at Lü's progress and could not believe that the man he met was the same Lü Meng he used to know.

110. *Chinsa* 進士 refers to a scholar who has passed the literary licentiate, one of the low-level civil service exams. Generally, in the civil service examination system called *kwagŏ* 科舉 (C. *keju*), one must pass either the literary licentiate or the classic licentiate (*saengwŏn* 生員) to take the higher, palace examination (*chŏnsi* 殿試).

111. Maiden Chang is a translation of "Chang Sojŏ" in the original text. "Sojŏ" seems to be *sojŏ* 小姐 (C. *xiaojie*) and frequently appears in heroic martial tales of the late Chosŏn. The term was originally used to refer to the daughter of a wealthy family or a young unmarried woman. However, *sojŏ* has had various connotations, from a young lady of the gentry to a concubine and housemaid or to a woman in the entertainment quarters. In the original text, it is not clear whether Sojŏ is used simply to indicate a *sojŏ* (young maiden) or as the name of the daughter. I translate Sojŏ as "maiden" throughout.

112. "Poetry and calligraphy" (*sisŏ* 詩書).

113. Kŏmun'go: a traditional Korean zither that has six strings.

114. "Tawdry nobleman who are actually beggars" is a translation of *kŏlgaek* 乞客, literally meaning "beggar-guests."

115. The original text says *sŏksang odong* 石上梧桐, meaning the Odong tree that grows on the rocks. Odong is a paulownia tree, also known as the Chinese phoenix or parasol tree. *Sŏksang odong* indicates a very strong paulownia tree, since it grows on the rocks. It is often considered the

best tree for making a Korean zither. The expression is frequently mentioned in *p'ansori* literature.

116. Hang-A 姮娥 (C. Heng E), also known as Sang-A 嫦娥 or 常娥 (C. Chang E) or So-A 素娥 (C. Su E), is a legendary fairy who dwells in the moon. Legend has it that Heng E was originally the wife of the archer Hou Yi 后羿. She stole and swallowed the elixir of immortality, which her husband had received from Xi Wangmu 西王母 (the Queen Mother of the West) for shooting down nine of the ten suns that had been searing the earth, and fled to the moon. She became the spirit of the moon, living a lonely life, accompanied by a hare who would pound the elixir with a mortar and pestle. It is also said that she later took the shape of a toad. For the earlier records of this legend, see Edward L. Shaughnessy, *Unearthing the Changes: Recently Discovered Manuscripts of the Yi Jing (I Ching) and Related Texts* (New York: Columbia University Press, 2014), 155–56.

117. The Ojak Bridge, literally "the Crow and Magpie Bridge" (Ojakkyo 烏鵲橋; C. Wuque qiao), is a famous rendezvous place in the legend of the Cowherd Boy and the Weaving Girl. The doomed couple, torn apart across the Milky Way, are allowed to meet once a year on the seventh night of the seventh month (*ch'ilsŏk* 七夕), and on this day crows and magpies make a bridge by stretching their wings so that the couple can meet on it. For further information on this legend and an English translation of its major texts, see Wilt Idema, *Filial Piety and Its Divine Rewards: The Legend of Dong Yong and Weaving Maiden with Related Texts* (Indianapolis: Hackett, 2009).

118. The Sosang 瀟湘 (C. Xiaoxiang) Rivers are the Xiao and Xiang Rivers near Dongting Lake (洞庭湖) in Hunan Province. The area produces spotted bamboo (斑竹), which is used for making flutes.

119. The original text contains the word *chiŭm* 知音, literally meaning "understanding the sound." The word, originating from the Chinese story of musician Yu Paega 俞伯牙 (C. Yu Boya) and his friend Chong Chagi 鐘子期 (C. Zhong Ziqi), also means "a true friend" or "one's other self." My translation of the passage focuses on expressing Cho Ung's desire to find a person who can understand his music, and thus his heart.

120. For a man's face being "as appealing as jade," see note 18, book 1.

121. A unicorn in the original text is *kirin* 麒麟 (C. *qilin*). In Chinese mythology, it is the unicorn (*kirin*) whose appearance foretells the imminent birth or death of a ruler or a sage. The famous story that a unicorn appeared to the pregnant mother of Confucius to announce the advent of a sage is referenced in this text.

122. A jadelike child: a translation of Kyŏnga 瓊兒 in the original text, following the interpretation by Yi Hŏnhong and Cho Hŭiung. It seems that Lady Wi refers to Maiden Chang as Kyŏnga.

123. "Striking a jade plate with a coral mallet": this expression is a trope describing a beautiful voice or beautiful music.

124. Jade girl (玉女 *ongnyŏ*; C. *yünü*): originally referring to a daughter of the Jade Emperor, or a heavenly maiden, the term later became widely used to describe a beautiful girl or a girl of true nobility.

125. This passage is from *yojo sungnyŏ kunja hogu* 窈窕淑女，君子好逑 in the song "Kwan'gwan chŏgu" 關關雎鳩. It is the first song in the first section of the *Book of Songs* (Shijing 詩經; K. Sigyŏng), titled "Chunam" 周南 (Airs of the Southern Zhou), a part of "Kukp'ung" 國風 (Airs of the States). This particular passage frequently appears in romantic narratives to connote desire for a love relationship or a physical union. The translation is a slightly revised version of Stephen Owen's, included in *An Anthology of Chinese Literature: Beginnings to 1911* (New York: Norton, 1996), 30–31.

126. The Six Rites (六禮) are the traditional rites for marriage, which began during the Spring and Autumn period (ca. 771–403 BCE). The rites consist of 1. "sending the first gift to the bride's home" (*napch'ae* 納采); 2. "asking the eight characters (八字; the year, month, day, and hour of birth time) of the bride" (*munmyŏng* 問名); 3. "consulting ancestors about whether the marriage would be auspicious" (*napkil* 納吉); 4. "sending betrothal gifts to the bride's family" (*napp'ye* 納幣); 5. "asking the bride's family for a wedding date" (*ch'ŏnggi* 請期); and 6. "welcoming the bride to her home" (*ch'inyŏng* 親迎).

127. This sentence, based on the *kyŏngp'an* edition, can also be interpreted as "Ung's lust (sexual desire) blinds his sense of propriety."

128. I, based on Yi Hŏnhong's interpretation, restore the Chinese text for this poem as follows: "洞簫將和玉女琴，/ 寂寞深閨狂夫至. / 金顏冶郎誰家兒，/ 張氏芳緣趙雄是. / 紋帳翠壁掛一袍，/ 奔到華筵弄佳姬. / 晨

風數語掩淚辭, / 消息茫茫不道時"; see Yi, *Cho Ung chŏn, Chŏk Sŏngŭi chŏn*, 95. "Kŭman yarang" 金顏冶郎 may be "Kŭmya arang" 今夜兒郎 (as in the 89-leaf edition at Ewha Womans University), which means "a boy tonight"; see Cho, *Cho Ung Chŏn*, 119.

129. The original text and the 1903 88-leaf and 97-leaf editions say a "blue dragon" (靑龍), but many other editions, including the 89-leaf Ewha Womans University edition and 80-leaf University of Tokyo edition, say "yellow dragon," which is the same as the one that appeared in Maiden Chang's dream.

130. Wisu 渭水 (C. Weishui) refers to the Wei River, located in west-central China's Gansu and Shaanxi Provinces. This is also the location where Kang T'aegong (Grand Duke Jiang) killed time by fishing; see note 104, book 1. *Samdal Wisu* 三達渭水 may also mean that Ung has learned three important aspects of life (e.g. past, present, and future lives in terms of the Buddhist teaching) at the Wei River with someone like Kang T'aegong.

131. *Yangdŭk Ch'ŏnji* (兩得天池). *Ch'ŏnji* means "Heaven Lake" (天池). For information on dragon-horses, see note 106, book 1. The original text says "Ch'ŏnjin," but I view it as "Ch'ŏnji," following the 89-leaf edition at Ewha Womans University.

132. The Chinese text in the original version would read *Kŭmsaeng Yŏsu* 金生麗水, literally meaning "Gold is produced in Yŏsu," a couplet seen in the *Thousand Character Text* (千字文)." This expression, like many others in this tale, frequently appears in Korean poetry and *p'ansori* literature, most famously in the *Tale of Ch'unhyang*. Yŏsu 麗水 (C. Lishui) is a river located in present-day Lijiang 丽江 city in Yunnan Province. This province is known for producing fine gold dust (麩金; C. *fujin*); see Hans Ulrich Vogel, *Marco Polo Was in China: New Evidence from Currencies, Salts, and Revenues* (Leiden: Brill, 2012), 243–48. A couplet, written by a certain Chong 鍾 (C. Zhong), contains the same passage as the one in the text: "The gold from Yŏsu has been the best for a thousand years; with its weight as heavy as Mount T'ae, it will last forever" (金生麗水千年秀, 重如泰山萬古存). It is not clear why Master Wŏlgyŏng brings up this passage, but one clue is that there is a *ch'ŏnji* named Pyŏkko Ch'ŏnji 碧沽天池 (C. Bigu Tianchi) near Yŏsu (Lijiang) that is known for its enchanting scenery.

133. The Chinese character for gold, *kŭm* 金 (C. *jin*), also means metal or metalware.

134. In Korean, the Chinese character for the tiger (*ho* 虎; C. *hu*) is a homophone for the character for "good" (*ho* 好; C. *hao*). This passage seems to reflect Korean people's familiarity with and affinity for tigers: they have been considered the most fearful animal, but are beloved by Koreans for their deep association with Korean folk culture and are even worshipped as guardian spirits.

135. *Chin* hour: 7–9 A.M.; see note 23, book 1.

136. "Making a bet": The original text says "making the bet of a lifetime," but it is unclear exactly what "the bet of a lifetime" means in the text.

137. The *Six Secret Teachings* and the *Three Summaries*: see note 104, book 1.

138. The Central State: the original text says *chungguk* 中國, which can mean both China and the Central State, or Middle Kingdom. Since it is unclear whether the word *chungguk* in the text means "China" as a country, I translate it based on the latter meaning "Central State," implying that it refers to Ung's country, the Great Country of Song. The Central State typically represents the Chinese civilization based on the central plain (中原), located on the lower reaches of the Yellow River. Due to the symbolic meaning of the region as the center of the world, the conqueror of this region gains the political hegemony over the entire Chinese land. For more on the central plain, see note 50, book 1.

139. The Kak Star (*kaksŏng* 角星; C. *jiaoxing*): the star Spica visible in the northern constellation of Virgo. In the East, this star is referred to as the small horn star of the blue dragon, while the Taegak Star (*taegaksŏng* 大角星), Arcturus in the constellation Boötes, is referred as the big horn star of the dragon. Because the Kak Star is located on the southeastern side of the Taegak Star, people often find the Kak Star with the naked eye by following the arc from the Taegak Star to it. In Korea, both the Kak and the Taegak stars are particularly bright in spring. In the city of Namwŏn, they have become the symbols of a famous romantic couple from the *Story of Ch'unhyang*, Sŏng Ch'unhyang (Kak Star) and Yi Mongnyŏng (Taegak Star); in the tale, they meet for the first time in spring.

140. Sŏbŏn 西蕃: literally, "Western Barbarians." The term Sŏbŏn commonly appears in the vernacular fiction of the late Chosŏn, along with the term *Kadal* 假韃 (Fake Northern Barbarians).

BOOK 2

1. This passage describes the practice of clearing a road before a person of high position arrives. When a high official made a trip, a crier would go ahead to inform the people on the street of his impending arrival. People would quickly respond to the shouting and step aside so that the official's sedan chairs could pass easily. For an official of extremely high rank, they knelt down to show respect until the officials had passed. It is interesting to see that the appearance of the ghost general mirrors the ways of the living.

2. Kwansŏ could be Guanxi 關西 or, following the *kyŏngp'an* edition, Guangxi 廣西.

3. "Wish-fulfilling Pearl" is *yŏŭiju* 如意珠 (C. *ruyizhu*), also known as Cintamani, a jewel believed to have supernatural power. In Buddhism, it can bring enlightenment and is often in the possession of the bodhisattvas and (different forms of) the Buddha. In the popular imagination of East Asia, dragons can wield special power through this magical jewel, which they always carry under their chins, and for this reason, they always fight over the jewel.

4. General of the left (*chwajanggun* 左將軍; C. *zuojiangjun*): a high military rank held by generals, along with general of the right (右), front (前), and rear (後), which were collectively called the Four Generals (*sajanggun* 四將軍). The generals were in the third rank (三品) during the Three Kingdoms period of China.

5. Grand field marshal (*taewŏnsu* 大元帥; C. *dayuanshuai*): a high military title superior to the rank of *wŏnsu* (marshal). According to Hucker's dictionary, it was one of the most eminent duty-assignment designations for military commanders on active campaign during the Song dynasty (960–1279); see Hucker, *Official Titles*, #6120, 475.

6. A god of war: the original text says *ch'onsin* 天神, literally meaning "gods of heaven." I have specified a god of war as most pertinent to the context.

7. The chief military officer (*chunggun* 中軍; *zhongjun*): *chunggun* refers to either the middle army or a head military officer. I translate the term depending on the context, but mostly based on the meaning of the latter; for more information, see Hucker, *Official Titles*, #1550, 189.

8. Permanently inking Chinese characters on one's forehead or other parts of a body was known as the "inking punishment," called *muk* 墨 (C. mo) or *kyŏng* (C. *qing*). It is one of five cruel punishments, along with the cutting off noses (*ŭi* 劓; C. *yi*), feet (*wŏl* 刖; C. *yue*), or genitals (*kung* 宮; C. *gong*), and various means of execution, such as boiling (*p'aeng* 烹; C. *peng*), beheading (*hyosu* 梟首; *xiaoshou*), strangulation (*kyo* 絞; C. *jiao*), and slow slicing (*nŭngji* 凌遲; C. *lingchi*).

9. The eight figures serve to create the symbolic presence of the spirits of dead generals by giving a physical form to them. This representation of the dead, known as *si* 尸 (C. *shi*), was common during ancestral worship and mourning/burial rituals in ancient China and Korea. *Si* was later gradually replaced with a memorial tablet. For more information, see Roel Sterckx, "Sacrifice and Sense," in *Food, Sacrifice, and Sagehood in Early China* (New York: Cambridge University Press, 2011), 83–121.

10. Supreme commander (*ch'ongdokchang* 總督將): in general, this title refers to a high-ranking general (rank 2a during Qing China) who is in charge of both military and nonmilitary matters in a certain region.

11. Chief commander (*yujinjang* 留陣將): this title refers to a military official in charge of each camp. The title *yujinjang* frequently appears in Korean (Chosŏn) texts rather than Chinese ones.

12. Prefect: a translation of the official title *chasa* 刺史, whose basic duty was to supervise all administrative units in a region.

13. Sŏgang 西江 (West River).

14. This is the translation of the old saying *hosa tama* 好事多魔.

15. Here "*ŭm* and *yang*" refers to the sexual relationship between a man and a woman; see note 75, book 1.

16. This passage reminds us of the legend of Hang-A, Goddess of the Moon; see note 116 in book 1.

17. Chief magistrates (*suryŏng* 守令): this refers to a governor or chief administrator at a local (prefecture or district/county) level.

18. "Five directions" (*obang* 五方) represents all directions, meaning the north, west, south, east, and center. Typically, in a ritual, one worships the five directions to summon ghosts after lighting the incense. "Banners of the Five Directions" (*obanggi* 五方旗) were first used as military banners and later integrated into Daoist and shamanic rituals

associated with the worship of the Spirit Generals of the Five Directions (*obang sinjang* 五方神將).

19. The original text has the expression "spirit like the frost," a Korean idiom that connotes vigorous strength, like that of a pine tree that has endured the frost.

20. I translate this sentence based on the Hoedong edition, which contains the phrase "having cleaned up my grave" at the beginning of this sentence. The expression "an inn of this world" refers to the first part of Yi Paek's (Li Bo) famous essay "Ch'un yayŏn toriwŏn sŏ" 春夜宴桃李園序 (Preface to the Evening Banquet in the Peach and Plum Garden), which reads: "Heaven and earth are an inn for all the myriad things" 夫天地者, 萬物之逆旅. The tomb in the text seems to mean a lodging place for General Hwang, much as heaven and earth are lodging places for all creation.

21. The poem in Chinese characters is as follows: "華山道士適期返 / 刀劍羌胡滿關山 / 汶汶天地未盡掃 / 快傑相逢有何關."

22. *Cangue* is a translation of *k'al* (C. *mujia* 木枷), a large, flat, rectangular wooden collar worn by a criminal as corporal punishment. It was used in Korea, China, and other parts of East Asia before the twentieth century.

23. Surveillance commissioner (*anch'alsa* 按察使): this title, also known in full as *chehyŏng anch'alsa sa* 提刑按察使司, refers to a high official (rank 3a) dispatched from the central government to each province (*to* 道; C. *dao*) to oversee the general conditions of local government officials; see Hucker, *Official Titles*, # 12; # 6446, 103; 495–96.

24. Marquis of Yangnam (Yangnamhu 梁南侯).

25. Misty moonlight of the O River (*ogang yŏnwŏl* 烏江煙月; C. *wujiang yanyue*): a reference to the last battle and death of Hang U (Xiang Yu), Hegemon King of Ch'o (Chu). After being defeated in battle by Yu Pang (Liu Bang), Hang killed himself in the area of the O River. Before killing himself, he was advised to cross the river and await another opportunity, but Hang U did not do so. His reason was that, because the soldiers from the area across the O River had all died in battle because of him, he didn't dare face their families.

26. Wŏltae's mission was to lure Cho Ung into accepting the title of marquis and staying in Sŏbŏn, but the message of her song was wrongly

focused on the futility of the title and on the death of Hang U, Hegemon King of Ch'o. Her allusion to the death of the famous general and nobleman Hang U offended Cho Ung and subtly mocked his efforts to return to, and fight for, his country. The *kyŏngp'an* edition has a slightly different and more elaborate version of this poem, which reads: "Who can value high the title of marquis, governing ten thousand households and worthy of one thousand gold ingots? / The Hegemon King of Ch'o, whose strength could topple mountains and whose spirit could dominate the world, / Died in vain. / Who can envy the wish of a young novice who has nothing in his hand? / May you change your mind so that you comfortably enjoy wealth and fame." Both poems encourage Ung to lead a realistic and comfortable life rather pursuing his aims.

27. "Moon terrace" is the literal translation of Wŏltae 月臺 in the original text (in the 80-leaf manuscript edition at the University of Tokyo). It is also the name of the singer Wŏltae. By placing Wŏltae's name poetically in the first part of her song, Kŭmnyŏn subtly contrasts herself with Wŏltae, who has failed to change Ung's mind.

28. One branch of the plum tree braving snow (*sŏlchungmae* 雪中梅): the image of the plum tree braving snow and frost has long been a literary trope that represents loyalty and true friendship.

29. Kŏl and Chu refer to the two last emperors of the Ha (Xia) and Sang (Shang) dynasties of China; see note 73 in book 1.

30. The fifth watch: 3–5 A.M., the last portion of night before the morning.

31. Hamji 咸池 (C. Xianchi): a legendary pond that the sun sets into in order to take a bath. It is also called "the peach blossom." This place first appears in the famous song "Iso" 離騷 (C. Lisao) in the *Songs of Chu* (Chuci 楚辭; K. Ch'osa) written by Kul Wŏn (C. Qu Yuan), which reads: "I had my horses drink water at the pond where the sun bathed, / And tied my reins to the mulberry tree of life (hibiscus)" 飲余馬於咸池兮, 總余轡乎扶桑.

32. "A soul that does not return" is a translation of *migwihon* 未歸魂, which indicates the death of a person in a strange land. Such a death is considered unusual and unfortunate.

33. Garrison commander (*pyŏlchang* 別將).

34. News of spring often refers to good news, and the good news in this context implies the return of Ung.

35. Willow trees (楊柳) in East Asian literature often represent parting, ordinariness, flexibility (its branch is easily bendable), or a prostitute or a brothel. The song contrasts the image of the plum tree with that of the willow to stress the fact that the plum blossoms endure the cold weather to bloom. For this reason, along with the pine tree, plum blossoms represent integrity and loyalty. In this song, the plum blossoms indicate the singing maid, since her name is Maehwa 梅花 (plum blossoms), while the news of spring refers to the good news that Ung and his troops will come to save the crown prince.

36. General of the main troop (chunggunjang 中軍將): the head of the middle army. Wŏnch'ung is also referred to as O Wŏnch'ung later in the story. I consider O his surname and insert it here.

37. The song, consisting of 88 lines in the original text, talks about all the historic events in the form of Cho Ung's time travel from the past to the present. In the original texts, events are described as though they are Ung's own experience or as though he witnesses them as an outsider. This song seems to have originated from or be associated with tan'ga (short songs) adopted into p'ansori performance songs, particularly those about ancient heroes, such as "Hongmunyŏn'ga" 鴻門宴歌 (Song of the Feast at the Hong Gate) and "Ch'ohan'ga" 楚漢歌 (Song of the States of Ch'o and Han).

38. The original text notes, "differentiating ch'ŏngt'ak." Ch'ŏngt'ak 清濁 generally connotes "purity and impurity," "good and bad," and "likes and dislikes," but what exactly ch'ŏngt'ak indicates in this passage is unclear. Given that this part of the song starts narrating the events in the prehistoric time of the Three Sovereigns and Five Emperors (三皇五帝), I translate this passage in relation to the achievements of Yellow Emperor (Hwangje 黄帝; C. Huangdi), the first of the Five Emperors, who divided sounds into surds (ch'ŏng 清) and sonants (t'ak 濁), and invented musical scales and instruments. There are different interpretations of who the so-called Three Sovereigns and Five Emperors were. According to one popular interpretation, the Three Sovereigns are Fuxi 伏羲 (K. Pokhŭi), Nüwa 女媧 (K. Yŏwa), and

Shennong 神農 (K. Sinnong), also known as Emperor Yan (K. Yŏm), and the Five Emperors are the Yellow Emperor, Emperor Zhuanxu 顓頊 (K. Chŏnuk), Emperor Ku 嚳 (K. Kok), Emperor Yao 堯 (K. Yo), and Emperor Shun 舜 (K. Sun).

39. This is a reference to the famous myth of "Nüwa (K. Yŏwa) Mending the Sky" (女媧補天). Legend has it that when the four corners of the sky collapsed, resulting in calamities and chaos on earth, Nüwa mended the cracks in the sky with ground rocks of five colors and made the legs of a turtle into four pillars supporting the corners of the repaired sky. Her work put an end to the disaster.

40. The original text includes an expression which can be identified as *yŏmje sesoe ijŏng purhyang* 炎帝世衰 以征不享 in "Oje pon'gi" 五帝本紀 (C. Wudi benji; the Annals of the Five Emperors) in the *Records of the Grand Historian*. My translation is based on the reference, which reads: "In the time of Hŏnwŏn, Sinnong (Emperor Yŏm) was enfeebled. The princes [feudal lords] waged wars against each other and brutally persecuted people, but Sinnong was not able to suppress them. Seeing this, Hŏnwŏn trained his army in using shields and spears, and conquered those defiant princes" 軒轅之時, 神農氏世衰. 諸侯相侵伐, 暴虐百姓, 而神農氏弗能征. 於是軒轅乃習用干戈, 以征不享[直]. Hŏnwŏn 軒轅 (C. Xuanyuan) is the name of the Yellow Emperor.

41. This passage refers to the work of Sinnong, who is also known for the development of agriculture and commerce.

42. This section refers to the flood control measures of Kon 鯀 (C. Gun) during the time of Emperor Yo 堯 (C. Yao). Gun was the father of Yu 禹 (K. U) or Da Yu 大禹 (Yu the great). While Gun, despite his nine years of effort, failed to control the floods, Yu accomplished his father's uncompleted work with thirteen years of toil. Emperor Shun (K. Sun) acknowledged Yu's work and made him the next emperor. The original text includes *kogwŏlsŏnggong* 告厥成功, a reference to "Hasŏ" 夏書 (Xiashu; the Book of Xia) in the *Book of Documents* (Shujing 書經; K. Sŏgyŏng), which reads: "Yu presented the dark scepter and announced the completion of his work" 禹錫玄圭, 告厥成功.

43. After suffering seven years of drought, Emperor T'ang 湯 (C. Tang) of the Sang (C. Shang) dynasty presented himself at the altar to heaven as a sacrificial offering. Considering the natural disaster to be his own

fault, he confessed his six wrongdoings and prayed sincerely for rain in the place called Sangnim 桑林 (C. Sanglin; Mulberry Grove). His prayer was answered before he had finished reciting it.

44.   Yi Yun 伊尹 (Yi Yin, 1648–1549 BCE) was the minister of the Sang dynasty and helped Emperor T'ang defeat Kŏl, the last ruler of the Ha (C. Xia) dynasty. Yi Yun was favored by Korean intellectuals such as Chŏng Tojŏn (1342–1398), who helped Yi Sŏnggye (1335–1408) found the Chosŏn dynasty. For information on Kŏl of Ha, see note 73, book 1.

45.   Both Sun the Great and Chŭng Sam are known for filial devotion. Sun the Great is Emperor Sun (C. Shun), who remained filial toward his blind father Ko Su 瞽瞍 (C. Gu Sou) and stepmother even though they both constantly treated him treacherously. Chŭng Sam 曾參 (Zeng Shen, 505–435 BCE), better known as Chŭngja 曾子 (C. Zengzi), was one of Confucius's favorite disciples. He served his parents well, particularly by understanding and achieving what his parents really wanted. His filial heart was highly praised by Confucius and was devoted to the Confucian teachings that he compiled under the title the *Classic of Filial Piety* (Xiaojing 孝經), which stresses filial piety as the root of all virtues.

46.   Yŏ Sang 呂尚 (C. Lü Shang): Kang T'aegong or T'aegong Mang; see note 104, book 1.

47.   This passage narrates the story of Paegi 伯夷 (C. Boyi) and Sukche 叔齊 (C. Shuqi). Paegi and Sukche were loyal subjects of the Sang dynasty. Having seen the usurpation of the Sang dynasty by King Mu 武 (C. Wu), who built the Chu 周 (C. Zhou) dynasty, Paegi and Sukche refused to eat the rice of the Chu dynasty and went to the Suyang 首陽 (C. Shouyang) Mountain, where they finally starved to death after living for a time on fiddleheads. They became symbols of the loyal subject during the dynastic transition.

48.   For Kul Wŏn's loyalty, see note 80, book 1.

49.   The original text has little information that would point to a possible allusion in this sentence, but it seems to narrate Confucius and his disciple Chagong's 子貢 (C. Zigong) mountainside encounter with a young woman who had lost her father-in-law, husband, and son to a tiger. When they asked her why she lived far up the mountain despite

such tragic deaths, she replied that it was because there was no oppressive government there. In response, Confucius famously said that "tyranny is more dreadful than a tiger" (苛政猛於虎). The related account is found in "Tan'gung ha" 檀弓下 in the *Book of Rites* (Yegi 禮記; C. Liji).

50. This passage talks about the death of Wang Kwang 王光, popularly known as Kae Chach'u 介子推 (C. Jie Zitui) or Kae Chich'u 介之推 (C. Jie Zhitui), a loyal subject from the State of Chin 晉 (Jin, eleventh century–376 BCE) during the Warring States period. When Prince Chungi 重耳 (C. Chong'er) began to starve to death while fleeing, Kae saved him by cutting off a piece of his own flesh and feeding it to him. The prince later became King Mun 文 of Chin and invited Kae to join him, but Kae wanted to live on Myŏn Mountain (綿山; C. Mianshan) with his mother. The king set a fire on the mountain to force him to come out, but only caused Kae to be burned to death. The king grieved, changed the mountain's name to the Kae Mountain, and decreed that no fire be used on the anniversary of Kae's death, a ruling that gave birth to the Cold Food Festival (Hansik chŏl 寒食節; C. Hanshi jie).

51. This passage describes the actions of Ye Yang 豫讓 (Yu Rang), who changed his identity to avenge his former master Chi Paek 智伯 (C. Zhi Bo) by killing Cho Yangja 趙襄子 (Zhao Xiangzi, d. 425 BCE). His plan failed, and when he was captured by Cho he killed himself after slashing Cho's clothes. The Changha 漳河 River (Zhang He; Zhang River) borders Hebei and Henan Provinces. The record of Ye Yang is found in "Cike liezhuan" 刺客列傳 (K. Chagaek yŏlchŏn; the Biographies of Assassins) in the *Records of the Grand Historian*.

52. These lines refer to the meeting in Minji 澠池 (C. Mianchi) between King Hyemun 惠文 of Cho 趙 (C. Zhao) and the king of Chin 秦 (C. Qin) during the Warring States period. At this meeting, the king of the powerful state of Chin asked the king of Cho to play the zither for him. When the king of Cho finished playing, In Sangyŏ 藺相如 (ca. third century BCE), who had escorted the king of Cho, boldly asked the king of Chin to play the pu 瓴 (C. fou), a musical instrument made of clay, for the king of Cho. The king of Chin refused the first time, but eventually played it. This episode shows how In's bravery and strategy helped to protect the dignity of the State of Cho.

53. This passage alludes to the story of Mo Su 毛遂 (Mao Sui, ca. 285–228 BCE), who helped Lord P'yŏngwŏn 平原 (C. Pingyuan) of the State of Cho 趙 (C. Zhao) resolve a military conflict. The State of Cho was between the two powerful states of Chin 秦 (C. Qin) and Ch'o 楚 (C. Chu), and one day the army of the State of Chin surrounded the capital of Cho. Lord P'yŏngwŏn decided to go to Ch'o with twenty retainers to seek relief. Mo Su recommended himself to be included in the twenty. When Lord P'yŏngwŏn couldn't persuade the king of Ch'o after half a day's discussion, Mo Su stepped forth and convinced the king of Ch'o to send his army to rescue Cho, by explaining the benefits Ch'o would get by doing so. The record of this event is found in "P'yŏngwŏn'gun U Kyŏng yŏlchŏn" 平原君虞卿列傳 (C. Pingyuanjun Yu Qing liezhuan) in the *Records of the Grand Historian*.

54. This section refers to the famous scene of the sending off of the assassin Hyŏng Ka 荊軻 (Jing Ke, d. 227 BCE) at the Yŏksu 易水 (Yishui; present-day Baoding 保定 city, Hebei). Hyŏng Ka worked for Prince Tan 丹 (C. Dan) of the State of Yŏn 燕 (C. Yan) and was planning to kill the king of Chin 秦 to help Yŏn. When people sent off Hyŏng Ka at the Yŏksu River, Hyŏng Ka sang these words: "The desolate wind blows over the cold Yŏksu River; a hero, once he leaves, will not return" 風蕭蕭兮易水寒, 壯士一去兮不復還. The related account is found in "Cike liezhuan" in the *Records of the Grand Historian*.

55. For information on the "deer of Chin" (秦鹿), see note 50 in book 1.

56. For information on the Feast at the Hong Gate, see note 89 in book 1.

57. This passage refers to "The Song of Ch'o on Four Sides" 四面楚歌 in the battle of Haeha 垓下 (Gaixia; present-day Lingbi 灵璧 county, Anhui) on Kyemyŏng 鷄鳴 Mountain. In this battle, Chang Ryang played the flute and ordered his soldiers to sing the Ch'o 楚 songs. The songs disrupted Hang U's soldiers by evoking their homesickness and became the main reason for the defeat of Hang U. Hang U killed himself, and the battle ended the dispute between Hang U and Yu Pang over China. Kyemyŏng Mountain is an old name of Chabang Mountain (子房山; C. Zifangshan), which was named after Chang Ryang's courtesy name "Chabang" and is located in present-day Xuzhou 徐州 city, Anhui. The name Kyemyŏng Mountain appears more commonly than Chabang Mountain in Korean texts about the Haeha battle,

particularly *p'ansori* literature. For Hang U, Yu Pang, and Chang Ryang, see notes 52 and 104, book 1.

58. This passage narrates an anecdotal story of General Han Sin 韓信 (Han Xin, 231–196 BCE) from Hoeŭm city (present-day, Huai'an 淮安 city, Jiangsu). Han Sin worked for Yu Pang and was known as one of three heroes of the Early Han dynasty, along with Chang Ryang (C. Zhang Liang) and So Ha (C. Xiao He, d. 193 BCE). Yet, before his successes, Han Sin had suffered from hunger and abuse due to his poor family background. The food from "the old lady washing clothes" in the text is often mentioned in literature to show the difficulties of Han's early life as well as to praise the lady's compassion and ability to recognize a potential hero. Han didn't forget to reward the lady; he gave her a thousand gold ingots when he returned to his hometown. The record can be found in "Hoeŭmhu yŏlchŏn," in the *Records of the Grand Historian*.

59. Ki Sin 紀信 (Ji Xin, ca. d. 204): general under Yu Pang. When Yu Pang was besieged in Hyŏngyang 滎陽 (Xingyang; present-day Zhengzhou, Henan) by Hang U's soldiers, Ki Sin presented an escape plan for Yu Pang; he volunteered to disguise himself as Yu Pang and to fake a surrender to Hang U. Yu Pang escaped as planned, and Ki Sin was burned to death by Hang U.

60. The Unicorn Hall (Kiringak 麒麟閣) was built during the reign of Han Emperor Mu 武 (Wu, r. 141–87 BCE). The hall displayed the portraits of eleven famous ministers on its walls during the time of Emperor Sŏn 宣 (Xuan, 91–49 BCE). Since then, the Unicorn Hall refers to a place in which the meritorious are honored (Kongsingak 功臣閣); see note 121, book 1.

61. "Burned jade and stone": the original text has a direct reference to *hwayŏm kon'gang oksŏk kubun* 火炎崑岡 玉石俱焚 in the chapter of "Yunjŏng" 胤征 of "Hasŏ" in the *Book of Documents*. The trope of "burning jade and stone together" is also seen in note 29, book 1.

62. The original text includes the expressions *mangji yŏun* 望之如雲 and *ch'wiji yŏil* 就之如日, which refer to the record of Emperor Yo 堯 in the "Oje pon'gi" 五帝本紀 (C. Wudi benji) in the *Records of the Grand Historian*. The expressions were used to describe people's attitude toward the benevolent Emperor Yo.

63. The *myo* 卯 (C. *mao*) hour: 5–7 A.M.

64. The original text mentions "three immortal souls" (*samhon* 三魂; C. *san-hun*). For the meaning of these three souls, see note 60, book 1.

65. This passage narrates the story of the treasured swords (寶劍) of the Chin 晉 (C. Jin) dynasty. Chang Hwa (Zhang Hua, 232–300 CE) saw that there was always a purple pneuma (紫氣) in the sky between the Dipper and Altair. Thinking it strange, he summoned the astronomer Noe Hwan 雷煥 (Lei Huan) to ask about it. Noe Hwan explained that the strange energy between the two stars is the essence of a treasure sword, which would be found in the P'ungsŏng 豐城 (C. Fengcheng) city of Yejang 豫章 (Yuzhang; present-day in Nanchang in Jiangxi). Chang appointed Noe as the magistrate of P'ungsŏng to find it. Noe Hwan discovered two treasure swords buried under the prison house, and on each sword a name was carved: Yongch'ŏn 龍泉 (C. Longquan) Sword, and T'aea 太阿 (C. Tai'e) Sword. Noe sent the former sword to Chang and kept the latter. After these swords were found, the purple pneuma disappeared. These two swords, however, disappeared after Chang and Noe died, and later transformed into two dragons flying into the sky. P'ungsŏng city belonged to the region of O 吳 (C. Wu), and, later on, swords from P'ungsŏng or the O area were regarded as among the best swords in China. A historical account for the swords is found of the "Chang Hwa chŏn" 張華傳 (Zhang Hua zhuan; the Biography of Zhang Hua), vol. 36 in the *Book of Jin* (晉書).

66. King Yama is Yŏmna Taewang 閻羅大王, also known as the king of the netherworld, underworld, or afterworld in English. In Chinese and Korean folk beliefs, he judges the dead and punishes them according to their deeds before death.

67. Minister of the right: the original text reads *ubogya* 右僕射 (C. *youpuye*), a rank similar to, or slightly lower than, that of *sangsŏryŏng* 尚書令 (C. *shangshuling*), one of the most powerful posts in the central government. There is also *chwabogya* 左僕射, meaning minister of the left; see Hucker, *Official Titles*, #4826, 394–95 (also in note 5, book 1). The position has existed in Korea since the Koryŏ dynasty (918–1392), and its rank has been between 2a and 1b.

68. Chegal Ryang 諸葛亮 (Zhuge Liang, 181–234): Chegal was a famous statesman and strategist of the State of Ch'ok 蜀 (Shu) during the

Three Kingdoms period of China. Chegal was also known for his strong command of Daoist magic.

69. Minister of the left (*chwabogya* 左僕射); see note 67, book 2.

70. The term "dragon robe" refers to the dress of emperors and kings.

71. Hamgok of Yŏnju: this place may refer to Hamgok 函谷 (C. Han'gu) in the Yŏnju 兗州 (C. Yanzhou) area. Yanzhou, located between the Yellow River (黃河) and the Ji River (濟水) (flowing from Henan through Shandong), is close to several places mentioned in the story, such as Sanyang and Mount T'ae Prefecture. Hamgok is a deep mountainous area, located in present-day Henan Province. Due to its strategic location, Hamgok was famous for many ancient battles, particularly those involving the State of Chin 秦 (C. Qin) and many other states during the Warring States period.

72. Sword Pavilion is Kŏmgak 劍閣 (C. Jiange), and Mount Iron is Ch'ŏlsan 鐵山 (C. Tieshan).

73. As in the cases of the two poems in book 1, the original text here has the Korean reading of Chinese texts followed by their interpretation in old Korean. Interestingly, unlike the previous two poems, this one shows occasional discrepancies or gaps between the Korean reading of the Chinese texts and the subsequent Korean explanation of them, which presents some challenges to restoring the complete Chinese characters. To date, despite scholars' efforts to restore the Chinese texts given here, many parts remained unexplained. However, my research shows that the Chinese text on which the original text is based is from "Hanbu" 恨賦 (Henfu; the Rhapsody on Resentment) by Kang Ŏm 江淹 (Jiang Yan, 444–505) of the Song (Liu) dynasty. The gaps between the Chinese text and the Korean explanation of the original text, as we will see, seem to be attributable to the complexity of the Korean appropriation of the Chinese text—that is, to the modification, misinterpretation, or even parody of meaning of the Chinese texts in translation. I keep both parts intact in this translation to illustrate the nature of the appreciation of the Chinese texts among general Korean (mostly late Chosŏn) audiences.

74. The meaning of this passage (the Korean explanation of the Chinese poem) is unclear, particularly due to the Korean word *chipp'in* in the original text. Scholars such as Cho Hŭiung and Yi Hŏnhong interpret this word as a variation of *kip'ŭn* ("deep"), and present the following

translation, "Deep thoughts are not many," while suggesting 深情已不灘 as the Chinese characters for this passage. I follow such an interpretation here. However, the word *chipp'in* may be interpreted differently, for example, as a short form of *chip'inŭn* ("figure out"), presenting an alternative interpretation that "there are not many I can discern in my heart." Further research is needed to verify the meaning of this passage.

75.   The Chinese text for the first writing and its translation are as follows: "By nature, I am a resentful person. The astonishment of heart never stopped. Thinking of ancient times, people died with their resentment kept inside" 僕本恨人, 心驚不已, 直念古者, 伏恨而死; see Jiang Yan, "Henfu," in *Liang Jiang Wentong wenji, Sibu congkan chubian suoben* (Taibei: Shangwu yinshuguan, 1967), v. 34, 1:5.

76.   The Chinese characters for this writing and its translation are as follows: "When the Emperor of Chin (C. Qin) wielded his sword, all feudal lords marched westward to the capital. When he subjugated the whole world, he unified the script and standardized the track gauge of wheeled vehicles" 秦帝按劍, 諸侯西馳. 削乎天下, 同文共規; see Jiang Yan, "Henfu," 5. This Chinese text comes right after the Chinese text cited in note 75. This use of Jiang Yan's "Henfu" shows that the Chinese literature of the Song (Liu) has been incorporated into the main text by the original author to evoke nostalgia among audiences for past heroes who lived during chaotic times and empathy for the deep sorrow hidden behind their spectacular accomplishments.

77.   The original text of this passage has *hok to hok pi*, and its Chinese characters seem to be 或跳或飛 ("Some were jumping and soaring into the air"). Yet some scholars interpret this passage as *hok no hok pi* 或怒 或悲 ("Some were angry and saddened"); see Cho Hŭiung, *Cho Ung chŏn*, 213.

BOOK 3

1.   See note 62, book 1.

2.   Mount Ak (Aksan 岳山; C. Yueshan): this seems to refer to Mount Yue, which is located in Baoji 宝鸡 in Shaanxi Province.

3.   The pavilions of the pass at Mount Kŏm (Kŏmgak 劍閣; C. Jiange): this pass is located in present-day Guangyuan 广元, Sichuan Province, also known as Jianmenguan 劍門關; it has seventy-two peaks and one narrow, high mountain path.

4. The Blue Donkey (青驢): this appears in the ancient tales of immortals and renowned figures. For example, in the *Hwarang seji* 花郎世紀 (the Annals of Hwarang), Prince Pojong (d. 621) of the Silla 新羅 dynasty (57 BCE–935 CE) used to ride a blue donkey and play the flute, which gave him the title of *chinsŏn kongja* 眞仙公子 (Prince of True Immortality).

5. White feather fan: a fan made of the wing and tail feathers of birds such as geese, pheasants, cranes, and peacocks. The image has been used for more than two thousand years among East Asian people, in denoting among officials, scholars, and generals. The fan is also associated with literary and religious (Daoist) tropes of magical power and immortality. For example, a white fan made of crane feathers often appears in descriptions of the most famous Chinese military strategist, Zhuge Liang (K. Chegal Ryang), evoking his magical talent and abilities.

6. Mount Oro (五老峰 or 五老山; C. Wulaofeng): this mountain is located in Yongji 永济 in Shanxi Province.

7. The hour of *o* 午: 11 A.M.–1 P.M.

8. The letter of the king of Wi only mentions Ung's mother. Yet, Ung's mother represents his family members also; later in the story, it turns out that Ung's wife and mother-in-law also came to Wi and waited for Ung.

9. Chamberlain for law enforcement (*chŏngwi* 廷尉; C. *tingwei*): an official who was in charge of recommending decisions on punishment and imprisonment of questionable cases reported by administrative units; see Hucker, *Official Titles*, #6767, 512.

10. Chamberlain for the National Treasury (*ch'isok naesa* 治粟內史): an official who was in charge of granaries.

11. General of the West Pass (*sŏgwanjang* 西關將): an official who was in charge of defending the western outskirts of the capital.

12. The Six Rites: see note 126, book 1.

13. The original passage has a reference to the song of the *Book of Songs* that appeared earlier in the story: "Gentle maiden, pure and fair / Fit match for a prince"; for more information, see note 125, book 1.

14. "To take a wedding bow" refers to part of wedding ceremony. The bride and groom formally kowtow to each other right after their entrance to the wedding hall.

15. "Plighting Troth (*chŏnan* 奠鴈; C. *dianyan*): a wedding ritual in which the groom brings a pair of wooden wild geese to the house of the bride and pours libations before them, as a symbol of faithful love.

16. The original text has *ŭndae*, which seems to refer to the Silver Terrace (銀臺). The Silver Terrace can mean a government office such as the Hallim Academy of Arts and Letters, or a place of immortals, particularly a palace of the Western Queen Mother. I translate based on the latter.

17. Hak Mountain (Haksan 鶴山).

18. Pyŏnyang: this place appears as Pŏnyang (藩陽) in the 80-leaf manuscript edition from the University of Tokyo.

19. There have been different interpretations of this passage. Cho Hŭiung and Yi Hŏnhong translate it as "the Jade Emperor lures people into this place," thinking the first word of this passage is *okche* 玉帝 (Jade Emperor). But I view it as *okkye* 玉溪 (Jadelike Stream), thinking that this passage describes the quiet and secluded scenery of the mountain, hinting at the location of the house. My translation here is based on " 玉溪百里清流" in the 80-leaf manuscript edition from the University of Tokyo, which makes more sense in the context.

20. The original text has the expression *puji ch'ŏn'go chihu* 不知天高地厚, a Chinese proverb, meaning "not knowing the immensity of heaven and earth."

21. See note 73, book 1.

22. The original text says "Ch'ŏnmyŏng." In this translation, I replace it with "masters" to reduce confusion. "Ch'ŏnmyŏng" is likely an error since Ung learned skills from Masters Wŏlgyŏng and Ch'ŏlgwan. In the context of "meeting by chance," it is more likely to indicate Wŏlgyŏng than Chŏlgwan. Another edition (the 89-leaf edition from Ewha Womans University) mentions only Ung's encounter with Ch'ŏnmyŏng, but not his learning under him.

23. General of the gentlemen-of-the-household (*chungnangjang* 中郎將): this position was in charge of the Three Corps (*samsŏ* 三署; C. *sanshu*) of court gentlemen (*rang* 郎; C. *lang*), that is, expectant appointees; see Hucker, *Official Titles*, #1581, 191. This Yi Hwang is different from the Yi Hwang of Sŏbŏn.

24. Commander in chief (*taesama* 大司馬; C. *dasima*): this position, which ranked as a minister, was responsible for all military personnel and activities; see Hucker, *Official Titles*, #6039, 471.

25. Consecrated helmet: this is my translation of the term *Pongch'ŏn t'ugu* in the original text. While *t'ugu* means a helmet, the meaning of *pongch'ŏn* 奉天 (Tribute to Heaven) can be various; it could be the name of the place where the helmet was made or a characteristic of a helmet. My translation is based on the latter.

26. See note 58, book 2.

27. P'aeng Wŏl 彭越 (Peng Yue, d. 196 BCE): a general and leader of the Late Qin and Early Han dynasties. He helped Liu Bang defeat Xiang Yu at the Battle of Gaixia and received the title of the king of Liang (梁王) for his contribution to Liu's victory. Peng Yue, like Han Xin (K. Han Sin), was well known for his military valor and accomplishment. Unfortunately, both Peng and Han were removed by Liu and his people after the Han dynasty was established.

28. East Pass (東關).

29. In the original text, a term for a spy (*ch'et'am* 體探) comes right after the general of the West Pass. I interpret this to mean that the spy belonged to the general of the West Pass.

30. Sŏju 西州 in the 80-leaf manuscript edition from the University of Tokyo.

31. Chang Tŏk 張德 in the 80-leaf manuscript edition from the University of Tokyo.

32. In the 80-leaf manuscript edition from the University of Tokyo, Kang Paek's (姜伯) father is named Kang Kil (姜吉).

33. Wi Kiltae 衛吉大 in the 80-leaf manuscript edition from the University of Tokyo.

34. Wi Yŏng appears as Wi Ryŏng (衛令) in the 80-leaf manuscript edition from the University of Tokyo.

35. Kwan Mountain (Kwansan 關山; Guanshan): this Kwansan could actually mean a mountain pass because *kwan* refers to passes. It could also simply indicate the name of a mountain near the capital city. There are places called Guanshan in China (Shandong, and Xi'an) and Taiwan.

36. See note 3, book 2.

37. Commander in chief (*sama* 司馬); *sama* is commonly an abbreviated reference to *taesama*.

38. Royal Sword is a translation of *ingŏm* 引劍, which refers to a sword bestowed by the emperor upon a commander. With this sword, the commander could execute any solider who disobeyed his order.

39. First Watch (ch'ogyŏng 初更): 7–9 P.M.

40. Iltae 一大, Idae 二大, and Samdae 三大.

41. Purple Star (chamisŏng 紫微星; ziweixing): literally meaning "purple (noble) rose star," this refers to the North Star, the most prominent star in the constellation known as Purple Forbidden Enclosure (chamiwŏn 紫微垣; ziweiyuan). Due to its central position, the star represents the character and state of the emperor in the world. For example, if the star loses its light, it indicates that misfortune will fall on the emperor; see also note 27, book 1.

42. "Wing under Samdae's left arm": wings are a Daoist trope often associated with becoming immortal (羽化而登仙). The human body becomes as light as a feather and ascends to heaven. In this text, Samdae's "wing" seems to refer to the Daoist magic with which Samdae was furnished, perhaps with the help of Daoist immortals.

43. Caged wagon: this means a wagon with bars or fencing on all four sides and above. It was referred to as hamgŏ 轞車 or 檻車 (C. jianche), and was used for transporting prisoners and animals.

44. Hwangja River: this river seems to be the large river Ung crossed with his mother when he escaped from the capital as an eight-year-old boy. The river is named the Yangja River (Yangzi 揚子 River) instead of the Hwangja River in the edition included in Chosŏn sosŏlchip, the collection of Korean novels published by Progress, a Moscow-based Soviet publisher, in 1966; see Chosŏn sosŏlchip, 428. But it appears as the Hwangp'a 黃波 River in the 80-leaf manuscript edition from the University of Tokyo.

45. Kadal 假韃 (Fake Northern Barbarians) or 加達; the Kadal, like the Sŏbŏn, were a northern barbarian tribe whose name appears frequently in the vernacular fiction of the Chosŏn dynasty; see also note 140, book 1.

46. The "Earth-Drumming Song" (擊壤歌): see note 2, book 1. The times of Emperors Yo 堯 (C. Yao) and Sun 舜 (C. Shun) represents the peaceful period in ancient Chinese history, which is also commonly signified by the common people's singing of the "Earth-Drumming Song."

47. Queen of chastity (貞淑王妃): there is no mention of the Wi princess, Ung's second wife, in the scenes of the Cho family's arrival in the capital city and the crown prince's giving rewards in either the original text or other wanp'an editions. In the kyŏngp'an edition, however, the

Wi princess also arrives in the city and is rewarded as a lady of chastity
(貞淑夫人).

48. Grand academician (太學士).

49. The *kyŏngp'an* edition enumerates the rewards in more detail; it includes
extensive descriptions of the rewards that Ung's family received, as well
as how Ung recalls and rewards all the people who helped him, his
mother, and the crown prince during his journey—such as the woman
in the Paekcha Village, Ung's Daoist masters, and the female enter-
tainer in Kyeryangdo.

50. See note 46, book 3.

51. In this last scene, the *kyŏngp'an* edition focuses on the continued bless-
ing and prosperity of Ung's family; for example, Ung has six sons and
three daughters from his two wives and one concubine, who all turn
out to be successful in their careers and marriages. It also shows how
Ung is filial to his mother and mother-in-law. He keeps the three-year
mourning period after their deaths, in accordance with the Confucian
funeral ritual, and soon thereafter he himself also dies. Finally, the story
ends with the emperor's death and ascension to the throne of his eldest
son (the crown prince). Both the *kyŏngp'an* and *wanp'an* editions conclude
by emphasizing that the new world Ung brings to the people is a har-
monious one. However, the *kyŏngp'an* edition focuses on the details of
the success and rewards of Ung's journey, whereas the *wanp'an* editions
present them rather briefly, as the finale to the long tale, and place more
emphasis on the value and meaning of Ung's journey. In addition, by
including the deaths of Cho Ung and of the emperor and describing
how their legacies continue within the family and the state, the *kyŏngp'an*
edition exemplifies Confucian thought. In contrast, the *wanp'an* editions end with Ung and the emperor still alive, suggesting that they
and the narrative will have a long eternal life among readers.

REFERENCES

Primary Original Texts

Cho Tongil. *Cho Tongil sojang kungmunhak yŏn'gu charyo.* Vol. 12. P'ilsabon sosŏl. Seoul: Pagijŏng, 1999.

Cho Ung chŏn. 104 leaves. n.p., 1857. In vol. 3 of *Kyŏngin kososŏl p'an'gakpon chŏnjip,* edited by Kim Tonguk, W. E. Skillend, and D. Bouchez, 147–99. Seoul: Nason sŏsil, 1975.

Cho Ung chŏn. 97 leaves. Wansan sin'gan, the *imjin* year (1892). Sogang University.

Cho Ung chŏn. 88 leaves. Wansan pungmun, the seventh year of Kwangmu (1903). Digital Hangeul Museum.

Cho Ung chŏn. 97 leaves. Wansan pugmun nae chunggan, the seventh year of Kwangmu (1903). National Library of Korea.

Cho Ung chŏn. 89 leaves. n.p., n.d. Ewha Womans University; also University of Tokyo (Ogura Collection).

Cho Ung chŏn. 80 leaves. Wannam sin'gan, the *musul* year (1898). C. V. Starr East Asian Library, University of California at Berkeley.

Cho Ung chŏn 趙熊傳. 80 leaves. Posŏng, Chŏlla-namdo, the *imja* year (1912?). University of Tokyo (Ogura Collection).

Cho Ung chŏn. 2 vols. Harvard-Yenching Library, Harvard University.

Cho(Tyo) Ung chŏn. Ansŏng, n.d. University of Tokyo (Toyo Bunko Collection).

Cho Ung chŏn. Seoul: Tongyang sŏwŏn, 1925; reprinted in *Adan mun'go ch'ongsŏ,* edited by Adan Mun'go Kihoeksil. Seoul: Hyŏnsil munhwa, 2007.

Ihwa Yŏja Taehakkyo Han'guk Munhwawŏn. *Han'guk kodae sosŏl ch'ongsŏ.* Seoul: T'ongmun'gwan, 1958.

Kim Tonguk, W. E. Skillend, and D. Bouchez, eds. *Kyŏngin kososŏl p'an'gakpon chŏnjip.* 5 vols. Seoul: Nason sŏsil, 1975.

Sin T'aesam, ed. *Cho Ung chŏn.* Seoul: Sech'ang sŏgwan, 1952.

Wŏlch'on Munhŏn Yŏn'guso, ed. *Han'gŭl p'ilsabon kososŏl charyo ch'ongsŏ.* Vol. 91. Seoul: Osŏngsa, 1986. Wŏn'gwang Taehakkyo Pak Sun-ho Kyosu sojangbon.

COLLATED MODERN KOREAN EDITIONS
AND TRANSLATIONS

Cho Hŭiung. *Kyŏngp'an Cho (Tyo) Ung chŏn.* Seoul: Chimanji, 2013.

——. *Cho (Tyo) Ung chŏn.* Seoul: Chimanji, 2009.

Hong Hyomin. *Cho Ung chŏn.* Seoul: Ŭryu munhwasa, 1962.

Kim Chaedu. *Cho Ung chŏn.* In *Chosŏn sosŏlchip: Hyŏndaeŏ p'an,* 311–527. Moscow: Progress, 1966.

Kim Kidong and Chŏn Kyut'ae. *Cho Ung chŏn, Chang Han chŏrhyogi.* Seoul: Sŏmundang, 1984.

Ku Inhwan. *Cho Ung chŏn.* Seoul: Sinwŏn munhwasa, 2004.

Yi Chuyŏng. "Han'guk kojŏn sosŏl ŭi tokcha." In Yi Sangt'aek et al., *Han'guk kojŏn sosŏl ŭi segye,* 107–29. Seoul: Tolbegae, 2005.

Yi Hŏnhong. *Cho Ung chŏn, Chŏk Sŏngŭi chŏn.* Seoul: Koryŏ taehakkyo minjok munhwa yŏn'guso, 1996.

Yi Myŏngnang. *Cho Ung chŏn.* Seoul: Ch'angbi, 2005.

SECONDARY SOURCES

Campbell, Joseph. *The Hero with a Thousand Faces.* 3d rev. ed. Novato, CA: New World Library, 2008.

Ch'ae Chegong. "Yŏ Sasŏ sŏ." In *Han'guk kososŏl kwallyŏn charyojip* II, edited by Muak Kososŏl Charyo Yŏn'guhoe. Seoul: Ihoe munhwasa, 2005.

Chia, Lucille. *Printing for Profit: The Commercial Publishers of Jianyang, Fujian (11–17th Centuries)*. Cambridge: Harvard University Asia Center, 2003.

Cho Hŭiung. "Cho Ung chŏn ibon'go mit kyojubo." *Ŏmunhak nonch'ong* (1993): 41–58.

——. "Cho Ung chŏn." In *Kojŏn sosŏl yŏn'gu*, edited by Hwagyŏng Kojŏn Munhak Yŏn'guhoe, 712–46. Seoul: Ilchisa, 1993.

——. "Han'guk sŏsa munhak ŭi konggan kaenyŏm." *Kojŏn munhak yŏn'gu* 1 (1971): 97–114.

——. *Kojŏn sosŏl ibon mongnok*. Seoul: Chimmundang, 1999.

——. *Kojŏn sosŏl yŏn'gu pojŏng*. 2 vols. Seoul: Pagijŏng, 2006.

——. "Kojŏn sosŏl yŏn'gu sŏsŏl (1)." *Han'guk ŏnŏ munhwa* 1 (1974): 19–47.

——. "17segi kungmun kojŏn sosŏl ŭi hyŏngsŏng e taehayŏ: Sukhyang chŏn ŭl chungsimŭro." *Ŏmunhak nonch'ong* 14 (1997): 19–31.

Cho Tongil. *Han'guk sosŏl ŭi iron*. Seoul: Chisiksanŏpsa, 1977.

Ch'oe Hosŏk. *Hwalchabon kojŏnsosŏl sŏji teit'ŏbeisŭ*. P'aju: Pogosa, 2017.

Ch'oe Sugyŏng. "Ch'ŏngdae chaejagain sosŏl ŭi yŏn'gu." PhD diss., Koryŏ University, 2001.

Ch'oe Yongch'ŏl and Pak Chaeyŏn, eds. *Chŏndŭng sinhwa*. Han'gŭl saenghwalsa charyo ch'ongsŏ/Pŏnyŏk kososŏl. Seoul: Hakkobang, 2009.

Chŏn Sanguk. "Sech'aek ch'ong mongnok e taehan yŏn'gu." *Yŏlsang kojŏn yŏn'gu* 30 (2009): 163–83.

Chŏn Sŏngun. "Cho Ung chŏn inmul hyŏngsang ŭi punjang." *Uriŏmun yŏn'gu* 44 (2012): 243–73.

Chŏng Pyŏngsŏl. "Chosŏn hugi ŭi Han'gŭl sosŏl param." *Han'guksa simin kangjwa* 8 (2005): 140–54.

——. "Chosŏn hugi Han'gŭl panggak sosŏl ŭi chŏn'gukchŏk yut'ong kanŭngsŏng e taehan siron." *Tasan'gwa hyŏndae* 3 (2010): 115–33.

——. *Chosŏn sidae sosŏl ŭi saengsan kwa yut'ong*. Seoul: Sŏul taehakkyo ch'ulp'an munhwawŏn, 2016.

Courant, Maurice. *Bibliographie coréenne: Tableau littéraire de la Corée, contenant la nomenclature des ouvrages publiés dans ce pays jusqu'en 1890 ainsi que la description et l'analyse détaillées des principaux d'entre ces ouvrages*. Paris: E. Leroux, 1894; *Han'guk sŏji*, translated by Yi Hŭijae. Seoul: Nuri Midiŏ, 1994.

Deuchler, Martina. *The Confucian Transformation of Korea: A Study of Society and Ideology*. Cambridge: Harvard University Asia Center, 1995.

——. "Propagating Female Virtues in Chosŏn Korea." In *Women and Confucian Cultures in Premodern China, Korea, and Japan*, edited by Dorothy Ko, JaHyun Kim Haboush, and Joan R. Piggott, 142–69. Berkeley: University of California Press, 2003.

Dillon, Michael, ed. *China: A Cultural and Historical Dictionary*. Richmond, Surrey: Curzon, 1998.

Haboush, JaHyun Kim. "Filial Emotions and Filial Values: Changing Patterns in The Discourse of Filiality in Late Chosŏn Korea." *Harvard Journal of Asiatic Studies* 55, no. 1 (1995): 129–77.

——. "Versions and Subversions: Patriarchy and Polygamy in Korean Narratives." In *Women and Confucian Cultures in Premodern China, Korea, and Japan*, edited by Dorothy Ko, JaHyun Kim Haboush, and Joan R. Piggott, 279–304. Berkeley: University of California Press, 2003.

Han'guk Chŏngsin Munhwa Yŏn'guwŏn. *Han'guk kojŏnsosŏl tokhae sajŏn*. Seoul: T'aehaksa 1999.

——. *Han'guk kososŏl mongnok*. Seoul: Han'guk Chŏngsin Munhwa Yŏn'guwŏn, 1983.

Han'guk Kojŏnmunhakhoe. *Han'guk sosŏlmunhak ŭi t'amgu*. Seoul: Chungang ch'ulp'an, 1981.

Han'guk Kojŏnsosŏl P'yŏnch'an Wiwŏnhoe. *Han'guk kojŏn sosŏllon*. Seoul: Saemunsa, 1990.

Han'guk Kososŏl Hakhoe. *Kojŏn sosŏl ŭi sot'ong kwa kyosŏp*. Seoul: Pogosa, 2013.

Han'guk Kososŏl Yŏn'guhoe. *Han'guk kososŏllon*. Seoul: Asea munhwasa, 1991.

Herman, David. *Storytelling and the Sciences of Mind*. Cambridge: MIT Press, 2013.

Hiltebeitel, Alf, and Barbara D Miller, eds. *Hair: Its Power and Meaning in Asian Cultures*. Albany: State University of New York Press, 1998.

Hŏ Kyun. *The Story of Hong Gildong*. Translated by Minsoo Kang. New York: Penguin, 2016.

Ho, Peng Yoke. *Chinese Mathematical Astrology: Reaching out to the Stars*. New York: RoutledgeCurzon, 2003.

——. *Li, Qi and Shu: An Introduction to Science and Civilization in China*. Hong Kong: Hong Kong University Press, 1985.

Hucker, Charles O. *A Dictionary of Official Titles in Imperial China*. Stanford: Stanford University Press, 1985.

Idema, Wilt L., ed. and trans. *Filial Piety and Its Divine Rewards: The Legend of Dong Yong and Weaving Maiden, with Related Texts*. Indianapolis: Hackett, 2009.

Im Ch'igyun. "Chosŏn hugi sosŏl ŭi chŏn'gae wa yŏsŏng ŭi yŏkhal." In vol. 5 of *Han'guk sŏsa munhaksa yŏn'gu*, edited by Sa Chaedong, 1675–93. Taejŏn: Chungang munhwasa, 1995.

——. "Han'guk kojŏn sosŏl ŭi hawi changnŭ wa yuhyŏng." In Yi Sangt'aek et al., *Han'guk kojŏn sosŏl ŭi segye*, 60–85. Seoul: Tolbegae, 2005.

Im Sŏngnae. *Yŏngung sosŏl ŭi yuhyŏng yŏn'gu*. Seoul: T'aehaksa, 1990.

Jiang Yan. *Liang Jiang Wentong wenji*. In vol. 34 of *Sibu congkan chubian suoben*. Taibei: Shangwu yinshuguan, 1967.

Jin Yiming. *Long xing jian*. Taibei: Yiwen wushu wenhua chuban, 2005.

Kan Hoyun. *Arŭmdaun uri kososŏl: Chŭlgŏun sangsang kwa haehak ŭro kadŭkhan Han'guk kososŏl ch'ŏnnyŏn ŭi segye*. P'aju: Kimyŏngsa, 2010.

Kang Myŏnggwan. *Chosŏn sidae munhak yesul ŭi saengsŏng konggan*. Seoul: Somyŏng, 1999.

Kim Chaeung. "Yŏngnam chiyŏk p'ilsabon kososŏl e nat'anan yŏsŏng hyangyuch'ŭng ŭi yongmang." *Han'guk kojŏn yŏsŏng munhak yŏn'gu* 16 (2008): 5–37.

Kim Chinyŏng. "Kojŏn sosŏl ŭi kyŏngjejŏk yut'ong kwa kŭ ŭimi." *Ŏmun yŏn'gu* 72 (2012): 161–83.

Kim Chŏngsuk. *Chosŏnhugi chaejagain sosŏl kwa t'ongsokchŏk Hanmunsosŏl*. Seoul: Pogosa, 2006.

Kim, Jinhee. "The Reception and the Place of Three Kingdoms in South Korea." In *Three Kingdoms and Chinese Culture*, edited by Kimberly Besio and Constantine Tung, 143–52. Albany: State University of New York Press, 2007.

Kim Kyunt'ae et al. *Han'guk kojŏnsosŏl ŭi ihae*. Seoul: Pagijŏng, 2012.

Kim, Hunggyu. *Understanding Korean Literature*. Translated by Robert J. Fouser. Armonk, NY: Sharpe, 1997.

Kim Myŏngsin. "Nongmoktan kwa Cho Ung chŏn pigyo yŏn'gu." *Chunggukhak nonch'ong* 19 (2006): 25–47.

Kim T'aejun. *Chosŏn sosŏlsa*. Kyŏngsŏng: Ch'ŏngjin sŏgwan, 1933. Viewable in Sogang University Loyola Library (www.library.sogang.ac.kr).

Kim Tai-jin, ed. and trans. *A Bibliographical Guide to Traditional Korean Sources*. Seoul: Asiatic Research Center, Korea University, 1976.

Kim Yongch'ŏl. "Yŏngung ŭi sigan/yŏngt'o kŭraep'ŭro pon Cho Ung chŏn: Han'guk ŭi kojŏn'gujo siron 1." *Inmun'gwahak* 51 (2013): 1–26.

Kim, Michael. "Literary Production, Circulating Libraries, and Private Publishing: The Popular Reception of Vernacular Fiction Texts in the Late Chosŏn Dynasty." *Journal of Korean Studies* 9, no. 1 (2004): 1–31.

King, Ross, and Si Nae Park, eds. *Score One for the Dancing Girl, and Other Selections from the "Kimun ch'onghwa": A Story Collection from Nineteenth-Century Korea.* Translated by Scarth Gale. Annotated by Donguk Kim. Toronto: University of Toronto Press, 2016.

Ko, Dorothy, JaHyun Kim Haboush, and Joan R. Piggott. *Women and Confucian Cultures in Premodern China, Korea, and Japan.* Berkeley: University of California Press, 2003.

Ko Misook, Jung Byungsul (Chŏng Pyŏngsŏl), and Jung Min. *History of Korean Literature: From Ancient Times to the Late Nineteenth Century.* Translated by Michael J. Pettid and Kil Cha. Seoul: Literature Translation Institute of Korea, 2016.

Kwon, Hyuk-chan. "From *Sanguo zhi yanyi* to *Samgukchi*: Domestication and Appropriation of Three Kingdoms in Korea." PhD diss., University of British Columbia, 2010.

Kyŏng Illam. "Cho Ung chŏn ŭi kasanghŭi hwaso suyong kwa kŭ ŭimi." *Inmunhak yŏn'gu* 85 (2011): 65–86.

Lee, Ki-baik. *A New History of Korea.* Translated by Edward W. Wagner and Edward J. Shultz. Cambridge: Harvard University Asia Center, 1988.

Lee, Peter H., ed. *Anthology of Korean Literature: From Early Times to the Nineteenth Century.* Honolulu: University of Hawai'i Press, 1981.

——, ed. *An Anthology of Traditional Korean Literature.* Honolulu: University of Hawai'i Press, 2017.

——, ed. *A History of Korean Literature.* Cambridge: Cambridge University Press, 2003.

——, trans. *A Korean Storyteller's Miscellany. The P'aegwan chapki of Ŏ Sukkwŏn.* Princeton: Princeton University Press, 1989.

——, trans. *The Record of the Black Dragon Year.* Seoul: Institute of Korean Culture, Korea University; Honolulu: Center for Korean Studies, University of Hawai'i Press, 2000.

——, ed. *Sourcebook of Korean Civilization.* Vol. 2: *From the Seventeenth Century to the Modern Period.* New York: Columbia University Press, 1996.

Legge, James, trans. *The Chinese Classics,* etc. Vol. 4: *The She King.* Taipei: Southern Materials Center, 1985.

Li, Xiaobing, ed. *China at War: An Encyclopedia*. Santa Barbara: ABC-CLIO, 2012.

Lindenberger, Herbert. *The History in Literature: On Value, Genre, Institutions*. New York: Columbia University Press, 1990.

Loewe, Michael. *The Government of the Qin and Han Empires 221 BCE–220 CE*. Indianapolis, IN: Hackett, 2006.

McMahon, Keith. *Misers, Shrews, and Polygamist: Sexuality and Male-Female Relations in Eighteenth-Century Chinese Fiction*. Durham: Duke University Press, 1995.

——. *Polygamy and Sublime Passion: Sexuality in China on the Verge of Modernity*. Honolulu: University of Hawai'i Press, 2010.

Minjok Munhaksa Yŏn'guso Kojŏn Sosŏlsa Yŏn'guban. *Much'yŏjin munhaksa ŭi pogwŏn: 16segi sosŏlsa*. Seoul: Somyŏngch'ulp'an, 2007.

Min Kwandong et al. *Chungguk t'ongsok sosŏl ŭi yuip kwa suyong*. Seoul: Hakkobang, 2014.

Muak Kososŏl Charyo Yŏn'guhoe, eds. *Han'guk kososŏl kwallyŏn charyojip I*. Seoul: T'aehaksa, 2001.

——, eds. *Han'guk kososŏl kwallyŏn charyojip II: 18segi*. Seoul: Ihoe munhwasa, 2005.

Nienhauser, William H., Jr. *Tang Dynasty Tales: A Guided Reader*. Singapore: World Scientific, 2010.

O Hwa (Wu Hua). "Yu Sorang chŏn ŭi kukchŏk munje e kwanhan koch'al." *Hanminjok ŏmunhak* 67 (2014): 221–50.

Ōtani Morishige. *Chosŏn hugi sosŏl tokcha yŏn'gu*. Seoul: Koryŏ taehakkyo minjok munhwa yŏn'guso, 1985.

——. *Han'guk kososŏl yŏn'gu*. Seoul: Kyŏngin munhwasa, 2010.

Owen, Stephen, ed. and trans. *An Anthology of Chinese Literature: Beginnings to 1911*. New York: Norton, 1996.

Pak Chaeyŏn. "Chosŏn sidae chaeja kain sosŏl ŭi chŏllae wa suyong: Saero palgultoen Paek(poek)kyuji rŭl chungsimŭro." *Chungguk ŏmunhak nonjip* 51 (2008): 463–95.

Pak Iryong. *Chosŏn sidae ŭi aejŏng sosŏl*. Seoul: Chimmundang, 1993.

Park, Eugene Y. *A Family of No Prominence: The Descendants of Pak Tŏkhwa and the Birth of Modern Korea*. Stanford: Stanford University Press, 2014.

Pettid, Michael J., ed. *Unyŏng-Jŏn: A Love Affair at the Royal Palace of Chosŏn Korea*. Translated by Kil Cha and Michael J. Pettid. Berkeley: Institute of East Asian Studies, University of California, Center for Korean Studies, 2009.

——, Gregory N. Evon, and Chan E. Park. *Premodern Korean Literary Prose: An Anthology.* New York: Columbia University Press, 2018.

Pratt, Keith, and Richard Rutt. *Korea: A Historical and Cultural Dictionary.* With additional material by James Hoare. Richmond, Surrey: Curzon, 1999.

Pregadio, Fabrizio, ed. *The Routledge Encyclopedia of Taoism.* 2 vols. New York: Routledge, 2008.

Ryu T'agil. *Wanp'an panggak sosŏl ŭi munhŏnhakchŏk yŏn'gu.* Taegu: Hangmunsa, 1981.

Sawyer, Ralph D., trans. *The Seven Military Classics of Ancient China.* Boulder: Westview, 1993.

Salmon, Claudine, ed. *Literary Migrations: Traditional Chinese Fiction in Asia.* Singapore: ISEAS, 2013.

Shaughnessy, Edward L. *Unearthing the Changes: Recently Discovered Manuscripts of the Yi Jing (I Ching) and Related Texts.* New York: Columbia University Press, 2014.

Shin, Michael D., ed. *Korean History in Maps: From Prehistory to the Twenty-First Century.* Cambridge: Cambridge University Press, 2014.

Sim Kyŏngho. "Cho Ung chŏn." In *Han'guk kojŏn sosŏl chakp'umnon,* edited by Wanam Kim Chinse Sŏnsaeng Hoegap Kinyŏm Nonmunjip Kanhaeng Wiwŏnhoe, 371–85. Seoul: Chimmundang, 1990.

Skillend, W. E. *Kodae Sosŏl: A Survey of Korean Traditional Style Popular Novels.* London: School of Oriental and African Studies, 1968.

So Chaeyŏng. "Imjin waeran kwa sosŏl munhak." In *Imjin waeran kwa Han'guk munhak,* edited by Kim T'aejun et al., 231–58. Seoul: Minŭmsa, 1992.

Sŏ Taesŏk. *Kundam sosŏl ŭi kujo wa paegyŏng.* Seoul: Ihwa yŏja taehakkyo ch'ulp'anbu, 1985.

Sterckx, Roel. *Food, Sacrifice, and Sagehood in Early China.* Cambridge: Cambridge University Press, 2011.

Strassberg, Richard E., trans. *Inscribed Landscapes: Travel Writing from Imperial China.* Berkeley: University of California Press, 1994.

T'ak Wŏnjŏng. *Choson hugi kojŏn sosŏl ŭi konggan mihak.* Seoul: Pogosa, 2013.

Vogel, Hans Ulrich. *Marco Polo Was in China: New Evidence from Currencies, Salts, and Revenues.* Leiden: Brill, 2012.

von Glahn, Richard. *The Sinister Way: The Divine and the Demonic in Chinese Religious Culture*. Berkeley: University of California Press, 2004.

Waley, Arthur, trans. *The Book of Songs*. London: Allen and Unwin, 1954.

Xiong, Victor Cunrui. *Historical Dictionary of Medieval China*. Lanham, MD: Rowman and Littlefield, 2017.

Yang, Shuhui, and Yunqin Yang, trans. *Stories to Caution the World: A Ming Dynasty Collection. Volume 2*. Compiled by Feng Menglong. Seattle: University of Washington Press, 2005.

Yi Ch'anghŏn. "Kojŏn sosŏl ŭi yut'ong yangsang e taehan il koch'al." In vol. 5 of *Han'guk sŏsa munhaksa yŏn'gu*, edited by Sa Chaedong, 1785–1809. Taejŏn: Chungang munhwasa, 1995.

——. "Kyŏngp'an panggak sosŏl Cho Ung chŏn p'anbon yŏn'gu." *Kososŏl yŏn'gu* 7 (1999): 175–204.

——. *Kyŏngp'an panggak sosŏl p'anbon yŏn'gu*. Seoul: T'aehaksa, 2000.

Yi Chuyŏng. "Han'guk kojŏn sosŏl ŭi tokcha." In Yi Sangt'aek et al., *Han'guk kojŏn sosŏul ŭi segye*, 107–29. Seoul: Tolbegae, 2005.

Yi Minhŭi. *Chosŏn ŭi pesŭt'ŭsellŏ: Chosŏn hugi sech'aegŏp ŭi paltal kwa sosŏl ŭi yuhaeng*. Seoul: P'ŭronesisŭ, 2007.

——. *16–19segi sŏjŏk chunggaesang kwa sosŏl sŏjŏk yut'ong kwan'gye yŏn'gu*. Seoul: Yŏngnak, 2007.

Yi Nŭngu. *Kososŏl yŏn'gu*. Seoul: Iu ch'ulp'an, 1978.

Yi Sangt'aek et al. *Han'guk kojŏn sosŏl ŭi segye*. Seoul: Tolbegae, 2005.

Yi Tŏngmu. *Ajŏng yugo*. In vol. 20 of *Ch'ŏngjanggwan chŏnsŏ*. DB of Korean Classics.

Yi Yunsŏk. *Chosŏn sidae sangŏp ch'ulp'an: Sŏmin ŭi toksŏ, chisik kwa orak ŭi taejunghwa*. Seoul: Minsogwŏn, 2016.

——. "Han'gŭl kososŏl ŭi t'ansaeng kwa yut'ong." *Inmun'gwahak* 105 (2015): 5–37.

——. "Panggakpon Cho Ung chŏn ŭi wŏnch'ŏn." *Tongbanghakchi* 166 (2014): 125–48.

——, Ōtani Morishige, and Chŏng Myŏnggi. *Sech'aek kososŏl yŏn'gu*. Seoul: Hyean, 2003.

Yu, Anthony C. *Comparative Journeys: Essays on Literature and Religion East and West*. New York: Columbia University Press, 2009.

——, ed. and trans. *The Journey to the West*. Chicago: University of Chicago Press, 2012.

Yu Ch'undong. "Wanp'an Cho Ung chŏn ŭi p'anbon." *Yŏlsang kojŏn yŏn'gu* 38 (2013): 37–62.

——. "Ilbon komajawa taehak tak'usok'u mun'go sojang Chosŏnjŏnjŏk kwa kososŏl e taehan yŏn'gu." *Han'gukhak nonjip* 48 (2012): 299–326.

ONLINE AND DIGITAL LIBRARY SOURCES

Academy of Korean Studies Digital Library and Dictionary

Center for Korean Studies Materials (Han'gukhak charyo center): kostma. korea.ac.kr

Chinese Erudition (Airusheng), Zhongguo jiben guji ku (Database of Chinese Classic Ancient Books)

Chinese Text Project: ctext.org

DB of Korean Classics (Han'guk kojŏn chonghap DB)

Digital Hangeul Museum: hangeulmeseum.org

Han'guk Yŏksa T'onghap Sisŭt'em: koreanhistory.or.kr

KRpia (Korean Database)

The Annals of the Chosŏn Dynasty: Sillok.history.go.kr